THE UNSELECTED JOURNALS OF *Emma M. Lion*

VOL. 8

BETH BROWER

THE UNSELECTED JOURNALS OF *Emma M. Lion*

VOL. 8

Rhysdon Press

This is a work of fiction. Names, characters, places and incidents either are the product of the author's imagination or are used fictitiously. Any resemblances to actual persons, living or dead, events, business establishments, or locales is entirely coincidental.

contact@rhysdonpress.com

Published by Rhysdon Press
Printed in the United States of America

Publishers Cataloging-in-Publication data. Brower, Beth.
The Unselected Journals of Emma M. Lion, Vol. 8: Beth Brower; p.cm.
ISBN 978-1-957492-03-2 1. Fiction Historical. 2. Fiction. I. Title.

Second Edition
10 9 8 7 6 5 4 3 2

978-1-957492-03-2

Text was set in Baskerville

Emma M. Lion

would like to dedicate these pages to

The Nephews

PREVIOUSLY MENTIONED PERSONS OF INTEREST

Emma M. Lion – *Myself, obviously. Owner of Lapis Lazuli House.*

Niall Pierce – *Photographer. Avenging Angel. More yet to…discuss.*

Young Hawkes – *Vicar and Reprobate. Knower of things. Keeper of secrets.*

Duke of Islington – *Accidental guardian. It was a corridor, not a closet.*

Archibald Flat – *Still a General Plague on mankind. Must one endure?*

Cousin Matilde – *Archibald's older sister. Dragon of a woman.*

Lady Eugenia Spencer – *Unyielding Aunt. Determined to rule us all.*

Damian Spencer – *Errant cousin. Currently…I've no idea, actually.*

Arabella Spencer – *Beauty of* The Season, *will become engaged…to someone.*

Parian – *Valet, Butler. Becoming something of a chum.*

Agnes – *Maid, Cook. Proud member of the S. S. C. S. S.*

The Roman – *Still not seen in person. However, he thinks I'm lovely.*

Mary Bairrage – *Good chum. Employed by telephone company and Prof. Fletcher.*

Jack Hollingstell – *Confidence man…still in my debt?*

Roland Sutherland – *Childhood nemesis turned gorgeous Sun God.*

Saffronia March – *Artist. Family friend. Fellow St. Crispian.*

Ben Chambers – *The Pirate. Waspish and insulting owner of The Hound.*

Lady Trewartha – *Gracious Hostess. Lives in Baron's Square.*

Reprobates Ten – *Striker, Capper, Quality Jones, Sargent, The Boy, Mastiff, Charlie Cross, Odysseus, Night Watchman, & Mighty Nigel Hawkes.*

Mr. Penury – *Banker encouraging me to find work. Soon.*

Mrs. Penury – *My serious banker's silent yet delightful wife.*

Professor Fletcher – *Widower. Masculine. ~~Cuts own hair.~~ Terrible glasses.*

Victoria Braithwaite – *New resident of St. Crispian's. In mourning.*

Gibbs – *Owner of The Cleopatra.*

Agnes Dowd – *My nonexistent chaperone.*

Lady Sheridan – *Aunt Eugenia's friend. Society Matron.*

Charles Goddard – *Tall. Skinny. Flagpole! My Unintended Intended. Sigh.*

Lord George West – *Potential husband for Arabella. Mourning his sweet pea.*

Annalise Clifford – *A friend in London.*

May Northgate – *A friend in London.*

Lady Mariana – *Islington's elder sister.*

Margaret "Maggie" Revel – *Islington's scandalous younger sister.*

Jonathan Revel – *Maggie's wealthy, American husband.*

Countess of Ellam – *From Norfolk, mother of the enchanting Lady Eloise Silver.*

Lady Eloise Silver – *Mysterious, ethereal, unexpected beauty.*

Maxwell Stuart – *January 31st 1861 – July 27th 1880*

May 1st

When I came down for breakfast this morning, I found Agnes happily fussing over the stove while Parian ate his breakfast at the table, a cup of steaming coffee at his side.

"Good morning!" I said with all the conviction any May first deserves.

"Morning, Miss," answered Agnes.

Parian did not look up, rather he mumbled a good morning at his plate.

"Has Mr. Pierce been in for his breakfast?" I asked. "I was hoping we might—"

Parian choked then, resulting in the need to hit his own chest with a closed fist.

I feel for the man.

I do.

Only, one would think he had discovered Pierce and I engaged in something far more nefarious than he, in fact, did.

Like operating a smugglers ring.

Or stealing our neighbours' pets on the regular.

All this to say, there are worse things than a kiss.

Certainly.

"No breakfast for Mr. Pierce, Miss," Agnes replied. "He asked for coffee and then a wagon came 'round to gather his supplies. He's taking photographs for the fair today. Mr. Flat has also gone, using the wagon that fetched Mr. Pierce to take his own trunks as well."

This gave me pause. And a delightful daydream of Cousin Archibald removing himself from the house altogether. "His own trunks?"

"Oh yes, Miss. Mr. Flat has a booth."

The full measure of an emotion filled me. But which?

Embarrassment? Apprehension? Dread?

I did not ask what he intended to do with said booth, but instead informed Agnes I would take my meal in the breakfast room. "You both are enjoying the fête all day I trust?"

Quick affirmations and a rush about Agnes helping the Society of St. Crispian's Senior Servants, while Parian is assigned to what he referred to as *The Muscle Crew*. "Moving chairs, setting up exhibitions, taking them down after, and the like."

"I'm certain they couldn't manage without you," I flattered.*

* Of course they could. I was attempting to bribe his silence with ~~obsequiousness~~ toadyism.

I have returned to my garret and finished preparing for the day. All is equanimity outside my window; a clement temperature and clean sunshine in place of last night's rain. As for myself, I am of a similar disposition. The pocket I sewed into my grey-blue walking skirt is well-made, and I'm wearing a clean white blouse to keep me cool. Twisting my hair up and capturing its unruly self with pins, I've an old straw hat which I've tilted to one side before securing it in place, *jaunt* being all intent and purpose.

Having patted Tybalt on the head seven times and delivered a scratch around each of his ears for good measure, I am off!

Later

Agnes returned an hour ago. She looked a triumph of the chin-held-high variety, for all her baked goods had sold at the Senior Servants booth. Parian has yet to return as he remained to help the men dismantle the structures, after which they will all gather at The Cleopatra for drinks on the house. (As if they hadn't already consumed several pints before the sun had set.)

Having spent my day—smiles, wonderments, arguments, confusions all—at Baron's Square, I have given my final hour to the window seat of my garret. It is dark, only light from the gas lamps glancing off the lane. I keep tracing my left palm with the fingers of my right hand. I've been thinking of what she said, the old woman.

I asked them—when we sat in Islington's garden—what they thought of fortunes and readings and premonitions, and if they were ever true and how one was to know when they were?

"Nonsense," Islington said in a confident manner, before adding, "but not always."

I'd frowned.

"Improbable and unrealistic," was Pierce's comment. "Or so one hopes."

Again, not entirely dismissive.

"Hawkes?" I enquired.

Hawkes was half turned away from the rest of us, reading. His response: "*Caveat emptor.*"

"What the hell does that mean?" asked Pierce.

Still more than a little put out by the afternoon's events, Hawkes turned the page of his book, ignoring the question.

Islington answered for him. "*Let the buyer beware.*"

I felt a full trembling go all the way up my back.

"*Fata volentem docunt, nolentem trahunt,*" Hawkes murmured.

Pierce and I looked towards Islington.

"*The fates lead the willing, and drag those who are unwilling.* More or less."

"Is that what happened this afternoon, Vicar?" Pierce said, in a sardonic tone of voice. "Fate dragging the unwilling?"

Hawkes turned the next page of his book, saying nothing.

And I was left with my question only partially answered, and a feeling the Romani woman may have spoken truth.

It is not the twenty-third, but I light a candle anyway.

For comfort.

For curiosity.

And courage, I hazard.

May 2nd

I've lain in bed three quarters of an hour, interrogating my memory that yesterday was as remarkable and unsettling as it was.

And yes, upon further inspection, it proves to be so.

I am going to rise, wash, dress myself, and then write it all down before a scattering of details can occur.

The May Day fair began at ten o'clock and a vigorous crowd was expected—according to Islington—drawing not only we St. Crispians, but many from surrounding neighbourhoods like Chalk Farm and St. John's Wood. Placing my spending money into my pocket, I locked the door of Lapis Lazuli House before setting off in anticipatory cheer.

Baron's Square was almost unrecognisable. Bunting and ribbons adorned everything, including Perseus and our weeping Medusa, the latter having ribbons tied to every one of the snakes on her head. The midnight rain had left a green feeling about the place, but everything was nearly dry. There were games of all sorts, tests of skill, more food and drink than one could imagine. A man was juggling assorted (and odd) objects, there was a tent for having one's fortune told, and a boxing ring on the ready—"There's a champion boxer'll be here all afternoon for the men to have a go," Mr. Havers had said. "Gibbs said so himself." As for said Gibbs and The Cleopatra, he had set up shop with a dozen round tables where patrons could sit and let the day pass.

I found Islington—wearing a light grey suit with a green waistcoat over his white shirt, hat held in his hand; not quite country fair, not quite London—standing with Lord Trewartha, who lifted his hat as I approached but explained he was on his way to speak with a man whose exhibit of venomous plants had been accidentally placed beside a game for children.

Islington was eyeing the masses before him, and it seemed he declared them good.

"You look pleased," I said, imitating his appraising gaze.

"It's come together better than I thought. The pony took sick, but we found another."

"There's a pony?"

He gave me an unwarranted side-eye. "For children, Lion."

~~I was not disappointed.~~

I was mildly disappointed.

"Don't overexert yourself today," I said, trying to discern if Islington still looked a trifle peaked.

"There are enough rumours regarding my health, as it is. I will present a hardy front."

"Even if it kills you?"

"Even if it kills me." He saw me open my mouth and attempted to outmaneuver. "Don't fuss."

"It has only been a fortnight since you collapsed, Islington. And as dapper as your clothing looks, I can't say you yet appear your usual self."

Islington *tsked.* "I'm fine, Lion. Hawkes has already read me the riot act."

"I wish I could have seen that."

A dismissive sound. "My constitution is robust."

"I know you think that by stating a thing it becomes absolute truth, but not even you can control *everything*."

"Life would be very different if I could, I assure you."

"Islington as God. How terrifying. Although I suppose you could have prevented our current tangle."

"Yes. I would prefer not to be fielding letter after impertinent letter asking me exactly who you are and why you are my ward."

"Oh dear." I glanced again at his face. "How many have you received?"

"Between two and three dozen. I've only answered the one."

"Whose?"

"My elder sister, Mariana."

"*Ah.*"

Another side-eye from Islington; I must be gaining ground in my mimicry.

"And yourself?" he asked.

"You mean interrogating letters?" I thought of the newspaper clip marked with a black question mark. Ominous, sitting there in my desk drawer, waiting. (Not that I am overly disturbed. It could have been sent by any number of Reprobates.) I simply answered with, "A handful."

"Sincere condolences, I'd imagine."

I grinned. "Oh, every one."

He laughed.

"I've not yet replied, as I can't quite think of what to say," I confessed.

"As little as possible, from my experience."

"Says the man whose sister eloped with an American."

He squinted in the midmorning sun. "Says the man whose sister eloped with an American."

"What did you tell her?"

"Maggie? Nothing."

"No, your elder sister."

"That your father was an important friend of mine, and I would explain the whole in a letter before we meet at Stonecrop come June."

It shouldn't have caught me by surprise, but it did. "Will she be there?"

"Yes. She often visits in June with her children, but this year she'll come alone. Mariana is expecting her sixth child and is in need of rest."

"Six children! Goodness."

"Hmm, yes," he answered. "After five nieces, I'm somewhat partial to the idea of another. Although perhaps I shall wish for a boy. It would be so very convenient to replace my lout of an heir once and for all. Thankfully he is in Europe, which means I am spared that measure of insufferable indolence for the time being."

Despite my curiosity, I vaulted over his comment back to the idea of meeting his sister come June. "Am I to assume you've told her I'll be among the party?"

"Certainly." Islington looked at me. "She is to chaperone the entire affair, as per the rules of my being a Male Guardian, as laid out by one Lady Spencer. And," he allowed, "society at large."

"*Ah.*"

"Indeed."

"We will bear our trial with grace." I looked about, suddenly eager to change the subject. "This is a proper fair. Look at all the games and merchants. Do you suppose the lawn will recover from the crowd? Heavens, is that man eating fire?"

"It will take a month for it to again look presentable," Islington replied, and we began to walk the perimeter. "Lady Trewartha is the one who always asks for a fire eater to be on hand. She says it gives her perspective."

I laughed. "Has the St. Crispian's May Day always been so... comprehensive?"

"Not when Traitors Road had province, which is why Baron's Square has taken permanent ownership. We're the committee that reliably makes money—and we donate the fireworks."

Crossing through a gaggle of sprinting children, we came to a stop by Squire Mason's house. There was a sign—surely not made by Pierce—which promised in purple paint, "Jubilant Photographs to Mark the Occasion."

Jubilant, Pierce did not look. He was ordering a family of seven children and their frazzled mother into place, a cigarette in his hand, a scowl on his face.

I smiled.

Pierce glanced in our direction, waved, took a draw from his cigarette, and told the six-year-old he would toss him in the fountain if the boy didn't stop pulling his sister's plait. The boy stopped. The mother seemed ready to hand the entire brood over to Pierce's discipline.

The mother seemed ready to hand herself over to Pierce, as well.

I tried not to look so very amused.

"On the count of three. Hold still now. One. Two. You there, stop twitching. One. Stop kicking up half the garden. One. Two." Pierce ducked beneath the black curtain as he held up the pan. "Three!"

Flash.

Squeals from the children.

Audible sigh of relief from Pierce.

A reminder for the mother to write down her address so the photograph could be delivered.

And they were sent off.

A boy helping Pierce—one of Toff's friends—carefully numbered the plate and set it in a specially made trunk on Pierce's direction, then he brought out a fresh plate for Pierce to load.

"I have the feeling you're going to exact revenge for my having asked you to do this," Islington said to Pierce as we approached.

"Have no doubt," Pierce replied, tossing his cigarette onto the ground and grinding it beneath the heel of his boot. "Only an hour in and already it's mad."

"You've been busy then?" I asked.

Pierce offered me half a smile with his answer. "This is the first break since we started. The Baron's Square Committee, or whatever you call it, is subsidising over half the cost of the photographs."

"That's a lovely thing to do," I said, turning to Islington.

"We thought it would be a novelty."

"An expensive novelty," I noted.

"We budget."

Pierce grunted.

"It's only until one o'clock," Islington added, looking at his watch. "Then, after capturing a few photographs for the historical society, Pierce will be free to enjoy toffee making to his heart's desire."

I looked back at the pleasant melee of Baron's Square. "Have either of you seen what Mr. Flat is up to?"

Pierce grinned. "Oh, it's a winner."

My stomach fell. "Please tell me I can still show my face?"

"He's in front of General Braithwaite's house, I believe," said Islington.

Just then a young man and young woman approached to have their portrait taken. They looked at Pierce as if he was to pronounce their vows.

"Make it all end," Pierce muttered before waving them in. "Here we are, stand here. You get one chance so listen carefully—"

And then Islington was picked off by a Mrs. Covings (also on the committee, it appears) who was fretting over the mess left by the pony.

"We have a boy for that," Islington said, looking about the mad dash of the square.

"Please do come and see where that boy is putting the…er…manure."

Thus, being left to my own devices, I decided to wind my way through the masses to General Braithwaite's house.

Cousin Archibald had secured himself a booth, and I discovered that he was not selling but exhibiting morning robes. There must be a law in Leviticus regarding the acceptable circumstances for the stoning of irritating relations or something very near it, but my Old Testament thoughts were brought to higher ground by the vision of Hawkes in conversation with the lunatic. Standing with his arms crossed, customary book beneath his arm, Hawkes was wearing an attentive expression, offering the occasional nod as Cousin Archibald showcased his Out and About Reminder—which he was wearing. A knot of people was gathered at the far side of the booth, staring at something between robes.

I offered a prayer of protection for ~~Hawkes~~ myself and approached.

"Hello, Cousin." I then glanced at Hawkes, who was not looking at me, rather studying a morning robe with a holy concentration. Uncertain if the balance of what had transpired between the two of us last Friday at Islington's was a credit or a debt, I hesitated in my greeting. Then a wisp of words, the echo of a sentence spoken not far from where we now stood, when Islington shared what had been said after Hawkes pulled me from the fountain in February.

Only she blew into St. Crispian's like a four-leaf clover, and I've trusted in that.

The thought came that if Hawkes had been willing to trust in our friendship like a four-leaf clover, I could trust in the mystery binding our lives—of which I understand nothing.

"Good morning, Hawkes," I said, watching his profile.

"You see what I have to put up with!" Cousin Archibald complained, his face oily in the morning sun, the sparse hairs on his head askew. "A man can't contribute to society without this Abomination coming forth."

This caused half the people knotted around the end of the booth to glance my way, curious, perhaps, to see the human expression of abomination.

Hawkes tilted his head slightly and finally looked towards me, his eyes not quite meeting mine. "I see, Miss Lion," he said, "you have a new pocket."

I blinked. "How could you tell? I thought the folds hid it quite well."

"You've a confidence that only comes with such an acquisition." Hawkes, finally looking me directly in the eye, gave a soft smile. It looked like relief. Our conversation in the Rabbit Room, the letter from my father, the unanswered questions, could be managed between we two. Hawkes and I took a parallel breath. Then his smile slid into something stronger.

"Stuff and nonsense," Cousin Archibald sneered in interruption. "He could see you were walking with your hand in your pocket. Unseemly! Women with pockets are a threat to the male sex."

Really?

Cousin Archibald had at last uttered something I thought I should know more about.

"Do expound."

"Why I—" came the sputtering and indignant reply. "You'll infect us all!"

"Very dangerous," murmured Hawkes. Then to Cousin Archibald, "As fine a collection of robes as I've ever seen. Thank you, Mr. Flat."

And as Hawkes walked past me, his gaze met mine and he winked.

It was so *unlike* Hawkes and yet so *Hawkesian*.

Cousin Archibald glowered as if I was the reason Hawkes had gone, then turned to the gawkers at his booth. "Might I interest you in this fine 1873 model," he said, picking up a purple and black silk morning robe. Polite dismissals, and then their attention returned to what I saw was Cousin Archibald's map of St. Crispian's.

"How clever of you, Cousin," I conceded. "The entire neighbourhood will be charmed."

"They come only for the map," he sniffed. "Very few wish to see the robes. I am surrounded by vermin."

"That you are. I, however, like that one." I pointed to a robe of pale pink and sea green swirls embroidered over by vertical gold stripes.

If irate were a colour, Cousin Archibald would wear it well. He picked up the robe and placed it behind his booth. "This is a bespoke design of which your craven soul does not deserve a viewing. Move along."

I wanted to retort that my inheritance had paid for said Bespoke Design but was determined not to ruin my day with the bleak reminder. "Craven soul," I repeated instead. "I'm falling into disrepute at an alarming rate. I'd best go and ask Hawkes to help sort out my immortal and—by your opinion—immoral soul."

"The devil will do that before long," was Archibald's response.

As I left Cousin Archibald's display, I glanced up at the windows of General Braithwaite's house. Unoccupied, but for the pale face of Victoria Braithwaite looking down over the scene.

We locked eyes.

A friendly smile did *not* seem the thing.

Neither did walking away, leaving her to long hours of grief and solitude.

I lifted a hand in recognition.

She looked away without acknowledgement, pronouncing silent judgement on the square before leaving the window. Wishing the unwanted weight of it all to go away, I went in search of something to eat.

The Middle of My Day Went Like So

- Fate placed me at a table with three Reprobates, who bought me sandwiches and lemonade and amusements until we went in our own directions.

- Mr. Harper was sitting at a table for the St. Crispian's *Gazette*, before him a stack of advertisements asking for brief submissions describing the various events of the May Day fair, to be printed in the June *Gazette*. Unpaid, of course.

"Miss Lion," he said, looking up from a newspaper he was reading.

"Mr. Harper," I replied.

"Do you also have something you would like to submit for the *Gazette's* consideration?"

"No," I replied. Then, slipping a folded advertisement into my pocket, I added, "Not yet, anyway. The day is still young, and I've yet to try hoop-la and wellie wanging."

A frown of consideration from Mr. Harper, followed by, "Then you'd best get to it, Miss Lion. Wellie wanging awaits." And he returned to a serious reading of his paper.

Well!

- I spent a few hours playing nearly every game on offer and won a small fishbowl but not, as fate would have it, a fish. My aim was not so good as that. Poor Tybalt.

By the tired hours of midafternoon, my hands were sticky from the heat, I had lost my fishbowl, perspiration had gathered inside the brim of my hat, and I could feel a few stray locks of hair pressed against my neck.

While attempting to throw a cricket ball into a shallow bucket of water, I saw Pierce removing the sign announcing photographs. Marking the sun, I wagered he'd let it go an hour past what was intended. Pierce saw my final toss (I'd missed half a dozen by then) and waited as I quit the game. Forfeiting all hope of winning new bootlaces from the Philosopher's Sole, I went to join him.

A perusal of my approaching person, and Pierce said, "Come sit in the shade."

I walked past him and into the garden between the two houses—shade, glorious shade—sitting on the small chair near his equipment. The boy who had been assisting him was gone.

"I assume you're finished for the day?"

I expected Pierce to begin packing as we conversed, as per usual. Instead, he tipped a trunk closed and sat on it, resting his elbows on his knees as his hands fiddled with a bit of string. My knees and his hands were less than twelve inches apart.

It felt like much more.

It felt like much less.

"Your cheeks and chin are a bit red," he said in response.

"Yes, well," I removed my hat and began to fan myself with it, "as I intend to see the day through, I'll have to remove my hat to balance the disaster."

He smiled.

A lock of Pierce's dark hair was falling across his forehead, his silver eyes looking especially bright in the afternoon shade. The moment was both comfortable and uncertain—a well-earned friendship having privately become more, finding itself in a public setting.

"So," I said, tossing my hat onto a nearby shrub for safekeeping.

"So," he replied, his silver eyes intent. We studied one another's expressions as if they were pieces in a game of backgammon. Having decided we are indeed courting, I'm not certain either of us knows which piece is to be moved next.

I attempted normalcy.

Of sorts.

Despite the rapid fire in my chest.

"How did it all turn out? The photographs, I mean?"

"Fine enough," he answered. "I was able to take some photographs out on the square for the historical society. Pleased whenever I caught a glimpse of you, as happens when you fancy someone."

My goodness gracious.

As happens when you fancy someone.

I replied with levity before ~~embarrassment~~ *too* much embarrassment could get in the way, "I accept all comments of similar ilk."

The smile that comes with releasing a quick breath. "Are you angling for a compliment?"

Yes. Under the circumstances.

"Niall, I have been told by Mr. Flat only this morning that I'm bound for hell. It was implied, at least. So, I am most assuredly in the market for a compliment."

Pierce tossed the string between his fingers onto the ground and looked up at me. "I fancy you, and I shouldn't worry about going to hell."

"Neither should I worry about your being overly sentimental, I see."

Pierce laughed.

"There you are," said Islington.

I straightened with a snap, as if I had been found out by Mrs. Wade, plotting shenanigans at Fortitude.

Pierce comfortably held his ~~ground~~ posture. "Islington," he said lightly. "Hawkes."

I—having forced an innocent smile onto my face (or attempted to, in any case)—turned to watch as the two entered the side garden.

"Warm for early May, isn't it?" Islington complained, pulling at his collar.

Hawkes looked from me to Pierce, then back again.

"Do fetch me my hat, Hawkes," I redirected.

He did.

Accompanied by a raised eyebrow, which I pointedly ignored.

"According to Mrs. Covings, I'm to set a good example," Islington stated. "Thus, I'm seeking a competitor for a sedate game of lawn bowling, as I refuse to be dragged into the tug of war."

"You can't participate in anything so strenuous, by any measure," Hawkes muttered.

"I'll challenge you, Islington," Pierce said, standing. "Only let me get my equipment in order."

"It went well, I presume?"

Pierce grunted. "If you ask me next year, I might just tell you to go to the devil."

Islington grinned, which is not his usual choice of smile. "Fortunate then that we only celebrate May Day every other year."

"This place is ludicrous."

"Admit you've grown fond of certain aspects," Hawkes said quietly.

We three looked at him.

Hawkes, still considering Pierce, tilted his head.

Pierce began to move his gaze in my direction but managed to stop himself. "Don't you have a sermon to give or a widow to cheer, Vicar?"

"A book to read," Hawkes replied. As he turned to leave, he said over his shoulder, "If any of you have yet to try the crockery smash, you should give it a go."

With Islington helping Pierce sort his equipment before lawn bowling, I decided to prove Hawkes's advice. Having never participated in a crockery smash, I can now testify it is jolly good fun.

The afternoon wore on. I tried my best at wellie wanging, ate my fill of a cream tea, and gawked my way through the exhibited collections—my favourites being the numismatist and the philatelist;

my least favourite being Cousin Archibald, the ridiculatist. By the time I had spent most of the coins in my pocket, the boxing ring had drawn a large crowd.

The benches on all four sides of the ring—a shorter bench in front, a taller in back—were filled with spectators (mostly men), with an additional three dozen standing about. A general cry went up as the smaller pugilist took an audible hit. Blood sprayed into the air, and I winced.

Snaking through the crowd, I saw that Pierce and Islington were sitting on one of the taller benches, Hawkes on the shorter bench in front, flanked by half a dozen Reprobates. The remaining Reprobates were standing about, none of them looking happy. I edged towards them—the scent of tobacco and cologne marking the crowd—and slid onto the bench beside Pierce, my toes just touching the worn grass beneath. I exchanged the currency of one smile.

He, turning to see who had joined him, returned my coin in kind.

Islington glanced beyond Pierce to me. "A bit bloody for a young woman, one would think."

He received a frown. "A touch tiring for an invalid, one would think," I replied.

"Been having a good time?" Pierce intervened, but as his focus was back on the ring, that is where I turned my eye. A man came to sit on my left. I shifted until I was quite close to Pierce, our arms pressed against one another. I have never before considered boxing a romantic thing, but it was the most enlivened I've ever felt during a sporting exhibition.

I digress.

As the crowd began to complain, I decided to pay some attention to the pugilistic display at hand.

It was, in a word, nauseating.

In the ring was a strongman, taller than his opponent by two hands at least. Black trousers, no gloves. His head was shaved, nose had been broken a time or seven, and to the shock of the other (five?) ladies present, he wore no shirt. He was muscle and fat by turns, creating one large, intimidating bloke. (A term bandied by my fellow spectators.)

The smaller man—a St. Crispian's native—was bleeding beneath his eye, knuckles swollen red, sweating profusely so that his linen shirt stuck to his body. He was struggling. The strongman was not. He swung at the smaller opponent, a solid hit, the latter collapsing onto one knee. Then the strongman stepped forward and punched down with all his might. One, two, three!

Vociferation rose around me.

Pierce swore and Islington looked *displeased*.

"Poor sportsmanship?" I asked.

"He's crossed that line three of the last four matches," Pierce said. "No one can touch him, but he's a brute."

"Bad form," Islington murmured. "Not how it's to be done."

Other critiques yelled around us were less genteel.

The Reprobates seemed agitated.

"Low show," Charlie Cross muttered as the match ended and the next challenger stepped into the ring; a bit bigger than the last, but still no physical equal to the strongman.

"Dog low," Night Watchman answered.

The Boy, smoking a cigarette, flicked his gaze to Hawkes. Then away. Then back to Hawkes. So I did the same. Hawkes was sitting nearly directly in front of me, book closed, shoulders tight and pulled forward. The next bout began. The St. Crispian made a few attempts to have a go at the strongman, but one answering swing, then a second, sent him stumbling backwards. He tripped. Fell to the ground. The strongman was on him, pummelling him flat until enough men jumped into the ring to pull him off.

Pierce swore again.

"There's your warning!" the judge called. "One more like that and you're finished for the day!"

The strongman spat on the ground. "Who's next?"

He was, I gather, making quite a bit of money. Or his manager was—a self-satisfied figure in a dark brown suit, two gold rings on his finger and a foul cigar in his mouth.

"Can't let him get away with that sort of behaviour," Mastiff said to Hawkes.

"Not in St. Crispian's," added Sargent.

"You gonna let this happen, Hawkes?"

"Hawkes, it's bad show all around."

"No honour, Hawkes."

"You've gotta do something."

"Gotta stop a brute that's hurting someone else."

The strongman was waiting for the next challenger—a man I recognised from Whereabouts, removing his jacket and waistcoat after paying his dues—as the former challenger was half dragged outside the ring, where an irritated Dr. Fairchild was attending to the others.

The Boy threw his cigarette butt at Hawkes's feet—causing Hawkes to look up—and said, "It's the right thing and you know it."

Hawkes, word-weaving, contemplative, quiet magic Hawkes, let his chin drop to his chest.

Then stood.

He was looking particularly worn.

Or particularly hungry.

Or tired.

Or elsewhere.

The Reprobates erupted in a cheer, The Boy's version being a clap, as he'd already another cigarette in his mouth. As Hawkes turned to face those of us sitting behind him, setting his book on the bench, his expression was resigned. Or was it, in hindsight, determined? Not making eye contact with Islington, Pierce, or me, he shrugged off his coat.

Pierce frowned.

Hawkes then removed his waistcoat, loosened his tie, removed his collar (not a religious collar, simply one a young man would wear), and rolled up his sleeves. He kept his braces in place—one vertical stripe of pale green beside a vertical stripe of pale blue.

I sat watching this process, trying to wrap my mind around what exactly was about to occur. What should have felt intimate was disrupted by a sense that somehow Hawkes was drawing himself further away from us all, into a steeled centre.

"What does he think he's doing?" muttered Pierce.

Islington glanced at Pierce then back to Hawkes, arms crossed and back straight, a curious light behind his expression.

Hawkes finished folding his clothing and placed it on the bench, then he lifted his book—pausing, his hands grasping both sides—

and looked at me.

The distance he'd set between us all was still in play, but his gaze was immediate.

"If you would, Miss Lion." And he handed me his copy of Newton's *Principia*. In Latin.

I nodded, and carefully took the book with my right hand, while placing my left reverently on the cover.

Only then did the tightness around Hawkes's eyes relax.

The strongman was finishing off his latest opponent—just as bloodied as the previous three I'd seen—but it was not the current fight which held most of the spectators' attention, rather the riot of bets churning around the match to come. Most of the outsiders went for the strongman, while most St. Crispians were siding with Hawkes. Charlie Cross paid Hawkes's dues.

"Young Hawkes can't win," said the man at my left side. "But I'd sure like to watch him try."

Even though my doubts agreed, it felt disloyal and I wished to pinch his arm.

The strongman was lifting his hands above his head in predetermined victory, despite the efforts of his manager to wipe away the blood running down the side of the pugilist's face. He looked hungry for the next fight, almost rabid. As his eyes fixed on Hawkes, his crooked grin grew even wider. For this vicar of ours looked too lean, too closely cut to the bone, hair pushed aside in a messy manner. Hawkes's blue eyes were darker than usual, and there was something to the way they narrowed…

Hawkes stepped into the ring.

My stomach dropped.

The noise which had been building and building was now at a frenzy.

Pierce was rubbing his hands together quickly before moving his knuckles along the bottom of his jaw. "I don't like this," he said, as if he were preparing to step in if necessary.

Islington was taut but said nothing.

Of all the spectators, The Reprobates Ten were the calmest. They stood jostling elbows, counting bets, with the occasional call of "Mighty Nigel", as if Hawkes were their favourite horse and was a full ten lengths ahead. Some of the Reprobates even removed flasks from their coat pockets and gave one another friendly toasts.

My own expression creased in surreal uncertainty as I returned my attention to Hawkes. He was loosening his shoulders, nodding along slightly as the judge reviewed the rules of the ring. The strongman's grin had turned into an unsettling twist. Nearly as unsettling was the fact that Hawkes looked both serious yet comfortable in the ring.

"*The raging rocks and shivering shocks shall break the locks of prison gates*," I quoted for good luck. And then I prayed that God would keep a steady eye on Hawkes.

Pierce was not taking his concerned gaze from the strongman, who had just growled, "Featherlight come to prove you can take a hit?"

All the cream tea and cakes I'd consumed grew unsettled in my stomach.

Hawkes, shirt partially untucked despite his braces, offered to shake his opponent's hand. But the strongman was beyond niceties; he spat on the ground. Our vicar cocked his head in a confident manner wholly foreign to any previous Knowledge of Hawkes.

The judge gave the call.

The bout began.

I held my breath so tightly it began to struggle against the hold.

Hawkes, brilliant, secretive, poetry-reading Hawkes. He was a head shorter than the strongman, hands lifted at the ready, yet fists relaxed. He managed his opponent like a sheepdog guiding a bull. All grace and liquid movement.

"Good feet," Pierce muttered.

Islington nodded.

The strongman charged forward and swung. But Hawkes was a spectre, there and then simply not. The strongman came back around; more force than intended. Hawkes danced aside then swung his fist at the fighter's left jaw, the noise of impact was drowned out by the roar outside the ring. St. Crispian's was out for blood, and Hawkes was going to lead the crusade. The strongman recovered quickly, stretched his jaw with an ominous glee, and went after Hawkes with more speed than he'd shown all afternoon. Hawkes feinted— as in dodged, a term I learned while watching—once, twice. The third blow hit, but Hawkes had pulled back enough to only absorb half the force. Still, it sent him flying back two steps against the ropes. The strongman came at him fast, but Hawkes flung himself out of harm's way.

Pierce whistled.

Islington nodded, this time to himself.

I realised I was gripping Pierce's arm.

A few more circles where only three of the swings found purchase.

Two for the strongman.

One for Hawkes.

The fight then entered a stage where more blows began to land. Both taking, both shaking them off. There was blood, and it was impossible to know where the blood came from. The strongman had speed and an obvious brute strength paired with hours of training. But Hawkes was taut, lean, disciplined. And with his shirt sticking to his body from sweat, one could see the power moving through his muscles like an engine. Precise, dangerous, almost frightening. For ten seconds there was uninterrupted hammering. Stomach, ribs, face as often as they could manage—the sounds as sickening as any I've heard.

Pierce's entire body leaned forward.

Islington was no longer nodding. His fists were clenched. His right knee was bouncing.

At one point Hawkes stumbled backwards, his knees giving out, dangerously low. The call of the crowd dropped with his body, then rose in frenzy as Hawkes yelled out, as if demanding his knees get him back on his feet.

The strongman was on Hawkes just as he had righted himself. The fighter swung with his right fist and missed, and Hawkes threw himself forward with a left hook, his entire body behind the ferocity of the swing. His fist connected. There was a gut-twisting crack as the man's nose broke.

Shouts.

Gasps.

The strongman's eyes bulging.

A pained look from Hawkes as he ended the fight with three hits to the man's torso. One, two. Three! And a final to the jaw.

The pugilist crumpled to the ground.

The judge called the match.

There may never be such a cheer raised in St. Crispian's again.

The Reprobates were through the ropes, surrounding Hawkes, but Hawkes had dropped down beside his opponent. Forcing his braces from his shoulders, Hawkes pulled his shirt off, tearing it in three strips and speaking urgently to Dr. Fairchild, who had rushed into the ring and pushed the Reprobates back, before kneeling on the other side of the unconscious fighter.

The judge cleared the ring of Reprobates, who happily began to collect their winnings.

It was a bloody mess.

Literally.

I am not attempting to sound like Pierce, who was astonished.

"Who the hell is Hawkes?" he asked.

Islington was sitting with a hard smile on his face, victory behind his steeled expression.

"Looks like the fights are done for the day," Pierce added.

Islington nodded. "Care for a wander to The Cleopatra booth?"

Pierce nodded, watching Hawkes and Dr. Fairchild trying to revive the strongman.

"Lion?" Islington asked, still not looking entirely thrilled I'd seen the whole thing.

I shook my head and held up Hawkes's book. "I'll wait until he's finished, then I'll come and find you both."

The strongman had regained consciousness.

I watched as Fairchild and Hawkes forced him to stay down, treating his injuries, setting his nose, wrapping his hands. All the while the manager was cursing at the judge, his cigar up and down in the side of his mouth. Some others—committee men from Whereabouts—stepped in and all was settled. The strongman was pulled to his feet, his manager then helping him to a nearby table. Thankfully, it was not long before they were gone.

Boxing ring abandoned, the crowd moving towards food and the entertainment of some hired musicians, I was the only one left sitting on a bench, watching Fairchild attend to Hawkes.

Fairchild asked him a question.

Hawkes gave a low answer.

Fairchild lifted Hawkes's chin towards the afternoon sun and looked in one eye then the next. A sharp, approving nod, saying one last thing to Hawkes before leaving.

Hawkes watched him go then, grimacing, rolled his right shoulder, and glanced back at the ring with an inscrutable expression. He seemed not to realise I yet waited, and only came to himself when the judge brought a clean, wet rag over to Hawkes while a few men began to dismantle the ring.

Hawkes half-distractedly began to wipe his face, and then he looked over to where I sat. He stilled, pressed his mouth into a line, causing fresh injury to a split lip, and—wiping the blood from his face where he'd a cut shaped like a half-moon at the top of his right cheekbone—he walked over to where I waited with his effects, still carefully holding his *Principia*.

His hair was pushed back away from his face. A line of blood crossed the bridge of his nose. He moved his jaw deliberately and made a slow hissing sound as he did so, then reached for his coat and waistcoat.

"Do you still have all your teeth?" I asked.

A raised eyebrow, a head tilt, and a nod, all in one synchronistic movement.

For having just come off the hero of St. Crispian's to the praise and respect of all—making his friends a fair amount of money to boot—Hawkes was looking decidedly down.

"That was—" I began. "I've never seen anything like it. Not that I know very much about the pugilist's art, but you were very, *very* good."

Hawkes shook out his coat, then slid his arms into the sleeves, pulling it over his bare shoulders and turning up the collar, as if to hide his strength. The waistcoat he half stuffed into his coat pocket, letting it hang out like a scarf. Then Hawkes looked again at me, his blue eyes—a tumble of ocean rather than a clear, even sky—meeting my green eyes in an unflinching manner.

"*Primum non nocere*," he said carefully.

"The first are not…born?" I attempted.

Hawkes blinked in momentary confusion, then a slow smile stole something from his dispirited expression. Shaking his head, he spoke in a tone I've never quite heard before. "*First, do no harm.*" The words were both bitter and sad.

I took in the swelling along his jaw, red and painful. "Is that what you feel happened?" I asked. "You did someone harm? Hmm. You put an end to more harm happening, from what I could see."

~~No answer.~~

No immediate answer.

Then Hawkes lifted his free hand to the bridge of his nose, a ginger touch with his fingers as he looked over his shoulder at the square, then back to me. "Thank you for guarding my book."

I ran my fingers along the smooth cover. "I've always thought it would be a jolly thing to read Newton's *Principia* in Latin, but I don't really know the language beyond certain popular phrases. As just exhibited. Quite clearly."

Hawkes tipped a small smile in my direction and held out his hand.

I knew that Hawkes was going to disappear. He would go home for a wash, a change of clothing (or restoration of clothing, rather), and then vanish. And when Hawkes means to vanish, one does not interfere. This is Understood Law inside the bounds of St. Crispian's.

But I couldn't help wondering if he needed something else.

If he needed reassurance.

To not get lost in the corridors of his own mind.

So I did what I thought best.

I took Newton's *Principia* hostage.

Latin and all.

I am yet uncertain if it was wrong or right. Regardless, it was the course I chose.

"I'm sorry, Hawkes, but once you have, ah, recovered and presented yourself back in Baron's Square, I'll return Newton."

One would think it impossible to startle Hawkes.

I can now give testimony in a court of law that it can be done.

His eyes widened as if to question if he'd heard right.

"I'm afraid, yes, you did hear me correctly just now," I reaffirmed.

A frown of consternation, Hawkes shook his extended hand, asking wordlessly for me to put aside this nonsense and return his book.

I pulled Newton to my chest and held him fast with both arms. (Terribly romantic, if one adores deceased physicists.) "Hawkes, I let you disappear on the regular, and I've lately refrained from asking questions pertinent to my own life per your request. Now, I understand you wish to slip between the fences of this world and deal with your ghosts in private, but this afternoon I think you should go find centre and then return, be with friends, and watch the fireworks. Forgive yourself for having let yourself down, even while you were holding others up. We both know you can keep your adoring parishioners at bay by simply hunching your shoulders and putting your nose into the *Principia*, so I don't feel my request is wholly untenable. I am not commanding you, rather I am establishing a benevolent dictatorship, in which a command may be given. Go home, sort yourself out, and return *post hoc*."

Hawkes gave me an even stare. "You are holding my book hostage?"

"You, rather," I replied. Then my courage somewhat slipped. "If you're not so very opposed to the idea." And just when he opened his mouth to say—I would imagine—that he was very much opposed and I'd better release Newton before God struck me down, I added, "And as it can't be appropriate *one iota*—did you see how I've inserted the Greek?—for me to speak in a public square with a man not properly clothed, I ask you simply cede this battle and join the three of us within the hour."

I finished with a smile, indicating I had sorted all very nicely.

"*Pati necesse est multa mortalibus mala*," said Hawkes.

"Yes, well, I am certain what you've said is true, however, I remain unmoved. You must let—on this rare occasion—someone intervene on your behalf. Emma M. Lion, patron saint of Scrappy Vicars everywhere. Not that *scrappy* is the most apt adjective. And neither am I calling myself a saint. Only, well, you understand… Now, I've a mind to have my fortune read. Newton and I will see you before long. On your way."

After a final appraisal of my face, Hawkes turned in honourable defeat, walking towards the top of Sterling Street, braces falling from his trousers, waistcoat still trailing from his coat pocket like an unsuccessful scarf. I am sure many a denizen of our fair neighbourhood was struck dumb at the sight.

As this entry is entirely gone off the rails in length, I should report little else.

However.

What came after must be written. And faced, at some juncture.

Agnes has only just brought a tray of tea and buttered bread up to the garret, and so I sally forth.

After tempting the wrath of every god by denying Hawkes his Newton, I found Islington and Pierce sitting in conversation with General Braithwaite and Lord Trewartha at a table near the booth of The Cleopatra. Their exchange? Amusing.

"Hello, hello. Have you found anything suitable to eat?" I asked Pierce, sitting down in the only unoccupied chair.

"How's Hawkes?" Islington asked.

"Hawkes has gone home to change clothing."

"I didn't realise we'd a bona fide pugilist preaching from the pulpit each Sunday," said Lord Trewartha.

"He never lost a bout at school," Islington supplied.

"Damn fine fighter." This was Pierce, his tone one of disbelief.

"I only heard tell!" General Braithwaite spat in frustration. "I've been keeping all the mongrel dogs out of the fountain!"

"There are dogs about?" I asked, lifting my hand to block the sun and scanning the late afternoon activity in the square. Always such a pleasant sight, a dog enjoying itself.

"He means the boys running about the place," said Pierce.

"*Ah.*"

Islington rolled his eyes.

"Yes, well, I'm holding Hawkes's book hostage until he returns. In the meantime, I'm going to have my palm read."

"Quite right," said General Braithwaite. "The Gypsies!"

"They're Romani," Pierce muttered under his breath.

"Rustled them up me'self!" General Braithwaite boasted. "A fine addition."

"Lady Trewartha has already been," Lord Trewartha said, "and was promised things we already have. Clever fakery, that."

"But harmless fun, the Gypsies!" added the General.

"Romani," repeated Pierce.

"Pardon?" General Braithwaite blustered.

"They are the Romani people," said Pierce.

"That's what I said! Gypsies!"

Islington redirected the conversation; I am not certain for whose sake. "Might I enquire after your niece, General? A difficult time, to be sure."

The General's bluster gave way to a thoughtful pull on his mustache. "She marches on stoically enough. Tried to get her to come out today but the girl insists she's in mourning and can't do nothing for six months. Is it really that long for a young thing?"

"A year, usually, for one's parents," Islington answered.

"All that bother? They're dead!" the General boomed. "Nothing else to be done."

"Then the half mourning," Islington added.

"Bloody inconvenient when she needs to be meeting the gents and shoving on to marriage. Bad luck, to have a woman in camp. Come to think of it, Islington, you need an heir, right as rain. Why not propose to the girl and we can be done with it?"

Pierce snorted and took a drink.

I made every effort not to do the same.

Islington did not bat an eye. "A compliment, General, but I am not looking at present."

"No? Too bad." The General glanced in Pierce's direction, frowned, and looked away and about the square.

I wondered if Victoria still watched from her uncle's window. She must be disappointed her entire Season is forfeit. I should visit her again. And hope she doesn't run me through with a lance.

"Gentlemen," I stood, "enjoy your pints. I will return with the promise of wealth and prestige."

Pierce tipped his glass. "To progress."

I crossed the square in a diagonal, passing the fountain, weaving through this and that, smiling at the occasional familiar face, avoiding a few others, and was almost at the tent set up outside the Romani wagon when Saffronia walked into the square from Sterling Street.

"Well met!" I ~~said~~ hailed (as it was more than a little too robust).

"Hello, Emma." She put a hand on her hip, to catch her breath. "How goes May Day?"

"When I tell you what you've missed, you'll be quite sorry for your late arrival. I'm having my palm read now. Care to join?"

Saffronia, a little paint on the side of her wrist, stepped right into the idea. "I've been curious as to what next comes my way, especially as the last Italian count has stopped writing. I am bereft of any suitors worth mentioning."

And so we waited in a line behind three other women.

Not wanting to speak of Hawkes's role in David and Goliath until we were alone, I talked of other things—light and airy as the afternoon. Strange, considering it all now after a night's sleep, that I'd had no premonition of what awaited.

That seems to be the nature of life, however.

Things that ought to come with warnings rarely do.

"Hello?" I greeted the waiting young woman when it was our turn to enter the tent.

"Sit, sit," she waved us into the two chairs before her.

We sat. I gazed about—pattern and colour and beads—while Saffronia paid the Romani woman and removed the glove on her right hand. Crossing one leg over the other, Saffronia leaned forward, her dark hair pulled back into a chignon beneath her hat, elegant profile catching the dimmed light of the tent, eyes all amusement. The young woman took Saffronia's hand and began to trace the palm. She looked bored and I didn't blame her. It had been a warm day, and the inside of the tent was stuffy. "Here, your heart line," she began. "Here, your head line. Here, your fate. Here, your life. We first return to your heart. There is a man."

Saffronia smiled slyly. "Do go on."

"He is on the path of your life but obscured by shadows."

"They always are."

"And he is wealthy. *Very* wealthy."

"They always are," I echoed with a grin.

The young woman continued to stare at Saffronia's palm. "And you will have a long life and enjoy the interests you pursue." She twisted Saffronia's hand to reveal the paint smudge. "And you will paint many things."

An older woman, treble the coins and jewellery hanging about her person, entered from the rear of the tent and settled down, watching.

"You will be happy wherever you go," our palmist continued, "but this man will only be happy again when he finds you."

"Well done, Saff," I murmured.

The young woman released Saffronia's hand then looked at me expectantly. Saffronia and I switched seats, and I removed the proper coin from my pocket, handing it to the young woman before I held out my right hand. Hawkes's book I kept on my lap.

She reached for my hand and pointed with her finger. "You will find love, and some money—"

It was then the older woman said something sharp to the girl, who stopped, looked at me with widened eyes, and practically yanked her hand away. I too pulled my hand back, but the older woman stood, dusting her skirt, then—nudging the young woman to move—she sat before me.

I held out my right hand.

She waved it away and indicated my left. When I gave it to her, the old woman frowned.

"Do you see something?" I ventured.

The woman tutted me to silence and began working my palm like dough. Then, as if having cleared something, she let out a sigh and settled, one worn thumb crossing my palm in thought.

"Men come into this tent hoping for money. And women," she raised her eyes to mine, "come wishing for love."

"And do you tell them what they want to hear or what you actually see?"

"Yes," the old woman replied. "We see plenty. We tell most what they want to hear. What we see and say may be in disharmony, for many do not want honesty. But others..."—she tapped my hand—"...it would be unkind to hide the truth. And so this is what I give you." She moved the tip of her finger to a point on my palm. "Not every person has what you have. Fewer than you might think. Do you see here?"

I shook my head. It looked like my hand and nothing more.

"You have the line of true love. But something has happened, despite your youth."

The muscles in my back tensed and I looked up at her wrinkled face, then down.

Saffronia had gone still, watching me.

"Your true love was—what's the word?—broken. Charred. Burned away. Like a tree in a storm hit by lightning. And he is no more."

All of me had gone still.

My stomach felt like lead. My mouth tasted dust.

Nothing moved inside the tent except the woman's hand moving across mine.

"But the tree," she lifted two knotted fingers, "did not die. It did not fall with him, for each side of the split trunk branched out with life. Where there was a single path, there are now two."

I could no longer hear the din and noise of the fair outside the tent.

"Two paths now leading to a love; both true. A different shape of happiness to be found with each. Which path you take? Depends on many things. What you choose. What they choose. A thousand other decisions, or possibly very few. One you would love deeply. One you would love completely. One sharp as a knife. One a game of mirrors. One more difficult. One less free. Both inheritors to the line that refused to die when your first heart was buried." She raised her eyes to my face. Beneath the weight of the gaze, I could feel my cheeks burning. I did not look back in return.

"We have many hearts in this life," she pressed, "but not all are so fortunate as you. For most, when the lightning strikes, everything burns."

I pulled my hand back. From instinct. Or surprise. Or fear.

She smacked her paper-thin lips in approbation. "You are wise. Take the truth you have been given and do not mingle it with flattery and trinkets."

Without a word, not even a thank you, I stood and left the tent.

Saffronia followed.

We came outside to a square no longer touched by sun, the air just taking on the slight pink cast of the May evening. Torches were being lit, and even more revellers were about. The general sense was of loosened enjoyment. And Saffronia and I standing in our silent pocket, discomfort and amazement wrapping about our ankles like a vine.

It felt as if the woman was still grasping my hand.

"Emma? Was she—? Your soldier—"

"Have you had your palm read before?" I interrupted in response.

"A time or two. Nothing so—"

"Uncanny," I said. It was as good a word to hide behind as any. I then swallowed, gripping Hawkes's book like it would stand guard over the slice of pain in my chest. "I was, we were— I'm going to look for Pierce and Islington now, to find a spot of dinner. Care to join? Hawkes will return." I sounded distracted. "Soon, I should hope."

Saffronia linked her arm through mine. "Only lead the way."

We found Islington and Pierce in fierce competition at ringala, a boisterous crowd gathered. The noise began to work something loose in my chest. I smiled as the two seemed to play up a rivalry for the sake of those watching. In the end, Pierce won by a single ring, and all went the way of cheers and hands clapping backs. Islington looked tired, too tired. As for myself, I put on a good show, but I could still feel the grip of the Romani woman and how the buried places of my soul wished to burst into confused tears for what had been said.

Islington and Pierce made their way out of the crowd and to where we stood.

"Islington," I said, "you've met Miss Saffronia March? She's an artist and—"

"Yes, Miss March, I admire your work." Islington held out his hand much in the same way he had when first meeting Pierce. (Islington's Artists Greeting, apparently.) "Last year I saw half a dozen of your pieces in Crenshaw's exhibit. I wished to add your *Piazza San Marco* to my collection, but another gentleman beat me off the line, I'm afraid."

"You sat for my friends and I nearly ten years ago, Your Grace," Saffronia replied.

"*Ah*. The portrait in the kitchen."

"The what?"

Wishing to avoid a conversation about Agnes's unrequited love, I intervened. "Shall we all find a table before hunting down some dinner?"

Crowded with tired fairgoers, we did manage to encounter a group leaving a simple wooden table on the darker edge of the square, enough chairs for us all.

I sat down feeling like weights had been dropped into my booted feet.

And the weights were chained to my heart.

"Shall we divide and conquer, Lion?" Islington asked, placing his hat to claim our stake.

I heard the words but did not understand them at first. "Pardon? Oh, um, yes."

"Leave Emma to her thoughts," Saffronia said. "I'll go after the meat pies if you and Mr. Pierce procure the drinks."

Islington nodded readily enough, but he noted the protective stance of Saffronia's words and gave a second, slower nod. "A ready plan."

Pierce, a glance at my face, placed a hand on Islington's shoulder. "Let's see what Gibbs has under the counter." And they left.

There I sat, caught between my external and internal atmospheres.

It was a picturesque evening, and an unknowable thing had just occurred.

The two somehow fit together well enough.

There is a certain evening hue, a blue tinged in cool green spread over warm pavement. I don't know a better description, but it was one of my father's favourite shades. ("Impossible to get right. No one's done it, far as I'm concerned," he'd say.) But that was how this May evening bedecked herself after the pink faded. And there I sat, on the edge furthest from the lights, my elbows before me on the table in a violation of everything Aunt Eugenia holds dear, chin in my hands, staring at the fête and seeing a tree split in two. Charred. Almost ash. But new green leaves emerging, despite…

Uncanny, indeed.

Unearthly.

Like a cosmic fabric folded over itself, half concealing, half revealing.

I scarcely noticed the shadow sliding into the chair at my side.

The delay of a moment, then awareness, and I turned, letting both my hands fall into my lap.

"Might I have my *Principia* back?" Hawkes said quietly.

I was so glad he'd come. I wished to throw my arms around him and ask what I was supposed to feel about it all.

Instead, I simply looked at him.

An other-world understanding crossed Hawkes's bruised face. He didn't speak—didn't need to for how his eyes narrowed. He reached for my hand, catching the edge of my palm and pressing his fingers around it. It felt as if he were dispelling the grip, dispensing with the uncertainty of the fortune, and placing a star in my hand.

My chin trembled, but I nodded.

Another squeeze and then he drew his hand away.

Still, it felt I was holding a light.

Wordlessly, I pushed *Principia* towards Hawkes.

A gift for a gift.

"*Pax*," I said, "for having held your book hostage. But I'm glad you're returned. You are forgiven for it being under the cover of darkness."

Hawkes lifted the book from the table. "*Pax potior bello*."

"It sounds as if you're speaking of mushrooms."

A rare Hawkesian grin split the growing dark, despite the cut on the side of his mouth. "I am not speaking of mushrooms," he answered. "*Peace is more desirable than war*."

"Yes, it is."

"And the palmistry? Were you promised what you wished?" He asked like he already knew it was the root of my wistful unsteadiness.

Leaning against the back of my rickety, wooden chair, I released a slow breath. "I have experienced something I can't quite understand."

Hawkes waited, then, "A state I've known."

"What do you do with it?"

"I wait on the shore of the mystery to see what the tide will bring."

And so we two sat in a companionable silence, listening to the sound of the tide move around our feet as we both waited on the shore of our respective mysteries.

Saffronia returned with an impressive half dozen meat pies, while Islington and Pierce—limping for the length of his day—followed behind, four pints between them.

"Hawkes," Pierce greeted, placing two pints on the table. "Let me go back and fetch something for you."

Hawkes slipped past the offer. "Thank you, no."

Pierce, accustomed to giving a man his way and not stepping on toes, shrugged. "Far be it from me to tell a man to eat, but anyone who fought the way you did needs stout food and a good drink. I'll only be a moment."

And he limped away while Islington and Saffronia distributed pies and pints about the table.

"Good gracious, Hawkes, what happened to your beautiful face?" Saffronia asked.

Hawkes gave Saffronia the rebuttal of an even stare, opened Newton's *Principia*, and began to read, prior moodiness returned.

"This afternoon we saw a variation on the theme of the good Samaritan, Miss March," Islington supplied. "More punches, fewer Levites. There was a pugilist, a bad apple. Hawkes put an end to his blood sport."

Hawkes turned a page without looking up.

"I ought to have quit my studio sooner," Saffronia said, her glance moving from Hawkes to me. "Now, are we supposed to eat these meat pies with our hands?"

We ate and talked—Saffronia, Pierce, and Islington carrying the weight of the conversation. The tightness in my chest continued to ease. Hawkes joined with the blue mood of the evening, digging his heels in silent irritation anytime his exploits were mentioned, causing more smiles about the table. It was just as it ought to have been.

At the end of the evening, we found ourselves on Islington's front steps, waiting for the famed fireworks. It seemed all of St. Crispian's and hundreds of other Londoners had crammed themselves into the square, some gathered around the fountain on blankets, others standing about in wait. We were lucky to have a relatively comfortable place to sit with the promise of an unimpeded view. Pierce was over in conversation with Gibbs while the rest of us waited in silence.

Until I noted Islington's hands were shaking. "Ought you be resting, Islington?" I asked.

But it was not Islington who answered.

It was Hawkes, delivering his judgement as he watched the sky. "I've told him five times to go inside."

"I will remind you all," Islington batted back, "that I rested well enough before the boxing." Then, "You fuss about so little, Hawkes, but when you do, you manage to become incredibly irksome."

Hawkes kept his eyes heavenward. "Yes, well, when you're a practicing physician you can contradict my orders."

Islington raised an eyebrow. "When you're a practicing physician you can dare give them. Until then, let me enjoy the fruits of my labour. It should be illegal to be an annoyance before fireworks. See how delightful I've chosen to be?"

"As sure a miracle as any."

At this Saffronia laughed. "Lemons from Young Hawkes. Who would have guessed?"

Hawkes tightened his expression. "*My heart is hardened, I cannot repent.*"

"Now we're in for it," muttered Islington.

"What?" I asked.

"He only quotes Dr. Faustus when he's tremendously put out."

We fell silent, all thinking, I'm sure, about Hawkes's reluctant moment of glory, as we were too tired and sunburnt to say much else. Pierce returned, sitting on the step below where I sat, his arms folded, legs stretched out to their full length, before saying, "Where did you learn to fight like that, Hawkes?"

"Eton," Islington and Hawkes said in unison.

That was when the fireworks began.

Shimmer and fire, autographing the sky with smoke.

A moment of awe for us all.

It was very nice.

Later, while Saffronia and I sat on the edge of the fountain, watching the men of St. Crispian's helping vendors and exhibitors take down booths, I thought about the day, absently running the finger of my right hand over my left palm.

"Did it bother you," Saffronia asked. "What the Romani woman said?"

I did not answer for a long while, finding Pierce's limping form in the torchlight shadows.

Through my head ran the words as well as I could remember them. Having committed them to paper, they form a sort of poem—line and metre forgotten, cipher intact.

Two paths leading to a love. Both true.
A different shape of happiness to be found with each.
Which path you take? Depends on many things.
What you choose. What they choose.
A thousand other decisions, or possibly very few.
One you would love deeply. One you would love completely.
One sharp as a knife. One a game of mirrors.
One more difficult. One less free.

Both inheritors to the line that refused to die when your first heart was buried.

"Emma?" Saffronia repeated gently.

"It shouldn't bother me, no. A very hopeful thought, if true."

"But not a simple one."

"No. Not simple at all."

It wasn't long after that Saffronia excused herself, and Islington sent his footman to fetch Pierce and I for a drink in his garden.

Islington's garden, that is.

Not the footman's.

May 3rd

Yesterday I spent nearly five hours writing in my journal.

My hand, neck, my entire body, if truth be told, is stiff.

Absurd.

I ran out of ink and had to open a new bottle (my last on hand), finding myself worn out only midway through the effort. During which I was not proper company. For what did it mean? Was it simply wild conjecture? How could she possibly have known…

And if it is true, who? Who is the man that I would love deeply? Who is the man that I would love completely? And might Pierce…?

Bother.

I determined to ignore the fortune.

I then proceeded to reread it seven times more.

Then I'd turned Pierce's photograph of Afghanistan to the wall in mild protest, and finished putting the events of the day on paper. Wise that Cousin Archibald stayed in his rooms, and just as well that Pierce had a dinner obligation.

However—despite my hand cramping from the Herculean effort—I thoroughly enjoyed writing all earlier events, especially Hawkes's unexpected moment of Divine Intervention. Afterward I felt somewhat…sorted. As if the writing had created a doorway for the fortune or prophecy or wildly lucky conjecture to walk through and say that I need not carry it with me everywhere.

So, taking a piece of paper, I wrote out the fortune and—with a sense of ceremony—folded it three times over and placed it in the back of my desk drawer, near the missive marked with the black question mark.

There are enough things to worry over.

This need not be one of them.

Washing my face and blowing out my candle, I went to sleep.

And the effort did indeed leave me with a sense of clarity. For I woke this morning feeling more like fresh, wind-blown linen. Which is to say cheerful, light, and a little wrinkled. I suppose the first of May agreed with me. Palmistry notwithstanding.

That being acknowledged, I wrote far too much.
(Ben Chambers would skin me alive.)
Fin.

May 4th

In light of recent pugilistic events, I dusted off my soul and went to church in great anticipation.

So, it seems, did everyone.

The church was full, almost every seat taken, with several parishioners standing along the walls. Hawkes's triumph had spread the length and breadth of St. Crispian's.

I assumed the space to Islington's left was fair game and after ~~delicately~~ tripping on my own dress while squeezing past half a dozen parishioners, I dropped down beside him.

"You might have sat nearer the edge of a pew," I breathed out.

"Good morning, Lion," he replied. There was a terseness in his tone not directed at me, and I surmised from the way he was sitting—arms in that half-crossed manner with one hand lifted, finger against his lips, thumb under his chin—that he was not a fan of crowds in church. What he said next was confirmation of the fact. "To think I could be home enjoying the quiet of my library."

I considered my fellow St. Crispians. We all looked fresher for our day in the sun, like a bouquet of flowers set in clear water, the blooms lifting their heads.

"Crowded, but cheerful," I said.

The side of Islington's mouth twitched.

The service began, a hymn sung, before Hawkes walked out of his vestry and took his place behind the lectern, face mottled with bruises and black reminders of half-healed cuts.

(Far worse than March's efforts at The Cleopatra.)

He looked at us all in resignation. Yet seeing the church as full as it has ever been, conflict skirted the shadows of his face. Hawkes lifted his fingers to the place between his eyebrows, as if attempting to rub away a headache. He sighed. The result being the entire congregation…well, falling into a fit of laughter.

It couldn't be helped.

It rolled and rolled and grew increasingly worse.

(Islington excepting.)

Just as things would quiet down, another wave of laughter would begin. And all the while Hawkes stood, tersely flipping through the pages of the Old Testament.

Looking, I surmise, for vengeance.

Finally, when silence prevailed, Hawkes let it stand on an uncomfortable leg before saying, "Over the course of the last few days, I have been given more requests for a particular sermon topic than ever before. The story of David and Goliath, on which I have no intention of discoursing today."

From the back, Quality Jones yelled, "You've already taught David and Goliath this week. Chapter and verse!"

Hoots and hollers and fresh laughter.

Islington smiled internally.

I could see it in his eyes.

Hawkes gave Quality Jones a look that was four parts long-suffering and one part withering, then proceeded with, "Seeing as how the church is filled, I thought to discourse on the question posed by Christ Jesus: Who is my neighbour?"

And off Hawkes went to the good Samaritan, leaving David to stand over the body of Goliath unsung.

It was a very good sermon, if subdued.

Hawkes kept the congregation an extra twenty minutes.

Later

This afternoon, Pierce and I sat reading in his studio. I was telling him how I'd been called to a council of war at Aunt Eugenia's On The Morrow, when Cousin Archibald walked in. I gaped at the man. Pierce lifted his eyes above his newspaper, then, the hint of a grimace, folded the paper into one hand and stood. "Good afternoon, Mr. Flat," he said, in a style imitating the name. "What might I do for you?"

Cousin Archibald lifted a book in hand. "I see we're having a Reading Sunday. Is the only place for me to sit beside *her*?" He indicated my person as I slowly, carefully, unfolded my feet from beneath me, sitting up as a proper human being should.

Pierce pressed his lips together in a bid for patience then said,

"Actually, Mr. Flat, if you would like my chair, I'll happily sit on the sofa."

So Pierce sat.

So Archibald sat.

I was a little flustered when Pierce settled closer to centre than his designated side. Cousin Archibald being present. But Pierce, unfolding his newspaper, glanced in my direction like an avenging angel, and smiled.

"Agnes is to bring tea," Cousin Archibald said, turning the page of an illustrated periodical about gentlemen's fashion.

Agnes did indeed bring tea.

May 5th

Cousin Archibald had his breakfast in the dining room this morning at the same time that Agnes, Parian, and I were attempting to capture a mouse that had run from the pantry to beneath the stove. All the while Tybalt sat like a sphinx, in elegant curiosity, as we did his work for him.

"You realise your days in this house are numbered, Tybalt. There are only so many opportunities for you to snag a fine mouse in this kitchen," I told him at one point, while Parian was using a fireplace poker and squealing every time he jabbed it behind the stove.

Tybalt refused to look at me, instead watching Parian's attempts with ever-widening eyes.

"Oh, Miss!" Agnes bewailed. (Bewailed or wailed? I'm not actually certain.)

"Ah ha!" This was Parian. He pulled out the poker, on which now hung an impaled mouse, ~~hanging limp~~ slightly twitching.

There was blood.

We all screamed.

The poker was dropped.

The mouse went flying.

We jumped away, Parian practically into my arms as he hemmed his mouth in disgust.

Cousin Archibald in the dining room began to yell, "What what what!!!"

By the time we'd all calmed enough to take a long breath and cast our eyes properly about the kitchen, both Tybalt and the mouse were gone.

Clever, clever cat.

The poker has been thoroughly disinfected.

Later

"Miss Lion," Agnes asked after she had scrubbed the kitchen floor. Twice. "Would you permit me to go to the haberdashery this afternoon?"

"I most heartily permit. Take all the time you need. Really, sometimes I think you'd be wise to leave for an errand and never return. But I'm always glad you do. I'll also be gone this afternoon, as I must subject myself to Aunt Eugenia's machinations."

"I didn't know Lady Spencer had machinations, Miss." Agnes gave me a nice albeit confused smile. "What exactly do they look like?"

"Untoward plots and plans, tangled in a mess of tar-stained rope, Agnes. At least according to the dictionary of Emma M. Lion."

Later

An Account of The Great and Terrible

We met neither in the First drawing room, nor the Second.

Nor the Third.

Nor the Fourth, thank goodness.

Instead, we were in Arabella's father's study.

A room ~~seldom~~ never used.

Aunt Eugenia was sitting behind the large mahogany desk—one she selected for her long-suffering husband. It is in a style so burdened with ornamentation it looks like a wealthy man, squat and uninterested, who couldn't be bothered to even think about moving. I almost offered it something to eat.

"Emma!" Aunt Eugenia said as I was shown into the room.

"Aunt Eugenia, how very determined you look behind that desk. I rather think you should wear it more often. Like a hat."

My aunt's expression steeled in such a manner I almost asked if she were a railroad. "I will not have you being ridiculous today, I will *not*. I have been working tirelessly with Lady Sheridan on a complex strategy far beyond your social capacity to understand."

"I blame her Irish father," Arabella murmured from the window seat. There was an open book on her lap, despite her eyes being closed.

"Hello, Arabella."

Aunt Eugenia sniffed. "I blame her Irish father for everything."

Everything! I thought to test this thesis. "Including the fall of the Roman Empire?"

"Had Ireland simply handed over their island," Aunt Eugenia stated, "Rome would have had a much easier time of it. Fewer wasted resources. They might have stood another five hundred years."

My expression was dubious. "You posit that Rome's ownership of Ireland would have somehow hindered the Vandals?"

"Don't sneer at empires that accomplished far more than you ever will, Emma. It's tiresome."

While Aunt Eugenia regained her composure, I joined Arabella on the window seat. As we exchanged a kiss on the cheek, Arabella grabbed my arm, holding me in place while she whispered, "I am going to extract from you the whole of this Islington charade." She tightened her hand as I tried to wriggle away. "Do not think you can avoid me forever."

It was then Aunt Eugenia saved me.

"Now. Lady Sheridan and I have been in closeted meetings over the topic of the Countess of Ellam and her hermit of a daughter." She cleared her throat. "And although we both know the truth of Arabella's pre-eminence in every way, much of London has been taken with the novelty. We cannot expect barbarians to judge with impartiality, and London is nothing if not a city of barbarians thinking themselves to be upper class. Say nothing, Emma. I've no interest in your thoughts on the subject. My own are *quite* sufficient." She cleared her throat. "My every intention was to hold a ball at the *end* of *The Season*, where we would announce Arabella's Engagement; however, necessity requires, nay, demands the vulgar moving of the ball forward in the social calendar. May is oversaturated, not only with Lady Sheridan's ball, but others that carry a weight worthy of consideration. Thus I have no choice but to settle for June. Now, Emma, your role will be the most vital—"

But I was fixated on the word June.

June.

My Stonecrop June.

"I'm sorry Aunt, but I will be in Derbyshire come June."

"—seeing as how you will be required to—"

"Aunt Eu—"

"—manipulate the Countess of Ellam and her daughter, both of whom will be invited—"

"Aunt Eugenia!"

She looked up at me with a self-righteous fury. "What could you possibly have to say!"

"I will be in Derbyshire all of June," I restated.

"I expect you here."

"Wonderful. Before and after June."

"Nonsense." And then Aunt Eugenia began a quarter-of-an-hour rant. In my opinion, it was excessive. There were several threats upon my life. I was left with the consolation that if I managed an escape to Stonecrop, I could disappear into the forest, living the remainder of my days as a poacher on Islington's estate.

I digress.

Only when Aunt Eugenia took a break in her diatribe to take in more oxygen did Arabella put a stop to it all. "Simply ask Emma to return for the last Saturday of the month, Mother, and it's sorted. Really, you've become such a spectacle."

"I am nothing of the sort." But she took another breath. Then another. "Very well, Emma. We will hold our ball on the twenty-eighth of June. No Ifs, Ands, or Buts."

"Seeing as how the twenty-eighth is the end of the month, I agree. You will find me an ever-useful tool in the dismal plot of Arabella's marriage. I should like a few days, by any means, to prepare myself for the hunt of all things Julius Caesar."

Aunt Eugenia stared at me for a full half minute. "We are all sent trials in this life, Emma. I've yet to understand why God placed so many of mine in your singular person."

Not knowing what one ought to say, I answered, "I aim to be singular."

Arabella smirked.

Aunt Eugenia ignored us both. "I've updated the list of May obligations. Here it is." And her maid magically stepped into view to take the paper from her hand and bring it to me. Expecting it to be the exact schedule she'd given both Roland and I in April, I was startled.

"Aunt Eugenia. There are eight events—balls, dinners, card parties, a tea! *Eight!*"

"Your point being?"

"That for the rest of the month you expect to see me one out of every three days! You've claimed May the 8th, 10th, 14th, 17th, 20th, 23rd, 24th, 28th! It's not simply astonishing, it's a vulgar misuse of anyone's schedule!"

She double tsked. "Nonsense. I'll not waste any time before you leave for Stonecrop on the Fourth."

"Pardon?" said I.

Arabella sighed with contentment.

"Islington writes you are to leave for Stonecrop on the fourth of June."

"Does he! Not even I am aware of that."

"Emma!" The second syllable higher than the first, as happens when she is exasperated. "As you are Little to No Help, I took it upon myself to write to the duke and enquire. He replied—in a brisk manner erring on the impolite—that you will be departing for Stonecrop on the fourth of June."

I gritted my teeth. "It can't come soon enough."

"I assure you, Emma, it can. Now, as for our handling of Lady Eloise Silver, these are the instructions I give you. First—"

Ah! Pierce, returning home, has just seen me through the window and asked, through pantomime, if I would care for a walk.

I would.

He's looking rather tall today.

Later

Apparently, Pierce took a portrait of a man with not one, but two glass eyeballs. He said it was rather a challenge to capture the image without the sitter appearing to be cross-eyed. Extraordinary!

May 6th

After watching Cousin Archibald snake out of the house this afternoon, and seeing as how I was caught up with the demands of unexpected correspondence—

Islington,

My aunt informs me we will break for Stonecrop on the fourth of June. I repeat: MY AUNT INFORMS ME. Now, I understand this is a great imposition (for us both). However, I do hope to know certain details before she drags them out of you.

I hope your day has been pleasant.

Lion

—I decided to spend some time curled in Hawkes's chair reading Plutarch.

That was until Mary came round at half past four.

"I need a dose of perspective and some of Agnes's biscuits," she announced after Parian showed her in.

Do not we all?

"Perspective?" I replied.

Mary grumbled something or other as she threw herself onto the green sofa. "I was supposed to deliver the typed proof of *A History of the East India Company* to Professor Fletcher's office, but he sent one of his students instead—a fellow so irritating I wish he were stupid. He's not. 'The old Prof didn't want to put you out,' he said. 'Asked me to fetch it myself.' *The old Prof?* It was the way he said it, Emma. I felt…" Mary pulled herself upright and looked into a philosophical distance. "I felt defensive. And horrified. In equal measure. All the while I've been expecting him to—"

Someone rather banged on the door.

We both started.

A second bang.

Parian was…well, I've no idea where he'd got himself off to. So I answered the door myself. What I found was a man—a comfortable frame, having missed a shave or two, cap sliding to one side—who said, "Miss Lion?" with a south-of-the-river accent.

"Speaking," I replied.

"I've a delivery for you. Shall I bring it in?"

"A delivery? I've not ordered anything."

I looked past him and towards his wagon, where a long, oblong something was wrapped in a sheet.

"It's for you, right as rain. There's a note." He pulled an envelope—rather smashed on one side—from his pocket.

I looked again at his wagon. "If you can guarantee it's not a corpse of some sort, I suppose you ought to bring it inside."

From that man's startled expression, the idea had never occurred.

"I wouldn't think so, Miss. Look at the shape. And no blood seeping through."

"Hmm, I see. A great comfort."

The mystery object was brought into the hall, then the drawing room, where Mary was waiting with a second cup of tea. After the man—with much complaining, and a fair amount of dragging as it was reasonably heavy—managed to place it in the centre of the floor, I went to Agnes for the kitchen purse and gave him a few coins for his pains before ushering him back outside. Returning to the drawing room, tapping the unopened envelope on one hand, I offered Mary my expression of intrigue.

"What, exactly, is this?" she asked.

"I've no idea, but here is our clue."

Sitting in my pink chair, I opened the envelope.

"Oh dear," I said.

"What?"

"It's from Tad Whitaker, of all people. You remember. Look at that handwriting. Atrocious. Let's see if we can decipher what it says:

Miss Lion,

I've never seen such a jolly good swing. You could have gone first team in cricket. Laura—

Shocking, he calls his mother by her Christian name.

—was determined to send the spoiled carpet to the ragman as we are moving house, but you were dashed disappointed to see it ruined, so I send it as a token of my regard.

An Admirer
Also, Tad Whitaker"

"An admirer of fifteen!" Mary grinned.

"Sixteen, I believe. This is merely a token of naive adoration. You remember me telling you of the uncle? Well, there was a previous scrape that involved a bottle of red ink. It ruined a carpet which, it seems, has now been sent to me. Shall we unroll the thing?"

"I don't see why not."

Everyone should have a friend like Mary.

We pushed back all the furniture and rolled up the very old, very sedate carpet that had likely lain unresponsive for two decades. Hauling and grunting the stained carpet into place, we then unwrapped the covering and rolled it out.

There it lay in all its glory. The compelling red lattice with exotic green leaves, hints of parrot blue. It was, on the whole, stunning.

With the exception of one dreadful ink stain.

"That's the scene of the crime?"

"Indeed."

"It's not so very…" she began.

But it was. The red ink had been worked at, leaving a garish, red-tinted mark extending beyond the original sin of it all. It looked very much like someone had been murdered on the carpet and the household staff had tried to cover it up.

"The carpet itself is large," Mary stated. "And expensive. Unless we marry well—dissolute viscounts for all—I don't foresee either of us owning anything of this quality in our lifetime."

"Which makes it all the more extraordinary that Tad delivered it to me."

"If only…" Mary sighed at the blemish.

"Why don't we move the furniture back into place and perhaps it will look less…?"

"No reason we shouldn't try," answered Mary, her tone laden with doubt.

And so we brought back my chair and Hawkes's chair and the side table. Then we—"Steady on, Mary, let us lift. One, two, three!"—moved the green sofa back into its place.

Everything fitted just as it should on the carpet, with a fashionable amount to spare. It set the colours in the room off like a kaleidoscope.

"Very nice with the yellow curtains," Mary stated. "I expected it to be garish, but I think you might just pull it off."

The ink stain was ~~mostly covered~~ partially covered by the green sofa.

I dusted my hands. "I'm beginning to like it."

"Just feel this pile. Luxury, Emma. That's what this is. But does it remind you of the Whitaker house?"

Upon a moment's serious reflection, I was happy to report that it did not. "The stain does, yes, poor dog. But the carpet makes me think of faraway places. I'm rather fond. And my aunt will hate it, which is a solid endorsement."

Mary and I finished our tea, pretending we were living in India and being courted by not one but three maharajas.

Each.

She did not again mention the professor.

Later

Lion,

Do you believe I find any interruption from your aunt acceptable? I do not. And yet, in the last four days I have been sent six separate queries, all written on a sickly peach paper:

What date do we leave for Stonecrop?
Do I have all of my teeth?
Do I give excessive amounts to the poor?
Have I decided which of the provided dates I will be dining at Spencer House?
Do I realise your English blood is sullied with both Portuguese and Irish descent?
When have I slated a house party for your aunt and some Select Friends?

I have only answered the first.

Islington

Later

Islington,

If I were not mandated to attend some function every three days this entire month, I would feel more pity. As it stands, I find comfort in our joint suffering.

I do apologise for the inappropriate questions levied at your person. I am, however, myself curious. Please answer each (now, while Toff waits) with all due haste.

Lion

Later

Lion,

June the 4th, details forthcoming.
Yes.
No one's business but my own.
Never, if it can be helped.
Information I found charming. Your undefeatable hair must hail from your Iberian family line.
Stonecrop is sacred ground. Invitations are painfully exclusive. And rightly so.

Islington

May 7th

Whereabouts Lane number 34 has been let!

It is, by all accounts, the young family Mrs. Morrow spoke of; father, mother, two children—boy and girl—who look to be about four and five. The removers arrived first, carrying in furniture and trunks and who knows what. And then came the family, the mother smartly dressed, directing the work while the father tried to be of help, the two children hanging off his arm and laughing. Then, at one point, crying. I found myself smiling along with the picture.

The girl looked up at my window and saw me spying. Having been found out, I lifted Tybalt from his sleeping curve—not pleased—and held him up to the window, moving his paw with my hand to indicate a wave.

Her eyes grew wide.

Thinking I ought to have a bit of fun, I disappeared from the window to snag the crown and sceptre given to me by the Reprobates. Returning in all my majesty, I sat perched in the window, an imperial expression in place when the girl dared look up again. She began to tug on her father's sleeve, but he was distracted by something his wife was saying. Finally, when he'd had enough of the children's antics, he took them down Whereabouts towards the Reed and Rite where I suspect they will be filled with scones and milk.

The mother looked to be relieved.

Later

Another wagon of possessions has arrived.

I spy a piano. They also have a globe.

I approve.

It isn't that I'm looking to become another Mrs. Morrow, but the idea of this fledgling family is...almost like watching the beginning of a story.

Later

I was expecting to invite Pierce for tea in the drawing room.

I was not expecting to push open the studio door and find Pierce sitting on the plum sofa, an array of telegrams on the low table.

There was a full glass of whisky before him, and a half-empty bottle at the ready.

His head was in his hands.

"Pierce, has someone died?" I said before I could think that, perhaps, *Is something wrong?* might be the better question.

Startled, Pierce looked up, eyes rimmed red from ~~too much alcohol~~ what must be a lack of sleep. "What?" he said, dropping his hands. "Oh, no. No." He moved a hand half an inch towards his glass. Stopping himself, he shook his head and looked down at the telegrams before him. The room felt uncertain, as if it could spin into a wobble at any moment. "Not yet, anyway," he muttered.

My stomach tightened.

Pierce picked up a telegram, seeing but not reading the words before him, then tossed it back onto the table. I took a step towards him, halted—still unsure of ~~what the rules of engagement are now that we're…~~ how to behave now that we've ~~decided to~~ decided. A fortifying breath, and I walked over and sat on the plum sofa, feeling his weight tipping me slightly towards his person.

~~It was not unpleasant.~~

It was not the time for such thoughts. However gravitationally sound.

"Pierce?"

"There's been a panic," he said, rubbing the bridge of his nose a moment before dropping his hand. "In New York."

A panic.

Of what sort and variety?

I made an attempt. "A panic after having come to a realisation that they are not able to rule themselves after all?"

His laugh was brief, coarse. "No, uh, financial." Now Pierce reached for his glass of whisky and took a drink. "As I'm sure you've read in the papers, the States have been in a bit of a recession these last two years."

As I'm sure you've read in the papers.

Question: Ought I read the papers more than I do?
Answer: Likely.
However: Books.

"I am afraid," I clasped my hands together in my lap, ignorant but apologetic, "that I have not been following the state of America's finances, calm, nervous, or otherwise."

Pierce ran a hand through his hair—not as tidy as it was earlier in the day when he'd had a client—and let a jaded smile escape. "It has not been ideal, but I've navigated the dip well enough, keeping my portfolio in the clear, holding steady. But it now looks like there was a scheme; certain banks were manipulating their numbers, Grant & Ward being among them. As it happens, I invested heavily in them last year, in tandem with a friend, Thomas Nast."

"Meaning?"

"Meaning, I have lost over seventy percent of my money." He stated it as passionless fact, but his eyes conveyed far more worry.

"Pierce!"

He lifted a hand across his face, pressing his forefinger and thumb against the corners of his eyes as if he'd a headache.

Disbelief. As if I could feel the crush of the loss. How could it have come about? Pierce, working so diligently, being so meticulous regarding his investments, all his efforts.

"The irony is," Pierce continued, breaking me out of my thoughts, "Jonathan Revel has been asking me to invest in the expansion of his and Maggie's business. I was hesitant. It sounded unsafe and far-fetched. Racehorses? But I cashed out some investments over a fortnight back—reluctantly mind you—and put twenty percent of my savings into the business. Now it looks like it's my most reliable investment."

There was nothing I could do. No help to be given. And a half-formed thought in my mind gave the abysmal advice that if I could make him laugh, smile at least, he could… He might… Well, I don't rightly know. But I chose to say, "Surely you mean your most stable investment?"

And then I kicked myself.

Metaphorically.

Pierce sat a moment, his expression an even, humourless stare, but then the edges of his eyes raised in a self-deprecatory amusement. "That was terrible, but yes, it is now my most stable investment, in all senses of the word."

He then laughed. And I grimaced out a silent apology.

"Do you—?"

"I'll be able to pay rent, Emma, of course," he interrupted. "And the other expenses."

"I'm not—"

But he interrupted again, more concerned with the fictional dialogue in his head than our actual conversation. "I'm good for it. I'm good for it," he repeated, as if convincing himself. "I won't make you regret—" Pierce picked up his glass and finished his drink. "I will prove to you," he stated, cutting the air in front of him with his free hand, "that I'm not an unsteady investment."

"I've never thought you were."

He didn't look at me.

"Pierce!" I grabbed his hand, forcing him out of his own head. "You'll set things aright. I'm sorry. I'm terribly sorry. I know, better than most, how it feels. Only, please, don't— Don't—"

His eyes narrowed as he studied my face, silver and exacting. "Don't drag you into this?"

I pulled my hand away. It was a stinging conjecture. "Don't assume I'm so very shallow."

He stilled, gaze intent on my face. "I don't."

I took a breath. "Then know I've no doubts regarding your capacity to weather the storm. Just as you've never doubted mine."

Pierce pursed his lips, then reached to reclaim my hand, catching it sideways. He gave it a squeeze, then ran his thumb over my knuckles. "Apologies."

With the two of us having avoided ~~demonstrative actions~~ most demonstrative actions all week, I'm afraid I rather let my heart skip with abandon.

"Well," I said, trying to regain my footing. "As you wait for more news, I propose a Fiduciary Tea."

"A what?" He looked at me.

"A Fiduciary Tea," I repeated, for footing. "We will take tea in the kitchen with whatever is on hand and try to throw some sunshine on our lot."

Pierce made a sound of discontent. "I'm not really in an acceptable state, Emma, if you'll forgive me. I've already…" He released my hand, motioning towards his worktable where another whisky bottle sat, also half empty and abandoned.

"*Ah*," I replied, the ducal tone covering for my not knowing what to say. "In that case I won't suggest a game of darts, as you might not have the surest throwing arm."

Pierce made a sound of agreement. He gathered up the telegrams before him and stood, as did I.

"I think it best I sleep this off, but do enjoy your tea."

Pierce hesitated, lifting his hand as if he would smooth away the worried lines of my face. But he then let his hand drop back to his side. "I've steady work coming in. I'll manage. The markets are always unpredictable. Gains can be made as fast as losses can be incurred." He spoke as if he were trying to convince himself. "Don't worry over me, Emma. Things will sort out. But I do hope they nail Ferdinand Ward to the wall, that son of a bitch."

I did not intend to raise both eyebrows.

However.

Pierce's smile was rueful. "Again, my apologies."

"Yes, well," I swallowed, "now you've made me worry for Ferdinand Ward."

"Get on with you," he said, waving me off with a painful grimace. He then laughed.

And so did I.

I need to send a note to Mr. Penury. It is time to take another serious look at my financial state and discuss another possible course of work. Although with Aunt Eugenia's schedule here beside me, penned in her extravagant style, I wonder how I'll very well find the time.

May 8th

I dreamt last night that Cousin Archibald stole all of Pierce's money. He was putting it into bags and throwing them out the window. I ran out onto the lane but could find nothing. It was an unsettling dream, me trying to convince him to say where it had all gone. The honest truth is that by the end I was shaking the Unfortunate Relation by the collar and demanding he tell me what he had done with all *my* money. "You can't have spent it all on clothes!" I was shouting.

A conversation with Hawkes on the matter of dreams would not go amiss.

Waking, washing my face, and sitting at my desk, head in my hands, I faced something I had not anticipated—my panic rising as the full force of the realisation presented itself.

My financial insecurity has been negated by Pierce's security.

I've unwittingly assumed, somehow, that one is connected to the other.

Yes, he lets Lapis Lazuli Minor and the studio. There is *that* financial tie. Only, I believe I've entwined my sense of stability with Pierce's. My urgency these last months has not equalled that of Mr. Penury.

I am certain this is why.

Later

Agnes and I conferred over the ink stain on the carpet.

"Is it possible to make it appear less...violent?" I asked.

Agnes knelt down and ran her hands along the stained portion of the carpet. She considered, pulled, and studied, and at one point removed a small pair of scissors from her pocket and snipped a sample or two. Finally, she stood and brushed off her skirt. "Miss, if you'll permit, I'll take these samples to the monthly meeting of the S. S. C. S. S. Someone there will know how to do the job."

"I leave it in your capable hands."

Upon leaving the drawing room, I was cornered by Cousin

Archibald, who has had a Terrible Encounter with a woman on Whereabouts Lane. I know not all the particulars, but it sounds as if he's met a female version of himself and it almost came to fisticuffs.

She has moved into Whereabouts Lane number 36.

He cannot abide the day.

I related what I knew of the affair to Pierce when he'd come to seek me out—stepping into the drawing room and changing the physics of the space. He was wearing his dark grey suit. Sitting on the green sofa, an arm resting comfortably across the back, he was clear-eyed and much improved from yesterday.

"Mr. Flat is a difficult man for me to stomach," he said. Then he frowned and tipped his head to the side. "You've a new carpet."

"Yes!"

"Colourful."

"In the most wonderful way, only don't look where your feet rest."

Which, of course, caused him to look immediately. He frowned.

Before he could think suspicious thoughts, I said, "Now you may surmise that someone has died—"

"Wrong shade to be blood," Pierce replied, very matter of fact.

> *Question*: How ~~comforted~~ discomfited ought I be by such a statement?
> *Answer*: I dared not ask.

"Agnes is going to do her best to remedy the stain," I supplied, "but is it so very terrible?"

"It's your house," Pierce answered, a shrug in accompaniment. "Do what you like."

Lovely, lovely philosophy.

"And how are you? That is, how are you feeling— Or rather, doing in regard to— Simply put, how are you?"

He smiled, a slight thing. "More on my feet after the shock of it all." Then, "I'm sorry, Emma. I'm sorry for the state you found me in."

"No, please don't apologise. There is no call for it. Have you...? That is to say, what will all this mean for you, going forward?"

Pierce carefully measured his expression. As if he felt he could err on either side of something. "It means the security I've worked for is gone. It means rebuilding. It means I continue to ingratiate myself with the over-stuffed, self-satisfied, upper class so they can reline my pockets."

"Gladiator sport."

A fast release of breath, the quietest of laughs. "Something along those lines."

"You'll still be able to come to Stonecrop in June?"

Pierce hesitated, but in a manner I wasn't expecting, as if the question had tapped into a different worry altogether. "I intend to come, but I can't stay the entire visit. Especially now. I need to accept every last commission and drum up more clients."

"Niall Pierce, the social butterfly."

He made a rueful sound. Then, "Speaking of, friends have invited me to dinner tomorrow night. A polite gathering, Mrs. Montgomery as hostess. Would you care to join?"

Would I care to join, he asked. Would I care to join?

Yes.

And no.

Why the hesitation?

~~Is it that I'm not curious about Pierce's friends?~~ I'm dreadfully curious.

Is it that I would feel out of my depth? If it is anything like the soirée I attended in December, I may not feel sufficiently sophisticated. Musing and philosophizing and arguing, throwing my arm over the shoulders of some artist the way that Pierce had so easily draped his over the shoulders of his sculptress friend.

What if I am terribly young and uninteresting in comparison?

What if I become a woman who ages into an uneventful existence, minding my business in all the wrong places and not minding it near enough in the essentials?

"You don't have to—" Pierce began.

"Yes! Of course," I said. "I was only envisioning myself in twenty depressing years, with a ring of keys about my waist and sagging jowls."

A sharp look born of confusion. "Why?"

"Because I'm not a sculptor." A sigh. "I would be happy to

accompany you to dinner tomorrow evening. If your friends are expecting the addition, that is. If it won't upset their table. That is, if there is a table. This may be a *joie de vivre* affair and I should be prepared to fling my limbs around the shoulders of some man in, what I admit to be, petty retribution."

Pierce absently picked at a stray thread on the sofa, an amused frown forming. "I understood one clear thing from what you've just said, which was that you will join me for dinner, after which I gathered you intend to fling your arm over the shoulders of some man as an act of retribution? Dare I ask for clarification?"

It did not sound as logical when he spoke it aloud. I quirked my mouth to the side. "Best leave it at invitation accepted."

His smile came with a narrowed gaze. "Right." Then, "I've been thinking, Emma, about how we might place a more respectable front on this experiment of ours. I was going to speak to you yesterday but was obviously sidetracked."

A flutter of some sort. Possibly palpitations. I replied, "Yes?"

"We spoke of how we received some protection from the authority, the *perceived* authority, of Mr. Flat."

"Unfortunately."

"I think, then, it is incumbent upon me," Pierce sighed, "to ingratiate myself with Mr. Flat. Making it appear to the neighbourhood that I've a stronger connection with him than I do. I'm not saying overmuch. Only, perhaps we go for a drink at The Cleopatra."

"He's banned, from what I recall."

"Is he? Damn."

"Perhaps Gibbs will make an exception?"

"And Mr. Flat will hound me every time he wishes to sneak in for a pint."

I snapped my fingers. "Tea at the Reed and Rite. Followed by a visit to The Hound. The long way round—up Whereabouts and the Diagonal, then down Traitors Road."

"Solid plan." Pierce smiled, mostly with his eyes. "Think it'll help?"

"The illusion that there is an adult male worth speaking to in Lapis Lazuli can't harm anything. Well, it might. The man's a lunatic. However, try we must. It isn't as if much bother has been made up until this point. All is above board with the diplomatic relations of Lapis Lazuli Minor and Lapis Lazuli House. Thus we soldier on."

"Circumspectly."

"Alas."

Later

This evening consisted of a dinner and card party, the first of Aunt Eugenia's excessive list of obligations. Worried as I was—the papers having splashed the news regarding Islington and myself about London—the guest list was small, rather old, and seemingly uninterested. Aunt Eugenia *did* field a few whispered questions from Lady Salisbury, in which I'd swear I heard Islington's name mentioned.

Sigh.

Thankfully, Roland was also in attendance. Try as Aunt Eugenia might to separate us during cards, Roland and I were determined to play at the same table. It took some maneuvering, but when Lord Salisbury took a turn for the worse (the fish had *not* agreed, his wife kept insisting), Roland was able to magnanimously step into his place. Suddenly, what had been a dreary affair was now a lively competition.

Correction came swiftly.

"The point of cards is not to have fun, Emma."

"What is the point then, Aunt?"

"If you're a man playing with men, it is to gamble responsibly. If you are a married woman playing with married women, it is to gossip. If you are a man playing with a woman, it is to rescue your female partner from folly. Which aligns with the sole role of a young woman."

"To be rescued from folly?"

"Yes, thereby spurring on a proposal. Do any of the previously mentioned aims warrant the laughter to which you and Roland subjected your partners this evening?"

It was a veritable relief to return to Lapis Lazuli.

May 9th

Parian came home with a fern today.

Cousin Archibald was in the drawing room writing to Cousin Matilde. Agnes was baking bread. And I was giving the stairs a solid sweep. Parian stood in the hall, fern in hand, waiting, I think, for us to notice this was a Ceremonial Moment. Deciding that if a man wants to celebrate a fern, he ought to celebrate a fern, I called Agnes in from the kitchen. (Cousin Archibald, I did not disturb.)

Parian did his best to hide how pleased he was, clearing his throat impatiently and asking Agnes if she would bring a small glass of water. Upon Agnes's return, the water was placed on the sideboard. "The woman who sold me this fern said they like to be welcomed with a sprinkle," he explained. "A soft rain to hail the new life in our midst."

My eyes went wide. As did Agnes's.

Parian nodded to himself, swallowed, and lifted the potted fern with one hand while reaching the fingers of his other hand into the glass of water. He then sprinkled the fronds in solemnity. It was… well, it was very like a baptism.

Agnes and I gripped one another's hands in an effort to maintain composure. Laughter very nearly escaped us both—Parian, concentrating on making the fern feel at home, was oblivious to it all.

"We greet you," he said to the fern, "and wish you long life."

"Amen," Agnes whispered.

Duty duly fulfilled, Parian looked relieved and back to his usual self. "I was thinking here, Miss." And he placed the fern on the far left of the sideboard, closest to the door. "It seems to have a pleasant amount of light."

"I think you are right, Parian," I answered. Then, "Have you thought of a name?"

Parian let out a breath, his head leaning to the side, eyebrows drawing together in consideration. "I suppose we could call it Fitz."

"Fitz?" Agnes and I both said in tandem. I continued with, "Is it a German fern?"

"No, no, English, I think. Fitzwilliam is the full name, but Fitz will do fine."

"It might want for more water than a sprinkling," Agnes said. "Let me get a plate to set beneath the pot."

Later

I THOUGHT WE COULD WALK DOWN TO KING HENRY'S AND HAIL A HANSOM.

That is the second time in my day the word hail *has been used.*

WHEN WAS THE FIRST?

Oh, when Parian baptized Fitz.

DARE I ASK: WHO IS FITZ?

The fern on the sideboard in the hall. Ah, that's right. You were not present when the household discussed Parian's purchase of a fern. It was terribly moving, the baptism. In its own heretical way.

HAVE I RECENTLY MENTIONED HOW WELL IT SUITS ME TO HAVE MY OWN FRONT DOOR AGAIN?

A laugh at that.

Are you almost ready?

YES. I'LL MEET YOU OUTSIDE IN QUARTER OF AN HOUR?

Which gives me enough time to find my gloves and say goodbye to Fitz.

Later

Our evening was absurdly pleasant.

And if I'd known who would be in attendance, I would have looked forward to the dinner, unequivocally.

The hansom cab took us to an address in Pimlico. The townhouse was narrow, tall, and tidy, every room done in a floral paper. One had the feeling of being in a private garden.

A maid opened the door, and we were ushered up to the first floor, where the Montgomerys greeted us at the doorway of their drawing room—already filled with half a dozen people in conversation. The Montgomerys were not part of the bonhomie set. He (English) is in shipping while she (American) tutors in French and Italian. He was shorter than Pierce, dark bronze hair, brown eyes. His wife was of similar height as her husband, auburn-haired and green-eyed. There were no awkward corners in the introductions. They were Pierce's friends, and I was welcome. Only once did Mrs. Montgomery (*Call me Eileen*, she said mere minutes into the evening) glance between Pierce and I with a look one female recognises in another.

As for the others in the room? A barrister and his wife, a clerk and his sister (who is engaged to a long-absent sailor), and two friends—young men who own a building firm. Mr. Montgomery explained that his aunt would soon arrive.

"You'll have to forgive my relation," he said to me when Pierce and Mrs. Montgomery were trading reminiscences. "She's a bit of an eccentric. The thing is—"

And then who should enter the room but Mrs. Penury!

Unexpected as a Greek climbing out of the belly of a horse.

To a Trojan, that is.

We of the modern world have had centuries to become accustomed to the idea.

"Mrs. Penury!" I exclaimed.

Her eyes lit on my person, and she brightened.

"You…know one another?" said Mr. Montgomery.

But she'd already crossed to where we stood, linked her arm through mine and, with an affectionate nod to her nephew, stole my company. The room was small, and so we made our way to the windows. She pointed through the glass. It was a lovely prospect, despite the encroaching shadows of evening—a church tower rising above a park of trees outlined by the gaslight, and rows of London houses happily living in a line.

"Very picturesque," I confirmed.

Mrs. Penury nodded, a touch more grey in her hair than I remembered there being. She pressed my arm lightly with the fingers of her gloved hand and looked at me expectantly.

"How am I?" I queried on her behalf. "Well." I considered my need to speak with Mr. Penury. "I've been meaning to visit your husband at the bank this week."

Mrs. Penury shook her head.

"Oh dear. Is he ill?"

A smile, followed by a single shake.

"He is elsewhere?"

A nod.

"And will return next week? No. Later this month? No. Next month? Ah, good. Well then, I won't spend a wasted trip. I'd like to see him before I head into Derbyshire. I'm going to Stonecrop, you see, for the month of June. What is Stonecrop? Why it's— Now, when I say this you mustn't think too much of it all. Stonecrop is the Duke of Islington's country seat."

A knowing, expectant, and rather direct look.

"*Ah.* You saw that business in the newspaper."

She nodded slowly, soft brown eyes unflinching, the edges of her mouth trying not to turn up like a paper just unrolled.

"Now," I began, falling into my usual habit of verbal disaster. "I have nothing to say, really, regarding what has been reported. Only Islington was a friend of my father's, a trusted friend. And yes—for all intents and purposes—he inhabits, er, a particular position in my life at present. But not in *that* way. A number of us are going up, not just me. Pierce—Mr. Pierce, that is—will help form the party. Do you remember him? He's over there, speaking with… I actually don't remember who that is. Anyway, Hawkes will be there too. Young Hawkes, the vicar. A respectable party, to have included a vicar. Speaking of respect, Islington's elder sister is to chaperone it all." I took a breath. "What of you, Mrs. Penury?" I rallied. "Anything of note?"

The creases around Mrs. Penury's eyes deepened, and she glanced back out of the window. Lifting her other hand to my arm, she gave it a gentle squeeze. I could not know what it was that weighed on her mind, but I placed my free hand to cover hers and said, "Life may tumble and jostle, now and again, but most things iron themselves out." I paused, "Isn't that right?"

Mrs. Penury nodded just as Pierce approached.

He greeted Mrs. Penury as he came near, extending his hand. She took it easily and he kissed her glove with equal and comfortable confidence. "A pleasure to see you again, Ma'am. And in circumstances where I hope I can redeem myself, as our first meeting was fairly informal."

I did the quick arithmetic of my days and recalled that the only time Pierce and Mrs. Penury had crossed paths was the end of last year, when Islington had raged against my ~~stalking~~ engaging in important, nay, vital! historical research of The Roman.

Who has been remarkably quiet this spring.

Perhaps he's been feeling unwell.

And went to Cornwall.

Or the south of France?

I digress.

The remainder of the guests having arrived, we were ushered up to the dining room on the next floor. There were a dozen of us, all told, a thoroughly convivial gathering. As for the Montgomerys, she and Pierce knew one another from New York, he and Pierce met on a boat to Morocco. Or from Morocco? Or possibly Egypt. That part of the tale I hadn't got straight before the conversation moved on.

At the end of the evening, Mrs. Penury insisted on taking Pierce and I back to Lapis Lazuli House in her carriage, a companionable drive where not much was said, save that which fitted contentedly with the late hour.

When we disembarked, she squeezed my hand.

May 10th

From What I Can Gather*, the family across the street is mostly settled.

> * From What I Can Gather: *The act of using the spyglass Arabella gifted me for Christmas to inspect the home across the lane. Verb. Also, a Noun.*

Mostly settled with two children appears to be a constant state of being run off one's feet. There is—Agnes reports—a cook, a man for odd jobs, and a maid. No governess to speak of, as the mother and maid care for the children in turns. It is rather charming, watching life across the way.

Later

> *Emma,*
>
> *You are to present yourself at Spencer House no later than seven o'clock to prepare for the Halton Ball. We leave at nine. Cooperation is all I need from you. Leave the rest of your perverse personality quite at home.*

Bully for that!

Aunt Eugenia's mandate continued, excessive in length. My given tasks are four-fold:

1. To ensure the remaining men on Arabella's list dance with her at least once. I really do not believe I shall have to maneuver anything in this regard. They will come. Bees, honey, and all that nonsense.

2. To avoid Lord Abernathy who, I was informed, had proposed to Arabella last week! "*The second of* The Season." The second?! Who was the first? "*He has, as I have long thought, too pleasing a face, too fine a*

figure, and would forever be something of a distraction. Arabella will be best suited by contrast, rather than complement." (Which I think is about the stupidest thing I've seen in writing.)

3. To coincidentally overhear any information which might be used against the Countess of Ellam and her daughter, Lady Eloise. This I have no intention of doing. That is not to say I am against hearing a fascinating thing, or even two. But I will not pass any information along to Aunt Eugenia. Manners must prevail! When they suit one's situation, that is.

4. To not embarrass Aunt Eugenia. Unlikely.

And I suppose I could add a fifth from the final note on Aunt Eugenia's instruction. "*If Islington is present, he may ask Arabella to dance, but only at a time of my choosing.*"

Considering this list, it struck me that there are people in this world—usually men—who are doing other things, like walking long, grass-lined roads and thinking poetry and spangled thoughts. Men like Whitman. Or those who study great lives of ages past, recording them for a thousand generations after. Men like Plutarch. Or men who toil in enchanted islands and cold places called Elsinore, weaving magic and tragedy, and selling the tale to those willing to approach the altar of the stage. Men like Shakespeare.

And here I sit. Beneath the thumb of an aunt who wishes me to wear this and curtsy that and manipulate him and discover gossip about her. I've a litany of such things ahead. And so while the previously mentioned have built direct lines between their lives and history, I'm skirting the edges of even my own time.

Bah!

And it isn't, I attempted to explain to Agnes when I communicated the whole with might and vexation just now in the kitchen, that I wish to step away from the day-to-day realities of a life. I *like* the day-to-day realities. Floors must be swept, tea consumed, and windows washed. Walks must be taken, and the purchases of ink (so very much ink) and twine and wood polish are to be made. It is not those things from which I wish to run away. Nor is it existence as a woman. I *like* being a woman. Now, would I rearrange several lopsided restraints? Of course. But my dissatisfaction of the moment comes from having a long list of mandates set by another, so long I cannot see the end of the shadow.

Oh, drat. Look at the time.

Speaking of shadows, I must now leave for Spencer House.

Tybalt, curled up on my bed, just gave a lazy yawn as if to imply I don't have to acquiesce to any of Aunt Eugenia's orders.

But what does he know?

Later

So this is what it means to have found oneself in the centre of the London rumour mill.

Dreadful.

The rise and swell of voices as one passes. The glances. A few outright stares.

We'd been greeted by the hosts and were making our way into the ballroom when I whispered to Arabella, "Are they speaking about me?"

"They're most certainly not speaking about Arabella," Aunt Eugenia hissed at my back. "Emma, I'm ashamed of you. *Ashamed.*"

"*...apparently he had to drag her from the floor for misconduct...*"

"*...but did anybody know he had a ward?*"

"*...Islington...*"

"*Always thought her look to be...*"

Aunt Eugenia's sentiments bothered me not at all, but the undiluted attention, the whispers?

A brutality.

I have taken my insignificance for granted.

One's anonymity is not a thing to give away.

It was not a grand shaming, by any measure. No wide swathes gave way about my person. I was not being cut by society. I was not a scandal. But I am now of interest, and any unrelated woman associated with an eligible man is bound to be made a target. I wanted to shout, "For heaven's sake, it is the year eighteen hundred and eighty-four. We've progressed beyond such old-fashioned gossip!"

Apparently, we have not.

Only how irksome, the interest in my presence. For the general atmosphere was all the warmth and noise of a May ball, with Arabella very soon becoming the centre of *much* male attention. There was no sign of the Countess of Ellam and her "eremite of a daughter." (Which, I must allow, was disappointing. She is such a singular, if unwilling, force of ancient beauty. Strike task three from the list.)

And Aunt Eugenia—seeing Arabella properly engaged in a dance—went quickly to Lady Sheridan's side to plot. (Plot, I say.)

It should have been a comic delight. But due to the Islington Debacle, I've lost my place as Bystander and Observer.

Bother.

Drat and bother.

Women who I've not spoken to in years presented themselves. I found myself considered by men who had walked past me before without a second glance.

And the overheard exchanges?

How maddening!

"*...cannot quite believe. The Duke of Islington? Guardian to the Spencer niece?*"

"*Lady Sheridan said she leads him on a merry dance...tries his soul...*"

"*Always thought she was too friendly...*"

"*Or not friendly enough...*"

But when I turned to glare at the gossipmongers, they'd already faded into the crowd.

Lead Islington on a merry dance?

I?

Emma Lion?

That is to say, I do.

Often.

But certainly *not* in the insinuated manner.

Looking back at the dance floor, I pressed my lips into a line of consternation.

A sigh and an honest consideration of the partners revealed both Annalise Clifford and May Northgate dancing—Annalise quite stoically with a widower on Arabella's approved list, May with a young gentleman to whom I've never been introduced. Roland was also on the floor. A rise of hope at the sight until I saw that his partner was Miss Hunt—*Miss Hunt*, of all people! Yes, she of the tinkling laugh, hunting for husbands right and left, wearing orange as if she could manage the thing. I almost marched out onto the floor and demanded Roland see a doctor.

But then, a beacon of light. For I was bookended by, "Hullo, hullo, hullo!"

"Old thing Emma."

"A nice gown that, not quite your colour."

"No matter, still a picture."

And I found myself sandwiched between the impish Brookstone twins.

Unexpected dazzle of life.

"Why I never—!" I began.

"Certainly not," Phineas said.

"Couldn't be helped," Oliver followed.

Reinforcements. "Are you back for the Season?"

"And you're"—Phineas was already dragging me into the waltz—"going to help make this Season bearable, old friend."

"As bearable as it can be, but what are you doing back in London? I thought your mother wanted you as far from the creaking marriage mart as you both could manage?"

"Yes, dear, but Father paid an impromptu visit to our lair of glorious indulgence in Rome. It wasn't two hours before we were packed up and ordered back to London."

A tap on the shoulder (yes, my shoulder) and I found myself dancing with Oliver. "We did manage to stop in Paris on the way," he picked up, as if it was he I'd been conversing with all along. "Only we decided to shimmy down a drainpipe—leaving Father none the wiser—to join your cousin Damian for a night of theatre, drinking, and dancing into the Seine."

"Into?"

"Well, the drinking preceded. Made climbing back up the drainpipe at dawn a tremendous task. Almost didn't survive."

"I can imagine."

After the dance, we met with Lady Brookstone, having a merry conversation until the boys disappeared into the library for "gambling of the whist variety."

"Their father is furious," Lady Brookstone said to me as we watched them go. "But he often is when it comes to Oliver and Phineas."

Lady Brookstone looked ready to ask me a question when she was approached by an old friend and was quite swept into another conversation.

It was in this moment, as I stood in the glow of rascality—thinking the Brookstone twins would have made natural-born Reprobates—that Charles Goddard appeared.

He fervently asked for a dance.

Before I could say otherwise, Aunt Eugenia had materialised at my side, "Of course she'll dance with you, and be lucky for the chance. Go along, Emma. Arabella is dancing with Lord Brexton, and I've no need of you at present. See how generous I can be when I make up my mind to do so?"

Charles Goddard secured my gloved hand and—with all the adoration he could muster—led me onto the floor.

"Had I known that the Duke of Islington was your guardian, Miss Lion, I would have paid him the proper respect, ingratiating myself in preparation for our nuptials."

"Oh, Charles, I'm sure the ingratiating would be irritating. Please leave the man alone."

"But if he must approve our—"

"Charles. There will be no wedding."

A frown. "I see. If I irritate Islington, he might dash all hopes. Best do as my mother advised and stay close to your aunt, Lady Spencer. We will see a way through this, Miss Lion, I promise you that."

And just as I opened my mouth to clarify my point, he launched into a lecture on best practices for raising boys of the sensitive soul.

He used himself as example.

It was painful, mortifying, and—dare I admit?—somewhat touching.

Over the next two hours, I danced with four men I lightly know, then again with Phineas, then finally Roland.

"Are you *trying* to be snared by a fortune hunter?" I demanded to know.

"It was an awkward business of timing and there was nothing to be done," Roland replied. "I would rather be polite than avoid all inconvenience. I've given her no false hope."

"Yes, however—"

"Don't make me wish I was dancing again with Miss Hunt, Emma."

"Roland, you wound me!"

A golden smile, then Roland asked, "Are you going to explain this Islington affair?"

At which moment I was convinced that the remainder of my life is going to be my explaining Islington to people.

"Dastardly business," I muttered.

"Pardon?"

With an acerbic smile on my face, I experimented with brevity. "He and my father were friends. My father liked him a good deal more than Aunt Eugenia, if you can imagine."

"I can," Roland said, dancing as if he truly did not remember that most of the females in the room were gazing at his person. "But why did you never say anything before?"

Thankfully, at that moment Lord West cut in.

I suppose he had given Islington's cutting in last Season a good deal of thought and decided it was something he might try.

"Miss Lion, I was hoping to speak with you—"

"Please do."

"Only," he fumbled as we fell into step mid-turn, his rhythm and mine never quite finding one another, "I now understand why Islington so elegantly warned me away."

I blinked.

It was not what I was expecting.

But continue he did. "As Islington is your guardian, it is his duty—"

"Lord West."

"—to take precautions. I, as you know, am the guardian of my greenhouse. The flowers therein are mine to shepherd and protect. I care deeply about their breeding. Cross-contamination must *not* be allowed. My friends do not always understand what I deem an acceptable pairing and what I do not. But I am considering the future, do you see? And you, Miss Lion—" he blinked up at me with his placid blue eyes. "You are Islington's greenhouse."

"Oh no!"

It spilled out.

"Or rather," Lord West corrected, "his prized flower in said greenhouse!"

I groaned.

Lord West looked taken aback. "Miss Lion? Are you quite well?"

"Not at all!"

"You look wilted, or as if you might weep."

"I very well might!"

And there we were, still hobbling disjointedly through it all.

The metaphor must have given the man courage, for he tried again. "Are you…fatigued?"

"I am, Lord West. Terribly. But I thank you for understanding that Islington will likely bar my marriage to anyone. Now. Might we spend the remainder of this dance on brighter topics, such as maladies which inflict the sweet pea?"

A tangent which proved effective.

I now know to keep powdery mildew from my greenhouse, at all costs.

When the ordeal was over, I avoided my aunt and her co-conspirators and made my way directly to the powder room. (Which I wished was a gun-and-powder room, where I might arm myself.)

Needless to say, by the time I'd ~~entered~~ clambered into Aunt Eugenia's carriage I was determined to follow Mr. Penury's advice from our first meeting. Sell Lapis Lazuli and settle in a forlorn country cottage.

"You were little help to Arabella," sniffed Aunt Eugenia. "Why, with all the speculation, I myself spent half the night confirming that Islington is, indeed, your guardian. What a glaring waste of my time."

I sighed loudly. So many whispers, cutting at one's ankles.

"You are now what you always wished to be," she continued, finger fully wagging. "A spectacle!"

"Mama, it is too ridiculous an hour in which to be lectured," Arabella yawned.

I closed my eyes in agreement and pretended to fall asleep.

May 11th

A smirking, misty, opinionated rain today. I woke too early and listened to the storm as I reminded myself that last night was the absurdity I remembered it to be.

Despite the delightful return of the Brookstone twins, I choose to believe the planets have misaligned against me.

Later

Hawkes was not in church today, a curate in his place.

Neither was Islington.

Nor Pierce. (Which was to be expected.)

They'd abandoned me, all.

I sat by Mrs. Tribly, who leaned over and whispered, "God is punishing us."

"What, exactly, do you believe he is punishing us for?" I asked.

"Giving Hawkes a hard time of it, love. The Bible says God is no respecter of persons. However, in Hawkes's case, I'm not so certain."

"God gives Hawkes preferential treatment, you mean?"

"It's not that, exactly," she whispered back. "More like, God frowns on those who make Hawkes's life harder. Here, love, have a biscuit."

She opened a small tin hidden beneath her hymnal and proffered a piece of shortbread. Which I waited ten seconds to consume, as seemed only right in church.

Later

I AM GOING UP TO ISLINGTON'S TO SEE SOME ROMAN ARMAMENT RECORDS HE'S GOTTEN A HOLD OF. CARE TO JOIN?

Yes! I plan to rail against Islington in person for having left me to the wolves.

I'LL MEET YOU OUTSIDE IN HALF AN HOUR.

Later

I would have considered impaling him if Islington hadn't have drifted off to sleep in his library—which meant that when Crosby directed Pierce and I into the room, our duke was looking young, innocent, and worn through.

Alas.

When he ~~woke~~ started awake at the sound of Crosby clearing his throat, Islington hastily stood and apologised profusely for having drifted off—"Still a touch tired from it all"—and ordered Crosby to bring refreshment, while inviting Pierce and I to sit with him on the sofas before the hearth.

"Again, pardon," said Islington, controlling what would have been a yawn. "Have you also come to see the armament records, Lion, or to throw a javelin at my person?"

"The second, mostly, and then circling back to the first. However, at the sight of your exhaustion—"

"Exhaustion? I dozed off on a rainy afternoon in my own library. Was church so very bad without my company?"

"Not especially, no. Mrs. Tribly and I ate an entire tin of shortbread. I left filled—literally and spiritually—despite Hawkes being absent."

"Where was Hawkes?" asked Pierce.

"I've no idea, but the shortbread was quite good." I turned back to Islington. "You threw me to the wolves."

"Did I?"

"Last night. At the Halton Ball."

"*Ah.*" He crossed his arms and frowned. "I'd believed my absence would be a help."

"While I was not outright bludgeoned, the whispers and stares were a touch—what is the phrase?—death by a thousand cuts?"

"Attention you did not relish, I'd imagine."

"I much prefer my anonymity."

"Don't we all," muttered Pierce.

"We were the talk of the *ton*, Islington. But I'll spare you the details. Especially Lord West's metaphor."

"Horrifying, I'm sure."

"Rather."

"A perusal of Roman armament records will ease the pain. Wouldn't you agree, Pierce?"

Later

We talked for so long that Islington invited us to stay for an early dinner. It was easy company and ~~an unexpected~~ an expected balm. Eventually, I did admit to Islington the nature of Lord West's metaphor.

He *was* horrified, saying, "More wine, I think."

As for Pierce, he placed the entire debacle in perspective with a few deft sentences. "Gossip and meanness have a way of making one feel beaten down, but they themselves are of small origin. They have no character. So keep yours intact and carry on."

"Hear, hear," from Islington.

I looked at Pierce, his silver eyes always sharper come night. His words held an earned gravity and, as a result, my worry moved to a smaller place.

May 12th

"Miss, *he's* here to see you."

"*He's* here? It sounds as if you're introducing *The Duke of Islington.*"

I was in the back garden doing a bit of…well, *gardening*. And when I say gardening, I use the term loosely. I was standing with a pair of kitchen shears before a rambling rose profusing itself violently along the wall, determined to quell its enthusiasm. I had yet to make a cut.

Profusing?

Not a word, I fear.

(Confirmed. I've looked in the dictionary and *profusing* is nowhere to be seen.)

I digress.

"Yes, Miss," Agnes confirmed.

I blew a strand of hair away from my face and considered the monster before me. "Good. He mentioned he might visit. Now, Agnes, does gardening *require* I suppress this rose?"

"It has gone a wee bit ramble, Miss, but you're supposed to prune it early spring. Or after the first bloom. Not now while it's covered in roses."

"Ah. Well." I looked about. "It can't be said I didn't attempt the thing. Islington is in the drawing room?"

"Yes, Miss."

I followed Agnes back into the kitchen and went straight to the drawing room, apron over my afternoon dress, shears still in my right hand.

Islington was not waiting politely (as he ought to have been).

No, he was standing, hat in hand, glaring at the carpet.

"Hello, Islington. You didn't tire of my company yesterday, I see."

"What is this?" he asked, looking at me as he motioned to the carpet with a flattened hand.

"It's a carpet, a very nice one. Quality is ever my watchword."

"It looks like something has been murdered."

"In a way, something was. Won't you please sit down so events don't find themselves repeated?" I snapped the shears in warning.

He looked at my ensemble, wild hair accompanied by perspiration on my brow, and asked, “Have you been shearing sheep?”

“Roses. Or, thinking about it. I’ve little idea what I’m about, despite having grown up in the country. My mother never let me near her flowers.” I collapsed into my pink chair.

Islington sat on the sofa, setting his hat and gloves at his side. He leaned forward just enough to continue his tedious scrutiny of my lovely carpet. “The stain makes one suspect a body is concealed hereabouts.”

“There soon will be,” I ~~snipped~~ answered patiently. “Besides, Pierce says it’s the wrong colour to be blood.” Islington did not appear to take comfort from the statement. “I was gifted this carpet,” I continued. “I like the design very much. And yes, there is the small matter of my having spilled red ink all over. So goes life. Is this a social call, or have you come with a specific purpose? Such as nagging?”

“It began as a social call but now I’m questioning whether we need to find you a new carpet.”

“I like *this* carpet.”

“Hmm.” All disapproval.

A polite segue was deemed necessary. “My aunt said three very unpleasant things about your person on Saturday.”

Islington, having partially reconciled to the stain beneath his feet, looked up at me, his hazel eyes clear. “I’m certain she did. She sent me a full list of events for May and asked to which I would be presenting myself and would I insist on creating A Stir.”

“I’d like to see that.”

“I don’t create stirs,” he elegantly replied.

I snorted, but Agnes entered. “Pardon me, Miss. I came to enquire if the duke should need anything.”

“Good afternoon, Agnes,” Islington charmed. “I don’t need anything, no. I’ll not be taking my tea for a few hours yet. I say, Agnes, does your expertise extend to the removal of ink?”

“I’ve already taken samples, Your Grace, per Miss Lion’s request, and am prepared to bring the matter before the Senior Servants. If there is a way to reclaim this carpet, the S. S. C. S. S. will know. We’ll not let you down.”

She curtsied rather deeply in the ducal direction and quit the room.

~~I refrained from making a long-suffering expression.~~

I did not. Long-suffering expression was made.

Islington, charm melting into a flat glare once he looked in my direction. "Why didn't you simply tell me you were arranging to have it cleaned?"

"I was amusing myself at your disapproval's expense. Shall we go for a walk?"

And so we went.

(Let me insert, the apron *was* removed.)

We walked through Regent's Park. A beautiful day for our pains.

"You seem agitated," I said.

"Do I?" he asked, looking into the distance but not seeing much of anything.

"It's only a stained carpet. Honestly, Isling—"

"Don't be absurd. I'm not bothered by the— The carpet has already escaped my thoughts. If you must know, I've had a letter from my sister."

"Which one?"

"My elder sister, Mariana, who writes to tell me to expect a visit from my youngest sister, Margaret, and her husband, in June."

"Isn't it customary to write the host oneself?" I enquired.

"Yes, if you're a thinking, rational human being. As it happens, too often if you ask me, Maggie doesn't want me to question anything. She wants to do as she pleases with no regard to anyone else. So she writes to Mariana, informing her when she plans to waltz—leap rather, as if from the basket of a hot air balloon—into our lives, expecting everyone to catch her, and fawn over her, adorning her with ribbons and crowns, as if we've been gifted a presence so vivid and dazzling we should cast every other concern or obligation aside and worship the inconsiderate flash of *joie de vivre* that is my sister Maggie."

It was unexpected.

Both the level of intimate detail and the emotion unmasked.

My next question may not have been the best. There were many threads I could have pulled in Islington's Tapestry of Irritation. But I chose this one: "Have you truly seen someone *leap* from a hot air balloon?"

It was a rather sharp impatience conveyed in the look that Islington gave in return. Followed by an unwilling smile and a sound of frustration that turned into a laugh. "*She* would have said the exact same thing," he said. And I couldn't tell if *she* was Maggie or someone else. Then he answered, "Only metaphorically, Lion. All this to say, our last week at Stonecrop will be graced with the presence of Mr. and Mrs. Jonathan Revel."

It was a mostly wonderful concept.

Despite the fact that the more I hear of his youngest sister, the more I'm afraid of her, even if she is—have I done the maths correctly?—two years my junior. "I thought you liked your brother-in-law? It certainly seemed so when you first spoke with Pierce."

"While I was not thrilled with the idea of the man, upon our actually meeting, I liked him on the spot. We get on well. He has his feet on the ground and seems to love Maggie despite her being absurdly mad. I can't imagine what we'd do without him. And I will be happy to see my sister, of course. Only she is determined for everything to enter her gravitational pull and most certainly *can* walk about with barbs."

"I can't imagine knowing a member of the Devereux family with *barbs*," I sauced.

He glanced sidelong at my face. "If you think I can be sharp, prepare yourself with some very thick armour."

On the whole, I feel more and less excited to meet this sister. Pierce, however, seems fond. And if necessary, I'll simply hide in his shadow.

Not that I am the sort to hide (too often) in the shadows of avoidance.

Only, if Maggie Revel is the sort to throw herself confidently from a hot air balloon (metaphorically), I'm not certain yet she won't try and bite off my finger.

May 13th

This morning I've had an honest conversation with Numa Pompilius.

I have been negligent.

It is not that I don't wish to finish the narrative of his life. I do.

Only, it will likely be helpful for me to return to the beginning (meaning that whole business of the Romans and Sabines debating how to proceed with the government). I've no desire to read a thing and not recall three-fourths due to any number of distractions.

To say that my attempts at scholarship are in shambles might be accurate.

Later

It Happened Like So

A knock came to the door late morning. Having met with Pierce across breakfast, helped Agnes put the bedclothes out on the line to dry, and returned from a glorious walk, I was sitting in the drawing room, returned to Rome and its post-Romulus confusion.

My day having been the model of industry, I felt willing—nay, practically ordained—to open the door when a knock sounded.

This I did.

To find a man I recognised as Plithco Wright standing before me.

"Good morning, Mr. Wright," I said.

"Ah, good morning, Miss Lion. I say, I know this is a bit odd, but we are fellow St. Crispians, and so I ask: does Hawkes happen to be here?"

"Hawkes?"

"Yes."

I was perplexed. "Did he tell you he would be?"

"No, only he's not been seen since that whole David and Goliath fiasco at the church, and I've been needing to speak with him."

Knitting my eyebrows, I commiserated. "I'm afraid I've not seen him in over a week."

Mr. Wright shrugged. "I thought you would know. Owing to that d'Artagnan business."

Just as I was about to open my mouth to ask what d'Artagnan business, he continued with, "I'll ask Gibbs again, although he's rather tight-lipped regarding Young Hawkes."

"A sturdy principle to uphold."

Mr. Wright pulled at his gloves and lifted his hat in my direction. "Good day."

"Good day," I replied in a rather automatic fashion.

He was gone.

And I was left standing at the open door of Lapis Lazuli asking myself whatever could it mean?

That *d'Artagnan* business?

Later

> *We've not yet had a letter from the Accidental Wife.*
>
> *DO YOU MEAN NICK STONE'S WIFE?*
>
> *The very same. Do you think this means they've decided to throw off London, and Tybalt is ours?*
>
> *I THINK IT MEANS THEY HAVE BEEN OCCUPIED AND TRUST WE WILL UNDERSTAND UNTIL THEY COME FETCH TYBALT AT THEIR EARLIEST CONVENIENCE.*
>
> *What a pessimistic view of the world.*
>
> *Pierce?*
>
> *YES?*
>
> *Have you heard anything about some d'Artagnan business or other?*
>
> *NO*

May 14th

This evening I attended a dinner with Aunt Eugenia and Arabella. It was at the home of Rutherford Crane, a widower friend of Aunt Eugenia's, whose sister played hostess to a small, exclusive gathering of wealthy, titled nonsense-speakers.

I braced myself for any unexpected thing.

Thankfully, the geriatrics outnumbered us all, and they'd little interest in me whatsoever.

Bless them.

I was the last to enter and exit every room, as usually happens, but I was paired with a gentleman of eighty with the tendency to let yell anything he had to say so that his companion might hear. His late wife, apparently, had been quite deaf.

"You Remind Me Of A Girl I Knew When I Was A Young Man!"

"My Wife Hated Those Curtains!"

"I Rather Like Peas!"

And at that moment, for my own entertainment, I replied, "I'm sorry, but I couldn't hear you."

"I SAID I RATHER LIKE PEAS!"

The entire table grimaced.

After the meal, in the drawing room, I was ordered to stand between Arabella and a "ghastly lamp which makes all women appear plain and sickly. It should have no great effect on your features, Emma." And so I stood like a Japanese screen, while Arabella flirted with Steward de Preiss and Lord Stringham—both on Aunt Eugenia's List—by turns.

The only bright spark of the evening was when Aunt Eugenia confided a deep dislike of a Lady Becker. "Can't stand the woman," she hissed ~~to~~ *at* me in the drawing room. "She judges All and Sundry in silence until, at regular intervals, she clangs out an opinion as if she were a bell. Most uncomfortable for those of us who prefer to share our judgements freely, without discretion."

Aunt Eugenia, tired from the dinner and the subsequent musical offerings—Arabella Spencer played the piano, Emma M. Lion did not—

was disapproving of both present prospects for Arabella.

"We shall strike Steward de Preiss from the list. Well, perhaps after I invite him over this week to propose to Arabella. As for Lord Stringham? He is *far* too in love. Why, he becomes a veritable milksop in Arabella's presence."

It was then Aunt Eugenia ordered the carriage to return to Spencer House before sending her coachman to go "well out of his way" to take me to Lapis Lazuli.

"It would be better if Miss Dowd were waiting at Spencer House to usher you home, Emma, with no inconvenience to the rest of us."

"It very well might, Emma," Arabella contributed from what I can only claim to be a perverse sense of self-entertainment at great cost to others. A dangerous game, as I am certain Aunt Eugenia would cut off at least three appendages were she to discover the truth.

To be clear, the appendages would be mine.

"Miss Dowd goes to bed quite early on the nights when I am acting as your agent on behalf of Arabella," I said, "as she wishes to preserve her energies to discipline my person, as needed, at Lapis Lazuli."

This seemed to meet with Aunt Eugenia's approval. "I do hope she doesn't leave a mark." Then, "At least not one that can be seen in a ball gown."

"Only a mark on my conscience, Aunt," I managed straight-faced. "A reminder that I will eventually pay for all falsehoods, which hang like the sword of Damocles. So says Miss Dowd."

"It is good and right she say such things. To keep you from Behaviours Natural to a person Like Yourself," came my aunt's reply. Then an aside, "A woman of sense, your Miss Dowd. I do like her a good deal."

"As do I," Arabella drawled.

"I should have her for tea, on a day when you are suitably subdued. Think on her counsel, Emma, as you are being driven home by Waits."

"I shall, Aunt. With gratitude and grace," I muttered at the window.

When I arrived home, Agnes and Parian were laughing over something in the kitchen. Cousin Archibald had eaten his dinner and then left to visit the Ericksons of Great Pulteney Street, who are in London. The door to Pierce's studio was ajar, marking the dim hall like a bookmark.

I quickly went upstairs, changed my clothing, and returned with my journal. Pierce was sitting on a stool at his worktable polishing two pairs of boots and one pair of black evening shoes.

"It's you," he said, when I pushed the door of his studio open the wider.

"It is I."

"How was dining with the upper echelons of society?"

"As you can imagine, having had a number of invitations yourself."

Pierce made a sound of pained agreement.

Looking to see if the curtains were drawn (they were), I entered. "It is late, but the entire house is still awake. Care for some company? Oh, hello Tybalt! Lovely cat. I see you beneath the chair."

Pierce—the steady movement of the small brush in his hand, the sound of the swish, swish—glanced up at me, happy.

I sat on the sofa and opened my journal, prepared to record the day.

"Pierce?"

"Hmmm?"

"Is anyone— That is, ought we…?"

He looked up at my question.

"That is to say, is anyone to know we are—for want of a more palatable word—courting?"

Pierce looked down, angling the shoe he was polishing, before glancing back up. "Is there anyone in particular you would like to tell?"

The notion gave me pause.

I thought about telling Islington. I didn't care for the image.

I thought about telling Hawkes.

> Emma: "Hawkes? I have something to tell you."
> Hawkes: "You have decided to become a professional sailor."
> Emma: "Well, no, actually. At least not in the near future, although I do support most professions which require hats. I'd like to tell you

that Pierce and I are, in fact, courting."
Hawkes: …
Emma: "We like one another a great deal."
Hawkes: …
Emma: "Won't you say something?"
Hawkes: "What should I say?"
Emma: "We could begin with how you knew my father?"
Hawkes: "Good day, Miss Lion."
Emma: "Hawkes, wait!"

I cannot even get Hawkes to do my bidding when I'm writing his words *for* him.

But I suspect he suspects, which I said aloud, for Pierce asked, "Who suspects?"

"Oh. Hawkes."

Pierce's hands slowed but they did not stop. "You may be right."

"Why the concurrence?"

"He invited me for a drink a few nights after the May Day fête."

"At The Cleopatra?"

"Yes."

"And?"

"He didn't say a word. Just sat across from me taking his pint slowly, sometimes looking around, sometimes watching me."

"What did you say? Was it very uncomfortable?"

"Not very, no. I had my own thoughts. Why bother companionable silence?"

Nice, in theory. However, there are times I prefer information to companionable silence.

May 15th

I am filled with regret.

And yet still believe I made the ~~right~~ best decision.

While I have a rather too comfortable relationship with my own foibles, this morning I did something quite without thinking. And I worry that it might come at the expense of another's peace. Another who means a great deal to me.

Meaning: Hawkes.

I tried to reverse the hasty act, but it was too late. Too many strings had become attached.

This afternoon, I was sorting the garret, telling Tybalt that he was the finest feline specimen known to man and would he please consider *not* going with Mrs. Jane Stone when she and her Accidental Husband come to collect him. (I argue this pending grief put me in a mind to *carpe diem*. And so Latin must bear a portion of the blame.) Among the detritus I cleared from my desk was the advertisement from the St. Crispian's *Gazette* on May Day, asking for any denizen of St. Crispian's to contribute a small article about the goings on of the fair. Opening my journal and reading through the day, it was clear what the most significant public event was: Hawkes taking down that brute of a fighter. The account brought back the pull of worry, the push of desperation, then shock! Amazement! Triumph!

Without thinking, I set a clean sheet of paper before me and rewrote the account—a few tucks here, a few pins there, and it was done. Such a noble, unexpected tale. Nothing could be more fitting for the upcoming *Gazette*.

The advertisement stated that all submissions were to be delivered to The Cleopatra by end of day on the 15th, so I put on an afternoon dress, my gloves, a hat even, and stepped out into the sunshine to deliver my contribution.

Gibbs was happy to see me, and upon enquiry, he directed me to a table near the back where Mr. Harper himself was enjoying a pint and reading a newspaper.

"Hello, Mr. Harper."

He glanced up, salt and pepper hair too dapper for his own good. "Miss Lion, please don't tell me you're here to ask more favours of the long-suffering *Gazette* committee?"

My smile was deliberately sweet. "It is the fifteenth of the month, Mr. Harper. Which, if your advert was correct, is the last day to submit something written about the fair." I held out the envelope in which I had placed my carefully folded account and set it on the table. "For your consideration."

He was looking at me with steady challenge when he said, "I've already had more than one rapturous description of the fireworks, Miss Lion."

"And I hope you will print them all," I replied before turning on my heel and exiting The Cleopatra.

Feeling Accomplished and Proficient for having contributed something towards the betterment of mankind, I took myself in the direction of Regent's Park for a lap of victory. Only something began working at the frayed end of my conscience. It worked and worked, pulling at this and that, until enough had unravelled for me to realise that I may have just betrayed Hawkes.

In an utterly insensitive manner.

A multitude of feelings rose up in my chest, all ending in the singular knowledge that I needed to protect him.

And I may not have.

I felt ill.

Turning myself around, I walked and ran, by turns, out of Regent's Park, across a corner of Primrose Hill, and back into St. Crispian's where I pushed through the door to The Cleopatra.

I noticed Gibbs pause out of the periphery of my eye, but my focus was on Mr. Harper, still reading his newspaper.

Relief.

I walked forward and opened my mouth to speak when he—without looking up—moved a folded piece of paper into my vision. Written on said piece of paper were the words: *No Gazette Submission Can Be Withdrawn Once Submitted.*

My heart sank with the long breath I let out.

I slumped onto the opposite bench in Mr. Harper's booth. "Mr. Harper."

"Yes, Miss Lion?"

"Might I please have the envelope back I gave to you not half an hour ago."

Eyes still on what he was reading, he lifted a finger and tapped it on his makeshift sign.

"There were no such parameters on the advertisement."

He tapped the sign again.

"Mr. Harper."

He looked up. "I am afraid once submitted, there is nothing I can do. The committee—"

"You run The Committee, Mr. Harper! For all intents and purposes, you *are* The Committee!"

A glass of lemonade was set before me.

I looked up to see Gibbs. He winked at me and walked back to the counter.

I made the resigned expression of one who has been given a small kindness in the depths of despair and took a sip of the lemonade.

"Miss Lion,"—Mr. Harper set down his paper—"I know you are friends with Young Hawkes. I also know Hawkes. And so I tell you this to ease any qualms you may have. There was only one story which was attempted more times than the fireworks display. Can you guess which?"

I may have taken another sip of lemonade, set my glass on the table, and slouched over my corset. This silent action was all the answer I gave.

"Most of the submissions were overdone, maudlin, and frankly a disservice to the pugilistic display at their core. Yours was quick, engaging, and humorous. If you are a true friend to Hawkes, you will leave your submission with me. Otherwise, a different version of events will be published, and it will—believe me—be doing our resident Prometheus little justice."

I grimaced.

"If Hawkes were here, you could ask him," Mr. Harper continued. "But he has not been in the neighbourhood these many days."

"He has not," I confirmed.

"Do you know why today is the deadline, Miss Lion?"

I shook my head.

"The typesetter of the *Gazette* is Mr. Byrd."

"The old gentleman who sits on the front right pew working out riddles in church?"

"The ancient gentleman who works out riddles in church. He's ninety-seven years old. If he does not begin to lay out the *Gazette* tomorrow morning, it will not be finished in time for the June printing. You must make your decision now. Embarrass Hawkes through the hands of others—which I will do without remorse—or discomfit him while giving a solid, suitable account of what he accomplished that day, preserved in dignity rather than fluffery for all generations to come."

If Pierce had been there to ask. Or Islington.

But no.

It would do no good to consult with another. I needed to ask myself, honestly, what was to be done.

I chose Hawkes's dignity.

"I expect my name to be withheld."

The wrinkles around Mr. Harper's eyes creased in victory.

Picking up my lemonade, I tipped my head back and drank what remained in a single, unladylike swig, stamping the glass onto the table with resigned finality.

"Good day, Mr. Harper. And I'm certain we both know *fluffery* is not a word."

And then I left.

When Pierce returned home and entered his studio, he found me sagging against a cushion on the plum sofa in philosophical angst, Tybalt stretched out beside me—asleep, ears twitching—unread Plutarch on my lap. For who can read about Numa Pompilius when they've betrayed, and yet saved from sentimental account, a friend.

"A pleasant surprise," Pierce said, crossing the room and easing the camera over his shoulder gently onto the table, placing beside it the large carrying case in his hand. "Long day of it, I gather. Should I ask Agnes for tea?"

"For heaven's sake, yes."

Tea was had.

Over the crumbs of a lemon cake, I made light conversation,

having already decided that I wished to keep the *Gazette* to myself for the present. There will be a reckoning in June, should the men read my account. Thankfully, I believe it to be a small chance that Islington murder me at Stonecrop. It's far too pleasant-sounding a place for that.

He'd wait until we'd returned to London.

When our conversation did turn towards Stonecrop, Pierce shared what he knows of the ongoing financial crisis in New York. Another series of telegrams has confirmed that, yes, his money is gone. "You're not to worry," he kept repeating. Then, "I know how to land on my feet, Emma. I know how to work."

"It's unfair," I told him.

"Life isn't without risk."

"No."

And I'd looked out of the window so I didn't see his face when he said, "I might not be at Stonecrop for as long as I'd planned."

I looked back at him.

He was waiting, watching.

"Of course. You have new considerations you must take into account." I abandoned my worried expression and smiled at Pierce. "You'll join us for what you're able, I'm sure."

May 16th

I had grand plans for my Friday afternoon and they did *not* include Victoria Braithwaite.

It happened when I visited The Keep and had begun scouring the shelves for Agnes's sewing box. No immediate results. (It was later discovered that Parian had absconded with the box that he might fix a loose button.) So I found the register and was reading through unclaimed entries when I heard a sniff.

Then another.

I blinked and looked about. Nothing.

Then peering around one of the centre tables, I saw a young woman in a black dress, sitting on a low stool like a raven crumpled on the ground.

It was Victoria Braithwaite.

She was crying.

Face splotched in red, tears she could not control, holding one gloved hand in front of her face to cover her embarrassment. I was hesitant to intrude. But one does not leave an Archnemesis in full mourning crumpled on the ground without a handkerchief. Not even Machiavelli would have suggested such a breach in etiquette. (The aforementioned statement is not necessarily true.)

"Victoria?" I attempted, withdrawing a clean handkerchief from my reticule.

She ignored me.

Another sniff.

I crouched down beside her.

"Victoria, are you all right?"

"Go away," she managed.

"Are you trying to find something? I can only imagine how… unsettling St. Crispian's can seem."

"Go away!" she repeated raggedly.

I did not go away. I placed my handkerchief in her twisting, tear-stained hands. She made as if to brush it away, then grabbed hold, her back to me as she sorted herself. There was a rolled-up rug nearby, which I dragged over and sat on, indecorousness for the sake of camaraderie. The handkerchief fully used, Victoria opened her mouth to speak but only a wail came out. She covered her mouth with both hands yet could not arrest the sob. Her shoulders shook and she tore off one cry after another. I threw both of my arms around Victoria and pulled her close. Much to my surprise, she let herself fall against me, utterly brokenhearted and weeping it all out.

I heard someone enter The Keep and had fashioned a disinviting frown by the time a ruddy-faced man appeared, whistling. I waved him off without unsettling the inconsolable Victoria. It took an unreasonable amount of time for him to understand the pantomime, but in the end he turned and disappeared. A second person entered, a maid not a year or two older than Agnes. She'd a more practiced eye, understanding then leaving before I had to shoo her away. With each intrusion, Victoria had grown more ashamed, crying harder, and so when I heard the third set of footsteps, uneven and strong, I leapt to my feet and said, "Really, cannot people stay away for five minutes altogether!"

My impatience dissipated when I realised I was looking at Pierce.

"Oh," I managed, a touch out of breath for my haste. "It's you."

Frozen in place, Pierce looked about to enquire, but he stopped himself upon seeing Victoria. A nod of comprehension and he left as quietly as he could manage.

Victoria was trying to make use of the now sodden handkerchief and so I wordlessly rummaged around the shelves until I found one that was clean and unadorned with any identifiable cipher. (One *has* learned their lesson about paying attention to ciphers on objects.)

I held out the orphaned handkerchief, which she accepted before going about the painful process of regaining composure. To give her privacy, I began glancing through the shelves. Once Victoria had sorted herself, she gathered her skirts and stood.

"Victoria—"

"Thank you for your help," she said, her voice anaemic yet sharp.

"I think—"

But she had moved past me.

I followed. "At least let me help you out of the Reed and Rite."

She paused, and half turned, letting her guard ~~drop~~ wander off a bit before nodding quickly.

Relieved, I linked my arm in hers. "We will enter the tearoom, smiling demurely as we keep our conversation low, heads bent towards one another in a manner that would be awkward to interrupt. Moving with steady but not undue speed, we will go up the stairs to the shop and straight out of the doors, turning right on Whereabouts Lane without hesitation. Once on the street I can—"

"Apologies," someone was saying just outside our field of vision. "The Keep is closed for maintenance. Come back in half an hour. Yes. Record verification, I believe. A quarterly task."

It was Pierce.

One more step and we could just see his profile.

A creak in the floor gave us away. Pierce, arms folded, leaned back and saw us, an even gaze between us two before he said, "Sorted?"

I nodded. "We only need to make our escape."

"The tearoom is relatively empty, but the shop is teeming with people. Follow me up the stairs and I'll see that you escape unnoticed."

"And then you'll join us back at Lapis Lazuli for tea?"

Pierce, after a pause, nodded. Working his way through the tearoom, Victoria and I followed at a small distance. Then once we were up the stairs, Pierce looked back at us both. His smile was a quiet scaffold. "Give me ten seconds, and when you hear a bit of a crash, slip across the room and out of the door."

Victoria was watching Pierce intensely, like he would save her from any eventuality.

I frowned. "What are you going to—?"

But Pierce had stepped out and…

Crash.

Grunt.

Rush of voices.

My heart jumped out a window and straight onto the pavement of my stomach.

"Good heavens, are you all right?" a man asked.

"He just took a terrible fall!" said an older woman.

"Isn't he the fellow with the limp?"

Then a muffled apology from one quasi-American photographer.

Pierce had fallen on his sword.

Closing my eyes, I tightened my arm around Victoria, and we swept across the now distracted Reed and Rite, while everyone's eyes were on Pierce regaining his footing.

~~I wanted to kiss the man.~~

~~I wanted to bludgeon the man.~~

~~I wanted to elope with the man.~~

I kept all wild and half-formed thoughts unspoken.

Victoria was looking over her shoulder, eyes wide, red-rimmed, and swollen. "Do you suppose he's all right?" she asked.

I led Victoria across the street and up the pavement, loosening my grip on her arm.

"I would wager he fell onto his good leg," I answered. "We have just witnessed a chivalry few men possess. An extra piece of cake for us all."

Victoria almost smiled when I said the word cake.

Entering Lapis Lazuli, I ushered Victoria into the drawing room—not to Hawkes's chair, but the green sofa—and went to the kitchen to ask Agnes if she could prepare tea an hour earlier than usual.

"*A consummate servant is ready to accommodate the unexpected with grace*," she quoted.

I shared a glance with Islington, The Portrait Of.

"A direct quote from the Society of St. Crispian's Senior Servants handbook, Miss."

"Heavens, do you have the entire thing memorized?"

Her face fell a fraction. "Almost, Miss Lion. But there is a tricky bit in the chapter on Managing the Unmanageable that I've still to commit to memory."

"Onward and upward, my dear Agnes. I shall do my best to let you practice the proficiencies outlined in said chapter."

She brightened. "Oh, Miss, you already do that so well!"

I frowned, then informed her that Pierce would be joining Victoria and myself for tea.

I've discovered that a silent Victoria Braithwaite, perched in black on my green sofa, is not the most comfortable of situations. Entering the drawing room, I hesitated before taking a seat in my chair. "The sunshine has been nice," I said, like a lame horse, hobbling my way through a field of rabbit holes.

Victoria obliged with a half nod, then sighed, glancing about the room.

"Have you been able to leave Colonel Braithwaite's house…?" I attempted.

"It's only been six weeks."

"Hmm, yes," I replied, not wringing my hands, but knotting them a bit. "I've no wish to make light of your mourning, but neither do I agree that a young woman isn't to be treated as human for the year after her parents have died, not allowed out to enjoy anything that might divert one's mind. You might find," I swallowed and followed Pierce's self-sacrificing example, "a few moments of respite here at Lapis Lazuli House. Or I might accompany you for a walk in Regent's Park."

She made a line of her mouth, then spoke with an equal measure of suspect cooperation. "I've told the General he is to find me a proper chaperone, so I might—as you say—accept the appropriate condolences or take a short, respectful walk in a park. She would then be ready to help me re-enter society, if…" And the words hung between us. If society would take her back.

The fact of the matter is that unless the General were to put up a rather sizable dowry, Victoria Braithwaite would not be a prize, her father having owed his entire fortune to creditors.

The newspapers had been cutting and cruel.

And, alas, accurate.

In that moment I thanked God I still had Lapis Lazuli.

I nodded along with the incompletion of her sentence, wishing Agnes would hurry, and that when Pierce arrived, it would be in a way that would not cause undue suspicion. We have enough due suspicion to battle as is.

Thankfully, Pierce thought the same. A knock came to the respectable front door.

And then Parian—miracle of miracles—was on hand to answer. I do not know if they two exchanged a glance but when Parian showed Pierce into the drawing room, it was as if it didn't happen on the daily.

Parian is becoming something of a chum.

"Good afternoon, Miss Lion. Miss Braithwaite," Pierce said, holding his hat and waiting for me to invite him to sit.

"Mr. Pierce," I stood, "welcome. I've asked Agnes to prepare a tea—which you've certainly earned. Would you care to…" I was going to direct Pierce to the gold chair, but Victoria shifted and made the other half of the green sofa so readily available that there was nothing for polite manners to do but accept.

Which Pierce did, a quick glance in my direction.

Thankfully, Agnes soon arrived with tea.

This allowed for a light back and forth. "Cream? Sugar?" and all the reliable nonsense tea provides. We sat in a few moments of quiet, my noticing how Pierce shifted in discomfort.

"I've not seen you again at church, Mr. Pierce," Victoria said. A question even the likes of myself thought forward, considering their lack of relationship. (Which ~~may be~~ is hypocritical considering ~~some~~ many of the questions I've before asked.)

Pierce answered with ease. "No, I don't often go. But how do you enjoy the services, Miss Braithwaite? Is the preaching of Young Hawkes to your liking?"

"Oh, yes," was her reply. There was a shine in Victoria's eyes of which I was suspect. And then, "Especially the readings he selects for Evensong."

"Evensong?" I blurted. "St. Crispian's holds Evensong services?"

"Only a day or two each week, but the days vary," Victoria replied. "The General receives a note from Mrs. Coverfield each Sunday afternoon with the pertinent information."

Pertinent information, she said.

As if that phrase should even come within a ten-mile radius of Hawkes.

I was not repenting of my act of kindness, of course not. But I had the uneasy feeling of having ceded some ground that Victoria had stepped right into. If Hawkes—Our Hawkes, My Hawkes—had mentioned the fact that he held an occasional Evensong, I might be much further along the path of virtue.

I lay my lack of Higher Road sentiment at the feet of my vicar entirely.

I digress. As a result of not having attended an Evensong in ages.

"Mr. Pierce," Victoria said, her eyes justifiably filled with gratitude, and a touch too winsome. "I cannot thank you enough, for both what you did today and the portraits you captured. I've— That is, my uncle has already commissioned frames and they are a tremendous comfort."

"Of course," Pierce replied, all sincerity.

As he should.

Sigh.

Victoria set her hand on the sofa, leaning half an inch in his direction, "And your note of condolence has been read and reread. Thank you, truly."

Pierce nodded, frowning. "We all need a kind word in due season."

It was then a knock came to the door, which Parian answered. I gave it no great thought, thinking it someone asking for a donation to some committee.

It was not.

For—and I never would have thought the sight of this man could bring joy—in walked Charles Goddard.

"Good heavens, Charles!" I said.

"Miss Lion! You are a picture. Oh, why, Miss Braithwaite," as he registered Victoria. "I'm happy to see you looking so well, by golly. Happy indeed." Then his gaze moved to Pierce. "Hell— Oh! You!"

"Good afternoon, Mr. Goddard," Pierce drawled.

"Mr. Goddard," I attempted. "Why don't you join us. Yes, right there is fine, on the green sofa."

And despite the look of slight alarm from every face that was not my own, I ushered him to sit smack dab in the middle of Pierce and Victoria Braithwaite. Three uncomfortable peas in a pod.

Charles Goddard looked at Pierce. "But aren't you…?"

"I think, Miss Lion," Victoria stood, "it was time I returned home. Thank you for the tea and," she hesitated, "everything else. Forgive my leaving just as you've arrived, Mr. Goddard," she said. "I'm sure my uncle is expecting me. Good afternoon, Mr. Pierce. Thank you, ever so much."

"Allow me to show you out," I said, and we quit the drawing room.

Parian was at the door, which he wordlessly opened.

"Goodbye, Victoria," I said.

"Good afternoon."

Parian closed the door after her. I stared at it for three counts and then I returned to the drawing room to find Pierce sitting relaxed and easy in the far corner of the green sofa, while Charles sat all edge-of-cushion-straight-lines on the opposite end. "Miss Lion?" he said, voice high.

"Mr. Goddard, how unexpected for you to visit. I thought my aunt had banned such behaviour. Ah, well. I was—with the help of Mr. Pierce here—ministering to Miss Braithwaite, who is in mourning. Now that we have done so, Mr. Pierce is going to be on his way, and as Miss Dowd—my chaperone—is not present, I am afraid I shan't be offering tea."

Charles Goddard was watching Pierce with a side-eyed expression even Islington might envy. "I wholly support your position, Miss Lion. We shall *both* leave you to your maiden privacy."

A flash of humour in Pierce's eyes (which I did my best to quell with a *Please Cooperate* expression of my own) as Charles Goddard stood and looked down at Pierce, saying, "I suppose you have some silver to polish?"

"Charles!" I said with a rush as I stood. "Let me see you to the door!"

Pierce also stood, no sense of rush, his shoulders looking particularly, ah, present, his gaze sharp.

The human flagpole that is Charles Goddard flinched. "Yes," he squeaked. "Yes, Miss Lion. A chaste goodbye at the door, rimmed-full with future promises." And he was moving to leave faster even than Victoria.

I followed, saw him through the hall and out the door, stepping out onto the stoop.

"Thank you, Charles."

"Miss Lion—"

"It is fortunate my aunt doesn't know you paid me a visit. And without Miss Dowd present! Charles, it really is too much."

"Miss Lion, I must confess—"

"Confess nothing," I said as if we were in a play, "for it will only cause you pain."

With a wave, I stepped back inside, and swung the door shut.

Really, I should become an actress.

The door to Pierce's studio now stood open, and that is where I found the man, standing near his table, opening a letter.

"How was exchanging sweet nothings with Charles Goddard?" he asked, without looking up.

"There were no rimmed-full promises made, maidenly or otherwise."

Now Pierce looked up, a long-suffering smile. "Tell me," he began, the hand that held the unread letter being the same he placed on the edge of the table, the paper folding unnaturally beneath his weight. "How is it that the moment Emma Lion becomes part of an equation—almost any equation—every ridiculous prospect becomes reality?"

I could admit to the truth of his claim.

Or.

I could insist such mishaps had nothing, whatsoever, to do with me.

Walking up to Pierce, I stopped six inches from his person. "Really, Pierce. You do exaggerate."

~~And I kissed him.~~

~~A simple thing. Innocent enough. Well executed.~~

I meant to kiss Pierce simply.

I went up on my tiptoes with such intentions.

However. Without Pierce making an immediate effort to bridge the gap in our heights, I couldn't manage the thing before losing my balance and, of necessity, grabbing hold of his arm. He anchored himself against his right hand, lifting his left hand to steady me as I—with the finesse of a dancer at The Drunken Duck—regained my balance.

"Case in point," he said.

"Well, it would be much easier if you would—" And I made a vague motion to imply he should bend his head forward.

He did.

And I managed to kiss him without falling over.

Pierce, following my lead, made no movement to complicate matters. But there was something on his mind, for when I stepped away, he almost reached out a hand to pull me back. Instead, eyes dark, he gave a sharp nod, seemingly having a conversation with himself.

I took a step back, then another three, crossing my arms. "I have a book to read," I stated. "But that was terribly good of you to have done."

Pierce raised an eyebrow.

"Meaning Victoria!" I clarified. "Coming to the aid of Victoria! Not—" And I waved a hand between us.

Silent albeit amused acknowledgement from Pierce, as I turned and very nearly ran straight into the partially open door. Thankfully, I dodged and, with one last glance over my shoulder, escaped into the hall.

Hearing Agnes whistling her way from the kitchen to the drawing room, I offered to help her gather the tea things.

Pierce left the house not long after. His limp more pronounced.

May 17th

Pierce was free this morning—well, free in the sense that he had been given an experimental but now broken camera from a friend—"Made by a French manufacturer," he said—and had dismantled the entire thing on his worktable to see if it could be fixed.

He was puzzling it out as I sat musing aloud on possible work suited for one Emma M. Lion.

"A barber?" I said, sitting on the plum sofa with my arms crossed introspectively.

"Aren't they usually male?"

"Hairdresser, then. I'd like to think I could cut something somewhere with a medium degree of flair."

"Hmm," Pierce replied, looking up from his work, hands covered in grease. "Most women of my acquaintance would not trust their hair to such a statement. But," he looked back down, "what do I know?"

Later

Mary and I have just now gone on a constitutional.

We spoke nothing of Professor Fletcher.

We did speak a little something of Jack. "Have you seen him?" I asked, attempting to recall when I'd last spoken with the scoundrel.

"He's been occupied with…something," Mary replied. "I've found it best I ask certain questions and not," she looked at me with a knowing smile, "ask others."

"Yes."

"How is Mr. Pierce?"

"Mr. Pierce does not think my becoming a barber is a viable future."

"Is Mr. Pierce a viable future?"

"It's amazing, isn't it? How the park is abloom come May?"

A smirk and a swing of her umbrella at a tulip, and we continued on our way.

Later

My indentured servitude with Aunt Eugenia continues.

Thankfully, this evening we were at the Clifford house, which meant Annalise was also bound to the affair.

"Do you see how my parents look ready to come to blows?" she whispered as we sat listening to a musical performance.

"I noticed how your father cleared his throat at dinner each time your mother made some sort of declaration."

"After you all leave, they'll have a right row. Father will swear to never host an evening again. Mother will argue that they have to marry me off somehow. And Father, who spent over half my dowry on an ill-advised investment, will march into his study and slam the door. So oft-rehearsed, they could perform it as a revue."

"My friend," I said, patting her hand, "I believe I would purchase a ticket."

May 18th

Hawkes was not in church again.

~~A pity, as I've missed him.~~ I've missed him terribly.

Islington was in attendance. He's also feeling Hawkes's loss. Or so I surmised from how he tapped an impatient finger after I whispered, "But where *is* Hawkes? He's been missing for weeks."

"He's otherwise engaged. Unfortunately."

"Islington, he's missed *two* consecutive sermons."

"Please be quiet."

"I'm always quiet in church."

An unnecessary and argumentative expression followed.

I made a face. "I've had a very *trying* few days."

Lady Trewartha waylaid Islington and I after the service.

She had questions.

"My husband and I were both acquainted with your father, Declan Lion," she stated, with what felt at the time to be flat suspicion.

I was expecting her to add: "He could not have possibly thought this a good idea."

To which I would have muttered: "Amen."

But Islington, unruffled, said, "Yes, I remember seeing the two of you at one of his exhibitions."

Her gaze narrowed. And just as I was about to launch into a speech—*You see, Lady Trewartha, my father felt Islington needed to be plagued*—she smiled. "I'm not surprised he chose you, Islington. A guardian of standing, of secure position, who isn't in the least stodgy."

A guffaw as my contribution. "He most certainly *is* stodgy."

Islington looked heavenward.

Lady Trewartha laughed. Then said to Islington, "Stewart asked me to tell you the first-century Roman marble has arrived. It is in better shape than he'd hoped."

"Ah!" Islington visibly brightened. "Wonderful!"

"He expects you tomorrow. Do try to come by. I prefer Stewart to engage with another excitable collector rather than having to field his enthusiasm myself."

"Happy to oblige, Lady Trewartha."

A gentle nod, the sort that tips sideways and forward—I've practiced in the mirror just now, and my attempts at mimicry make me look like I'm plotting something—and she patted me on the shoulder.

"I don't *like* her thinking you're my guardian," I said to Islington as we left the churchyard. "It feels deceptive and uncomfortable."

"It is deceptive."

"And uncomfortable."

He adjusted his hat. "If you hadn't dragged me into a closet—"

"It was a corridor."

"—none of this would have happened. Maddening as all this has become"—Islington waved an impatient hand—"we must remember Stonecrop."

"I can't, as I've not yet been, but I will remember the Alamo."

Islington glanced at me in surprise. We were on the corner of Sterling and Whereabouts now, having come to a full stop before parting ways. "Did you just invoke the Alamo?"

"I did."

A smirk rising.

"My father would say that from time to time," I defended.

"Hmm," was the response I received. Then, "Pierce and I spoke of it only last week at The Cleopatra. I thought perhaps he—"

"Did you! So *he* remembers the Alamo? I'll ask him to teach me."

A curious light in Islington's eyes. "Lion, just what exactly do you believe the Alamo to be?"

"I always assumed it was a sort of dance. Like the *Allemande*. I mentioned it to the dancing master Aunt Eugenia engaged the summer I was fifteen, only he seemed confused."

Islington laughed. Very definitively *at* me.

"What, pray," I gritted through my teeth, "is the Alamo?"

When Islington composed himself, he managed, "Pierce will explain."

Then he laughed again.

Islington is an incurable elitist.

Later

~~Mary and I spent the afternoon planning for my visit to Stonecrop.~~

Mary and I spent the afternoon lazily reading in the garret. She in the window seat, I in the nearby chair. She only escaped Miss Lamb's boarding house because she swore she was visiting a feeble-minded friend to read the Bible.

"You've scribbled in all your books," she said, my entire library stacked at her feet. "Which is no surprise, as you tried to do the same with most of your schoolbooks—a whipping or two for your efforts. Returning to the point, you've written in each except your father's Shakespeare."

"Of course," I replied, turning a page in my *Plutarch*. "It's a work of art." I looked past Mary and out the open window, "Mother read the Bible every night and Father read Shakespeare. Those are the two books whose notes are primarily written in my mind."

"No inking over the word of God?"

"I didn't say that exactly," I confessed. "I've included several asides, general impressions, or humble complaints."

"Humble complaints?"

I tapped the cover of the book in my hand. "For example, why was Sarah chastised for laughing at the angel who told her she would bear a child. At ninety! I would have fallen about in absolute stitches, promise or no promise, mind you! The angel would have had to repeat himself three, possibly four, times. I know there is the business of faith in God's promises, and believing angels is wise to do, but I feel there was some justifiable amusement to be had."

"Which is why God tucked you quietly away in St. Crispian's rather than in the line of biblical matriarchs."

"Hmm," I agreed with a nod.

Mary then picked up my Bible and began to seek out all marginalia.

She began laughing. "You've given the story of Ehud stabbing Eglon top marks!"

"Mary, the King of Moab was so large that when he was stabbed with an eighteen-inch dagger, it was sucked into his body. I will always give such a story top marks."

It took Mary quarter of an hour to quiet down and continue reading.

Later

What, exactly, is the Alamo?

I HAVE A BOOK ON THE TOPIC I'LL LET YOU BORROW.

So it is not a dance.

I can hear Pierce laughing through the wall.

May 19th

When I went into the breakfast room this morning, there was a book with a snip of black ribbon marking a chapter about the Mexican-American War.

The Alamo is *not* a dance.

Later

Pierce had three clients this afternoon. I know this, for Agnes and I had an honest discussion regarding the household budget, and where we might squeeze out a touch more use.

"Like a lemon, Miss Lion?"

I pulled my tongue back against the tension of tart anticipation, as if I'd actually had a taste of lemon juice. "Yes, Agnes. Budgeting is rather like a lemon. Now, how much sugar did you say we consume each week?"

Parian walked in with a question, glanced at the paper of figures between Agnes and I, turned and was out of the drawing room without saying a word.

Wise man.

I sighed and looked back out of the window.

"Two more clients are leaving Lapis Lazuli Minor. A mother and daughter, I'd guess. Heavens, the woman's hat has a rather ambitious number of feathers, hasn't it?"

"We might consider the regularity of our poultry," Agnes frowned.

"We might."

"Miss Lion?"

"Yes, Agnes?"

"While Mr. Pierce has been covering most of the butcher, he's not paid nary a penny for the fishmonger. Do you think he would be angry if—"

A knock on the door of the drawing room and Pierce entered.

"What sorts of mischief are we up to today," he asked.

Agnes, convicted by the guilt of her suggestion, pinked. Her nearly invisible Scottish accent flared into existence. "Noothing of any kind. Noothing, Mr. Pierce. I certainly wasn't thinking we reduce your particular favourites, Mr. Pierce. Never you worry, now. Who needs fish anyhow?"

"I, uh," he looked confused. "Fish, Agnes?"

Agnes picked up the papers from the table and, with a curtsy, quit the room.

"Is Agnes all right?" Pierce asked, having watched her abrupt exit with bemusement.

"She will be. Care to sit?"

"Yes, um, at the Reed and Rite. I was wondering if I could take you for tea. It marks one year since we…it being your mother's birthday."

The nineteenth of May.

"Oh, goodness." I put my face in my hands. "I've been rushing about marking every day of the calendar with the sole focus of surviving this month." I looked up. "Of course it is my mother's birthday. The Reed and Rite would be lovely."

Quarter of an hour later, we left Lapis Lazuli House. He'd changed his clothes, wearing his dark brown suit with a fresh shirt, change of tie, and waistcoat. He'd also run a comb through his hair.

"You're cutting a smart figure," I said.

"I'd like to impress your mother."

"Seeing as she is deceased, I think she'd only be difficult to impress if we were to marry."

It simply flew from my mouth like a barn swallow.

And I, experiencing sudden and undulating waves of ~~terror~~ ~~disbelief~~ ~~shock~~ mortification, lifted a hand to my face and strangled out, "I did not intend to say that."

"So I've guessed by the expression of blind panic on your face."

Letting my hand drop, I swivelled my gaze to Pierce. "Said panic has *nothing*, or at least very *little* to do with your person. Ah. Rather, yourself. Your person is more than— As is yourself!"

Calamity.

Two men were walking up the lane, and then a woman not far behind them. "Shall we cross the street to finish untangling this conversation?" I half whispered.

A nod from Pierce, who seemed perfectly fine waiting for me to dig myself out of the verbal trench in which I'd so haphazardly placed myself. "I am not ready, is all," I said quietly, as we crossed the cobbles. "We've only just begun courting. But when I *am*, I'm not assuming we— You must— But there are clearly— What I mean to say— A lady doesn't curse in the street, does she? She doesn't curse at all. Nor does she accidentally half propose. Perhaps I should start. The swearing, I mean. A good *damnation* would fit this bill just now." I took in a gulp of air.

A maddening calm from Pierce. He slowed his pace. We were almost at the doors of the Reed and Rite. "Emma," he said so only I could hear, "I assume we both realise that, yes, marriage would be the question if this persists. But with all that banking business in New York, I'm not ready either." Someone walked out of the Reed and Rite as Pierce came to a full stop, causing me to do the same. We waited until we were alone again, then the sharp certainty in his expression softened. "We have time."

It was grounding.

His composure a remedy to my half-flung panic.

The door of the Reed and Rite opened again, and out came Mrs. Ribbits. She walked past without any consideration of we two, blinking her round eyes as she placed a liquorice candy in her mouth followed directly by a lemon sour.

Pierce grinned at the oddity, then, "Shall we go in then?"

The Reed and Rite was more than a little busy. Our table in the corner was not immediately available, but as Pierce and I were about to sit elsewhere, it became so, and I practically raced to secure the spot. Pierce followed.

It was not long before our order was given, and—after a few nonchalant comments referring to the passersby on the street—the serving girl arrived with tea, only to stumble, drop nearly everything without ceremony, and cause the teapot to splash right onto the table.

The serving girl moved quickly.

Pierce moved quicker.

He stood, using the tablecloth to help prevent disaster, carefully soaking up the tea while the serving girl picked up a broken teacup from the floor and left to find a clean tablecloth. Pierce was precise in his work, careful, glancing at me to make certain I hadn't been splashed upon.

"You unscathed?"

I nodded.

And then Pierce, bundling the stained tablecloth in the centre of the table, sat back down in his own chair, a slight grimace as he put weight on his leg.

The serving girl returned and our table was set afresh. Along with not only a replacement of our tea but a veritable tower of pastries. (Jack would have been pleased.) "Compliments of the Reed and Rite. I'm terribly sorry."

She hurried away and Pierce and I began to sort our table.

"Isn't she Jape's niece?" I said to Pierce as I handed him his tea while he was passing me a plate with a scone smothered in strawberry preserves.

"I've no idea."

"Well. A small moment of excitement, but excitement nonetheless," I said.

Pierce smiled, lines around his silver eyes creasing. "Tell me something about your mother."

I had just taken ~~too large~~ a bite of the aforementioned scone, and so I considered his question until I could swallow. Then, "She was a fine person. Raised in a home with high expectations."

"A burden for her?"

I shook my head. "No, actually. I believe she was content with many aspects of her life and what her future would ask. She was fit for purpose, as it were. No great desire to change the shape of her world."

"What happened?"

"*Ah.*"

Imitate the devil and he appeareth, for down the stairs came Islington, a wrapped parcel from the Reed and Rite shop in his hand. Seeing Pierce and I, he raised his chin in recognition, then—after being greeted by an older gentleman I don't know—wound his way to our corner table.

"Well met," he said, looking between us.

"Hello, Islington" I said.

"You'll join, I expect?" Pierce motioned towards a chair at the empty table beside ours.

"Gladly." Islington maneuvered the chair and, after setting it down, took a seat. "I was going to stop off at Lapis Lazuli just now." Light enquiry into our day, a report on his own, while the serving girl brought Islington a cup and saucer, with a fresh pot of tea and some additional pastries.

I offered to prepare Islington's tea despite the Alamo—he looked tired.

"Thank you," Islington replied, as I handed a cup and saucer his way. A single sip and Islington sighed with satisfaction, setting his cup down. Something had been restored. "I didn't interrupt anything, did I?"

"Emma was telling me about her mother," Pierce replied, taking a flask from his jacket pocket and splashing a swallow into his tea.

Islington's interest was piqued. By the statement, not the flask. "I rather liked your mother. We only met a few times, but she was always gracious."

"You can imagine how she despaired of me," I replied.

"No need to imagine," Islington replied.

I picked up my butter knife. "I am armed, Islington."

"Someday I'll fence with you, Emma, but not at the Reed and Rite."

I brightened. "Will you really?"

"Certainly." Islington made eye contact. "We have plenty of foils at Stonecrop."

"Well, wonderful!" I then smiled at Pierce. "Did you hear that? Islington is going to give me a sword."

"I didn't say that."

Pierce took a sip of his tea. "Implied, I'm afraid."

A guffaw from our resident duke. Then, "You were saying about your mother?"

"Today is her birthday."

The edge of Islington's eyes pulled tight. Grief understands grief. "May is a pleasant month for a birthday."

"It is." Preparing myself another cup, I considered all the lines that make up the weaving of my mother's memory. Her loss feels particularly unjust, for at thirteen there is only so much a child can understand about her mother. There were conversations that couldn't have been had, and if they had been attempted, would not have been understood. "I was telling Pierce how she had no aspirations to throw off the directives of her life. She was the beloved second daughter of a wealthy man, she had status and—I believe, anyway—beauty."

"What changed her mind?" Pierce asked.

"She went to a house party in the country, at the home of my father's English cousins. He had been wrangled over from Ireland for a visit. That is where they met."

"Love at first sight?" Islington asked.

It was irritation, rather. And I said so. "But he was too charming to stand against."

"I'd like to see anyone who could stand against Declan Lion."

"How did you first meet my father?" I asked.

Islington did not answer immediately, lifting his chin as he considered. "A December evening, here in St. Crispian's. I was twenty years of age, in need of someone wiser than I." Then he—and with great talent—shifted the conversation away from the question. It went to broader places, before settling on Hawkes.

"I haven't seen him at The Cleopatra all week," Pierce said.

"He'll return before long." Islington said, none too worried.

"Has he ever done this before?" I asked.

Islington's hazel eyes took the reflection of the window. "Hawkes always has his reasons."

It was then that The d'Artagnan Business came to mind and I opened my mouth to enquire if Islington knew anything of it, when we were interrupted by Mr. Spout.

By the time we'd wrested our conversation back, the question had fled.

Later

Pierce just asked me what I'd be doing tomorrow evening. Being in the process of scratching around a reclining Tybalt's ears, I somewhat distractedly replied that I had to attend a ball with Aunt Eugenia.

"That's too bad."

I looked at him. "Did you have something else in mind?"

"I was given tickets to a comic performance at the Adelphi."

The thought sounded wonderful. "No way to escape my aunt, I'm afraid. Too cruel. Will you ask Chambers?"

"Chambers at a vaudeville? That sounds like a special sort of hell, doesn't it? I'll ask Islington when I see him tonight."

"Tonight?"

"I'm meeting him at his club."

"*When sorrows come, they come not single spies, but in battalions*," I complained.

"To which sorrow exactly are you referring?"

"My missing the enjoyments of which you all so freely partake."

"*I that do bring the news made not the match*."

I sat up straight in my chair. "Pierce."

"Hmm?" he replied, taking a sip of whisky.

"You quoted Shakespeare."

"Is that Shakespeare? I read it in the paper last week."

It was almost unbearable, Pierce quoting Shakespeare.

The joyful tang of an unexpected pairing.

My new aim in life is to do everything possible to ensure it happens again.

Tybalt placed an expectant paw on my still hand, to remind me there were more important considerations in this world than photographers.

May 20th

Word is the Countess of Ellam has been hosting a spate of private occasions at her townhouse in Berkeley Square rather than attending the most desired events of London. It is, and I quote, "A shocking exercise of hubris and bad taste, especially for a woman who resides in Northumberland most of the year." Lady Carleton pulled Aunt Eugenia to the side upon our arrival at her ball to discuss the rumour.

"The countess and her daughter did not accept an invitation for this evening," Aunt Eugenia whispered to Arabella and I as we stepped into the freshly buzzing ballroom. "Lady Carleton was not disappointed, likely feeling her own daughter—daughters I should say, for she has the misfortune of having produced three in sequence—will look better for the lack of comparison. But then she ought not have invited Arabella."

A young couple, with whom I've no acquaintance but who are known to Arabella, has eloped, and both their parents have cut them off. Irrevocably. It ruled nearly all conversation. And so while still met with bald-faced curiosity, I was only asked to my face a dozen times regarding The Islington Connection.

I learned to recognise the expression of curiosity and slip through the maze of guests as often as it could be managed. Most of the men who asked me to dance were not well known to me, seeing as how neither Islington, Roland, Charles Goddard, nor Lord West were present.

But Annalise Clifford and May Northgate were.

"My aunt demanded I ask you about Islington, you know," May said. "What am I to tell her?"

Annalise laughed. "My mother says Islington was drunk, and you were begging him to get a hold of himself."

The story stopped me short.

A flattering portrait of a desperate Miss Lion. As entertaining as it would have been to let it stand, I defended Islington, "He was *not* drunk, he was taken ill."

We three were interrupted when May was asked for a dance.

And then Annalise.

I was content to wait just out of the grasp of my aunt, watching Arabella dance with Steward de Preiss, despite him having been Removed from Serious Consideration.

I now stare out of the window of my garret, the long evening having come to an abrupt close when Aunt Eugenia declared, "Emma, I'm tired. Go and tell Arabella we're leaving."

It is far enough into late spring that the gaslight shows dark, cutout leaves on the branches of the trees in view. Moody and pleasant, and I've a warm cup of tea at the ready.

No ghosts.

No pirates.

No one coming.

No one going.

I've been moving my fingers along the glossy, black leather of my journal and thinking any number of things. The month is getting away from me. It's practically sprinting away. My studies? Paltry at best. A trusted routine of walks, time to pleasantly stretch my internal philosophies? Woefully ignored. My time has not wholly been my own, in unpleasant and, yes, some very pleasant ways. I'm beginning to think that the catawampus nature of these days is due to Hawkes being so long absent.

Or am I simply being cursed for half disregarding the May Day fortune?

Or cursed for half regarding it?

I don't want to read the fortune again, and wonder what might apply to Pierce and what might not. For I've grown accustomed, to the expectation of his company, the feeling of his unknowable, storied life undergirding mine, the masculine way of his, the sense of storm, how he moves undeterred through his work, how he looks up to find me, how something in his face relaxes when he does, how it is now habit for him to smile. The way his hand feels on the side of my neck when…

Well.

And what of my own questions?

I've not yet been brave enough to look too far into that strange, internal country of my heart, to see what has battered its way through the gates, and what has not. But it feels as if there is a confirmation there, of complicated, tangled courage.

Hearts are intricate stretches of land.

Mine is no exception.

Hmm. Looking out of the window just now confirms my earlier suspicion.

St. Crispian's *has* tarnished without Hawkes.

It is untended, grown unruly and too wild.

May 21st

The telling must be accurate.

And not simply to explain away having done something unquestionably beyond the acceptable boundaries laid out by society. But also because the peculiar events of the afternoon deserve such attention. In preparation, I have purchased more ink.

I walked up Traitors Road this afternoon with nary a thought for anything but stretching my legs in the sunshine as I took in the neighbourhood. I'd passed The Cleopatra and rounded the corner onto the Diagonal when someone called out, "Miss Lion!"

I half spun and managed to nearly trip on a chipped section of pavement, but Toff caught my arm and made certain I didn't fall.

"Hello, Toff," I said once I was steady on my feet, lifting my hands to my hat and pinning it back into place. "Do you need something?"

"Gibbs, Miss." Toff doffed his cap. (What a jolly little sentence that is.) "He would like to speak with you."

"Gibbs of Cleopatra fame?"

"Yes, Miss. Says he needs your help with something important."

An image of the black sludge that is *The Cleopatra* left muddy footprints across my brain. "Hmmm," I replied, sounding unconvinced. "I assume he wishes to speak with me now?"

Toff nodded.

"All right, then."

I rounded the corner and entered The Cleopatra.

Gibbs was in fine form, rather imposing figure that he is, cleaning glasses and circling his own thoughts.

"Hello, Gibbs."

"Miss Lion," he replied without looking up. "Can I get you anything? It's on the house."

"Well, then. How about a lemonade?"

Gibbs shook his head. "How abouts I mix you up something far better, Miss, if you'll allow."

"Will it be slodgy and gutter-esque? If so, no thank you."

A harrumph and Gibbs went about seeing to my drink while I considered the company. Only a few men sat in calm corners sharing an early drink, keeping lazy conversation in the late afternoon sunlight puddling across the pub.

"Here you are, Miss Lion." And the sound of a glass set down on the counter.

I turned and looked at what waited before me.

A thin, but tall glass. Delicate in feeling as well as shape. Whatever filled the glass was the softest, sparkling gold—and there were candied violets floating at the top. The glass itself looked like summer frost in the sunlight.

"Gibbs, it's beautiful!"

He shrugged. "Something a mite more interesting than your lemonade, Miss."

I took a thoughtful sip. My expression betrayed the unexpected punch of bitter until a flood of sweet rose beneath. I released a slow breath.

"That…is certainly something other than lemonade."

"But you like it?"

A second sip confirmed the fact. "Very much. What's it called?"

"As to that,"—Gibbs pulled a pint for a man who had come up to the counter, expertly tilting the glass to keep down the foam before handing it over—"it used to be called The Cora."

"Used to be called?"

Gibbs shrugged, wiping down the tap. "Before she went off and married a blacksmith. Don't make it much these days."

"Ah. I'm sorry, Gibbs."

He shrugged. "If you like, I'll give it your name."

"The Emma?"

"The Emma," he stated.

"What about The Lion?" I parried.

"I've already got one of those, named after your father."

"Really?" I could feel my eyes brighten. "Might I have one?"

A laugh. "Not today. It's…not for the faint of heart. You have a day when your world has crumbled down about you and I'll serve you The Lion, no questions asked. But this here, tart and sweet altogether is The Emma, and forever it will be."

A great honour I wasn't certain I deserved. I said as much.

"Miss Lion, you put down a full Cleopatra amid a hostile crowd. With guts and flair. I like you, and I like your friends. But also, if you run off with a blacksmith, I won't care two dog's tails. Hell, I'd even lift a glass to you. Now, if you *were* to run off with a blacksmith, I know of a bloke or two who'd be—"

But then Gibbs was interrupted by a rowdy set crashing through the door, patting the statue of Cleopatra on the head as they called out for ale. Terribly poor timing as I wished to hear more of the bloke (or two) who would be (insert yet undisclosed desperate emotion) if I ran off with a blacksmith. But Gibbs did not return to the subject, and I am not so forward as to ask for clarification.

Alas.

Alack.

"But here's why I called you in, Miss Lion." And from under the counter Gibbs withdrew a stack of letters.

I picked up the letter that slid nearest me. On the envelope was written *F.N. Hawkes*. The next letter was addressed to just *Hawkes*, as was the next. There were a total of seven letters.

(None, I noticed, scented with pear.)

"He hasn't been in to collect his letters, Miss Lion, and I don't like to keep them here too long. Makes me uncomfortable and the like. You never know what will disappear here in St. Crispian's. And so I was wondering if you would place them in his room next door."

"I—"

But Gibbs had pulled a key from under the counter and set it before me.

I took the key, lifting it in my hand, my finger tracing the blue ribbon tied through the ornate pattern. Frowning, I pulled the ribbon straight with my gloved fingers. For scrawled in black ink was the following:

This key is not to be given to anyone except Islington.

Then added to the end in a midnight blue ink,

And Miss Emma M. Lion.

"Hawkes has his correspondence sent to The Cleopatra," Gibbs explained. "And I have this here key to his room, but I've only permission to give it to Islington. And now you. No one else, for any reason. I was hoping you might take these up now, so no one finds their way into Hawkes's business, seeing how Islington is in Kent for a few days."

"What is Islington doing in Kent!"

A shrug from Gibbs.

I considered the script on the ribbon, the same hand which had written Imperterritus all those years ago.

"I am a young, unmarried woman, Gibbs. I cannot enter Hawkes's personal room."

Gibbs shrugged. "He's not there miss, all of St. Crispian's knows it."

"It's the principle."

"Miss Lion, only last night I found Moody Matthews trying to peel open the corner of that there letter. I can't vouch for their safety if I leave the counter to find a cask or break a fight. Now, I have instruction to let Islington take Hawkes's post up to his room. Your name has since been added to the key. What else do you propose I do about it?"

"Hide them away! Keep them in your breast pocket!"

He looked at me. As if I weren't being a Good Sport by simply accepting my reputation-rumpling assignment. "Things go awry in St. Crispian's, when the more important rules aren't kept," Gibbs said.

"Rules like guarding Hawkes's correspondence?"

"Rules like guarding Hawkes's correspondence."

My hand closed. I almost took his letters home to my garret. Then the horrible picture of Cousin Archibald finding them, slicing them open with the same knife he'd used to butter a scone, and sniffing as he read, a nose in need of a handkerchief about to drip onto the page. I sighed. "If you'll set straight any rumour, I'll—discreetly, mind—see the letters safely stowed."

Gibbs nodded. "Good on you, Miss Lion. A weight off my shoulders. Say, do you know where Hawkes has gotten himself off to? He usually tells me when he's going to be away."

I looked down at the object in hand.

The key felt holy.

Keep thy friend under thy own life's key, indeed.

"No idea, I'm afraid."

A grunt from Gibbs, who then turned his attention to a pair of gentlemen who had just entered The Cleopatra.

> *This key is not to be given to anyone except Islington. And Miss Emma M. Lion.*

Sitting there with my task, I felt bigger than myself, somehow. Greater for Hawkes's trust. Picking up my glass, I finished The Emma, clearing my throat as tears came to my eyes, sweetness chasing it all down.

"Phew," I muttered. Picking up the letters, I said, "Thank you, Gibbs," and saw myself out.

There stood I, before the door that led to Hawkes's life; uncertain, key in one hand, letters in the other. I have—in my short life—done many a thing to incur wrath from Comportment Gods of every stripe. Thus I was well aware that my having a key to the private room of a young man—however much of a vicar he may be—is not The Thing.

Even if he was known to be elsewhere.

However.

Hawkes had placed two names on this key, full trust given to enter and operate on his behalf.

I clutched the stack of letters in my hand.

Taking a step forward, I reached my hand out and placed it on the knob of the boarding house door where Hawkes resides.

It opened.

I looked inside, noting a worn rug in the entry and a staircase ahead, leading to the three floors above. Not feeling it particularly right for me to wander the halls attempting to open the rooms of who knows how many men, I felt myself to be in a quandary.

Then the sound of footsteps behind me on the pavement caused me to jump back, pulling closed the door and taking on the appearance of an innocent student of architecture. Then I saw who was approaching.

"Mastiff!"

Mastiff, the largest and quietest of Reprobates came to a stop beside me. His nod fully conveyed a "Hello, Miss Lion."

"I find I need your help, Mastiff."

Again a nod.

"You see, Hawkes has not been about—"

Mastiff nodded and smiled.

"—and I am one of two entrusted with the key to his room."

Mastiff waited, his clear eyes intent on mine.

"Now, you see, these letters must be placed in his room, and perhaps you—"

Mastiff delivered a light shrug.

Hmmm.

I'm not yet fluent in Reprobate.

"Does that mean yes?"

"Can't do it, Miss Lion."

"Pardon?" I said.

"If Hawkes put only two names on that key, there are two names on that key. You have to go in yourself."

"Heavens," I said. "But I don't even know which room is his, exactly. I suppose," I glanced up, "it belongs to those two windows of which I've seen you all hanging out? What was it, the second floor?"

"Yes'm. Go up the stairs to the second floor. You'll find his door in the corridor on the left."

"And you're certain you can't do it for me?"

Mastiff shook his head. "Can't. Protocols, bylaws, and all that. Besides, I'm in preparation for the midsummer games which means I can't speak to Hawkes for the seven days of purification. There was an agreement made."

"Midsummer games? Purification?"

Mastiff nodded.

"And are the consequences so dire if you were to fraternize with Hawkes?"

"Not just him. Any man of the cloth. I'd be booted out altogether."

"Ah. I see." I did not. "What room is he in?"

"773."

I frowned. "Room 773?"

Mastiff nodded.

"Surely the building is too small for such a number. Wouldn't you think he'd live in 5 or 6 perhaps?"

"773, Miss Lion." Mastiff gave me a half bow and continued down the street.

Well!

I turned to look at the door.

Then I counted to seven.

And for good measure counted again, but to twenty-one.

Glancing about and seeing I'd the attention of no one, I turned the knob, slipped inside the vestibule, and closed the door behind me with a discretion anyone would envy.

Not a soul was coming or going, so I made my way up the stairs, tripping on the hem of my skirt twice in my haste. Turning to the left I saw a room 13, then a 5, and lastly, the door with 773. Just as Mastiff said.

There was a note nailed to the door, threatening certain death and signed by Sargent and Night Watchman. My hands were shaking too much to smile as I took Hawkes's key, inserted it into the lock, and let myself in, closing the door behind me and leaning back against it for support.

I had managed the feat.

I had found my way into Hawkes's room.

Or rather, upon looking about, I'd found myself inside a pocket of Hawkes's soul.

The late afternoon light splashed gold over everything, and it took a moment for my eyes to adjust, but when they did, I lifted my right hand—the hand that held the key—and placed it over my heart.

I have loved the spaces of my friends—Islington's library, Pierce's studio, Saffronia's Thrush's Victory, Mary's haphazard room filled with papers and strewn bits of clothing, and even the atelier of The Hound—but this room, this very small room, made me feel something I'd not experienced before.

It was dear.

It was to be safeguarded.

I felt the desire to take off my shoes.

In the corner to my left was a bed, neatly made but having been laid atop of, a book left where a person had been. Then two windows a few feet apart, and a simple washstand in the corner, a mirror on the wall, shaving paraphernalia beside a bowl filled with clear but days-old water. The wall ahead of me allowed a single window in the middle, the view rising just above The Cleopatra to the rooftops, trees, and sky beyond. To the left of the window was a bookshelf, humble but absolutely burdened with books, improperly stuffed atop and around, stacks rising towards the ceiling, balancing by fey magic or some other sort of impossible physics. On the right side of the window, and straight ahead from where I stood at the door, was a desk—with three straight legs and a fourth, ornately carved and clearly taken from another piece of furniture. A chair of deep brown wood waited before it, scarf draping over its back. And then on the final wall to my right was another bookshelf, as bursting with books as the first, and then a line of pegs where a few old but well-cared-for jackets hung.

It was not a large room, smaller than my garret; however, it felt immense. As if it were an entire world. My eyes returned to the laden bookshelves, a beloved jungle of words.

Where to begin? It was a question I asked myself and almost believed I could answer. However, Hawkes had not given his permission. My task was to bring his correspondence, place it on his desk, and to leave again.

Without tampering.

Without imposing.

~~And so that is what I did.~~

And so that is what I tried to do.

(And I say full marks for a near gallant effort.)

However.

Taking a step forward, then two, I reached out my hand and ran my fingers along the book spines on the shelf to my right. But honour bound me to my task.

I placed the letters on Hawkes's desk.

Then. Well, I sat down.

I sat on the chair to see how ~~he~~ it felt. I took off my gloves and placed my hands on the surface worn smooth. I paused at an ink stain, long ago spilt. I felt a dent in the wood with my fingertip. I did not open the single drawer, a thing for which I expect to be fully rewarded in this life or the next. And it was while I entertained this thought that I glanced up at the paraphernalia Hawkes had pinned to the wall just above. Newspaper clippings, bits of writing, a small painting of a place I did not know, a line of Latin written in Hawkes's hand, two in Greek, and one in a language I did not recognise. My eyes traced this collection—important enough to pin to the wall and consider day in and day out. One of the newspaper articles caught my eye. It was about that horrible business with the Fenian society, the bomb left in the luggage room of Victoria Station in February.

There was another article about the arrest of John Daly in Birkenhead.

I know Pierce has been following the details keenly, greatly upset by them.

I frowned, and, lifting the clipping with my finger, I scanned the clipping pinned below. An older article, from October of last year, when two bombs had exploded in the underground. No one killed, but many injured.

Unease.

And disbelief.

And then worry.

Was Hawkes an Irish revolutionary? Was he secretly fighting against the English government to secure independence for Ireland? Was it possible?

Everything in me said that yes, it *was* possible.

But was it true?

I sat with my elbows anchored on Hawkes's desk, my face in my hands, wondering if—

"Is it so depressing a place?" a voice said at my back.

I spun round in the chair, gripping the back as I looked to see Hawkes (Hawkes!) standing in the doorway, shoulder against the doorframe, unreadable expression on his face.

Strange as it may seem, it was almost like meeting a person for the first time.

Hawkes was tired, hair mussed in its accustomed way, head bent despite his gaze being lifted to watch my movements. His eyes were a complicated blue, the articulation of his face masculine, quiet, lovely. The softness that usually surrounds him was wearing thin. He felt resigned and yet wild beneath a faux-tamed exterior. A glimpse is all, then the layers of distance rushed in like the tide. I blinked, and it was Hawkes. My Hawkes. Straddling the line of mystery and wisdom, a brown travelling satchel thrown over his blue coat, the leather strap a diagonal line across his chest. His hands were in his pockets, his trousers were rolled up twice so as not to get dirty from the street, and his right shoe was balancing its tip as he crossed his ankle while placing all his weight on his left leg.

I could not tell how far he had come. But it felt a great distance.

"You did," I ~~said~~ scraped out, feeling explicably nervous, "put my name on the key." And I held up his key in my defence.

This caused Hawkes to lift his chin. His eyes captured the afternoon light. "*Keep thy friend under thy own life's key.*"

How good of him. For the Shakespeare was grounding.

Hawkes stepped into the room, closing the door behind him. He looked like he was trying to solve an equation. Moving carefully, slowly, he lifted the satchel from his shoulder and set it on the foot of his bed, stretching one of his shoulders and running a hand through his hair. He sighed, a personal sound of relief.

"You see, I brought up your letters," I said rather quickly, trying to push the impropriety away. "Gibbs sent me. Said it had to be done. And if I took them home, then Cousin Archibald would get butter on the envelope and not use a handkerchief while sneaking a read. There was nothing for it but to bring them here." I pointed to the letters neatly stacked on the edge of the desk.

"Thank you."

And Hawkes sat down on the side of his bed, leaning forward so his elbows were on his knees, hands laced together, chin resting on his knuckles. He was watching me.

"No one saw me come in," I blurted.

"No, they didn't," Hawkes confirmed, in that somewhat maddening tone of all-knowing. I asked myself in that moment—requiring an honest answer—if this man looked like a revolutionary of any sort.

Of radical preaching of poetry, the answer was yes.

"Hawkes—" I glanced towards the articles pinned on the board. "Are you— That is, do you— Is there anything you feel you would like to…confess?"

The flicker of a smile, mostly come from the back of his eyes. "You're asking if I am a member of the Irish Fenian Society."

I feigned amusement. "No. Heavens, no!" A laugh. "Certainly not. You wouldn't blow anyone up for any reason. *I believe.* I hope. But yes, now that you suggest the question, I think a concrete answer might…not be a terrible thing to have? And then I'll return your key and room and…privacy. That is, I *am* very happy to see you. We've missed you terribly. Everyone, but the three of us especially. St. Crispian's has been falling apart by the hour. Unexpected inconveniences. Invasions of the trying sort. I'm so *delighted* to see you returned. Only please don't be secretly living a life of chaos and crime—unless you're a forger. I've already given that some thought and feel it would go hand in hand with your work in the church. Not that the core principles of the two professions would align, per se, but I would think you might have the time to master the knack of replicating any number of documents in between the writing of sermons. And now I'm going to try to figure out a way out of this speech. Hmmm. How about the weather? The afternoon sun is so glorious, scarcely a cloud to strangle it away. Such a pleasant thing. The sunshine, not strangulation." I clapped a hand over my mouth to stop the disaster.

"I am not a forger," he said. It was delivered with the arrival of a genuine smile.

Before I could express mostly relief and some disappointment, he continued.

"I am what I say I am, Emma Lion—a vicar."

"So you are *not* an Irish revolutionary?"

"I am not an Irish revolutionary, but I care about the island, a great deal. And I visit some of these men in prison, with a friend who is a Catholic priest."

My relief that Hawkes was not building any sort of bomb rather, well, exploded out of me. "Then where on earth have you been!" I almost shouted.

Hawkes laughed.

He ducked his head, face in his hands a moment, before rubbing his tired eyes and looking back up at me. "I have been a guest."

"A guest? In a…gaol?"

"A very nice one. I was a guest of the family of the one whose letter you so gallantly saved. That is all I will say of the matter."

Hawkes, being so honest however cryptic.

I opened my mouth in ~~surprise~~ a most unladylike manner. And then closed it.

Things had gone far enough.

"Hawkes, it would be prudent for me to leave."

"Not yet."

"Pardon?"

He rubbed his left eye and yawned. "If you leave now, you'll be seen. Best to wait a few minutes." He looked at me and shook his head. "It should be clarified, I never intended you to come into my room…barring some great emergency."

"Ah." How awkward.

Hawkes pressed his lips together and tilted his head in concordance. "I am not so careless, Emma. I would not place you and your reputation in this particular position."

"How do you know?"

A blink. "I would hope to know such things about myself."

"No, how do you know I'll be seen if I leave now?"

A shrug. A shrug!

And so I, turning the chair to face the rest of the room, i.e., Hawkes, settled in for a quarter of an hour.

It felt far more scandalous than The Drunken Duck.

Hawkes looked as if he wished he could lie down to sleep, but as there was a young woman ~~accidentally~~ in his room, he'd better stay sitting. His eyes were heavy, his shoulders releasing into a slump. Then, he looked up. A sudden focus.

"What are you taking to Stonecrop?" he asked.

What was I taking to Stonecrop?

Well!

My often-dormant sartorial mind bloomed like a bud in water. "It's a grand effort to live up to the formality of the place while keeping a country—*ergo* comfortable—aesthetic. Agnes has been cleaning my skirts and blouses, for walking, and I've an afternoon—"

Hawkes batted my words away like a fly. (I do not think Hawkes dislikes the sartorial, but I had clearly misunderstood.) He rephrased. "What *books* are you taking to Stonecrop?"

"Ah. I see we're going straight to the important questions."

A nod.

"I've begun anew with Numa Pompilius, as I keep— But do not look so worried! I will make it to Pericles!"

"Do not bring Plutarch to Stonecrop," he said.

"Do not bring Plutarch…?"

A shake of the head from Hawkes. "It is not a mismatch by any means, only this is your first visit. It should be set apart." Then a fixed expression of decision. He stood, giving all attendance to the bookshelf just behind me on the wall. I turned in my chair to watch. His hands moved like those of an artist. No, perhaps those of a physician—prodding carefully, testing, watching. He withdrew a volume, then another. Opening the first, he frowned and put it back on the shelf.

"Not up to Stonecrop's standards?" I asked.

"Some worthy verse." Hawkes glanced at me. "Only it's in the original Greek."

Ah. Well then. But rather than admitting defeat, I quipped, "My Greek is excellent."

He paused. "Is it?"

"Yes. I've got so far as to know that there is a letter shaped like a triangle. Delta Philo Zeta something or other."

One of his rarer smiles, then.

Hawkes withdrew a slim volume, then, tapping it on his hand, put it back. "The exact volume you need isn't here. I'll—" He paused. "You can leave now."

"I can… Oh! Yes, of course." And I stood, replacing my gloves and doing my best not to cast a final glance at his room.

Hawkes opened the door, stepped into the corridor, and turned, waiting to see me out. I followed him, down the two flights of stairs and through the small vestibule.

No one came.

No one went.

Not a sound to be heard, as if Hawkes suspended time.

He opened the door, looked out, then with a tilt of his head, motioned me to follow. I did. Closing the door behind me, we were once again rooted on the solid ground of Traitors Road. A relief! As if the very street was letting out a breath. And then a few people emerged, someone entering The Cleopatra, someone leaving.

Hawkes, a slight breeze catching the tousle of his hair, bent his shoulders forward in their familiar way, a book I hadn't realised he'd taken beneath his arm.

He looked at me, so very much his St. Crispian's self. "Thank you for the letters."

"Of course. I'm sorry I misunderstood. I'm— I'm sorry I entered your room."

Although I wasn't sorry to have seen it. I wasn't sorry at all.

A thought, a random memory from months past. Then, "Hawkes?"

He waited.

"You told me once you had a painting of my father's. Only it wasn't in your room."

"It was not," he said, measuring my reaction even as I felt him remeasuring a careful distance between us.

"But what…is it of? And where is it?"

He smiled at me in a manner one might even argue is a sliver of Reprobate. And turning on his heel, he passed The Cleopatra, crossed the street, and disappeared into the churchyard.

More than a little rearranged from the whole affair, I walked slowly home.

If truth be told, it did not cross my mind to confess to Hawkes in the moment that I'd sold his pugilistic tale for naught. Or, depending on the slant, that I'd saved him from the embarrassment of a mawkish report.

Perhaps Sunday, after church.

When one feels they ought to do good and be good.

Later

All that mysticism and intrigue, and yet I found myself scrubbing the kitchen floor while Agnes kneaded bread and talked about the virtue of us possibly investing in half a dozen chickens.

Later

"It was a good day," Pierce said that evening. "I can't explain why." A shrug. "Like something finally standing up straight."

"Oh, yes!" I replied. "Hawkes! Hawkes has returned. I saw him this afternoon."

Pierce smiled to himself. "Good," he answered. Then a nod. "Maybe I'll go up to The Cleopatra later and buy him a pint."

May 22nd

The facts of the matter are these: Professor Fletcher has invited Mary (and myself) to Oxford for a reception tomorrow evening, with scholars gathered to hear him speak on *The History of the East India Company*. Mary (and I) are to stay at his sister's house. Mary (Emma included) will catch an afternoon train on Friday and return on Saturday.

I've not yet had the details from Mary herself, as she sent a note round implying that ~~if I would please consider~~ I must attend, no matter what, and that failure to support her at this juncture would result in her murdering me in my bed.

Therein lies the problem. I do not wish to die at such a young age.

But I am due to dine with Aunt Eugenia and Arabella tomorrow evening at Lady Sheridan's, followed by a ball the evening after.

However, if I aid Mary (I must), then the likelihood of Aunt Eugenia ending my life is…great. (A shame, really. I feel I've potential for a life north of mediocre.)

Perhaps if I promise to return in time for the ball on Saturday evening, the scales of my survival might tip towards life. If not, if this leads to my inevitable death, I ought to choose the best way to spend my final days on earth.

The obvious answer being Oxford.

And so I sit here at the kitchen table to compose a note to Aunt Eugenia.

> *Dear Aunt Eugenia,*
>
> *I am ill and will be unable to attend the dinner. I expect my situation to be one of short duration, and aim to be back in your service for the ball on Saturday evening.*
>
> *Sincerely,*
> *Emma M. Lion, a young woman with much life yet to live*

"But, Miss," Agnes said, eyes wide at my indiscretion. "My mother says lies grow like bindweed. You never can extract them from your soul!"

"It's *not* a lie, Agnes," I replied. "I *am* ill. I am ill-used. If Aunt Eugenia were to enquire after the nature of my illness, I would specify. Now, what does one wear to an academic reception in the '*city of dreaming spires*'?"

May 23rd

The journey to Oxford should have been nothing but pleasant anticipation—myself and Mary setting off for the great Bastion of Academia by train, green fields stretching towards the west, thick, philosophical thoughts billowing (yes, *billowing*, Mr. Chambers) as our combined gaze caught on the roofs of cottages and intermittent church steeples among the trees.

It was an accumulation of schoolgirl dreams.

Or ought to have been.

Mary, however, was in a state of emotional dishevelment.

Mary: "When he asked me, Emma…"

Emma: "Yes?"

Mary: *Clears throat.* "When he asked if I'd be willing to travel to Oxford—would I mind, he asked. 'Would you mind, Miss Bairrage, joining in the little reception? I'll be giving a short speech about the whole thing, but as your work has been so invaluable, I would want you to have the opportunity to meet others in the field'—all the while I stood there like a mute, staring. Do you wish to know why?"

Emma: "Why." *It was not a question, merely a placeholder prodding her on.*

Mary: "The man was just back from a game of cricket, faculty versus students."

Emma: *Envisions Professor Fletcher in his office, the starched shirt tucked into white trousers, somewhat scuffed from play.* "Don't tell me he wore the small collar turned down?"

Mary: "Bowtie *un*tied, Emma. As for the collar, the top button was—"

Emma: "Mary, don't say it."

Mary: "—undone."

Emma: *Swallows and shakes her head, looking out the window.* "Given the evidence, I'm to trust he was not wearing his spectacles?"

Mary: *Remains speechless, which says enough.*

Emma: "Cap?"

Mary: "Red and white stripes, pushed back on his head just so."

Emma: *Looking back at her chum.* "Mary, you have been given a trial beyond the capacities of most. But I believe you can."

Mary: "Can what?"

Emma: "I'm not sure what you can do exactly, but I will give you the solid shoulder of camaradic support through it all."

Mary: "Is camaradic a word?"

Emma: "No, it isn't, but the concept still stands."

And so we held mocks, practicing every situation we could imagine wherein Professor Fletcher might engage Mary in conversation.

"Might I please pretend he is wearing his horrible spectacles?"

"No, Mary," I firmly replied. "We prepare only for the most debilitating of circumstances."

Our consolation was that we would be in Oxford less than sixteen hours, and a full half of those would be sleeping. (The previous sentence was also our great sorrow, as this insufficient dip of the toe in such a storied place felt, and still feels, cruel. Especially now that I've seen it.)

Arriving at the station, we gathered our bags and walked out to Botley Road, turning—as per instruction—left, across the bridge and into the fabled, scholarly city. It was, in a word, dreamlike. Much of the architecture a honey limestone, the buildings comfortable in centuries of companionship. Mary had the direction written on a piece of paper, and so onward, onward, until finding ourselves on one Magpie Lane.

Charming.

We'd each packed sparingly, yet my handbag still felt heavy as I waited for Mary to lift her hand, take a fortifying breath, and give a resolute knock.

Well done chap, thought I.

When the door opened, we were met by a woman who looked to be in her mid-thirties. (Pierce's age, I suppose.) She did not wear spectacles, her hair was neat but non-fussed, and her dress was a practical sailor blue.

"Miss Mary Bairrage and Miss Emma Lion," she stated.

"Yes," we both said, nodding and imagining ourselves an equal of confidence and self-possession.

A smile broke over her face. It looked familiar. An appraising eye over us both, a lingering glance for Mary, and she stepped back. "I'm Miss Fletcher. Up the stairs and to the left is your room. Settle yourselves for an hour, recuperate from your journey, and then we will have tea."

Our room looks over the lane.

And what a view. Oh, I don't know how to describe these streets. As if every surface were patinaed with hundreds of years of words and thoughts and equations! And history and intelligent argument and green fields not so distant.

I do not know what to say other than Oxford makes a transcendent first impression.

Later

Tonight was a banner night! What an intelligent, heady gathering. ~~And to think that this entire while…~~

Steady on.

I should reveal my great surprise properly.

First and foremost, I must record that Professor Fletcher entered looking—through no fault of his own—like a refreshed specimen of Ideal Man.

He also entered with an attentive sister.

(The two facts are related, I believe.)

(I saw her brush a bit of lint from his shoulder.)

(Distracted as he was, he took no notice.)

As much as this will sound offensively conventional, the men were wearing a tremendous amount of tweed. It is not a stereotype but a truth. And there is nothing for it but to record the fact. The men wore tweed and smoked pipes, eccentrics saturated in their particular field of study, hair like bird feathers more often than not. There were a few wives on arms, some of which looked bored. (The wives, not the arms.)

But then!

Glory be.

There were also entire collections of female academic specimens.

Sensible colours, with a few bold souls throwing their lots in with brighter hues. Solid shoes, for the most part. Earned spectacles. The women dressed with variation yet belonging. All with the wicked glint of knowledge in their eyes.

The professor and I stood, a drink in hand, exchanging pleasantries—he nervous to give his speech, I somewhat dazed from the scholarly glory of it all. Mary had been kidnapped by three Fletcher sisters who appeared to be making detailed observations of her mind. I asked the professor, "Are there so many female academicians in Oxford? I didn't think any of the colleges allowed women among their numbers."

Professor Fletcher blinked and said, "Pardon?" And I realised he'd been watching Mary. My question caught up with him. "Well, Miss Lion, that is to say, as a result of the Sisters Fletcher, the OWLS have come out in force."

The owls?

Envisioning an entire cadre of the feathered things lining Botley Road, I said, "When you say owls, professor…?"

"Oh, yes! I would have thought you'd have known their reputation, being the sort of intelligent, thinking woman you are,"—

In that moment, I almost threw Pierce over, betrayed Mary, and proposed marriage myself.

—"but the OWLS are from the Oxford Women's League of Scholars. Quite a formidable group. I, thankfully, have been accepted into their number as an honorary attachment, as it were, due to the fact that full half of my sisters help run the organization."

The Oxford Women's League of Scholars.

How wonderful!

Someone came to greet Professor Fletcher, and I made my way towards a few knotted parliaments of OWLS, wondering if I'd be brave enough to engage.

And there, standing among them, was none other than Miss Dowd.

My Miss Dowd.

My Agnes Dowd!

It was her, right as rain and clear as day. Her cheeks were less full. (Had she stuffed them?) Her teeth were more pleasing altogether.

(Had she worn a false set or dyed them somehow?) Her hair far less, shall I say, German governess? She wore a scholarly dress buttoned right up to her chin, but her movements were far too comfortable to be thought of as unyielding.

I approached.

I caught her eye, she gave a second glance and smiled. So I closed the distance between us, trying to not look too… What is the scholarly version of an ingénue?

"Miss Dowd!"

"Miss Lion," she greeted. She looked both older and younger by turns.

"But you're— And Jack! You really are… Did you arrive by train?"

"I live here, Miss Lion. The academic accessibility—or rather my attempts to gain such accessibility—suits my particular fields of study."

I blinked in blissful amazement. "Which are?"

"Chemistry and English Law."

"Good heavens! How does Jack—?"

She lifted a hand. "Mr. Hollingstell and I have our own professional arrangement. Let me simply say that I am happy you have found your way to Oxford. It is no great surprise, but a pleasant one nonetheless."

I opened my mouth to enquire more but we were in that moment herded towards our seats so the lecture could begin.

Professor Fletcher, once he removed his spectacles, did a crack shot job of it all. Commanding, knowledgeable, flexible when questions were asked. He did recognise the invaluable work of one Miss Mary Bairrage, having her stand to receive the accolades of all.

I've never seen such an expression on Mary's face.

I was bursting with secondhand pride myself.

And when it had all come to an end, and Professor Fletcher was accompanying his sister, myself, and Mary back to Magpie Lane, his sister and I happened to find ourselves walking ahead discussing the history of the region, while Mary and the professor fell behind, keeping their own conversation.

Returning from the water closet later that evening, and seeing Mary lying awake in her bed, I said nothing, blowing out her lamp and keeping mine low so I could write the evening in my journal. She is now asleep, and I am wondering when they will be brave enough to confront their feelings for one another.

May 24th

This evening at Somerset House was lavish and fashionable and lively.

It proved itself to be a success, especially as the weather cooperated, being neither too cool, nor too warm, with a sense of favoured existence for those present. We were at one of the premier events of the season and weren't we all so very glad?

Islington was in attendance.

Which meant that when he and I greeted one another, we were observed by a dozen people in the near vicinity.

"You look very put together," I said. "Is it because you knew you would be under scrutiny?"

I expected him to say, "I always look put together."

He said rather, "I'm always under scrutiny."

In an instant, it put certain things in perspective.

"How terrible."

"What?" he asked, straightening the cuff of his shirt while looking about the ballroom.

"I've been having a grand sense of injustice on my behalf for becoming the centre of so much unwanted attention. I've not thought how you have always borne the same."

Islington, hazel eyes clear, looked back to my face.

He said nothing.

I, therefore, provided his answer for him. "Thank you, Lion, for your philosophical consideration of my situation in life."

His expression relaxed into amusement. "Thank you, Lion."

"You're welcome. Are you going to ask me to dance?"

"You wish to parade before everyone's curiosity?"

A frown. "I suppose you're right. Please, let us not."

"Right, then. I'm off to play cards in the library, while you…"

"Avoid my aunt. Oh look, she's seen us. Go, Islington, while you can. I'll gallantly cut her off at the pass. She is *my* relation, after all."

"A mystery how you two could be related."

I turned and bestowed my loveliest smile. "That is the most

wonderful thing you have ever said to me."

"Likely, yes." Then Islington wished me luck and disappeared.

I was happy for him.

I really was.

Sigh.

And so the evening progressed, my dancing a few dances here, a few there, luring Lord Stringham into the clutches of Aunt Eugenia so she could speak offhand of Arabella's beauty and dowry. He found both to be of great interest.

And all the while I was thinking about women who huddle around tables as they discuss their fields of interest, writing monographs on topics such as, *Glacial Forces in the Geological Record*. I was picturing the ready use of a bicycle along limestone alleyways, connecting one storied street of academia with another. I was thinking of the eight Fletcher women who are forces in their own right. And how some are married. And some are not. Some have children. And some do not. Each circumstance slightly different from the next, yet they all carry their minds with them no matter. And I wished to rip Aunt Eugenia's demands on my time right out of the book and begin anew. For the overextended pageantry of *The Season* felt inane.

Worse.

It felt asinine.

One unexpected *ergo* pleasant thing did occur.

Well, in actuality there were two.

The first was Islington leaving the library long enough to enjoy a conversation on the terrace.

Emma: "Why were you in Kent?"
Islington: "Why do you seem surprised I've other friends?"
Emma: "Do you?"

And the second, which came after.

For I was curtly asked to dance by a young man named Mr. Hazel.

He looked tremendously unhappy to do so.

We had been standing side by side, both staring blankly at the floor before us when a woman approached him and whispered something. His response was brusque. Hers a gentle but stubborn rebuttal. The man, nonplussed, looked to his left, then his right.

Which is where I stood, pretending not to be ~~enjoying~~ watching his dismay.

The dance on the floor ended. The next soon to begin.

The woman then turned to me with all charm. "Pardon, Miss Lion, you may not remember. I am Lady Cross. We have been introduced, but it was ages ago at a garden party. You were—if I recall—only just out of the schoolroom."

I had no recollection of the introduction but was willing to own it.

I liked something in her eyes. "Kind of you to remember, Lady Cross."

She brightened. "Might I introduce you to my brother, Mr. Hazel."

Said brother was now standing with his hands clasped behind his back, subdued as any stoic would be in the circumstances.

"He is visiting for the summer, and I am trying to help him meet interesting people."

Mr. Hazel thought it introduction enough. He said, "Forgive me, Miss Lion. Only I have to find a partner for this dashed dance, if you'll oblige."

Having been addressed directly, I was able to stare at him without pretending otherwise.

Aunt Eugenia was in discussion with Cynthia Goddard, and so I was free to accept.

"I don't mind a dashed dance now and then," I smiled, and walked onto the floor, my reluctant partner following. His sister looked at me like I had hung the moon—despite my use of the word dashed.

EMMA M. LION'S CONVERSATION WITH ONE MR. HAZEL
Stalwart Brother if Malcontent Dance Partner

The waltz began. We neither of us said anything. But one can only maintain tight silence for so long in a ballroom. I decided to sally forth into troubled waters, saying only, "If you like, we can be stoic throughout."

A full minute passed. Then, "Forgive my brusque request. Only my sister insists I dance once at every ball to which she drags me. I simply aim to finish the ordeal and be done with the obligation."

"Nothing to forgive, Mr. Hazel," I replied. "I only regret to say that you picked the longest waltz of the evening. We will be on the floor a full twenty minutes."

His gaze swivelled to mine, eyes widening in disbelief. "Is that so? Da—" He caught himself, but with a grimace. "How very disappointing."

I laughed.

And the corner of his mouth twitched with indecision between self-puncturing amusement and grave displeasure.

"We will endure it as best we can," I stated with a regained solemnity.

Looking like he was in complete agreeance, he said, "I'm not so bad-tempered as that."

"I perfectly understand the shackles of familial mandates, Mr. Hazel, I assure you. I will do my very best to prove that you have placed your faith in the correct partner."

"Hmm," he said, looking over my shoulder a moment then back at me. "I'm rubbish at the sort of talk one makes while dancing."

"If unusual conversation is what you need to see the task through, you have picked the right partner. For conversations imposed upon me this Season alone include but are not limited to the diseases which inflict the sweet pea and the perils of applying the strap to a sensitive child."

He frowned. "You jest."

"Quite often, but not now. When dancing with a friend, I speak of far more pleasant themes: coercion, what *some* consider to be my poor behaviour, escaping one's father via Parisian drainpipe, Greek gods, the avoidance of proposals, and the ills of the common mustache—a rodent seen in abundance tonight. Happy you're not sporting one this evening."

"I shaved my beard only last week."

"Well done. Though the beard is more forgivable than the mustache on most men."

"I am appeasing my sister, who holds similar views."

"For someone who seems rather terse, I applaud your acquiescence on several fronts."

"Yes, well…" He fell silent.

I took the silence as an opportunity to study his person.

He would have looked more at home in a military uniform than in a ballroom. Taller than Islington and Hawkes but not so tall as Pierce, strength pulled tight somehow. Hair an unremarkable brown, eyes cold blue. He was a man I could see levelling a pistol with one hand—without any hesitation or nonsense. The skin along his jaw was marked, as if he'd survived a childhood disease, adding to the gravity of his person. A few more nicks and scars for overall effect. He did not look amicable, but one might just be lucky to count him as friend.

"Are you finished?" he broke into my thoughts.

"Finished? Oh. Pardon. I was staring. Only if we're not to speak at all I need to speculate over something."

"What are your speculations?"

"There is something rather militant about you, but I simply cannot see you in a redcoat. Shall we assume the navy rather than army?"

His eyes narrowed.

"Am I correct?"

"Three years."

This divination was a moment of grand accomplishment in my young life. I continued. "I would guess you to be the sort to confidently shoot a gun. A pistol. With one hand. Like in a gothic novel. How close is that guess?"

He pressed his lips together. "Not far from centre."

"Ha! I also assume you're from the north."

"I came down only to be with my sister."

"Whom you love. Otherwise, you wouldn't have capitulated."

"Hmm."

I almost said, *I also suggest the possibility of a tragic past.*

Instead, I said, "Let's have it then."

"What?" he replied.

"*Your* assertions of *me*. Come now. I can't have been the only one making grand assessment."

He glanced down at me, then looked over my head. "Yours is not a wealthy family."

"I'm wearing my cousin's most fashionable hand-me-down dress. How could you possibly guess it wasn't mine?"

"I didn't." He spoke with weight, as if he were handing me a stone. "I'd wager you were raised in the country, but not beneath the tutelage of a strict governess."

"Bravo!"

"I grew up in the country. I recognise a vicar's daughter, or the daughter of a gentleman with little means but intelligence. It is of them you remind me. There's nothing about you that's stale, or too practiced."

"Praise I will take."

"Not like some of these vipers. That blonde over there practically falls over from the weight of her own self-importance."

I glanced over my shoulder to see Arabella.

Ha!

"You mean Miss Spencer? She's my cousin."

"Another offence at my tally," he stated. But he was not shaken.

"Arabella has a mother with whom she must contend, so I wouldn't judge her too harshly."

"But I do. I judge most of them harshly."

"Would you care the same done for yourself?"

"It happens often enough."

"And you're only here to please your sister, at any rate."

"That is my sole purpose for being in London, yes." Then, "But we're straying from the game. I have more assertions of your character."

"Dreadful."

"You think you're a wit."

"I've never claimed to be one. I am, however, more than a little deft with humour."

"You wouldn't want to be anybody else."

"Would anyone?"

"Several. Most of the young women in the room wish they were your cousin. At least one wishes she were you."

"Now I know you're fabricating the whole."

"It's true. She was watching you like she would crawl into the freedom of your life at any moment."

"Free! Ha. How is my life free?"

"You don't act as if you've any chains."

I frowned. "How can one be disagreeable after a compliment such as that?"

Our dance ended and Mr. Hazel returned to his sister's side, answered a few pressing questions, then disappeared in the direction of the library. Our meeting gave me something interesting to think about on the drive home.

I forgot to light a candle last night.

May 25th

Hawkes was in church.

No one dared say a word about David. Or Goliath.

Or even dared smile, really.

All were on their best behaviour as no one wished to drive Hawkes away again.

It was not, I believe, any more comfortable for our vicar.

Later

WHAT BARGAIN DID YOU MAKE TO TROUNCE ME IN THREE CONSECUTIVE GAMES OF DARTS?

One can't help native talent. You can avenge yourself after I return from the church.

I THOUGHT YOU ALREADY ATTENDED SERVICE TODAY.

I am going to Evensong. Mrs. Coverfield said this week's services are this evening and Thursday. I choose today as I'm liable to forget during the week.

It is also high time I face Hawkes as I've a sin to confess which may have ramifications on his life.

SOUNDS OMINOUS.

Later

Evensong was lovely.

The service itself was quiet, three hymns, two readings, and a prayer. Lasting twenty minutes at most. Victoria was *not* present. As the fifteen or so parishioners were filtering out into the early evening, Hawkes bidding them a good night, I sat stubbornly in my pew until he returned inside. He then walked down the aisle and sat on the pew in front of me, looking up at the rose window.

"Hawkes, I have something to confess."

"I know."

"Are my indiscretions so very apparent?"

Hawkes, looking to his left—I could more easily see his profile—said, "You are here, I think, to speak of the *Gazette*."

He *was* aware. "I'm terribly sorry."

A long, lonely minute soldiered on until, quietly, Hawkes said, "It was my own doing, Emma. I chose to publicly intervene in the fight."

"A thing which has brought much joy and gladness. It was very Psalms fifty-one, verse eight." Hawkes glanced over his shoulder, and so I, having practiced for this very eventuality, quoted, "*Make me to hear joy and gladness; that the bones which thou hast broken may rejoice.*"

Hawkes sat a moment, then he lifted his hand to pinch the bridge of his nose, thereby hiding a slight line of amusement.

Or would it be a line of slight amusement?

No, I believe I was correct in the first.

The line was slight.

The amusement?

Likely vast.

"Is that everything on your mind?" he asked.

I sighed. "I'm tired, Hawkes. My aunt's demands are legion."

He waited.

"And last night was very fine and monied and aesthetically pleasing."

He waited.

"Only," I sighed again, "I went to Oxford for the first time on Friday and I find myself changed. Or rather, something in me that has been dormant, or limping along, is now trying to run and it has no place to go. I've neglected my studies all the month long. I can't find order in my day. And therefore, am left with an unsatisfied taste on my tongue. That, I suppose, is how I feel."

Hawkes had fully turned when I'd said the name Oxford, twisting himself comfortably, leaning his left elbow on the back of the pew.

"I love that small but great city," he said, his voice so quiet and thick, I almost did not hear the words. Then, louder, and meant for me, "Coleridge, Miss Lion, is what I think you need."

"Do I?"

"*Yet I detest these scented rooms.*"

I sat a moment then said, "Well, perhaps *detest* is too strong a word."

Hawkes smiled and continued,

Hark! The deep buzz of vanity and hate!
Scornful, yet envious, with self-torturing sneer
My lady eyes some maid of humbler state,
While the pert captain, or the primmer priest,
Prattles accordant scandal in her ear.

O give me, from this heartless scene released,
To hear our old musician, blind and gray,
(Whom, stretching from my nurses arms I kissed,)
His Scottish tunes and warlike marches play,
By moonshine, on the balmy summer-night,
The while I dance amid the tedded hay
With merry maids, whose ringlets toss in light.

He trailed off, into a different thought, a separate weight from that which I'd carried into the church.

We allowed silence its place.

Until, "How's Pierce?"

It was not what I was expecting. "Pierce? Himself. He has his concerns but is not…concerning. I find him…" I swallowed. "He's well."

A pause, and then Hawkes said, "Tell him I'll look for him at The Cleopatra tomorrow night."

"I will."

And as Hawkes stood, walking towards his vestry now waiting in shadows, I heard him repeat,

By moonshine, on the balmy summer-night,
The while I dance amid the tedded hay
With merry maids, whose ringlets toss in light.

I left fortified with beauty.

May 26th

Sackcloth and ashes.

I was not prepared.

Tybalt is gone.

Tybalt has been taken away and all of Lapis Lazuli House is in full mourning.

I suppose I ought to record the basic facts, as I am tired and sad. To have finally met the Accidental Wife but be too distraught to appreciate the moment!

I am in need of sustenance, something sweet before I can go on.

Later

Oh dear. I found Agnes crying in the pantry.

I joined, sitting on the floor eating shortbread and weeping.

Parian found us, blinked a few times, then asked Agnes what it was again she needed him to fetch from the greengrocer.

Onward with my account, I suppose.

He is not a man I would readily trust, though she clearly does. (This is in reference to Mr. Pierce's friend and his Accidental Wife, not the greengrocer and Agnes.) If the Accidental Wife did not appear to be quietly strong and very present of mind, I might be worried. All this isn't to say I don't like the man. I find him fascinating. And appealing, in a way that isn't altogether comforting. I believe him to be the sort of man who keeps most things in the realm of absolute privacy. Observing he and Pierce in conversation was intriguing. For his stiff, controlled demeanour relaxed against the friendship.

Mr. Nicholas Stone is of a height with Pierce. In fact, while the details of the men are different, they feel as if they were both cut out of the same cloth. How to describe the difference? Mr. Stone is a man born with a raw energy, strong, the kind that serves farm labourers, stonemasons, and dock workers well. But there is an overlaying elegance. Be that inherited or studied, I've no idea. Some force took him from whatever childhood was his and placed him among those of wealth and prestige. I recognise the elite cut in his clothing, the quality of his watch, the clean, masculine scent of his cologne. He is well-mannered but without any obligatory sense he has to live up to the ideals of others.

My father twice read me *The Count of Monte Cristo*, once in the final year of his life. And this Mr. Stone reminds me of a taller Edmond Dantès. He appears both to be a gentleman's gentleman, and a blokes's bloke, by turns. Perhaps a sense of self-preservation spurs him on to meticulously watching everything and everyone.

All these descriptors feel wildly assumptive, but there it is.

My sad attempt.

Jane, on the other hand, is also highly intelligent. She is certainly not as striking as her husband, yet I think her companionship would be more pleasant. No, not pleasant. That isn't the word. Refreshing, rather, in a quiet way. With her hair a soft harvest gold and dark blue eyes, she is lovelier upon inspection, like a meadow of field grass and flowers. Her speech is self-assured without being sharp, and her self-control evident.

One wishes to spend time in her company.

While she may not be as arresting as he, he is not as clear and judicial as she.

If they were flowers, they would be an unexpected complement and likely surprise the recipient.

As for the thievery itself…

Thus Tragedy Fell

It was Agnes who fetched me from the garret.

"Miss Lion," she said, wringing her apron in her hands. "Mr. Pierce has sent me to tell you it's all his fault, that he'd spoken with his friend at a club earlier this week and knew they were coming but forgot to tell you as he'd broken a plate and had to write to a client about recapturing their image, and it had completely flown out of his mind. But they are all waiting."

"Breathe, Agnes!" I commanded. "You're turning blue."

Agnes took a breath.

Then two more.

"Miss, they've come to take Tybalt away."

"What?!"

I glanced over to the bed where Tybalt was asleep, stretched out as far as his paws could reach, a smile over the muzzy sound of his steady purr.

The hour of tragedy had fallen.

"Tell them I will be down with Tybalt momentarily," I replied.

After Agnes left, I walked over to my bed and sat, Tybalt's stretched form curling into a half-moon. I scratched his head, behind one ear then the other, as he sleepily dozed.

I bent down and kissed him between his ears, then lifted his little head just so and kissed his cheeks, pressing down the whiskers as I did so. A final kiss on the bridge of his nose, which was when he pulled his head away, opened his eyes, and delivered a fierce yawn, blinking slowly at me.

Twice.

He fought as I picked him up, and I was halfway down the stairs when he managed to work his way loose and bound ahead. When we came to the hall, he loped his way towards the kitchen, assuming Agnes was going to give him some sort of reward for his bothering to exist.

I watched him go, then confronted my fate, pausing in the threshold of the drawing room.

There stood Pierce and Mr. Nicholas Stone by the fireplace, each with his arms folded. It was impossible not to note their similarities in height and colouring. This observation came in the same split second Mr. Stone looked at me. Something about his eyes was strange. I couldn't tell why, being too far away to understand the nuance of their colour. After looking at me, he glanced towards a woman who stood on the other side of the room, studying one of my father's paintings.

She was taller than I by an inch, wearing cornflower blue, her hair set in a simple, high style. Her dress sported fewer flounces than what is currently being endured. (It was a dress I would have considered for myself.) A frown of concentration on her face, she leaned towards the painting—a watercolour of Cambridgeshire.

Then two things in tandem.

She, perhaps feeling my gaze—or her husband's—began to turn herself around and Pierce said, "Miss Lion, let me introduce you to my friends. Mr. Nicholas Stone and his wife Jane—" we were all shifting as he spoke, until we were making up the corners of a misshapen rectangle. Nods and small greetings, the kind of moment that sounds like a flutter of wings and then is gone.

"Welcome to Lapis Lazuli House," I said as sincerely as I could. "I'm afraid Tybalt has disappeared into the kitchen where the cook is feeding him his last meal. Final meal in Lapis Lazuli House, I should say. No intention to poison Tybalt before he leaves. If you don't mind waiting only a moment. Please have a seat." And I motioned Mr. and Mrs. Stone to the green sofa, then I sat in my pink chair, Pierce in Hawkes's gold.

I think Pierce and Mr. Stone would have wished to continue with their personal conversation, but both acquiesced to polite expectation. Leaving them to lightly simmer, I addressed the Accidental Wife.

"Your travels went well, I trust?"

She had a ready nod, a smile on its heels. "Illuminating to be sure. But we are happy to be home. I cannot thank you enough for your having taken care of Tybalt in my unexpected absence."

Unexpected how, I wished to say.

"Of course," I said. "The kindness was yours. Tybalt was reliable in his service. He will be very— That is to say, I shall miss his company."

Mr. Stone shifted, not impatiently but like he was a man always chafing at the bit, a man used to holding the reins. Mrs. Stone—Jane—understood the wait, that we could not let Tybalt go without spoiling him to offer our thanks. Not that her patience was an easy thing. After all, she had loved that cat for years before he invaded my garret.

Mr. Stone looked at his pocket watch.

I was liking him and disliking him by turns.

Pierce was tapping his toe absently on the carpet. Unintended, but still a small irritant.

It was then I decided something must be done.

"Pierce, why don't you take Mr. Stone to your studio and show him some recent work. Or old work for that matter, I don't care. Perhaps a drink? Mrs. Stone, how about you and I go to the kitchen, and we can have a cup of tea while fawning over Tybalt. This staid politeness doesn't seem to be the inherent setting for anyone present."

This. This speech was what won me an appraising glance from Mr. Stone. He weighed my person and found me not wanting too very much.

"Sound idea," Pierce answered. "We'll not be long."

"No, nor we," I replied, and we all stood. The tethered lines of the room loosened. Mrs. Stone kept her burgeoning smile under wraps as I said, "Follow me, Mrs. Stone, and I'll lead you to the feline in question. Likely long finished with his treat and lying near the stove."

With a last glance towards her husband, she followed.

"Clearly Pierce and Mr. Stone were wishing to continue their conversation," I said as we walked down the hall to the stairs leading down into the kitchen. "And were not appreciating the silent negotiations inherent in the Exchange of a Beloved Cat."

"Yes," Jane Stone said with a laugh. "Both were attempting—one might say painfully—to be polite."

We entered the kitchen—"Agnes, we are here for some tea at the table"—and there lay Tybalt, with the recumbent ease of a cat bathing himself after a satisfactory meal. I heard Jane's intake of breath and took a step to the side, giving her a full view.

Tybalt looked at us both. Then—if such a thing were possible for a cat—performed a pantomime of surprise, glancing from Jane to me then back again. His eyes went wide, and he was up, crouched and watching. He meowed at Jane. It sounded like disillusionment and abandonment.

She took two steps towards him, bent down and held out her hand, restraining her movements when she wished to scoop him up into her arms. But Tybalt would have none of it. He moved from a crouch to sitting up with judgement. Then, a single meow pronouncing a displeased verdict. She had left him and he was going to demand a tax before any affection could be exchanged. Without a look at either of us, he scampered off to the pantry.

"I suppose I deserve that," she said, watching him disappear.

And I laughed.

We took tea at the table. Enjoyable as it was, our conversation never did breach any personal fences. I discovered nothing of her scampering off to Europe. Despite that, I liked this Jane Stone more and more, for her answers were never boring, even when they revealed absolutely nothing.

Most of our joint attention was spent watching Tybalt slink back out of the pantry, and then hold court midfloor, his eyes moving from Jane to me and back.

Jane watched him with a knowing eye, and at one point said, "It is fair of you, Tybalt, to treat me so. I don't expect loyalty without remonstration."

"I will also take no offence for your having someone else in your life," I added, in case.

Tybalt didn't seem to need permission from either of us. He shifted his position until he was sitting like the Sphinx and then he gave her a slow blink. And, in that moment, I knew he would be leaving with Jane Stone. It wasn't long before Tybalt had launched himself onto her lap. Rolling purrs too loud to ignore, he nuzzled his face against her hand, over and over, occasionally doing a full turn before sitting down for more scratches.

I couldn't help myself.

It slithered out of my mouth like a jealous snake. "Laying it on a bit thick now, Tybalt? It's not as if you've been a wholly unwilling participant in the luxurious life of Lapis Lazuli House."

It sounded on the edge of bitter. And it was. Enough zing for a lemon custard.

Bad form.

I was saved, it must be recorded, by Jane giving the most gracious laugh I've ever heard.

It was not long after, they were gone. All three of them.

"We'll get another cat," Pierce said, as we watched their carriage making its way down Whereabouts. But I put up my hand.

“Not a word, Pierce, until we have completed an acceptable period of mourning.”

“He isn’t dead, Emma,” Pierce said, half a smile. “Nick said he’d have us around for dinner sometime. You’ll see him then.”

“When you’re in distress on the other side of the wall, I shall send no message of comfort, nary a one.”

“I’m going to miss the cat, Emma, only…”

“Only?”

“He was never ours to begin with. Some things have to be let go. They weren’t made to stay.”

“Let us philosophize another time, shall we? For now, I propose a woeful walk. Brace yourself. I expect it to be several miles. No mention of Tybalt or any other cat. If we happen to cross paths with a feline, we are to solemnly nod. And no petting of any dog. That would be disloyal.”

In the end, Pierce could not resist scrunching around the ears of a hound that had escaped its lead and was running the park as happy as any living creature could.

“It would make you feel better to do the same,” he argued.

“I will not bend.”

I confess, I did give the dog a pat on the head.

May 27th

I have just had one of the oddest conversations of my life. Which, for the layman, might mean very little, but for Emma M. Lion, means a good deal. It was dreadfully timed, as I am in Full Mourning over Tybalt and will likely never recover.

A man by the name of Lord Croixton accosted me on Primrose Hill. He's long been whispered of by the mamas of the *ton* when they believed their daughters and nieces weren't listening.

(We always were.)

The encounter began with a shadow—a rather dark one—falling across my page. I looked up to see a man I did not immediately recognise. I was told a lady knows how to put her unique personal touch to everyday interactions, setting herself apart. And so instead of saying, "May I help you?" I said, "I do believe you've chosen to stand between me and the sun."

He did not move. "I believe I saw you the other evening at Somerset House."

"I was there." And for good measure, "We were not formally introduced, which I believe is a prerequisite of some kind when blocking a lady's sun."

"No lady wants sun," he remarked. And he sat. "You are the niece of Lady Eugenia Spencer, are you not?"

"I am."

"Cousin to Miss Spencer."

Ah, I thought. Arabella. Goddess Divine.

"And you are?" I glanced around to see if our *tête-á-tête* was being observed.

"Lord Croixton. Your name?"

Some conventions I follow. Some I do not. But this was wholly unacceptable. A reputation like his? I know not to play with such fire.

"Lady Spencer's niece," I finally answered.

He made a gruff sound. "I've watched you. Coy is not what you usually wear."

"Not coyness." I slammed my Plutarch shut. "Healthy distrust, rather. Even I, the smallest player on London's societal stage, know your reputation."

He chuckled, confidently swinging the end of his cane above the ground. "Yet you remain in my company."

"It is my bench. I remain, you may go."

His answering smile was too experienced.

I wager he's approaching sixty, and he looks like what his reputation reports him to be—a man who drinks well, indulges, and entertains corrupt politicians whose wives wait at home, resigned to the fact they married weak men.

"I have a favour to ask of you, Lady Spencer's niece."

"Shocking."

"How is this for shocking: I wish to be introduced to your cousin. I cannot simply approach *her* in a park. It would be unseemly."

Villain.

"No."

"Come now, I don't expect you to make the introduction. I have plenty of seemingly reputable men in my pocket. But once the introduction is made, I wish you to aid me, and in return I will make it worth your while."

"Are you speaking of bribes?"

"Certainly. Jewellery, money, advantages."

It was said in a way that made me feel cheapened somehow.

I stood, Plutarch and pen gathered like a sword and shield. "Good day."

"Your assistance is all I ask for."

"Never."

He stood and set his cane into the ground as if claiming a nation for himself. "I can see you are entertained with the small shocks in your life and so I will speak plainly. See if you can keep from blushing. I am in need of an heir; therefore I need a wife. A beautiful woman with little inclination to meddle. Your cousin is extraordinarily handsome and when she is my wife, I will either treat you as beloved cousin, privy to the privileges my position affords, or control every halfpenny that passes through her hands, with the determination that you should see none of it and little of her. There is the choice before you, Miss Lion. Good day."

Before I could so much as spit in his direction he had walked away, as if the world and all its kingdoms were waiting to crumble at his feet.

I was angry.

I *am* angry.

Let the man think Aunt Eugenia Spencer is like the other society matrons.

May 28th

Perhaps Aunt Eugenia *is* like other society matrons after all.

I am all fury.

How could she be so…so…blind? So foolish?

This afternoon's tea was hosted by Aunt Eugenia, and so I *voluntarily* took myself early to Spencer House, requested a private audience, and shared the whole, ending with, "Even his name sounds like the villain in some novel."

But Aunt Eugenia had not looked as outraged as I fully expected. No, she sat tapping her finger with interest. "I'll give you his name is rrrridiculously spelled. Croixton! Why not CROYTON, as it's pronounced, and be done with the business of silent letters. Persons—of the male sex especially—with excessive Xs are all suspect."

"Aunt Eugenia, the man is abhorrent!"

"Abhorrent is a strong word, usually reserved for the violently poor."

"I am upset, as I have also just lost someone very dear to my heart, but I believe this man to be—"

"Don't tell me it's someone I know!"

"What?" I paused. "Oh, it was Tybalt."

Association with the cat at Lapis Lazuli House failed to cross her mind. "Oh, Emma! I hope you've not entertained the idea of marrying a man named Tybalt. Why, I can't think of a more horrid name."

"I will promise you, Aunt, to never marry Tybalt. I can't, anyway, as I've lost him."

"Well that's a relief. How did he go? Illness? Accident?"

I was dumbfounded.

I'm often amused by Aunt Eugenia's behaviour, but this was too much. I stared at her a moment and then said, "He was kidnapped, actually."

"Kidnapped!" Her eyes went round. "Worse than I'd imagined. Are they asking for money? Tell his family not to pay a farthing. Why, my grandfather was held up twice by highwaymen in his day. *Twice*!

It's best that this Tybalt's people are not willing to pay the ransom on anyone. Lose the occasional member of the family so the family fortune Remains Intact."

"Noted, Aunt. As for Arabella—"

"Kidnapped!" she continued. "I should think you would want to steer clear of a man named Tybalt who allows himself to be kidnapped."

"Aunt Eugenia—"

"Who kidnapped him, pray?"

"What? Oh, the woman he used to live with and her new husband."

A gasp. Then vapours. Of the worst sort and kind. "What is happening to the morality of England!" Aunt Eugenia demanded.

"Aunt Eugenia! Arabella must not suffer introduction to Lord Croixton. Do we agree on this matter!"

"My dear Emma, I've narrowed Arabella's choices down to three and have no intention of adding to the list."

I was not comforted by the calculating expression on her face.

May 29th

Lion,

I've already confirmed with Hawkes and Pierce that we will discuss our plans for Stonecrop on Sunday afternoon. Pierce offered his studio and suggested we dine at Lapis Lazuli. He was to check with you and Agnes. If she would be so good as to send Mrs. Knowlls and Crosby her menu, they will be sure to send me with a nice pairing or two from the cellar.

Thank the powers that be that May is come to an end.
I can already smell the fresh earth of Stonecrop.

Islington

Later

Islington,

Do not tempt fate. May has not come to an end. May is almost come to an end. This is an important distinction.

Agnes informs me she has already been in communication with Mrs. Knowlls, making me believe neither of our staffs believe we are quite up to snuff when it comes to managing the details of a dinner.

I worry I am holding too tightly to the hope of Stonecrop.
Please let it meet every expectation.
I'm feeling desperate.

Lion

Later

Lion,

There is no such thing as too tight a hope of Stonecrop. I cannot imagine it will be anything to you but a refuge.

My staff is very fond, but I most assuredly agree they none of them believe I am quite up to snuff. They imagine me lost without them. To be fair, it is likely a correct opinion.

Islington

May 30th

Today Arabella took me to tea. We were at Claridge's. She ordered a full complement and then settled back in her chair and blinked slowly at me like a cat. (A painful reminder, which did not improve my mood.)

"Mama told me of your encounter in the park."

Of course she did.

"And what do you make of it?" I asked.

Arabella smiled. "It interests me."

"Lord Croixton?"

"Not him, *per se*, but rather the game of it all. I find it amusing."

I do not.

I said as much, including, "Are you merely a prize, Arabella, for some degenerate man to chase after? A Helen? Is that all you are?"

"Nations burned for Helen."

Tea arrived then and we waited, Arabella looking smugly beautiful while I fretted with my fingers and the edge of the tablecloth. Once we were again alone, she prepared each of us a cup, stirring slowly. "You remember the name at the top of my mother's list?"

"Steward de Preiss?"

"He's been demoted, remember."

"George West?"

"George West, whom you once accused of being a pill bug, somehow cutting out Lord Stringham."

"That does not mean you should find yourself a corrupt, unprincipled—"

She stopped me right there with a little more spirit than she is accustomed to having…or showing.

"Oh, what man isn't? Are they all so *good* in your estimation? Name one that isn't also an imbecile."

"Roland Sutherland."

"Roland!" She scoffed. "Roland is like a well-fed puppy. We would never marry one another. Not good enough. Who else?"

I thought of Islington, the standard of personal integrity to which he holds himself, or how Pierce delivers measured opinion, earned by a desire to understand, not simply know. Men, and good men. And then there is Hawkes, a bright force, a tide.

I almost spoke of them all, but a selfishness reared its head.

Or a protectiveness.

I'm uncertain how to parse the two.

Arabella has the men of London at her feet, and I wish to keep my dear friends from her golden gaze.

It was not my finest moment, but neither was it my worst.

I settled with an instance of lukewarm morality.

"There are better men than Lord Croixton," I finally said. "Don't encourage him."

"Better marry an idiot than a hedonist?"

"Yes. If it comes to that."

"It will," Arabella said lightly. "It's either one kind or the other for me, as I've limited choice in the matter. Mama's list is comprised of both. Luckily for you, she is especially adept at finding the idiots."

It was meant to make me laugh.

I did not.

May 31st

Today was not as clear as one would like. The yellow-tinged air of a dirty city warming towards the complicated smells of late spring. The day wore on. Evening, with Pierce being gone, was not a lift, and despite my not having slept particularly well last night, here I am again, awake.

The late hours of the night are not—I admit—an ideal hour to grow philosophical.

Arabella is my chief concern. All related thoughts end with the realisation that a good deal of life is watching those we love consider the stupidest of possibilities.

Why would God trust humankind if—in the end—we are all fools?

It defies comprehension.

My worry over Arabella has led me right down the thorn-strewn path of worrying over everyone else for whom I care. Beginning with a working irritation on behalf of one who has a past of miles and far nations and injury and struggle, of which I know little or nothing. Who despite his best efforts, is now put at risk because someone across an ocean rolled false dice.

And some have been shattered by old hurts, but we've no idea how they formed.

And some keep their distance and their mystery, despite writing names on keys.

And betimes the very streets of home, i.e., St. Crispian's, usually charming and whimsical and fallible in the most lovely way, begin to feel cramped, small, and smudged. And there isn't any other place one would wish to live, which makes the sense of being trapped all the worse.

And Roman ghosts *never* appear to those who want them, and libraries are sold from ignorance, and cats are stolen, and the thinnest of relational chains can change the course of one's entire security.

To think, there are people in this world who know things, and speak several languages, and fill their days with meaning, and have sufficient funds, and live above the machinations of tiresome aunts and cousins, who might choose to be fools even though they are not.

Which circles one back to one's initial worry: Arabella.

To quote my father, "Bother and damnation!"

Perhaps I've lent a weary mind too much rope.

But is not the month of May supposed to be a clear, green propulsion of all things new and brilliant? To be renewed but also have some faultless sun bless such a renewal? Yet here I sit on the final day of the month, exhausted—body, mind, and spirit.

I suppose Shakespeare finds fit purpose here. *Rough winds do shake the darling buds of May.*

Such has been the tumults.

But there now. Perhaps it is time to take some advice of the Islington variety. "Remember Stonecrop," he had said.

Stonecrop.

The promise of acres and acres of woods and skies, and the sort of recorded history in which very few families are steeped. Stonecrop sounds like a verb, meaning the reclamation of serenity which, by birthright, should belong to May.

June it will have to be.

And why not?

Did not Shakespeare also write, *When June comes dancing o'er the death of May*?

Well then.

May has exacted a good many things.

So come, June, come, and tell me every secret.

June 1st

Rain this morning, and Agnes and I in the kitchen early, discussing all I will need for Stonecrop. After reciting a few passages regarding Preparing One's Person for a Country Visit (courtesy of the S. S. C. S. S.), Agnes paused and watched the rain draw lines down the window.

"The London rain is fine enough, Miss, but there is nothing like the storms of home. All sudden-like. Murky colours filling the sky. The rain itself an impatience, like it has rushed for miles and miles only to come crashing at the door." A sigh. And then, while I was still speechless over the poetry of her heart articulated, Agnes cheerily said, "I've been washing and sewing and thinking of everything you're going to need. Time in the country requires a '*different sartorial and predatorial mind*' than that of the city."

Agnes returned to her boiling kettle, and lifted it from the stove with a thick, knitted tea cloth. I was going to enquire after the predatorial aspect of that comment, but another thought struck. Like the lightning in Agnes's storm. Something, I am ashamed to say, that I've not truly given much consideration—which has been neglectful on my part.

"Agnes, you know I leave on Wednesday for Stonecrop."

"Isn't that what we've been speaking of just now, Miss Lion?"

"Yes, of course. But Agnes, how long has it been since you've seen your mother?"

"In the flesh, Miss Lion?"

"Er, yes, Agnes. In person."

"According to the manual of the S. S. C. S. S., I am not supposed to discuss time away from family."

"How long, Agnes?" I pressed.

She placed a cup of tea before me. "Two years, Miss."

A painful twist. I ought to have already asked.

I stirred some sugar into my tea. "Any siblings?"

"Two brothers and a sister."

"Fortunate," I replied.

No reply.

"Your mother is well, I take it. Your father?"

There was no complication in Agnes's face when she answered. "Dead, Miss Lion, these five years. I've come into service to help my mother care for the littles."

"I see. How about you help me prepare for Thursday, and then you yourself get on a train and spend the rest of June at home in Scotland."

Now came conflict, a flush beneath her freckles. "I'd just as soon stay and keep Lapis Lazuli running like clockwork, Miss."

"Agnes, if you have a reason you would rather not visit home, I will respect that, but if you're merely falling on your sword…"

A crease between eyebrows. "But I haven't got a sword, Miss?"

"No, Agnes. That is to say, do you miss your family?"

She pinked. "Of course."

"Do you wish to see them?"

"Only I think I should stay—"

"Agnes, go and visit your mother. I will still pay your wage for the entire month of June. And," I lifted a finger, "I shall purchase your ticket for the train. I've been needing to visit my banker, by any means, and he's only now returned to London. I'll secure the funds for your journey while there."

She looked startled. And then the reason for her hesitancy spilled out. "But Miss Lion, I know as well as you that no such thing can be afforded! And I don't want to risk losing my position because you realise that you really shouldn't be keeping Parian and I on as staff. That it's daft you try."

Agnes really did look like the last thing she wished me to understand was that I could not truly afford her services. "I—" I pulled my hands away from my teacup. "I've just been assuming that Islington was going to foot the bill for my train ticket to Derbyshire. Which frees up some monies." I slapped my hand onto the table in exaggeration. "You will have your train ticket. Visit your mother. Do…whatever one does in Scotland. And I'll make certain Parian takes care of all and sundry here."

"But Miss, the ideal lady of the house should never let a servant leave for so long, absent or no."

"Of all the— I should be embarrassed, you know, to live up to these so-called ideals laid out by the S. S. C. S. S."

"Oh, I shouldn't fear, Miss," Agnes said. "You'll never manage to live up to *all* the ideals of a lady of the house." And she—a promised train ticket in her proverbial pocket—happily began to clear the table.

Well!

Later

Hawkes, having read no poetry last week (a penance we were all asked to pay), did recite several passages from *The Faerie Queene* in service today. It was preceded by some verses from Jeremiah. And so we went from,

> *The heart is deceitful above all things, and desperately wicked: who can know it?*

To

> *Ah, gentle knight, thy vows are often crossed,*
> *And oftentimes must be renewed again.*

It was not until nearly five o'clock that we four convened in Pierce's studio to discuss our plans for Stonecrop.

I—having survived a scuffle with Cousin Archibald on the stair between the first and second floors, in which he insisted I had gone into his room—"*like a highwayman!*"—and set everything in disarray—was entering Pierce's studio while yelling over my shoulder, "I cannot yet walk through doors!"

To which Islington replied, "A great comfort to us all."

"Oh, hello!"

For there they three were, engaged in some sporting and unusual game, where they all threw their first dart at the same time, and then took turns attempting to dislodge the efforts of their opponents. Jackets had been removed, and were laid over Pierce's leather chair. Even Hawkes looked recovered from the solemnity he had taken to the pulpit. The room was what one would expect from a young men's dormitory at school or, perhaps, that of a younger gentlemen's club.

(Speculation, of course, my never having entered either.)

"Are you joining, Lion?" Islington asked.

I watched as Pierce threw a dart dead centre.

Hawkes followed suit.

"I suppose I'd better, if only to lower expectations."

And so we discussed all Pertinent Stonecrop Information while throwing darts into the board before us, smirking in victory when any of us managed to stick or knock loose the attempts of our opponents.

The Established Facts Are These

- We (Islington, Hawkes, and I) leave on Wednesday, June the fourth.

- The train departs at a quarter after eleven, and so Islington will arrive at Lapis Lazuli around ten o'clock in the morning.

> Emma: "Any limitations on what I can bring?"
> Islington: "Bring whatever will make you comfortable. This is not intended to be a stuffy visit, by any means, Lion."
> Emma: "And you will be providing the foils?"
> Hawkes, muttering: "Is that a reference to sport or literature?"

- Pierce's schedule has been rearranged, and so he is remaining in London the first half of the month, but is to join us on June the seventeenth.

> Pierce: "I might have to head down to London for an odd day, but I should be able to spend the final fortnight of June at Stonecrop."
> Emma: "It's a long way away, the seventeenth."

- Islington's sister, the Countess of Mirrenthorpe, is to operate as chaperone.

Islington: "There will also be a lady's maid provided, Lion, so you'll not need to bring Agnes, unless you specifically wish for her company."
Emma: "Agnes is going to stay the month with her mother, actually."
Hawkes: *A nod of approval.*
Pierce: "Parian is to keep the house from burning down?"
Emma: "In theory, yes. Do what you can to help keep Cousin Archibald from…well, anything too drastic."
Pierce: *Throws a dart.* "Incentive to rearrange my obligations and come to Stonecrop early."
Hawkes: "*I wandered lonely as a cloud.*"

- Islington's sister Maggie and her husband, Jonathan Revel, will be joining us for three days in the final week, before they head to the Continent.

Pierce: "I look forward to seeing them both."
Hawkes: *A sound of agreement.*
Emma: "I'm rather worried she might…impale something. Seeing as how she leaps from hot air balloons."
Pierce: "Does she really?"
Islington and Emma simultaneously: "Figuratively."
Pierce: "I've seen Maggie line up a dozen whisky bottles, full to the brim, and shoot ten of them at first go from a hundred paces."
Islington: *Gives a side-eye of superb make.*
Emma: "Oh dear."

- Stonecrop is, as has been testified, a most glorious place.

Islington: "A veritable Eden."
Hawkes: "Amen."
Emma: "So I can fully expect snakes?"

Hawkes was the first to leave, disappearing on some unspoken errand in the parish—but not before slipping a wrapped parcel into my hand, "Your reading for Stonecrop," he said quietly. "Wait to open it."

Islington stayed until half past the hour and then, when he was ready to leave, I saw him to the door.

"Lion," he said as we stood in the hall. "I am going to tell you something which might be presumptuous."

A presumptuous Islington.

I awaited with a measure of glee.

"When we are at Stonecrop, Hawkes will forget himself. Meaning, he will allow more familiarity." Islington was watching my face intently. "The intense camaraderie you sense in him now will rise to the surface, and the book of Hawkes might open, if slightly."

The Book of Hawkes.

"But why does it sound like you're issuing a warning?"

"Because," Islington said, pulling on his gloves and putting on his hat, "you will miss it when we return to London. And despite Hawkes being steady as ever, it will feel as if he has taken something away. He hasn't, only he doesn't realise how much he gives." A small pause. "And I make no effort to call his attention to the fact."

Ah.

"So I am to bask in The Book of Hawkes while it is opened, but not tell Hawkes that he left it so, preparing for the pain of when the book closes upon our return to London."

"Exactly."

I lifted my hand in salute. "I understand the commission you have set before me."

"One salutes with the opposite hand, Lion."

Needless to record, I made a great show of flinging open my door and ordering Islington out.

June 2nd

As I promised Agnes, I was waiting on the steps of the bank this morning when Mr. Penury arrived. It was all, "Hello, Miss Lion" and "Good Day, Mr. Penury." Then I was taken inside, beyond the disapproving glare of the young man who works as secretary—who remarked I'd not scheduled an appointment—and into Mr. Penury's office, where he removed his hat, set his cane in the corner, and twisted the ends of his mustache as he sat himself down.

"What can I do for you, Miss Lion? Have you come to tell me you've secured work?"

"May was a great deal of work, Mr. Penury, alas none of it was paid. I've come to purchase a train ticket and withdraw a month's worth of household funds."

"To where, pray tell, are you travelling?"

"As to that, I informed Mrs. Penury at a dinner last month, but wasn't certain she would tell you, er, pantomime any of the information in your direction. I'm travelling to Derbyshire. But that's neither here nor there. Well, it is *there*, actually. If one were to be technical. But the train ticket will be to Scotland."

Here, Mr. Penury went from a pleasant smile to a nervous flinch. "You're not…"

"Yes, Mr. Penury?"

"Now." And he placed his hands on the desk before him, lacing his fingers. "Miss Lion, I try not to interfere with the moral decisions of your life—"

"*Moral* decisions? Heavens. I try not to interfere with them either."

"—however, I cannot endorse the idea of you eloping with a man of any kind. Even if he is this duke of yours."

"Duke? Of *mine*?"

"Miss Lion. With whom are you travelling to Derbyshire?"

"Well, the Duke of Islington."

"See there."

"Yes. I mean, no! I'm not eloping with *anyone*, least of all Islington. In very fact, should the day ever come when we were to become engaged—secretly or otherwise—I would visit this office and eat my hat. Before your very eyes, Mr. Penury. Not that I'm against the idea of elopement for the desperate. A useful recourse in the correct circumstance, I'm sure. Now, as for the ticket to Scotland—"

"So you do not plan to elope?"

"In the near future? No."

"And there are no plans for marriage between you and the Duke of Islington?"

"I should say not!"

A *tsk*. "Pity. A proper wedding between you would have tidied up a great many things."

"He's not even—" I was going to blurt out *my guardian*, which would have sunk all the ships in our small navy, and so I turned rudder and said, "—the…style of man to which…I am accustomed."

Now true concern shone in Mr. Penury's face. "To which *style* of man are you accustomed, Miss Lion?"

How angular this conversation had suddenly become.

Mrs. Penury was going to be utterly delighted.

As to which style of man I am accustomed? I'm not accustomed to any, thank you. Not even brooding photographers. Pierce looking up at me, smile delayed half a second, silver eyes direct and unflinching. Accustomed?

Emma is unaccustomed, rather.

Now, if the men in question were fictional, I might have a good deal to say.

"Mr. Penury, I am living the life of a near-innocent single young woman. The train ticket to Scotland is for Agnes. Agnes the cook, that is. My cook. Which means Parian will need to control the household purse. I also would not mind a small amount of spending money, that I might purchase a new straw hat, among other things."

Mr. Penury appeared vastly relieved. "On the condition that you and I seriously discuss your prospects when you return."

"That we shall."

"This is no game, Miss Lion. Work must be found, and soon."

"Yes, Mr. Penury."

"Wonderful, Miss Lion."

Wonderful, indeed, Mr. Penury.

June 3rd

Emma,

I expect you at Spencer House at eleven o'clock sharp.

Aunt Eugenia

Later

Aunt Eugenia,

As I leave tomorrow, I fear I cannot accommodate your request.

Sincerely,
Emma

Later

Emma,

I would like to pay you a visit this morning. Be a good sport and walk about the park with me. You're leaving me alone in the clutches of the old girl, so you should oblige.

Roland

Later

Roland,

Your request is a gem in comparison to the demand made by Aunt Eugenia. If you would be willing to amend your request and escort me on errands about St. Crispian's, I would be happy for your company.

Emma

Later

EMMA,

YOU WILL PRESENT YOURSELF AT SPENCER HOUSE AT ELEVEN O'CLOCK SHARP. HAVE I MADE MYSELF ABUNDANTLY CLEAR?

EUGENIA SPENCER

Later

Emma,

Capital! Shall we say eleven o'clock?

Roland

Later

Roland,

I have been MANDATED to Aunt Eugenia's. If you will arrive at Spencer House—with carriage—by noon, we can swiftly retreat to St. Crispian's. I will think of you at least twice while I'm away if you do this.

Emma

Later

Emma,

I am ever at your service.

Roland

Later

Roland and I—he from true amusement and I from the terror of being received into my aunt's Third drawing room, wondering if she would lock me inside The Whole of June—were somewhat giddy over a luncheon at Everett's.

"When she forced you to state the names of all Queen Victoria's children in under seven seconds, proving your loyalty to the crown," Roland said, his smile illuminating the table, "I thought I might fall over from the hilarity of it all."

"Vicky, Bertie, Alice, Alfred, Helena, Louise, Arthur, Leopold, Beatrice!" I rushed in triumph.

"Brava! Although it took you quarter of an hour to get the names in the right order."

"Considering I'll not see Arabella 'til the month's end, I needed to contribute to her happiness in some way or another. Promise me you'll keep a weather eye out, Roland." I had, after half a minute of serious consideration, informed Roland regarding my exchange with Lord Croixton, and Roland—sunny disposition of the immortal—had the good sense to say, "You're right to worry, Emma. That man and I share a few clubs in common. He isn't..."

"Exactly. Promise me you'll prevent any untoward introductions. If needs be, bury the man alive in a coffin and find an obliging churchyard. I would offer up St. Crispian's, only I believe the knowledge that I'd helped you bury a man alive not one hundred yards from where I sit in church might interfere with my worship."

After tea, we walked up Whereabouts, where first we visited the Philosopher's Sole. "Bootlaces and polish!" Followed by a dip into the Reed and Rite. "Ink, grey thread, white thread, a new...well, I'll see to that myself, thank you, and envelopes. Handkerchiefs, also, which Agnes insists I embroider with my initials. Do you embroider? Pity."

Roland was a good sport. Attentive but not too attentive, available to carry any wrapped parcel but not too close at one's heels.

All went well. But then it was time for my final errand.

~~Roland and I stepped into The Hound.~~

Roland entered The Hound before me, I entering on his coattails.

"Good afternoon," I heard Ben Chambers say, followed by, "If you need any help, only… Pardon me sir, but is that miscreant bothering you?"

At which point I stopped trying to hide behind Roland and—with all the grace of a three-legged dog—I straightened myself, seeing Mr. Chambers and Stevens in the far corner unpacking a box of what appeared to be pomades.

"I beg your pardon?" Roland asked in confusion.

"I am Mr. Sutherland's guardian angel," I said, "ensuring you don't take it into your mind to steal something off his person."

"I take it you two are…friends?" Roland said.

Chambers—looking for all the world like The Pirate I know him to be—said, "Inmates, rather, in the jail called life." Then, wordlessly instructing Stevens to continue, he limped in our direction and took his place behind the counter.

"What is it you wish to wheedle out of me today, Miss Lion?" It was lacking half of his usual bite.

"I am very nearly out of my stationery and the Reed and Rite's supply is low. What remains is too…"

"Shoddy."

"…slick, I suppose."

Chambers then said, "*What has Athens to do with Jerusalem?*"

I was caught up short.

Athens? Jerusalem?

"Pardon?" I asked Chambers.

Chambers considered the sad excuse for a scholar before him and said, "You should read more."

A sore point. "I *try.*"

Chambers tapped his fingers impatiently.

Turning to Roland—Harrow then Cambridge—for enlightenment, I found him distracted by a display.

"Roland, what has Athens to do with Jerusalem?"

"Tertullian, I think. Is this Moroccan leather?" Roland pivoted to asking Chambers, holding up a small pocketbook.

"Moroccan leather, marbled edges, as you see, and three ribbons for marking important pages."

Roland considered it with a nod and then, pocketbook in hand, continued to peruse The Hound's offerings.

I turned back to Chambers. "I've no idea what Athens has to do with Jerusalem, Mr. Chambers. Neither do I have any idea what London has to do with Jericho. But I would like to purchase some simple, creamy stationery."

Mr. Chambers looked at me a hard moment, as if there were several cutting phrases at the ready and he was merely choosing the sharpest. However, touching the top of his eyepatch with his fingers, he kept his mouth sewn closed and offered only a single nod.

How unexpected.

It felt like progress in our ~~friendship~~ ~~relationship~~ encountership.

Chambers then disappeared into his back room.

"Have you seen this, Emma? From Africa."

I glanced towards Roland, who was holding up a grotesquely large beetle set behind glass. "You are never to bring such a thing into my house," I stated. "We are beyond such pranks."

Roland, the joy of his nine-year-old self shining through, then lifted an exotic coiled snake, framed in ornate gold. "And this one?"

"The poison dried in the glands," said Chambers, coming through the curtain with the stationery in hand. "Best not to remove it from behind the glass."

Roland looked impressed.

I thought it good that Cousin Archibald had no such information.

(Has Cousin Archibald such information?)

Chambers said something, but I was distracted.

"Forgive me," I said. "I was imagining myself being murdered over tea."

"Emma!" Roland called. He was at the wall of books. "Have you seen these?"

A nod as Roland turned back to the peerlessly bound books. "Now," I looked at Chambers who himself was eyeing Roland; suspicious of the enthusiasm, no doubt.

"A…relative?" he said.

"A variation on the theme," I said, almost impatiently. "He is my cousin's second cousin on her father's side and first cousin once removed or something or other on her mother's. You know how the upper classes like to keep hold of their wealth by marrying in repetitious patterns."

A sound of ~~disdain~~ amusement from Chambers.

Then, "Emma! I'm buying you a book for your month in the country." Roland crossed the shop and placed a book on the counter before me, beaming. "You are to become a naturalist!"

And apparently I am. For there on the counter lay,

The Ferns of Great Britain,
and Their Allies.

Further inspection of the title page revealed the allies to be *The Club-Mosses, Pepperworts, and Horsetails*.

"Well," I said, "if one is to have allies, I suppose the club-mosses, pepperworts, and horsetails are as solid as they come."

Chambers snorted, but Roland simply looked on expectantly. "Do you already own the book?"

"As I'm no botanist in training, I do not. But I'm certain I will become an expert before the month is out."

"Huzzah!" Roland cheered for himself, having accomplished something which should not have been too very difficult—that being the adding of a unique volume to my small library.

"Shall I wrap the book, Sir?" Chambers enquired.

"Of course," Roland answered, tossing the red leather pocketbook onto the counter. "I'll take this as well. And another day, I would be interested in discussing a bespoke pair of riding gloves."

"Happy to oblige," Chambers said.

Chambers disappeared into his back room and Roland, who had opened *The Ferns of Great Britain and Their Allies*, began to read aloud, "'*One may often observe that persons who are fond of nature, and who have yet never studied Botany systematically, are desirous of commencing that study with Ferns.*' There now! This ought to do it!"

I like ferns a great deal.

I do.

However.

I usually envision myself walking the countryside with a few stanzas in my pocket, not an illustration of the marsh fern.

When Chambers returned with paper, he wrapped the book in green, the pocketbook in goldenrod.

Roland paid for both purchases.

I was about to pay for my stationery when I was distracted by a handsome pith helmet.

I recognise it was more than a little foolish, considering the priorities of the Lapis Lazuli budget.

However.

I was so taken by the thing—the jaunty shape, its green and scarlet band, the metal spike at the top looking exploratory. I expected Chambers to argue or deny me the purchase altogether. Instead, he explained that the helmet was made of a light-weighted wood which allowed it to keep one cool while blocking some amount of sun.

"Useful for a month in the country, I should think," I said, picking the helmet up and placing it on my head.

Chambers, adjusting his eyepatch, almost laughed.

"Well, that's a lively look," said Roland.

That was the convincing argument. I paid Chambers, saying, "*Incepto ne desistam*," and walked out of The Hound, book, stationery, and pith helmet in hand.

Later

Pierce and I were able to eat dinner together this evening. A relief as Pierce has to leave early for a commission some distance outside of London. Just as well. Agnes and I will no doubt be running about the place attempting to ensure I have everything I need and no more.

"But in this moment," I said, as we slowly ate our meal, "we have stillness."

"What are you most looking forward to at Stonecrop?" Pierce asked. He was watching my face with an expression akin to gentleness.

It is a potent threat, the process of caring for someone at increasing intervals. I looked past him to manage the catch in my chest. "I suppose the vastness afforded in the country. All of May was a race. Against my aunt. Against time. Against the portions of life which were simply too much, even if many of them are good. I am saturated and ready to bleed out the intensity of the colour. I intend to trap serenity, if I can catch it."

"I hope you do," Pierce replied, his finger circling the base of his wineglass.

And then I said, "It is a pity you won't be there the entire first fortnight. It won't feel quite set until it is the four of us."

"The time will pass pleasantly enough," Pierce replied. "I'll be anxious to join."

I did not want to leave Pierce in London. For sitting with him felt like a current beyond my own. The feeling of stepping into a river and staying long enough that the water begins to shift one's feet. The current took an unexpected dip when Pierce said, "I've told Chambers."

"Told Chambers what?" And then, "Oh. Oh!"

Pierce's eyes slightly narrowed, even as he shifted his head to the left and gave a nod. It was truthful and apologetic. "We did think we should begin to tell certain people."

The whole of our interaction at The Hound earlier this afternoon paraded through my mind. "Is that why he was so pleasant?"

"Was he?" Pierce asked. Tone doubtful.

"Not by anyone else's standards. Only he...was not so caustic?"

"Sounds like Chambers."

Later

IT WILL BE STRANGE, YOU BEING GONE.

June 4th

> *We need the tonic of wildness… At the same time that we are earnest to explore and learn all things, we require that all things be mysterious and unexplorable, that land and sea be infinitely wild, unsurveyed and unfathomed by us because unfathomable. We can never have enough of nature.*
>
> *– Henry David Thoreau*

Stonecrop.

What words to describe this place?

None of the fussy, forward-flung language which could be applied to the rushed morning at Lapis Lazuli. The last-minute instructions to Parian and Agnes, the latter of whom will be leaving in two days for Scotland. The snide exultations of Cousin Archibald, who was counting every minute aloud until I left. The painful realisation that no one had to account for Tybalt. And all the soot and grime of London growing too warm.

But into all that hullabaloo a sense of holiday came with Islington, whose usual temperament was now met with unbound enthusiasm. When I came out of the house, he was showing his man and Parian where to place my trunk and case, turning to me with a youthfulness I don't recall ever having quite seen before.

"Lion," he said, followed by a smile—the sort one tries to keep hold of but might lose to joy at any moment. "Your effects are secured."

"We're off, then," I replied, my answering smile taking cue from his.

"That we are."

"And Hawkes?"

"I've his trunk here, but he's to meet us at the train. Speaking of, I've our tickets already secured." That was the moment Islington saw the pith helmet in my hand. His smile twitched to one side. "Are you," he said, taking great care to keep his voice steady, "planning to hunt a zebra while in Derbyshire?"

"After consultation with Mr. Chambers of The Hound, I have selected this hat for outdoor use, Islington."

"You say Chambers was the consultant? One would think he'd be the opposing counsel."

(Yes, one would think.)

(However.)

That was when I swung my pith helmet in Islington's direction, which he avoided with grace while opening the door to his carriage and offering me a hand as I ~~entered~~ scrambled inside, settling both my satchel and helmet at my side.

"There is at Stonecrop a wide-brimmed straw hat for your use," said Islington, clearing his throat, "which you might find more, ah, agreeable according to actual circumstance."

"Thank you, although I did also bring a hat of my own. I'm not a complete barbarian."

"Still to be determined."

And we were off.

As soon as we arrived at Victoria Station, Islington instructed his man to see our luggage was sorted and we simply waltzed into the station, finding the platform without the burden of managing our effects.

And there—in the hive of coming and going, of calls and smoke—waited Hawkes.

Book in one hand, wrapped parcel beneath his other arm, a half-moon scar on his cheek from May the first, satchel strapped over his chest at a diagonal like a soldier. Yet the expression behind his eyes was not militant. It was that of a dreamer.

"Hawkes," Islington called as we approached.

And Hawkes, shifting his gaze from a distant world to the present, looked about until he found us. "Well met," he said as we came near.

And we were.

The train compartment was comfortable, private, and both Islington and Hawkes insisted I sit beside the window, forward-facing so that I might—

This won't do.

I must rein in my meandering pen if the account is ever to arrive at Stonecrop. I cannot spend the entire month of June writing. Abbreviation is ever my watchword!

Suffice it to say, the journey by train felt like a rush of cloud and clang and green, taking us to a place which operated outside the regular passage of ordered time.

At some point, Hawkes had slipped the quote from one Henry David Thoreau into my coat pocket.

Tonic of wildness.

Unexplorable.

Wild.

Unfathomable.

The closer and closer we came to Islington's home country, the more rolling hills delivered us into deep, tree-laden dales which would intermittently break open into large pastures and small villages, tucked against a hill here or along a stretch of tree-bound fields there.

Across from me, Islington waited in a growing contentment.

Beside me, Hawkes looked as if there was blessed relief to be had and, finally, he might find it.

The empty seat in our compartment carried the ghost of Pierce.

The hills were growing steeper, a craggy green welcoming us into several layers of secrets. We stopped at Whatstandwell and Cromford and Matlock until finally, the train called at Lockwell, and we disembarked. It was a village of grey stone, all the marks of time and age and flood. The station was near the river, and Lockwell was built up both banks, rising with the forested hills.

"The drive to Stonecrop is half an hour," Islington said. "Mind if we press on? Or would you like to seek refreshment here in Lockwell?"

"Press on," I said.

And there, like clockwork, appeared Islington's driver with a coach, another driver with a wagon, and two footmen, the drivers being greeted by their duke, the footmen removing our personal effects from the train and transferring them to the wagon, a few grins between them both.

So on we went.

Hawkes sank into the cushions of the coach, closing his eyes. It was the most at rest I have ever seen Hawkes. I smiled, and looked towards Islington, expecting him to be looking out the window, lord over all he surveyed. Instead, he was watching me.

"Are you making certain I don't desecrate your holy ground?"

"No," he replied. "I want to see the moment it happens."

"What happens?"

"Magic," murmured Hawkes. But then he shifted, turned his head towards the light of the window, and opened his eyes.

I also looked, feeling Hawkes's gaze wandering over my shoulder. The clouds were thick with rain having gone and come again, but not without some breaks of open sky demanding their measure of glory. A Constable sky, my father would have said. And so it was in this misted, grey rain day—split by rebellious stripes of illuminated sky—that I saw my first glimpse.

Or thought I did.

For what appeared over ridge and tree was a tower. A cloud-strewn, ancient tower limned with sun, the glancing hint of something red, something green. Then it was gone, trees blocking the view. I rubbed my eyes, then lifted my hands to the glass, resting my fingers on the bottom for an anchor as I peered through the low clouds. Another break in the trees and the spectre of a tower.

More trees.

My mouth opened. "What—"

Islington grinned.

Hawkes smiled and nudged my arm with his elbow.

And then it broke. An entire vision. Unexpected as a mirage in the distance, for I was not looking at one grand house, but also a second. Or the ghost of a second.

"What on earth—?"

And Islington—bless his ducal soul—laughed.

How best to write it out?

Do I begin with the historical context or simply describe the unexpected aesthetic?

For there, beyond an easy river stood Stonecrop, its tall, honey limestone, Palladian architecture set against a gently rising slope. And behind it, higher up on the slope and separated from the grand house with cloud and a sense of dream, the remains of the old Stonecrop, initially built in the twelfth century, a squared southerly stone tower rising above the half a dozen rooms still intact, before crumbling into a long line of ruins towards the woods on the left.

And from the old tower flew a red and green banner.

Raised for the arrival of the Duke of Islington.

"Welcome to Stonecrop," Islington said, as we drove beneath the archway of a gatehouse, following a well-ordered ribbon of road down a flawless drive.

Grand.

And glorious.

I've never seen the like.

No traditional line of servants waited to greet Islington, but as the coach came to a stop before the house—the most magnificent pillars rising—a woman stood waiting atop the stairs. She wore a cranberry red gown, her dark hair pulled elegantly back from her face to the nape of her neck rather than imitating the more popular styles. She watched our coach come to a stop without expression. Then, as if mimicking the changeable weather of the day, a smile broke, her lips tilting upward.

Islington was quickly out of the coach, waiting near the door and holding out his hand—"Lion?"—to help me alight. I stepped out onto the warm-toned gravel of the pristine drive. Closer inspection confirmed Islington's sister to be a handsome woman, similar hazel eyes—hers more gold than green. And I found in her the same mettle that makes up Islington's disapproval. "Oh dear," I muttered, suddenly aware that my hair had attempted to escape in several places, and my clothing was more than a little wrinkled.

"You look fine," Hawkes murmured at my back, having followed me out of the coach. But Islington's sister was not looking at me. She saw only her brother.

"If it isn't our mother's favourite son," she said.

"Our father's least favourite child, rather," he gave in answer.

No rebuttal came save a wry expression followed by, "Welcome home, Henry."

Noting that Hawkes had offered me his arm, Islington began up the stairs towards his sister. She waited with clear affection. As Islington came to the top of the stairs, it was straight into her arms. Although he was taller than his sister, the way they held each other made it clear she had served as a protector of sorts.

A kiss on her cheek before he pulled away.

By this time Hawkes and I had followed.

"Hawkes!" she exclaimed, drawing him into a likewise sisterly embrace. Then I was brought into the loose circle and Islington was making introductions.

"Mariana, this is Miss Emma Lion. Miss Lion, my elder sister, Lady Mariana, Countess of Mirrenthorpe."

She held out her hand with a terrifyingly direct appraisal. "So this is Henry's unexpected ward."

I took her hand a brief moment and very elegantly said, "I—er, I see he's…told you the whole?"

"Yes," she replied, "he told me the whole."

"Oh dear," I sighed. "Better he than Lady Frankland, I suppose. Otherwise you would wonder how he ended up in my arms. Twice. To say nothing of the rest of the pantomime in the servants' corridor!"

Islington cleared his throat.

"*Ah*," the countess said, looking towards Islington. "I see you did *not* tell me the whole."

"Yes, well," Islington brushed her words away like a fly, "it was a disaster. Why don't you see Hawkes and Miss Lion to their rooms, and we can all meet for dinner at six? Ah! Crosby! Have you seen Clarke?"

And Islington began to exchange a few words with his butler.

The countess resumed hostess duties. "Hawkes, your belongings are now being taken to the old tower, as is only right, and Miss Lion," she turned graciously towards me, "January is prepared for your comfort. As I always stay in February, we might—"

"I wrote that Miss Lion was to be in the south tower," Islington interrupted, turning away from his conversation with Crosby.

The countess seemed surprised. "The south tower?"

"Yes, I asked it be prepared."

There was a suspended moment between them before she said, "Yes, I noticed the room has been prepared, only I thought Mrs. Harrison had made a mistake."

Islington shook his head. "No mistake."

She hesitated. "You're certain, Henry?"

"I thought Lion—Miss Lion, that is—would enjoy the unmatched view." His words were too light. He had dared not give them place to land. He turned back to Crosby and the countess turned to me, an additional layer of (unwished-for) appraisal. "It is well both rooms were prepared, Miss Lion." Her smile was generous. "You will be quite comfortable in the south tower. Accompany us as far as you'll go, Hawkes?"

A nod then to the woman I assume is the housekeeper, who rushed away, no doubt sending a footman to correct where my things were being taken.

I can't remember everything that was said as we calmly walked the great house, except the countess's assurance I was not to worry about getting lost. "Exceptional staff. Very helpful." We went up a grand stone staircase, beneath carved arches, three glass windows rising above my own numb astonishment. "The new house," the countess was saying, "was built right as the neo-Palladian movement was sweeping England, but not so far past the European baroque for there to still be a rather excessive amount of ornamentation."

"I see."

We entered a first-floor sweep of corridor, full of windows on the west, a wide hallway, and then a series of apartments—one after the other—all named after a different month of the year.

"My brother ought to have moved into our father's suite, but has still retained his apartments here"—she motioned towards a closed door—"in July. I cannot blame him, as I've never surrendered my ownership of February. When Mr. Pierce arrives, we will have October prepared for his comfort." She frowned then—and thinking of it now, it was because my room was up a corner staircase from the latter half of the corridor rather than closer to the beginning and her own apartment.

Hawkes was following with such an undefended comfortability, that I kept stealing glances. It was like seeing something for the first time, but not being given the definition as to its meaning.

At the end of The Calendar—which is the name of the entire corridor of apartments—there sits a morning room which, being neither the library nor the small library, only has two shelves of books. It is decorated in turquoise and soft green, with the bookshelves protected along the wall closest to the door, while the windows on the south wall feel more like a sunroom, for reading or gazing out over the expanse of lawn, lake, garden, and woodland.

"A place you might enjoy spending some of your leisure hours, Miss Lion. And below this is a covered portico where we often take tea. You are, of course, very welcome to read any book you like in the main library on the ground floor. That library is Henry's preference, and where he does a majority of his work. There is a smaller if you're hoping for solitude. Now." And we stepped back out into the corridor, where we turned left and entered a stairwell. "Your rooms are up, Miss Lion, while Hawkes will go down to the ground floor and walk the Glass Walk up to the old tower."

"Walk the Glass Walk?"

But Hawkes had already disappeared, and I did not want to press the countess for details.

Up we went.

The stairs led us to a landing with a door slightly ajar, which the countess pushed open to reveal a tall-windowed water closet, with every necessity provided including a large copper bath. "This is for your private use," she said. "Isla will see you have anything you need. Now, up to your room." And so another flight of stairs and another door, through which the countess welcomed me.

"Will it suit?" she asked.

I started forward. A comfortable size, squared, windows on all sides, the design was all pale green and cream, and it looked for a moment like a brave sun had thrown off the clouds to break the windows with complicated light. Beyond the glass, an unimpeded view.

"I've… That is to say, Your Ladyship—"

"Mariana, please." She moved her hand across the freshly pressed bed linen, looking about as if her mind saw a different room. "Do call me Mariana, Miss Lion," she repeated. "Now, I will leave you to settle. Your trunk and case are there. I find most guests prefer to unpack their own belongings, but if you prefer help, certainly do ask. Only choose the gown you will wear this evening and lay it across the bed. Isla—your maid for the duration of your stay—will see the wrinkles out. While you're at supper, she will take the trunk and case away. However, if you should need them at any time, please inform Isla and she will see you accommodated. Now," Mariana smiled kindly, "rest or wander as you wish. Isla will meet you here at half past five to help you dress for supper. I know it's fashionable in London to call the evening meal dinner, but Stonecrop usually considers any tradition of the last two hundred years modern, and so supper it is. We will meet in the green drawing room on the ground floor, as Henry prefers to use the adjoining family dining room when we are not a large party."

She considered me now, earning my own gentle scrutiny in return. However formidable the mettle of which she was wrought, there was habitual warmth. And I liked her eyes. "The design of Henry's Stonecrop is to make every guest feel they are returning home. So be at your leisure, Miss Lion. Until this evening." And she slipped from the room, leaving me to the comforts, and the windows, and the memories of which I knew nothing.

I liked the simplicity of what I saw. The bed was against the north wall, flanked by windows, a side table at the ready. Windows on the west, with a comfortable window seat—a place to avoid on a hot summer's afternoon, but glorious come evening. And beneath one of the windows to the south, a writing desk, which—upon further inspection—offered plenty of paper, ink, pens, fresh nibs, envelopes, a case filled with pencils and even a small sketchbook for drawing.

"Very accommodating," I said to myself as I closed the drawers and glanced around.

There was also an armoire, a washstand with a bowl and pitcher, and a French *bijouterie*—delicate carvings detailed with gold leaf, not too large, and beneath the glass top lay a collection of beads.

Ancient beads.

Some parts of longer strands, others singular.

Compelling, lovely.

Beads of jade, amber, lapis lazuli, three of gold, and other stones

I did not recognise. Curious, I tapped the glass with my fingers and glanced about the room. There was nothing to adorn the walls. No paintings, no drawings.

On the windowsill above the desk waited a wrapped gift, sent ahead it seems, with a note written in Islington's architectural hand,

For your first wanderings of Stonecrop.

When I opened the gift, I found a small brown volume with the most beautiful natural patterns in gold entitled:

British Ferns and Their Allies:
An Abridgment of The "Popular History of British Ferns,"
and Comprising the
Ferns, Club-Mosses, Pepperworts, & Horsetails.

I stared with amazement.

It couldn't be!

Opening the cover, I noted author and date. Whereas Roland's gift had been written by one Anne Pratt, this volume was penned by a man by the name of Thomas Moore (not the Catholic martyr, I trust), who also penned *The Handbook of British Ferns*, *The Ferns of Great Britain and Ireland*, *Nature Printed*, and *The Octavo Nature-Printed British Ferns*.

I cannot imagine a life so very dedicated to the fern!

Yet, here I stand. The owner of not one, but two books on the topic!

And as amazed as I am that Roland cannot gift a book without there being a twin, I am *astounded* how consistent a fern's allies are.

Club-Mosses, Pepperworts, & Horsetails, indeed!

The cruel jest bestowed by fate is that Islington's gift is a much more desirable size for traipsing about the country.

It was a reminder that I'd packed Hawkes's gift in my case, to open upon my arrival at Stonecrop. As enchanted as I am with my ferns, I was hoping it was not a third repetition.

Botany *can* be taken too far.

I needn't have worried. For when I unwrapped the brown paper,

I found myself holding a painterly sky-blue volume of Wordsworth's poetry. It was one of the most beautiful covers I'd ever seen. Opening the book, I found a page with a scarlet ribbon, a single line marked.

The first line of the small poem.

In these fair vales hath many a Tree

I placed the volume on my bedside table with the *British Ferns and Their Allies*. A current of anticipatory contentment. I looked up and out of the windows. The tower stood at a timeless height, and it was with a ~~mature curiosity~~ rising giddiness that I was drawn out of my room and up the final set of stairs to the roof. The door was locked, but there was a key hanging from the wall—and having been given permission to wander at will?

Well!

I unlocked the door, slipped the key into my pocket, and stepped up the remaining half flight that brought me atop the south tower.

What to write!

A dreamscape, a sanctuary, the feeling of tangling with low clouds and grey wind. As I turned about, my hair whipped around, responding to the wildness.

I couldn't help but think,

I wish I were a girl again, half savage and hardy, and free.

But then I could hear the haunting question that follows,

Why am I so changed? I'm sure I should be myself were I once among the heather on those hills.

I don't really know why I did it, but as I stood at the balustrade, placing my hands on the stone, I shouted. The wind carried the sound of my voice—it turned and dipped.

I shouted again.

And once more for good measure.

Perhaps the tongue of angels is wrought when shouting into the wind.

Laughing, almost crying for the relief, I looked about. Miles of world, a forever expanse of hills and trees, eager green swathes of June marking the land. Turning, I found myself looking towards the ancient tower rising up the hill. And there, perched on one of the high stones, sat Hawkes, taking in the same glory.

There was enough distance I could see his form but little else.

I waved.

Unless it was a trick of the light, he tilted his head and saluted in my direction.

A full smile, and I turned back, breathing it all in.

The glory of old stones and woods and fields finding their way to the river about me.

When I left the tower, I did not replace the key by the door, but rather kept it in my pocket.

Later

The staff appear loyal to the bone and excessively fond of the family. My maid being no exception. Isla is accomplished, polite, and correct.

She is also, I believe, suspicious.

I am welcome…to a point.

It Begs the Question:

How long has it been since Islington brought a single female to Stonecrop?

Isla did help me dress for dinner, taking my gown away—the shimmering gown Arabella discarded last year—and returning it with nary a wrinkle. My hair caused her a double bother, but determination won the day. I was styled far more fashionably than I prefer, so I intend to manage myself most days.

Isla explained the most direct route to the green drawing room, and the instruction proved helpful, for I found myself in the correct place at the correct time, Islington looking sharp as a sword as he stood in conversation with the housekeeper. His hair was combed back with a shine, the cut of his black suit perfection, the crispest collar matched only by the brightness of his eyes. If one couldn't recognise his underlining happiness, one might think him insufferable.

"Lion!" he greeted with enthusiasm I'm not certain I warrant.

"Islington!" I sallied in return. The housekeeper, a Mrs. Harrison, had already disappeared, the mark of excellence in household staff. "Why you look positively radiant."

"I had a good hour with the hounds before changing for dinner."

"More restorative than mineral water."

"Quite." But he was in earnest. "I should introduce them to you tomorrow, if you're not allergic."

"I'm allergic on principle, but not in actuality. I will meet your oft-spoken hounds with equanimity, for your having given me the most glorious room in the house."

He poured me an aperitif—not sloe gin—and looked truly chuffed. Chuffed, I say.

"That room has its own particular brand of being. It is a simple room," Islington described, "but in the correct way. Like a brook. More akin to artless beauty than gilded ornamentation." A pause, Islington scanning my face then taking in my person as a whole. "Are you sporting a new hairstyle?"

"Not intentionally, no, but there was no stopping Isla."

"Ah. You were assigned Isla. A boon. Also," he very nearly grinned, "I wish you luck."

"She saw my gowns—I only brought three, I'm sorry to say—and with the determination of a stoic martyr selected my finest for this evening, then reformed the character of my hair, determined to make me worth your table."

A guffaw. "You've never once questioned if you were worth my table."

"I didn't say *I* cared one jot, Islington."

"I daresay you don't."

"Please note that I most certainly am worth a few pounds more than your table. You who first asked me to dine at your house under false pretences."

"When was—*Ah*. That was in rather poor jest. And yet," he smiled, "I've no regrets."

"A line I intend to repeat every time I do something particularly irksome."

"Like the reading of my journal?"

Sore point, but yes. "I was thinking of my accidentally pushing you into a river or stealing your horse."

"You would threaten my horse?"

"As for the sword you promised me."

"Speaking of threats—"

"I fully expect to stab you should the need arise."

It was in this rather unfortunate moment that a throat cleared, and Islington and I turned away from the window to see ~~the countess~~ Mariana, standing placidly in the doorway.

"Good evening," she said. Then, "I should hate to think Caesar has brought Brutus with him to Stonecrop."

"I— That is—"

I felt…an indescribable sensation of wrong-footedness.

But Islington laughed. "My chances of survival are high, I assure you. I don't believe Lion knows how to wield a knife, let alone a sword."

A glare from me.

In London I would have given a retort about the dining hall at Fortitude.

However.

Silent observation was made by Mariana before she asked if my room was to my liking.

To which I politely replied that yes, it was.

Hawkes soon appeared, not wearing anything half so formal as the rest of us, and we four went in to dinner.

I like Islington's sister. She is not easily readable, but one instinctively wishes for her approbation all the same. "Wealth, cleverness, and praise are not the same as excellence of character, Emma," my mother used to tell me.

To which my father would say under his breath, "But *do* also be clever, if you can."

I recognise this excellence in the countess.

The evening would have been unbearably perfect if Pierce had been present, leaning back in the duality of confidence and disquiet that sometimes marks his company. Exchanging interests with Islington, pronouncing something on Hawkes's head to see if the latter could be moved from his meditative silence, and glancing towards me as if, just possibly, happiness were a thing to be found.

I sit at the desk, window before me pushed open.

And what a chorus of crickets and owls can be heard, even from the tower.

The clouds tonight are moving in a deep ocean sky, a few bright glimpses of starlight now and then. What was the exact door that opened, I wonder, and when was the opening, that brought me to such a night?

June 5th

This morning I woke to the low convincing of a cello. It was just before dawn. The sound was faint; enough so that I might have just stayed abed—but it talked me out of my comfort. Forcing myself from beneath the blankets, I wrapped my robe and shawl about me. Cool air was waiting when I opened my door, and the music was growing up the stairwell like a vine. I crept down and down, until I was looking out into the window-laden corridor outside of The Calendar apartments.

The musician played with a sense of exclusionary focus, finishing one piece and beginning another. Hawkes would tell me later the first was a transcription of Requiem by Mozart and the second was a new composition by Gabriel Fauré called "Élégie in C Minor."

I did not know the second, for my musical education is lacking. Not that I don't have deep appreciation and great interest, but I've attended a limited number of musical performances, and I don't play a note of anything. My mother did. The piano. But my father could never afford an instrument, so I only ever heard her play in the houses of others.

I digress.

Looking about to ensure I was alone, my plaited hair having loosened into a wild halo of a braid, I took a watchful, cautious step. Two steps. Three. Then another.

And sitting in one of the generous windowsills across from July was Hawkes. He was dressed in trousers, a half-tucked white shirt, a pair of braces holding it all together. Stockinged feet, no shoes.

I Repeat the Important Facts

- The music hailed from July.
- Yes, Islington. Duke. Of.
- Apparently, Islington plays the cello. With provocative emotion.
- And yes, I—having descended into the corridor—believed I would be alone.

- I was not expecting any sort of vicar to be present, even Hawkes.

The entire scene should have sent me flying back down the corridor and up my tower stairs to pay for my sins. (A priest of the Catholic persuasion might have given me five Hail Marys. Hawkes? Five stanzas of Wordsworth.) However, the round depth of the cello rooted me where I was.

I recognised the next piece. It was Bach and I couldn't bear to not hear it.

Hawkes opened his eyes.

As if he fully expected to see my person standing there.

A smile, the rare appearance of Hawkes's dimple, the passing of his fingers through his unruly hair. He topped it off with a nod and reclosed his eyes.

I, in return, pulled my robe tighter round my person and—keeping a maidenly distance—sat down against the door of September, my shawl very properly covering my feet.

I've never considered the cello as companion for dawn. One would think to pair it with falling evening, with deepest night. But the instrument did seem to understand the dream state just before waking.

Islington played another selection of music.

Then another.

And finally—the corridor lighter and lighter in the growing day—I was startled from my trance by the door to July swinging open. Islington, in the action of leaving his rooms, fully dressed in rather fine country ware, was arrested at the sight of his audience.

He looked at Hawkes.

He frowned and glanced over and down at me.

I could feel September shrinking and sidestepping, leaving me exposed. A surprise, as September is not a fickle month.

"Ah," he said. Then, "Breakfast in half an hour, I should think." Then he stepped back into his room and closed his door.

Finding I was, indeed, quite hungry, I said, "I believe he's right, Hawkes. Allow me to scramble to my feet unobserved, if you will."

Hawkes placed a flattened hand before his eyes, which did not hide a somewhat elfin smile, and waited until I'd not only scrambled to my feet but run the length of the corridor to my tower stairs.

Later

The breakfast room at Stonecrop.

It is the only way to begin a day.

I will live there.

I will die there.

A full wall of windows broken only by French doors leading out to a colonnade the length of the house and overlooking the courtyard garden between Old Stonecrop and New Stonecrop. Sunshine splashing over the room like a merry fountain. The walls are soft yellow, neither too thick with cream nor too thin with lemon juice.

I was the last of the party to be ready for the day, as Islington and Hawkes were already sitting down. Surprisingly, ~~the countess~~ Mariana (she corrected) was also at the breakfast table rather than in her rooms, which is the usual custom for married (and certainly expecting) women.

"Miss Lion," she greeted when I was seated, my plate a sad comparison to Islington's and Hawkes's—veritable mounds of eggs, streaky bacon, and toast.

Hawkes, of course, had a book open on the table, reading as he ate.

Had we three been alone, I would have guffawed in jest.

As Islington's sister was present, I did not.

(One must uphold standards.)

Returning to Mariana. "Miss Lion," she began, "there are a variety of entertainments and—"

Islington raised his right hand to silence his sister, even as he was using his left hand to dab the side of his mouth with a napkin. "No guidance."

"Really, Henry. I am only providing—"

"Mariana."

She ignored her brother. "Miss Lion, you will find a full selection of—"

"Lion," Islington interrupted, "when was the last time you felt absolute and sustained freedom?"

Hawkes glanced up from the pages of his book to watch the exchange.

"Well," I thought, "in my garret—"

"*Sustained*," Islington clarified, "meaning days and days of the stuff."

I blinked. "Stonecrop Islington is shockingly at ease in his world. What have you done with London Islington? Is he locked in a closet somewhere?"

To which Hawkes murmured, "A corridor."

At which Mariana cleared her throat in an entertained manner.

Islington half scowled at both Hawkes and myself. "Only answer the question, Lion."

I, setting my silverware down, looked past Islington and over the garden. "I would say the summers at Spencer Court in Berkshire, only…"

"Your aunt?"

"My aunt. So freedom, yes. But absolute, sustained and unbound? My parents' cottage in Cambridgeshire."

"Too long, wouldn't you agree, Hawkes?"

Hawkes, who had returned to his book, nodded an assent.

"Therefore," Islington proclaimed, raising his arms as if he were readying himself to conduct an orchestra, "I give you freedom. Wander. The grounds are at your full disposal, as is the house. Every entertainment, ah, *almost* every entertainment you can dream of is on offer, you need only ask. Painting, riding, shooting of various kinds, reading, walking. This will be a month of following your own star and you will return to London a new man."

"That would be astonishing."

Islington laughed.

"Am I not to begin my visit with a house tour followed by a turn in the garden, as is the custom of my limited experience attending parties at grand houses?"

"Not at Stonecrop," Islington said, continuing to impale his eggs with excessive happiness. And yes, excessive is the correct word for what I witnessed. He looked ready to stride off in any given direction.

"As for house tours," Mariana inserted, "we keep a strict Rainy

Day Policy, Miss Lion."

"Rainy Day Policy?"

"Yes, the first day we're encumbered with too much rain to make the outdoors enticing, I will give you a formal tour of the house."

"A visit to Stonecrop should begin with liberal access to the gardens, the fields, the woods," Islington said. "*All things that love the sun are out of doors*."

"Tennyson?" I asked.

"Wordsworth," Hawkes gave answer, turning the page of his book. Then, looking up into a distance the rest of us could not see,

> *All things that love the sun are out of doors;*
> *The sky rejoices in the morning's birth;*
> *The grass is bright with rain-drops;—on the moors*
> *The hare is running races in her mirth;*
> *And with her feet she from the plashy earth*
> *Raises a mist, that, glittering in the sun,*
> *Runs with her all the way, wherever she doth run.*

As tempted as I was to lose myself in the gorgeous cadence of Hawkes's voice and the fresh leaning verse, to cry out, "Plashy! What a word!", there were principles at stake. I looked directly at Islington. "You dare invoke a verse that has a hare '*running races in her mirth*'? You of Rabbit Room infamy?"

"*Runs with her all the way, wherever she doth run*," Islington echoed without compunction.

I, seeing from the corner of my eye that Mariana had raised an eyebrow, chose not to reply, slowly lowering my knife as if I'd merely meant to butter a scone all along.

Mariana said, "A lovely day ahead, *I believe*."

Stonecrop might just very well be a riot.

Later

I honestly do not know what to think.

Islington has a tribe of hounds—beloved, beautiful, sleek, and adoring. As for why this is a problem for one Emma M. Lion?

Well.

It all began with my following Islington into the stables, where he took me to see a new litter of pups. "At four weeks old, they'll break your heart." And he melted, positively melted, at the sight. Crouching down, crooning and tussling, speaking to them as if they were expected to change the world. I was introduced to the proud mother, Iris.

It was then Hawkes appeared, possibly having sensed something he would not wish to miss.

And further into the kennel we went.

Of Islington's glorious pack there are twenty-six in all. There is usually a litter or three each season. "A single hound kept each year, the rest sold," he said with some regret.

One particular hound stayed at his side with the fidelity of a knight errant returned home to her liege. She was aged, dignified, and looked at Islington as if he were her pup grown. Islington went about saying names, "…Cicero, Jasper, True…" and so on, until he reached down a hand and, patting his most loyal dog said, "this is, *ah*, Emma."

I looked down at the dog.

She looked up at me.

Hawkes, leaning against a nearby doorway, watched with undisguised enjoyment.

I looked back up at Islington.

He was waiting with…well, I can't rightly say what sort of expression it was.

"Your most beloved hound is called *Emma*?"

He held up both hands. "She is fourteen years old."

"But…*Emma*?"

"There was a full litter we kept, years ago now. My sister had the naming of the five puppies. And so I was left to raise Jane, Marianne, Fitzwilliam, Henry, and, er, Emma."

The only saving grace was that there was also a Henry. I said as much.

"The handsomest of the lot. Deceased now, unfortunately."

Crossing my arms, I looked back down at the hound in question, who was now both suspicious of me and protective of Islington. She made some sort of snort with her glorious nose and lifted both ears, all without breaking eye contact.

"Have you ever"—this to Islington—"mixed the two of us?"

"Don't be absurd."

"Is this why we fell into such an easy friendship? I reminded you of…a beloved dog?"

"No," Islington scowled but it was conquered with a laugh. A laugh too gleeful, at that. "And there was nothing easy about falling into our friendship."

That is how Islington ended up feigning a run before striding out of the kennel, my following behind, with half a dozen dogs running along for the joy of it all.

"I never said it wasn't diverting," he called over his shoulder.

"You're going to rot, Islington. I don't exactly know where, but at some time, some place, you will rot!"

This was the moment Mariana stepped out into the courtyard between the stables and kennel.

Blast and rollick, as the boys of Stoicism would say.

But Islington was already out onto a path heading towards the north wood, hounds in joyous tow, and Hawkes—at that moment—was walking past me, book beneath his arm, hands in pockets. Thus I was simply swept along, smiling at Mariana politely as I escaped.

A Note on Stonecrop Islington

How do I describe? Islington looks taller in the country, and oh so very capable of a landed, pastoral existence. As if one could place a wineglass, or a cricket bat, or a walking stick in his hand, and they would all fit in equal measure.

Later

There are two dragons on the Devereux family crest because twins run in the family line. That is what Mariana explained when she showed me both the medieval crest and the "modern" crest commissioned by her great-grandfather in the earlier part of this century. Oft times skipping a generation or two (the twins, *not* the grandfather—although that is a fascinating twist to reincarnation if I've ever heard one), the return of family twins is always viewed favourably. On the rare occasion twins have been born two generations in a row, it is considered auspicious by the Devereux clan.

The green dragon is *passant.*

The red dragon is rather terrifying.

Both have claws, clearly.

June 6th

Every morning should begin with a cello.

Later

While Islington is seeing to business with his steward, I am going to ~~record a simple description~~ *begin* a simple description of Stonecrop and its immediate surrounds. (It may take some time, and more than one day's journaling.) After which, we are going searching for Hawkes, who wandered off yesterday afternoon with a rucksack filled with whatever Mrs. Knowlls donated to the glorious cause, and simply did not return.

There had been one bemusing exchange before he left.

"Hawkes," Mariana had said, "will you please allow me a few evenings of propriety before you kidnap the whole?"

Hawkes, considering, nodded, then said, "I should wait for Pierce, in any case."

"As this is Mr. Pierce's first visit, you're going to leave the impression we are perfect heathens."

"He's a rather perfect heathen," I said mostly to myself—a poor, out-loud habit, developed, I imagine, from too many solitary hours in a garret. Freezing in realisation before looking up and finding everyone's eyes upon me, I added, "Meaning, I don't believe he'll mind anything too unorthodox."

Bother.

I'm a perfect heathen.

Later, when we'd decided to go snare ourselves a vicar in the wild, Islington told me to ready my boots and hat—"A rational hat preferably, unless you insist on looking ridiculous."

Fully envisioning myself walking Derbyshire in The Pith, I answered, "Will he bite, do you suspect, our Young Hawkes, having gone feral overnight?"

Islington had given me a side-eye and strode—strode!—towards the stables.

I MAKE MY FIRST REPORT ON STONECROP
The Ruins of Old Stonecrop and The Courtyard Garden

As previously recorded, New Stonecrop was built in the late 1700s, down the slight slope of hill that ran before the Old Stonecrop. The Old Stonecrop originated in the 1200s, and was built of limestone, later squared on the corners with what Islington calls millstone grit.

"Permission was sought from the crown for several stages of building, including the addition of battlements along the wall," Islington said, as we stood in the courtyard garden looking up at what remains of Old Stonecrop.

"Why?"

"Why? The king would not wish for a fortress to be built in bonny old England if he wasn't absolutely convinced those walls would be *for* him rather than against him. However, the Devereux family *did* receive royal permission, and Old Stonecrop became what she was. According to the drawings done after the fire—which I'll show you when Pierce arrives, as I know he'll have an interest. As the fire broke out, most sections of the north roof falling prey to the destruction, we were left with only the main tower still standing on the south, as well as the adjoining rooms on both the ground and first floors—the old hall, a small armoury, with a bedroom and gallery above. And, of course, the aforementioned tower, which has been commandeered by Hawkes and never rightfully returned."

"Why not rebuild the north?" I asked, looking towards the crumbling wall of stone.

"Much of the stone was ransacked and hauled away. The bulk of this thievery happening a few years after the fire, when the family was spending their time elsewhere."

"I am impressed with the audacity."

"Impressive or no, when the duke discovered what had happened, he took swift action. Thirteen men were hanged in Lockwell."

"Hanged!" I sputtered. "What year was the fire?"

"Seventeen hundred and thirteen."

"Brutal."

"Barbaric times."

I looked at the profile of Old Stonecrop on the hill. On the north a desolate arch, with a crumble of stone grown over with *Erigeron*, which began to form the ruins of a wall, a few abandoned doorways, the stone growing taller and taller until it became what was left of the intact building, ending in the tall, squared tower—where above flew the red and green standard of the House of Devereux.

"And so after the house burned and then was pillaged, and the Duke of Islington did his duty by hanging thirteen poor men who were clearly threats to his wealth and status"—a side-eye from Islington at this comment—"what happened? The duke did not wish to rebuild the original Stonecrop?"

"No," Islington answered. "He was a great student of architecture, and the Palladian style had come to England, with those of great wealth setting up new monuments to their fortune. The tenth duke commissioned another Stonecrop, down the hill from the old, which would turn his interest and fortune into a legacy. As a man of modernity and innovation, he almost couldn't believe his luck. It was his son, my grandfather, who begged him to keep the remains of Old Stonecrop intact, to restore what had been spared by the fire and incorporate it as an almost fairytale rising out of the mist above the new house. I'm certainly glad he did. And between the ruins and New Stonecrop, he created this courtyard garden."

And Islington lifted his hands, as if to say: Behold!

I beheld.

And it is, in all honesty, the most wonderful garden.

A large square, the tower falling into ruins bordering the east, the Palladian Stonecrop bordering the west. To the north a walkway covered with a series of large, patiently spaced stairs with arches running the length. As for what makes up the border to the south? It began as a mimic of the arched walkway on the north; however, Islington's grandfather took it into his mind to turn it into a corridor, connecting the old building with the new by a sequence of large windows, with five sets of French doors set evenly along on both sides, allowing a cross breeze when desired. It became known as the Glass Walk, often home to large potted palms and other vegetation from more exotic climes.

The garden itself is not a tribute to other formal gardens of the time, nor is it a braver, looser ode to the English cottage garden. It is an enchanting balance between the two, with woven knots of boxwood patterns for structure in the centre and the four corners, the intervening squares left with drifts of romantic, heart-reaching flowers. As Old Stonecrop is higher up on a gentle slope, the garden is terraced, with gravel paths and stone steps allowing easy passage.

Perhaps my favourite detail is a stream, diverted from the river north of the property, which enters beneath the north walk and meets the circle of a stone fountain in the centre before continuing its straight course to the Glass Walk, where it drops below and reappears on the other side, making its way down to the lake.

Along the back of New Stonecrop is the long colonnade where one might walk or mingle during a ball, overlooking the courtyard garden. There are five wide sets of stairs between garden and colonnade, and beneath said colonnade is a covered porch, a cool walkway for a private *tête-á-tête*.

Enough description.

It is time to go a-Hawkes Hunting.

> Emma: "Exactly how does one find a Hawkes gone to ground?"
> Islington: "One wanders. And then one is found."

Later

How to describe the woods and fields around Stonecrop?

How to describe that light and sound claim kinship here in a way never before felt?

How to describe the feeling of deep, cool air, puddling in the crags of stone? The trees, comfortable in their wealth of green?

How does one write the bend in the river which is wide and deep, and set below a sharp jutting rock from which to leap? Lined with ferns and shaded by mighty trees accustomed to drinking deeply?

How does one account for the fact that of all the thousands of acres belonging to Stonecrop, it would be in a small-path-side-twist of a place where one would come across Hawkes, sitting in the comfortable crook of a tree, book open, eyes closed?

And as much as I love St. Crispian's, I'm beginning to wonder how one ever leaves this place.

June 7th

Islington asked if I would like to go out for a ride with him. I, holding up my butterfly net, a jar for collecting, and my satchel—filled with two books, my journal, and enough food to keep me wandering the day long, told him I was too occupied to find any enjoyment on the back of a horse.

"I would love to fence, however, at your second or third earliest convenience."

"There is a horse here who would prove the perfect mount," he replied instead, avoiding the idea of my running at him with a foil. "She's strong, a good head, not afraid of a run."

"I will give her my consideration. But do enjoy yourself, Islington!"

As for myself, I've disappeared into some of the fields kept round by snags and lays of woods. There has been less reading than I'd originally intended, for the sky is a glorious oil painting—the artist having added enough white for a most ethereal blue. And with the June greens—deeper in the trees, lighter in the grasses that brush against my skirt—it is a day for chasing winged things.

Later

There is an ancient oak wood.

I have found it, and am enchanted.

The whispering chill of Puck's fingers moves along the back of my neck. The gossamer encounter of spiders' webs, echoes of the faerie folk gossiping over the estrangement between Oberon and Titania. A fool of an actor is poised to become the plaything of creatures more powerful than he. The distant call of Hermia. The defence from Helena. I move from one enchantment to the next while the Duke of Athens sits none the wiser on his throne.

And here in this fascination, I have stumbled upon Hawkes. Lying beneath a long stretch of oak branches on the edge of the ancient wood. He is asleep in the grass, one arm beneath his head while his other hand rests on his chest. One leg is bent, his foot anchored on the ground, while the other is stretched out straight, like a root reaching for water. His lips are slightly parted in sleep. There are sounds through the undergrowth, the flit of bird from branch to branch, the false rainfall sound of a summer breeze rustling the leaves far above.

This is a place that knows every old thing.

Just Now

"Hello, Emma," Hawkes said, eyes still closed, not having moved at all. I am reclining against the trunk of the oak tree whose branches he sleeps beneath.

"How did you know it was I sitting here?" I asked after a minute had passed.

"Because," he took in a breath, his hand rising with his chest, "you slip through time."

He was soon again asleep.

And I was left thinking that was perhaps the loveliest spell I'd ever heard.

Later

"How was your afternoon?" Islington enquired as I joined him on the south portico for tea. He was looking refreshed, having bathed and dressed himself in the soft colours of proper country attire. "Did you secure any butterflies?"

"I am going to become a naturalist."

A single nod from Islington. "And what will be your particular field of study?"

"Oh, butterflies, or grasses, or dormice, or Hawkes—Hawkes of the religious variety, not the bird."

"I take it you came across the old oak wood?"

"And all enchantments therein. This cake is very good, you know."

"I quite enjoy cake."

"Who doesn't enjoy cake?" I replied with words Islington has used before. "I must say that Stonecrop is not what I expected."

"How so?"

"I've not been party to endless gatherings in the country, but I have attended more than a few. With my aunt."

"*Ah.*"

"Quite. But you know how they are. There are schedules, activities, forced games, and programmes in the evenings. A societal checklist dictates what is done and the order in which it *is* done. Stately, structural, all the promise of respite without true freedom. At least that is how it has felt for me. A young man's experience might be different in this regard—all hunting and shooting and sport."

Islington answered that his parents hosted more formal country parties, but that he, as a bachelor, had not yet seen the need. "I've invited very few here in the last ten years. I needed to reclaim that which it had once given me."

"Which was?"

"Solitude of the deepest kind," Islington shrugged. "Independence of soul not simply of choice, a natural line of beauty, serendipity."

I thought of those words later, as I stood atop the south tower before supper. Deep solitude. Independence of soul. Beauty. Serendipity.

And cake, I should add.

The cake has been *very* good.

June 8th

Today is Visiting Sunday.

> *Query*: What is Visiting Sunday?
>
> *Answer*: The Devereux family discovered long ago that if they wished to spend an undisturbed period of time at Stonecrop, they needed to make the neighbourhood feel tended. Rather like a garden. And so the concept of Visiting Sunday came into being. After church on the first Sunday of any prolonged stay, the entire parish is invited to Stonecrop for a luncheon. Any Devereux present is to make themselves amicably available for conversation.

"It's usually delightful," Mariana said.

"Quite," Islington replied. "But delightfully trying if you don't have any connection to the neighbours, which is why we always prepare a basket for any guests in our party."

> *Query*: What is in said basket?
>
> *Answer*: The basket is prepared by Mrs. Knowlls and stored in the vestry by the vicar—an obliging man nearing fifty years of age, named Vicar Snail. Yes! Snail! The happiest name for a country vicar, I am certain. As for the basket, it contains all the food a guest might wish to consume as they spend time hiding in the woods around Stonecrop for the length of three or four hours.

"Three hours are usually sufficient," said Mariana. "And then you can hide in Old Stonecrop."

"Five, if you value your sanity," Islington rejoined.

Which is why at breakfast this morning, Hawkes said, "Miss Lion, I would entreat you to change your polished shoes for sturdy boots. We are taking a sabbatical directly after church."

Query: Was it a novel experience to sit beside Hawkes in church?

Answer: Yes. There he sat, head bent, listening to the sermon while silently thumbing through his Bible. The pages are well-broken, like a team of thoroughbred horses.

I attempted to see if Hawkes had any bit of ridiculousness scribbled in the margins.

He did not.

I did not volunteer to show him my Bible, thinking that the drinking song scribbled beside verse five in the one hundred and forty-ninth chapter of the Psalms might not pass clerical muster.

Then again, Hawkes *is* a Reprobate.

Having escaped directly after the service, we are now sitting beneath a large willow near the swimming bend in the river, I leaning against the base of the tree, while Hawkes sits near the bank, reading the book of— Oh, he's just closed his Bible and is reaching for another volume. What will it be? He's lifted his Coleridge. No, he's put it back down. Now he's opened his *Meditations*. Marcus Aurelius has won the round. (I should like to read *Meditations*. Father had a copy.) Now Hawkes is reaching through the knapsack and fishing out…a plum! (Cultivated in a Stonecrop greenhouse.)

Polishing it on the sleeve of his coat, Hawkes—

Why there!

How charming.

Hawkes almost bit into the plum before pausing, glancing over his shoulder at me, and then—wordlessly—tossing it in my direction.

With little finesse, I've managed to catch the fruit.

He has now fished out a second plum, and we enjoy the fruits of our labours in silence.

Later

What an afternoon!

We did not traverse much ground physically. Most of the afternoon was spent at the river bend, each lost in the pages of our books. Once in a while a pebble of words would be thrown into the stillness.

Hawkes quoting this or I reading that.

We would let the words ripple, and then return to our own pages.

In the end—luncheon lazily consumed, pages turned, and a quiet yet competitive bout of skipping rocks—we prepared to leave. I took—with permission—Hawkes's Coleridge, securing it in my satchel beside Wordsworth and my mother's Bible.

Placing my straw hat on my head—the Pith Hat not *quite* the thing for a church service—I looked over at Hawkes. He was standing beside me on the bank staring at the water, eyes half lidded, lost to his own thoughts.

"How does one manage, Hawkes?"

He did not ask what. He simply waited for whatever words would follow.

"May took hold of my life and ran raggedly about London. Not only May. Before that. April. March! How does one ever manage to become master of their own fate? Is it even possible?"

"Quietly," Hawkes said.

"Quietly," I repeated, then, "*Quietly*?"

I waited for him to expound. He did not.

"Quietly," I repeated to myself.

And we struck out for Stonecrop.

As we walked, there came the sound of distant thunder. A storm was rolling through the dales. I'd scarcely noticed how the light had pulled itself down beneath the leaves of the great trees, how they seemed to glow with the threat of storm to come. And instead of returning the way we came, back down through the young wood and through the churchyard, we followed a path along the back hill, coming out on the edge of the ruins, slipping into the courtyard garden and passing blooms trembling in anticipatory glory. Rain was coming, and every living thing was in wait. Down a bit of stair in the southwest corner, and through an arched passage leading beneath the Glass Walk, we came out onto the stretch of lawn near the house, a view of the lake unfolding.

And there on the south portico sat Mariana. Islington stood nearby. And beside him? Another figure. Taller, habitually pensive, compelling.

Then the smell of round summer rain.

The sound of thunder.

Cold drops from the first volley.

Pierce.

Pierce, who was not supposed to be at Stonecrop for another ten days, was standing on the portico, in conversation with Islington.

And I'd been gone when he'd arrived.

The looseness of these first days was about my ankles. Add a summer storm to the remembrance of bramble rambling and what have you to expect but a good run?

Run I did.

I don't believe I have run so since I was a girl at school. Across and up the lawn. Then a sudden uppercut of wind, the rain connecting solitary points into something stronger, the start of a downpour, and I slowed myself.

Pure, euphoric drink.

I laughed, walking up the stairs, hands on my waist.

"You're half wet through, Miss Lion," said Mariana, and Islington made a motion to someone waiting near the threshold to bring me a shawl. And there was Pierce, sharp in his charcoal grey suit. He seemed almost hungry to see me, but we both caught ourselves, blunting the moment. "Miss Lion," he said, and he sounded like he had last year at this time; polite, not overly familiar.

"Mr. Pierce," I replied, catching my breath. "Ought I be worried that you've come to tell me Lapis Lazuli has, indeed, burned to the ground?"

"Rest assured everything is as it should be. I had two unexpected days due to a change of schedule, and Islington insisted I come if that were the case."

Pierce had come, his presence more palpable than ever.

Strange—knowing his expression so well. The moment when one recognises, not simply discovers.

~~And had Mariana not been standing there, I might have thrown my arms around him.~~

~~(Islington and Hawkes, notwithstanding?)~~

Pierce was not outwardly agitated, but I did note he was not entirely relaxed. He carried with him the feeling of one glancing occasionally over their shoulder, but for what? Perhaps Pierce is uncomfortable with the very grand expressions of Islington's wealth, although I would not think this would put him off his ease. He has enough friends who inhabit the elite rooms of society.

"Well," I suppressed every thought crowding my mind, "we are glad you could join the company as a preview of things to come."

Pierce smiled—and I, catching my breath, half turned, focusing on the rain as it insisted on becoming something stronger. A useful distraction.

Pierce, in my periphery, took a brief glance at my person, before clearing his throat and looking past where I stood. "I was telling Islington that Stonecrop isn't too threadbare a place. And I was about to apologise to the countess for my having disturbed Visiting Sunday—"

Mariana tutted. "We are the ones to apologise, Mr. Pierce. You endured the neighbourhood with equanimity."

Hawkes had not run, and was now a few paces from the stairs, protecting his books beneath his coat, while carrying my straw hat.

I'd not noticed it had been lost.

He walked up to join us on the portico.

"Hawkes," Pierce greeted evenly. Hawkes, having surmounted the stairs, wordlessly offered me my hat while tucking his books beneath his arm and lifting his now free hand to shake Pierce's. I noticed a five-pound note pass between them, from Hawkes to Pierce. A wager to which I was not privy. They both kept a straight face, thinking the exchange unnoticed.

A crack of lightning, then thunder—"Heavens," Mariana murmured—and we all turned to watch the full impact of the storm. It was as if we were watching the fall of the world.

How very good, to have Pierce with us.

The storm passed, and then Mariana—telling Pierce we would meet in the green drawing room at six o'clock for supper—excused herself to lie down. Hawkes made his way towards his tower. As for Islington, Crosby had arrived to speak with him regarding…something.

It was then natural for me to ask Pierce if he would like to see the gardens, for him to say that yes, he would, and for us to find our way to the lower wood trail instead, slipping into the shaded understory still dripping with the last of the rain now puddling into mud.

We looked at one another.

"Hello," I said.

A full comprehension for us both: that we'd been more than a little homesick for one another's company.

"Emma," as if he were speaking a pleasant thought aloud. His eyes silver as the spent rain as his gaze canvassed my face. Whatever had prevented him feeling entirely at his ease only moments ago, was lessening. And when he spoke, I could feel the words ordering themselves in a way my mind would ever remember. "I've long developed a habit of not growing accustomed to people, Emma Lion, but I have found the last few days ill-fitting without you."

Pierce stepped closer, his hand taking mine, and we began to walk, his thumb moving across the knuckles of my hand before tightening his grip.

It may have been the first time we were ever truly alone, and in this aloneness, Pierce kissed me like he had that first evening.

And I thought that perhaps, perhaps we…

I thought that if Pierce would…

If…

I found, I suppose, a readiness to cede some of the internal ground I've so carefully kept.

June 9th

No one had thought to tell Pierce. And so this morning when I was sitting on the stairs—mostly hidden from view—and Hawkes was half sleeping in his place on the window seat across from July, both of us in the daze of low notes and early morning, the door of October opened. Pierce, already having dressed himself, looked out in question.

He saw Hawkes.

He said something.

Hawkes replied.

Pierce, crossing his arms, leaned a shoulder against his doorway.

And I kept thinking of the four corners of the earth.

Later

My vision for the day included wild wandering with as many Pierces, Islingtons, and Hawkeses as I could persuade into the far-flung fields. Which is why at breakfast, when Mariana proposed a morning of embroidery and conversation followed by a private luncheon, just we two women, I felt more than a little deflated.

"The men can fend for themselves, Miss Lion."

All three men in question—wordlessly eating their breakfast with a robustness I'd thought endearing, but now that I was being locked out of their games, I found irritating—gave me some form of a sympathetic look.

Rotten luck, Pierce seemed to say.

I'm terribly sorry, Islington conveyed.

As for Hawkes? Well. His glance was made of one word: *Vicissitudes*.

Later

Mariana is the queen of amicable yet choreographed exchange. Our conversation was by no means a muslin affair, all flimsy gauze, nothing substantial. No. The woman has a sharp mind and a wealth of information. She executed this middle ground of conversation pleasantly and deliberately.

~~Upon review, I do not believe I made any very untoward contribution.~~ ~~I do not believe~~ I made untoward contribution.

For there did come a moment when I said, "Oh yes, we four discussed a similar topic in the graveyard on All Hallows' Eve." Whereupon, after a moment's reflection caused by the slight hitch in Mariana's embroidery, I added, "A thing which did not happen too terribly late as there were still plenty of men drinking at The Cleopatra across Traitors Road." This comment not seeming to have helped, I added, "Whenever Islington is present, most things remain in the highest order of decorum. Why, even the night he, Pierce, and I spoke by the fountain until— Ah, well. The time doesn't matter. I only mean to say that he certainly keeps me…us, that is, firmly in hand. But not— Rather, *in line*. Your brother can certainly be very cross. That is to say, what do you think of this orange I've selected for the fox? I intend to make Hawkes a banner." And clearing my throat, I'd returned to my work.

"A lovely shade for a fox." Mariana guided our conversation away from graveyards and The Cleopatra. A thing for which I—and my hinge of a tongue—am grateful.

Luncheon was pleasant and uneventful. After which, another session of embroidery ensued.

Hawkes's fox began to take shape.

(Hawkes the Fox!)

Finally, Mariana said, "Whew! What a day. We shall need a week outdoors to compensate. How about we step out onto the south portico for some tea?"

After Mariana gave brief instruction to a maid, we wandered out onto the pillared portico, Mariana holding her lower back and I stretching my fingers. Looking over the lawn, we were graced with the sight of Islington, Pierce, and Hawkes in a three-man version of cricket.

Only, not quite.

It was more as if three boys were doing their best to work out a game. Nary a jacket to be seen, their shirtsleeves rolled up, Hawkes wearing a pair of braces, Pierce limping but giving it no notice, holding the bat and calling something at Islington, who grinned in return as he prepared to bowl.

Mariana, easing down into her chair, laughed at the sight. "Henry looks seventeen."

Sitting beside her, I gazed longingly out over the lawn. My heart constricted then expanded in an absurd manner. Irrational, perhaps, to feel such conviction that they are mine and I theirs.

Tea was delivered, and Mariana set about preparing something for us both. It was only when I felt her scrutiny that I realised how unconcealed and open my expression was.

"Do you play, Miss Lion?" she asked, handing me a saucer balancing a cup of tea.

"Pardon," I replied, watching Hawkes take a swing at Islington's bowl. A solid hit. "Oh, yes. My father taught me, and we played often in the back meadow. Recently I've only used my skills to— Er, that is, not recently, no."

We took the rest of the tea in silence, until Islington called up, "Are you trying to behave like you're far more proper than you are because of my sister, Lion, or will you join?"

Mariana gave no outside indication of her judgement. And I—not having the day I'd initially envisioned—took my cue from Islington's invitation.

"If you'll excuse me, I'd better go and teach the men how to play cricket."

I was down the stairs and onto the lawn without looking back, the men now standing in a loose knot.

"Can you bowl with your leg?" Islington was asking Pierce.

"Better than I can full out run. Here, take the bat, Emma. Let's see how my arm fares this morning."

Three false starts, and a few jangled wickets, but I finally sent one ball over Pierce's head, Islington running after it. Another hit or two among half a dozen bowls, one veering drastically towards the lake.

It was Hawkes who dove in after.

June 10th

Pierce had brought with him the St. Crispian's *Gazette*.

It was shared round and commented on, including an article about our very own David battling Goliath on the second page.

"The frippery about the symbolism of the fireworks is trying," said Islington, "but I quite like what this fellow had to say about Hawkes and the pugilist. Apologies, Hawkes, but it is well written."

"Who is it by?" asked Pierce.

"There's no name. Harper himself, do you think?"

"Likely. He did one hell of a job with the retelling."

I felt the flush of embarrassment and a—rather unexpected—flush of pride.

Hawkes—ignoring all comments—did steal an amused and long-suffering glance in my direction.

Later

Hawkes told me not to dress for supper.

I was standing in the centre of the courtyard garden watching the ripple of the stream entering the fountain, the shadows of the house stretching over where I stood, the scent of irises and early roses overpowering any other plants in bloom. It *is* the loveliest garden I have ever seen.

I had Wordsworth with me, staring at the water as I repeated,

Where will they stop, those breathing Powers,
The Spirits of the new-born flowers?
They wander with the breeze, they wind
Where'er the streams a passage find.

Seeing movement, the undulating blink of interchanging shadow and light, and I looked up, the taste of poetry still on my tongue. There was the figure of Hawkes, walking down the Glass Walk, his hair rustling in the breeze allowed in by a set of open doors. Loose limbed and happy, the legs of his trousers rolled up in a boyish manner, Hawkes was summer carelessness personified.

At the next open set of doors, he stepped out into the garden, following a path until he'd come to where I stood. "Do not dress for supper this evening," he said.

I glanced down at my dress, more than a little marked from my morning walk in the woods. "I am afraid there are limits even my unruly self cannot—or should not, as the case may be—sink below. Are you seeking revenge for my having immortalized your battle in print?"

"We meet in the kitchens at six o'clock. Be prepared for walking. I've warned the others."

"Is there need for warning?"

Hawkes smiled at me, slipped his hands into his pockets, rocked back on his feet, and said,

That every day should leave some part
Free for a sabbath of the heart.

And Hawkes was off. Disappearing. As if he walks around corners none of us can see.

I thought nothing more of it all (I thought a great deal of it but had drawn no conclusions). The late afternoon began to stretch itself awake like a cat having napped all day.

An Important Aside

Stonecrop does have cats. Islington calls them the Marauders. They have no individual names, but a specific mandate to kill any mouse or rat on the premises. They take their vocation quite seriously and are less friendly with us humans. They have a job to do and will get it done, come hell or high water.

I Resume My Tale

Leaving the courtyard garden, I soon found myself in Pierce's company. We wandered about the stables and then over to a bench in the apostle garden. What exactly is an apostle garden, one might ask?

The one being Emma M. Lion not five days ago. An apostle garden, apparently, is a garden flanked by twelve trees—often of the clipped, evergreen variety—six on each side. The Stonecrop version is agreeable for sitting, with white petaled flowers lining the very same long borders which host each and every pruned apostle.

I'd asked days ago if they'd been given names.

Islington said no.

Mariana said she did not believe they had.

Hawkes had looked up from his book, given a subtle nod, winked—of all things—and resumed reading.

This afternoon, Pierce and I sat on a bench near Simon the Zealot.

"Which train do you take tomorrow?" I asked Pierce.

"The earliest I can."

A nod. "You're back on the seventeenth?"

"Fortunately," Pierce said. "Mr. Flat has decided we're to spend time together while the Meddlesome Harpy is gone from the house—man to man, he calls it."

I laughed.

I've just come upstairs to rest, write, and change my stockings, retying the laces of my worn brown boots (faithfully cleaned and polished every night by Isla, bless her). I then brushed off my skirt, pinned a straw hat over my hair, removed it, and readied myself with the Pith Helmet instead. Then—as a last-minute addition—I set my satchel near the door, Wordsworth inside.

Later

A constellation only takes shape when one maps the whole. And so I begin with the first star of the evening and work my way to the last, despite my endless rumination on questions asked and questions given.

Hawkes was packing a knapsack to the brim when I arrived in the kitchens, looking about to see very few members of the kitchen staff, as there was no formal dinner in the offing. Knowing better than to ask questions, I simply sat and watched Hawkes work. Islington arrived with a wooden walking stick, like one of the adventurers reported in the illustrated newspapers I see from time to time in London.

"To the Matterhorn, is it?" I asked.

"So amusing, Lion. I see you are wearing your pith helmet?"

Pierce arrived, running the backs of his fingers over the edge of his chin. "Are we off then?"

We walked out four miles, until the vibrant blue of early night began to deepen, and we had crested a hill which looked out over wild fields and distant treelines. There waited an old fire ring, stones accustomed to their place. Hawkes motioned to Islington, and they set about placing the firewood Pierce and Islington had carried in the ring, flint and steel at the ready. I—leaning with the aid of Islington's walking stick (which I had conveniently stolen) was gazing out over the distance. Nothing else in sight. No building. No herds. Not another human on the horizon. Only we four, a clear night above, and two satchels of provisions.

An Important Aside

Hawkes and Pierce are each acquainted with fire.

It responds to them both.

I Resume My Tale

Like a magician, Hawkes pulled bread and fruit, and then a meat pie and cheese from the two satchels, canteens of water, and a pilfered bottle of wine, with four tin tumblers of dubious make.

There came a sense of merriment.

We four sages, letting our words run out ahead of us. Comfort and laughter and lingering over our allotted portions of the feast.

It grew late, into the velvet time of night. No wind to speak of, which allowed the meandering smoke to follow a silent path upward. We surrounded the fire like the four cardinal directions. Islington and Pierce reclining in the grass with both Hawkes and I sitting on opposite sides of the bonfire, he with a book open before him. That is when Islington began asking his questions.

"Bonfires?" he asked.

"Glorious," I said.

"Primal," answered Pierce.

"Prometheus."

We all looked at Hawkes. He, after a moment of silence, looked up as if only now remembering we were all there. After looking at each of us he said simply, "You know I never answer Islington's questions." Then, "But, yes, Prometheus."

Islington gave Hawkes a raised eyebrow then he offered another question. "Inland or coast?"

"Coast." Hawkes's murmur sounded like a wave breaking on the shore, as he sat turning the page of the book in his hand.

We all stilled.

Hawkes followed his own answer with a quiet, "Though the woods and streams are also essential to the soul. That is the last you'll hear from me on the subject of Islington's questions."

"Coast," I volunteered my answer next. "If one must choose."

Hawkes gave me a nod of approbation.

"Inland," Pierce said thoughtfully. "For most of my life I would have answered, without hesitation, on the side of the ocean. But I'm weary of the waves. This time—this year, at least—I wish nothing but calm, solid earth."

A nod from me as I watched the fire, then I looked back towards Islington.

He gazed upward, the entire night sky a prophecy. "Stonecrop lies at the heart of this sea-bound island, and my own heart has never found anything comparable." Then something crossed his mind, enough of a trespass that his face drew a thoughtful frown. He opened his mouth and closed it again, shaking his head once.

"You know you've found an interesting question," Pierce drawled, "when you try to bury it before the asking."

Islington pulled his bottom lip between his teeth then lifted both brows as he tilted his head in an acquiescing nod. "Children?" he asked, with as vulnerable a tone as I've ever heard him speak.

Hawkes lifted his head, thoughtfully measuring all our expressions. I hoped Islington would lead the charge on such an unexpectedly personal question, one with myriad surrounding implications.

Alas.

Islington cast his gaze around the circle.

"I've…always thought, yes," I measured out slowly. "A life like the one I was given. A child or two. Books. Candles in the windows come evening." I twisted a piece of grass between my fingers. "What say you?" I asked Islington, unable to look at Pierce.

Islington, with a thousand years of ancestors lending an ear, replied from his position. "It is expected, a duty. A thing I must do. A thing I want, only…" Islington waved it off. "When the timing for such a thing strikes the suitable hour. Pierce?"

"No," said Pierce. It came with the firmness of established decision. I did not look up to see his face and could not tell if he looked my way or not. I admit now it felt like I'd been bruised by the premeditation of his answer. "I don't wish to have a child," Pierce continued. "No good would come of it. There are others better suited for the task."

I opened my mouth, to disagree I think, although I could not—would not, have uttered a word in present company. I wasn't— Well, it felt presumptuous to assume.

Hawkes soon saved us all.

Shifting half away from the fire, he lay on his back and—lifting a hand to his chest, the other holding tightly to his closed book—he began to recite a poem.

Calm is the fragrant air, and loth to lose
Day's grateful warmth, tho' moist with falling dews.
Look for the stars, you'll say that there are none;
Look up a second time, and, one by one,
You mark them twinkling out with silvery light,
And wonder how they could elude the sight!

And after his voice had stilled, lingering in our memory long enough for the sounds of night to ease back into focus, we wordlessly began to pack up our things. Pierce kicked out the fire, pouring an untouched canteen of water over the embers. And through the cool swathes of night air, we made our silent way back to Stonecrop.

Did you mean what you said? I wished to ask Pierce, who had kept his own introspective company the long walk back. *And if so, why? And if so, might you change your mind?*

But I knew I couldn't.

Not now.

Not yet.

June 11th

Pierce left before dawn. Hawkes accompanied him to the station and has not yet returned. We commented on Pierce's departure at breakfast. Even Mariana said she looked forward to his return.

Near the end of breakfast, I was handed a note by a footman. It was written on green paper.

"*Ah*," said Islington, when he glanced up.

Then Mariana, her eyes noting the colour of the note in my hand, also said, "*Ah*." Then, "We are terribly sorry, Miss Lion. Only remember, there was nothing we could do."

"I was going to ask you to ride out this morning," said Islington.

"I'm not a stellar horsewoman," I replied, "but I would be willing to try."

"Only, now you're spoken for."

"Am I?"

"There's nothing I can do, Lion. Not even the Devereuxs can rule every roost."

"Am I doing something with chickens?"

Mariana laughed.

I opened the note.

You are expected in the greenhouse at ten o'clock this morning.

Later

I stepped into the greenhouse at five to the hour and found myself at the mercy of a gardener who is eighty-seven if he is a day. "Horace Walpole," he said. "But not *that* Horace Walpole."

After I'd assured him that I did not expect to find a deceased prime minister in Islington's greenhouse, he informed me that—as a guest of Stonecrop—he was going to put me to work. "If you can't handle a day in the garden, you best think twice about coming back."

"Heavens. Do you prove all of Islington's guests in such a manner?"

"Not all. But I been watching and you just might be a decent."

"A decent?"

"Undergardener."

"Heavens. I'm rot at gardening, to be sure. That is, I've never given it much time. My mother banned me from her flower garden, you see, and I've not learned a thing since."

"Which is why I said *under*gardener, Miss Lion. You follow instruction, plain and contrite like, and you'll do just fine."

And that is how I spent the morning working alongside Horace (but not *that* Horace) Walpole, replanting some small topiary boxwoods into larger pots and hunting the greenhouse for snails.

A "Not the best I've seen, Miss, but not the worst neither," for my pains.

June 12th

Rain, and such a rain! One wouldn't have known it from last night, but a few hours before dawn a wind mounted the unexpected assault. When the hour arrived to go down for breakfast, it was a battle in full swing, bullets of water shaking the windows.

It was decided that the Rainy Day Policy was to be enforced, and so Mariana would show me the whole of Stonecrop. When I write *me*, it is because no one else was present or available.

Islington had to leave for business in Lockwell, despite the sodden roads, and Hawkes was nowhere to be found.

"He's likely half drowning himself swimming at the bend," Islington answered when I enquired.

"In this barrage of cold rain?"

"Hawkes will swim in any weather."

The cipher that is Hawkes is given another dimension.

I am now going to meet Mariana by the front door where she will tell me the entire history of the Devereux family while showing me every secret passage in the house.

At least that is my hope.

Later

The rain persists, while I sit in my tower among the clouds like a worried crow. Mariana shared a trove of history and lore, all of which fascinated to no end. But that was before we ended the tour in the picture gallery. Now I'm biting my fingernails (truly abominable of me) while I consider what I was *not* told.

The Devereux family has a more extensive history than I could imagine possible. There are no less than twenty-four volumes in the library which compose an abridged version of the family.

To save the reader time.

Twenty-four!

Stonecrop is interesting to no end. Such a sprawl of window, ornament, and stone. There *are* certain secret passages, although—as the building is not medieval—there is a disappointing practicality about the two I was shown.

"Are there others?"

"You will have to discover this for yourself, Miss Lion."

Which was a suitably enticing response.

Then we entered the picture gallery.

Overwhelming. Stately. The walls a deep, dusty red. Gloriously mantled gold frames. Centuries of paintings. The works of great masters mixed with portraits of the family.

Awe.

Wonder.

While Mariana gave an abbreviated history—in the practiced low tones of the upper echelons—we worked our way through the gallery. They were a handsome lot, the Devereuxs, if not daunting. The way they peered down from all their elevated and judgemental glory. There was one of Islington that I'd swear had been commissioned within the last five years.

One portrait was of his mother.

One was of his father.

The housekeeper, Mrs. Harrison, came to speak with Mariana, and I was left to wander at my own will. Wander I did, introducing myself silently to the array of figures still parading the walls despite having long left the earth. At the far end of the gallery, at eye level, waited a peculiar painting. It captured my interest, I suppose, for the background was a light green fading to blue, as if the subjects were sitting in an idealized garden.

In the painting there were three figures.

On the left side, a young woman with chestnut brown hair, her eyes also brown with such warmth, such richness, they leaned towards the red-amber tones of a polished instrument. Unusual. I've never seen the like. My sense was that she was contained, quiet, but that she ordered her world. She sat looking at me, a confidence that comes from inner character, rather than any exterior trappings of prestige. This was why I thought she was not a Devereux.

On the right side was another young woman, leaning towards the centre, her expression clear, direct, honest, a surprising sense of magnetism conveyed. Her hair was Devereux dark, her eyes green. It was not only strength she seemed to carry, it was joy.

Between the two of them sat a young man. He was leaning forward, his arm intertwined with the second young woman, their shoulders almost touching, while between his fingers wove a ribbon from the dress of the young woman on the left. Dark hair, hazel eyes almost green. He was young. He looked no older than seventeen.

And the young man was Islington.

It is one of the most arresting portraits I've ever seen.

Of movement and abundance, of confidence unshaken.

Life had come a-calling and these three had answered.

It looked as if they shared amusement.

I would wager they shared secrets.

Something about the three of them pricked the skin on the back of my neck like a haunting. I knew what I was gazing at, but I could not give it a name. It was only later that I realised exactly why it was so familiar.

Alchemy.

The three of them.

As if they had no need of anyone else in the world.

So captivated, I did not realise Mariana had finished speaking with the housekeeper and was now standing behind me.

"It is well done," she said.

I turned, stepping back on a diagonal so we were standing side by side. "Extraordinarily so. Now this is Islington," I asserted.

"Yes."

A triumphant smile on my part. "Ever himself."

"It has never been a problem for Henry to know who he is. A saving grace."

"And the young woman on the left?"

"She was…a lifelong friend."

"Does she still live in the neighbourhood?"

Mariana's hazel eyes seemed to pull a curtain closed. "She became a countess, in Austria."

The answer struck me as strange, and when I looked back at the young woman, I realised why. For while her bearing matched those of her companions, her clothing was less fine, her jewellery insignificant. She was not in the same category of wealth or status as the Devereuxs.

A countess?

What must life be for her now?

"And the other young woman? She and Islington so complement, one would think them twins." It was said lightly, almost a laugh.

The muscles in Mariana's neck drew tighter as she took in a breath—a deep cut expertly sealed over. "Tea?"

There was a silence between her singly spoken question and what I managed to cobble together on its heels. "Certainly," I replied. "Of course. You've been on your feet far too long, I'm sure."

With a gracious smile, Mariana turned and walked out of the room.

I glanced once more at the portrait, my eyes landing on Islington.

The unspoken pain I have seen in him, the shattered glass I'd recognised in February, was not yet marring his young face in the portrait.

June 13th

I returned to the picture gallery this morning, staring at the portrait. Last night, I'd decided to call it *The Three Fates*.

They were all waiting for me to come back.

Islington, sitting centre, happy and secure.

The now countess ruling her determined kingdom of one, the ribbon of her gown entwined with Islington's fingers.

And the third.

Not a cousin, I think.

No, I would wager Lapis Lazuli House that she is his sister.

Which, if either, of the two young women is named Hannah?

Which would haunt him on a night of fever?

Frowning—having left the portrait gallery, and in the process of making my way across the hall—I caught sight of the Devereux coat of arms in the ornament of the grand staircase and remembered. The Devereux family is known for their twins.

I did not go in to breakfast.

Instead, I found myself wandering down to the church.

The door was unlocked, but it was empty, and I sat on the back pew looking up at the red, green, and gold stained-glass windows, thinking of the portrait. Poised, young, and painted not long before some unspeakable tragedy.

Later

There is a maze at Stonecrop!

There are two, actually.

Now the irksome part. The smaller maze—simple, with roses and white benches tucked around every corner—takes only ten minutes with no effort. A thing which is fine in and of itself. Only, it is called The Ladies' Maze.

The second maze is quite large—the largest in England, if one is to believe Islington. No clues. No balls of yarn to mark one's place. It is a challenge, and a robust challenge at that, which has a tower in the centre with a grotto beneath. It is called The Gentlemen's Maze.

I gave it my best effort this afternoon, but did not manage the thing. I will formulate a plan for my next attempt.

"We once lost a baron for half a day. Thankfully, a footman had seen him wander in and he was eventually retrieved."

"But why the names, Islington? Why is it always assumed that ladies want the facile?"

"They have thus been called for two hundred and fifty years, Lion. I make no such assumptions."

Hmm.

Later

A RECORD OF LETTERS BETWEEN:
London and Stonecrop

Dear Emma,

It has been an unseasonably warm June and all of London feels out of joint. I, finding heat and stuff and claustrophobia in my studio, have been taking a near-daily pilgrimage to Hampstead Heath. Only yesterday, I found myself painting in Highgate Cemetary. When the living irritate, best to spend time with the dead.

I saw Mr. Pierce the other night at a soirée hosted by a friend. He approached me—a slight surprise—and we spent a pleasant half hour discussing light in our respective mediums. He said he'd seen you at Stonecrop, that you were well, and he would be returning to join your party later this month. May you be experiencing something of the fantastic. And may you avoid any Italian count who may come your way. One of mine has recently appeared in London and I'm finding it inconvenient at present.

An exhibition is being organized, set to begin in September, and I've had not three, not four, but five of my pieces selected. We shall go together, and you can tell me how superior my work is to all else. Be they true or not, I believe my pride can manage the compliments.

Until soon,
Saffronia

Emma,

Chum, you owe me a king's ransom. I have been fully roped into being you and it's dreadfully inconvenient.

At one point the other night, Aunt Eugenia turned to me and said, "Emma!" Then appeared shocked to find myself standing there. "Oh, Roland! You've become such a disappointment in such a short period of time!"

"You mean the amount of time Emma has been away?"

"Come to think of it, yes! I suppose finding Emma at the root of the problem should come as no surprise."

"Mother," Arabella then said, "if Emma knew what was good for her, she would marry this duke and move as far away from you as possible."

"Don't talk nonsense, Arabella! Your cousin does enough of that as is. Emma is never to rise above her or your station. Now, Roland, take Arabella back out onto the ballroom floor and make certain to smile in the vicinity of Lord Abernathy.

But not Lord Stansbury. I've struck him from the list."

The old girl is also on somewhat of a rampage over the Countess of Ellam and her daughter, Lady Eloise—with whom I am having a rather difficult time getting acquainted. Many of the gentlemen feel the same. I've never seen such a beauty. She's the talk of every club. You don't, by any chance, know her to an introducible degree?

Enjoy Stonecrop and tell Islington he's missed at Brooks's.

Yours,
Roland

Roland,

I am so very grateful for your playing surrogate, I cannot even claim irritation at your summoning the ghost that is Aunt Eugenia into my summer Eden.

As for Lady Eloise, you do realise that we women roll our eyes each time every man in the room falls over himself due to a new beauty? To answer your question, I do not know her at all. Now, please continue to watch for any mischief from Lord Croixton. Let us hope his interest was passing.

I gave your regards to Islington, who said, "Ah, Sutherland. Solid chap. I've heard he has a near-perfect German Pointer." Which, Roland, I can testify is High Compliment.

Your chum in absence,
Emma

Dear Saff,

Do you have any idea of the history and architecture of Stonecrop? I think you would find yourself approving. It's walking through an oil painting a thousand times a day. But sometimes, when the clouds sweep low and the wind ripples the entire landscape, it's more of a watercolour. The trees keep their coolness, the fields their warmth. And I, moving about in a constant state of wonder.

Is this how you feel about Italy (counts excluded)?

Emma

Dear Mary,

You and I would create Holy Terror of the best variety and kind if we were let loose on the gardens of Stonecrop. Islington has asked if I would like to ride out with him one morning, and I—with all the trappings of a resolute explorer—keep telling him, "Perhaps tomorrow."

I like horses. I truly do. Only, I wonder if the night we broke out of Fortitude to steal Farmer Strawhun's gelding and went on a wild gallop before being thrown several feet—you breaking your arm, I spraining a wrist—has anything to do with my reluctance to try the sport again.

That and I have a strong aversion to the idea of breaking my neck in a fox hunt.

Emma

June 14th

Hawkes took a very early train to London to give a sermon.

He won't return until tomorrow.

He intends to see Pierce.

I am glad.

Later

Islington, his faithful hound (must I say the name?), and I went for a walk into Lockwell. It was more diversion than errand, but we did pay a visit to his old steward, the father of his current model. Emma (the faithful hound, that is) lay on the hearth while we three visited. A pleasant offering of tea, bread, and jam, accompanied by talk of the estate, then, now, and in the future.

Islington was a man in his element. Not a detail he couldn't discuss at length, turning to me to clarify or explain what may not have been understood by a layman.

The steward appeared *very* pleased that I was enjoying my stay and took an interest.

"Why do you spend so much of the year in London, when you're clearly invested in the workings of your estate?" I asked as we were walking back to Stonecrop.

Islington's hound seconded the question, lifting both her ears and tilting her head as if she'd wondered the very same thing.

"I'm at Stonecrop more than you might guess, often coming up for a few days before returning to St. Crispian's," he replied, adjusting his hat. "London boasts many advantages which align with particular interests. And I have my friendships there, of course. To be truthful, Stonecrop has not always been a simple place for me. However, I'm pleased to have—"

He paused in speaking then, gaze on the road ahead. Walking towards us was a man. Of an age with Islington, I'd imagine. He was not of equal rank or fortune, but there was a self-respect independent of class. As we drew closer, it was clear they owned some variation of acquaintance, for they greeted one another in a manner usually reserved for one deeply disliked. That is to say, a stiff politeness.

They did not shake hands.

They did not speak.

There was no introduction.

The man—taut, flint-like, with the intensity of an untamed creature—continued on his way.

Islington made no remark on the silent exchange. He instead asked if I knew the history of the far field, and would I like to hear it? But before Islington could dig deep into the theories behind crop rotation, I asked, "Do you know that man well?"

"We shared some growing-up years."

"His name?"

"Kennedy. Sean Kennedy."

"Why the cold greeting?"

Islington removed his hat, running the fingers of his gloved hand through his hair. "Was it a cold greeting?"

"Spare me, Islington. I'm neither blind nor stupid."

"I think you overestimate the enthusiasm with which men should greet one another."

"So you like this Mr. Sean Kennedy?"

"I can't say I know the sort of man he's grown into. He seems an adequate fellow. We live very different lives in very different places. I scarcely see him more than once a year, if that. There's nothing on which to comment."

"It *felt* as if there was a past."

The hound at my side looked between us.

"We both grew up in the area," Islington answered. "There may have been a disagreement or two, but that is years ago now."

"*Ah.*"

"Everyone is allowed a past, Lion," Islington said.

"Everyone except young women," I said. "We can't afford one."

I expected a jolly romp of a spar.

Islington of St. Crispian's, responding with spirit.

Islington of Stonecrop did neither. It was as if he'd taken my words and paired them with some long-faded event. The house was in view before he spoke again.

It was about crop rotation.

Later

Goodness. I don't know if it is the afternoon rain, the house feeling too large for a cose, or my mention of Islington's St. Crispian's penchant for scrapping with one Emma M. Lion, but I have the most tremendous sense of homesickness.

I miss my garret.

I miss Whereabouts Lane.

I miss my familiar ghosts, and notes through the wall, and dinners at Islington's, and sermons in ~~my~~ our very own church built on the Celtic burial mound, and Agnes repeating the most absurd maternal counsel. Stonecrop is lovely. A jewel, really. One I hope to keep. But one can love many places and still miss home.

Things have grown very quiet with only Mariana and Islington in this large house. Perhaps I will bully them into playing the piano and cello, respectively. Music might balance the melancholy of a damp, isolated day.

I've just had a glimpse of one of the Marauders.

I wonder how Tybalt fares.

Sad, really, to think he is no longer prowling the west garret.

Later

I was right. The music—for after a small amount of needling, Mariana and Islington obliged—has left me settled.

Strange, I've heard it many times now, but this was my first time *watching* Islington play.

He has a relationship with the instrument, one trusting enough to be lost to everything else. A curiosity that he's never mentioned it before.

June 15th

After church, luncheon, and having a lie down, I left the house midafternoon for a walk in a pleasant pocket of the day. I walked into the woods north of the house, *British Ferns and Their Allies*, my journal, Wordsworth, and Coleridge in hand. It was not long before I heard something lower than birdcall, and smoother than the rustling of leaves above a woodland streamlet.

It was the sound of Islington's cello.

He had only begun to play a few moments before I trespassed on the particular path that led to the copse, and when I saw the accompanying hint of movement, I pulled myself behind a tree, sinking along the trunk until I was crouched low enough to dare look again.

There, through the branches and low shrubs, I could see the figure of Islington playing his cello. Jacket removed and thrown to the side, his sleeves rolled up while he played, black waistcoat still buttoned with the unspoken decorum I've come to expect—even here, in his inner fortress. He played as if he dared not allow the looseness of the June woodland to steal the notes before he claimed them his own.

I settled myself more comfortably and thought that as I had so enjoyed last evening, I would only listen to one song. Possibly two. But after he finished the piece, I was surprised to see him resting his cello and reaching for something on the ground near at hand. It was a bottle of wine, from which he poured a glass. More surprising was that he'd begun to talk to himself. No, not himself; he'd begun to speak to another. Pausing in intervals as if to listen to whatever answer his companion might have. Only, no voice gave response.

This continued a few minutes more, Islington speaking quite seriously, until the glass was set down and up came the cello. He played something less bright—made of undercurrents and shadows—and then he resumed conversation. Such earnestness, broken only when he smiled at himself. I could hear the tone but none of the words, for which I was relieved. He spoke and spoke until he'd said everything he wished. Or needed to say.

~~My respect for Islington's privacy...~~ My fear of being discovered soon prompted me on my way. And I, well, that is to say, I crawled down the path a good stretch before daring to stand and hastily return to the house. When Isla saw my skirt, her eyes widened.

Later

Islington and Mariana are supping with a friend of their mother's, who entreated them at church. Islington, duty bound, accepted but politely declined on my behalf—"As proof of my friendship, I've spared you the tediousness of it all."—and quarter of an hour after they left, I decided another woodland walk would fit the order of the coming evening. Following the same trail from this afternoon, I returned to my spot of indecorous eavesdropping, walking into the grove where Islington had held his ritual.

There was a gravestone, and on the gravestone was a name.

Hannah Devereux

July 15th, 1853 – October 3rd, 1873

There was little trace Islington had been there. Nothing but some tramped grass and a stain of red before the gravestone where Islington must have shared his spoils. 1853 would have been the year Islington was born, which means that, yes, he and Hannah were twins, and she died when they were twenty years old, and it is so painful he cannot even speak of her existence.

Later—after Islington and Mariana had returned, and Hawkes's train from London had arrived—we sat reading in the library, making the occasional comment here or there. And I realised two things.

Islington's birthday is July 15th.

Julius Caesar day in St. Crispian's is July 15th.

I recalled sitting beside him at last year's performance, how we had sparred, and given one another a bit of a run. I could feel my cheeks turning an inconvenient pink.

"Nothing to add, Lion?" Islington said, breaking into my thoughts.

"Cat got your tongue?"

I looked up. Mariana and Islington were both looking at me. Hawkes was still reading.

"Ah, terribly sorry. I'm afraid I was giving preference to my own thoughts just now. You were, last I knew, speaking of the hounds…?"

At this Mariana raised a delighted eyebrow while Islington raised one with no delight whatsoever.

June 16th

A day without restraints, nature spending miles and miles on herself. No one fussing over one's whereabouts or schedule or preferences. All day I walked, the wide-brimmed straw hat on my head, white blouse indecorously rolled up at the sleeves. My arms are turning a lovely brown and Aunt Eugenia will skin me alive for my Iberian heritage taking a summer stand.

Enough dour London thoughts.

This is a day of breeze and cloud.

Stonecrop is for wandering philosophy.

I've been miles in every direction, butterfly net in hand, a jar for my findings. It feels a crime, and during my stay at Stonecrop I've found myself letting the vast majority of my butterflies go. But I have kept three.

A small heath.

A green hairstreak.

And a marsh fritillary.

Islington had found a board in the attic, to which I have pinned my butterflies, the third only this morning as he watched, frowning. "I think it is meant to appear more, ah, elegant. Like so."

And as I watched him redo my work, I almost blurted out that I knew his birthday! That I knew he had a twin sister. That she was dead. And I knew.

But I did not.

Instead, Islington looked up at me, his eyes more lovely green than gold, and said, "Are you feeling quite yourself, Lion? Or is your disturbed expression due to the fact that we've not yet brought out the foils? I'll teach you this afternoon, if you'd like, after I return from the blacksmith's."

"Pardon? No! I'm feeling wonderful." And I was. "I look forward to our fencing, but I'm set for a day of far walking and long thoughts."

"Do you see how I pinned that butterfly?"

"Perfectly done. Bravo. You're a marvel."

His eyebrows drew together. "You're certain you're well?"

"Quite."

As I set out, I reminded myself that Islington was looking better than I've ever seen him since we became acquainted, and I relaxed into my outdoor scheme.

Later

Comfortable, deep afternoon, when I returned to the great house to find Islington and Hawkes shooting archery behind the stables. I sat beside Mariana, who watched from the shade, tea at the ready.

"Have you caught any more butterflies, Miss Lion?"

I showed her my jar where a single common blue lay. "I am deeply conflicted."

Mariana laughed. "I'm happy you've had a pleasant day. Your nose is very pink. I'll send Isla up with some cream before supper."

I lifted my fingers to my nose, feeling the dusty satisfaction of many miles beneath a generous sun. "I'll sleep well tonight, I should think."

"I daresay you will."

As I watched Islington and Hawkes battle, I could feel Mariana watching me, her astute, often undisclosed thoughts kept to herself.

June 17th

Pierce has returned!

"Well met," was tossed about, the men clapping one another on the back. And after luncheon, lawn croquet.

Pandemonium, joy, and a few arguments requiring independent rulings from Mariana.

Our second game of lawn croquet is soon to begin. Islington, Pierce, and I have formed a confederacy against Hawkes.

Later

Hawkes.

He trounced us in the second game.

I wished to say to him, "*The villainy you teach me I will execute.*"

Later

Pierce and Islington spent a few hours in the library before ~~dinner~~ supper. Hawkes was nowhere to be seen, having raised his fist in silent victory before taking himself to the bend for a solitary swim. Mariana was with Mrs. Knowlls in the kitchens before returning to the morning room where she spends much of her time.

As for myself? I was hunting Marauders.

Determined to catalogue how many prowlers are in Islington's employ.

"Islington," I said before I began, he and Pierce standing at a desk with several architectural plans ready for their amateur enthusiasm, "before I embark on a small personal project, I must ask if you think it rather likely or rather unlikely that I will be invited back to Stonecrop."

Emma the Hound, lying on the floor of the library, rolled her head to watch his reply.

(I could not tell if she was for or against.)

Pierce bent down and gave the hound a scratch around her ears, her interest in me subsequently lost.

Islington looked at my pith helmet happily in place on my head. "Have you enjoyed yourself?"

"Immensely. Stonecrop has been a revelation. Several, rather."

"Then your chances of return are high."

"Splendid. My task might take several visits." And I turned to leave the library.

"Where are you— What task?" he called.

"I'm cataloguing Marauders!" I ~~answered~~ yelled in return.

Rather than consulting Mrs. Harrison—who usually feeds the noble creatures—I decided I wanted to stalk their territory—inside and out—making my record from observation. Pith helmet, satchel, paper and pencil, and a pair of binoculars I ~~borrowed~~ stole from Islington's desk, I was ready.

My initial report includes the following:

There is a black-and-white prowling the attic, sex unknown.

Two grey tabbies are stretched before the ovens, one male, one female. They appear to be a year old.

There was a sighting of an orange mackerel tabby, followed by a chase which comprised two corridors and three staircases, but no effectual contact was made.

I *was* able to stalk a female calico up to the ruins of Old Stonecrop, and—reaching into my soul for patience I do not by nature possess—I crept Ever. So. Slowly.

Triumph!

For I discovered her returning to a litter of no less than seven kittens, hidden among the stones.

She hissed and clawed herself into a twisting dance when I dared approach, but I—armed with Hawkes's Coleridge and an apple—sat myself down in the visible distance for an hour until the calico knew I meant no harm. A jar of sardines (from Mrs. Knowlls, who says the Marauders are essential for keeping the kitchens clean) proved an appropriate white flag, which resulted in the proud mother—after a luxurious bath—introducing me to her brood.

The thought crossed my mind that perhaps…

But as I studied the small, pinched faces, I saw seven lovely cats-to-be who did not feel as if they belonged to either me or Lapis Lazuli House.

They are Stonecrop Marauders, and it is not my place to change that.

June 18th

Ill-fated.
Unfortunate.
Star-crossed.
Disastrous.
Grievous.

All words to describe the day. And yet… I can't help wondering if *purging, brutal, cleansing* are the words to be found among the ruins. I wish to sleep, but I have the strain of the day lacing my veins. And thinking back, I realise that Pierce only said yes for me.

He would have declined.

He'd attempted as much. But I'd wanted him there and so he'd given way, choosing what I wished over what he did not.

How painfully unexpected.

I cannot tell if I ought to wish it had not happened, or if knowing is a relief. For not everything in an unspoken past can remain in the dark. Some things are too damaging not to come to light, despite a painful sun.

Best write it all out, I suppose—exorcise the demons.

It was Islington who proposed the ramble during breakfast.

"The day couldn't be more suited for the purpose," he said, or something very like. "We cut through the back fields, a long stretch of woodland, back out into pastureland, and have lunch in the small village of Nettle. It's not tied to the Stonecrop estate in any official manner, which is part of the enjoyment. The Thistle and Flag is a particularly pleasant place for a meal. Then we wander back with enough time to rest before supper."

"A jaunt sounds just the thing for the day," I replied.

"That's what I was thinking," Islington replied. "A long stretch of the legs. What say you, Pierce?"

I'd looked up. Pierce's expression was not wholly free, his hands holding the cutlery with a disproportionate grip.

"Are you opposed to the idea?" Islington asked.

Eyeing his coffee as if he blamed it for not being something else,

Pierce spoke tightly. "Are there more interesting destinations? Ruins or prospects? Both preferable to a mere country village."

"There's the pleasant rub." Islington was assured of his soon-to-be victory. "Prospects are had along the walk, as well as the ruins of the oldest church in the county. Nettle merely provides a point of destination. The Thistle and Flag is on the edge of the village, offering a hearty meal and respite before we come back again."

"Pierce," I said, "doesn't it sound idyllic down to the soles of your boots?"

"It sounds like blisters," he replied, not looking at me.

"Have you spoken with Hawkes?" I asked Islington.

"He's already readying a rucksack of supplies."

"Then it's done." I looked at Pierce, having no reason not to consider the entire venture in a bright light. "A long, empty walk, Pierce. Prospects. Ruins. Woodland paths. Please join, or it won't be the same." Then it struck me, the reason why he might be less than enthusiastic. "Oh! Has your leg been bothering you this week? I'd not noticed a significant—"

"Not at all," Pierce cut my words off swiftly. "My leg is what it is, but I'm fit for a country walk. Only I wasn't…" He frowned, a thought behind his silver eyes, perhaps the battle of his wishing to give me what I'd asked for. "If most of the day will be spent walking the countryside, with very little time in the village, I will acquiesce for the sake of pleasing one Emma Lion." Then he smiled.

It was not easy, his expression. Nor settled.

"Brilliant," said Islington, who had stood to serve himself additional breakfast and therefore had not observed. "Three quarters of an hour, shall we say?"

The walk to Nettle unspooled like a ribbon in a field of tall grasses—a path which bent and curved in unexpected ways. I was in high spirits, as was Islington. Hawkes looked distracted in the best sense. Pierce walked along beside me without complaint, his limp manageable. Having decided to come, he held no qualms.

My own perspective was that the four of us were unconquerable.

Only, a few hours in, while going down towards the river and into a new line of trees, not far outside the village, Pierce had slowed.

"Is it your leg?" I asked.

"What? No. I'm—fine, really."

"You look pale."

And he did, his eyes scanning the place as if something lived in the shadows.

Thirsty, dusty, but with a sense of undefeatable well-being, we piled into the Thistle and Flag, finding ourselves to the table furthest from the door. Nettle was a sleepy village, and there were few in the dining room. Pierce sat in the corner. His paleness had transformed into awareness as he watched anyone coming or going. Although he took care to speak as he usually would, his easy cadence did not match the watchful measure of his eyes.

If Hawkes or Islington noticed something amiss, they've not since said. But at one point, I almost reached my hand to his, to stop him from worrying his thumb over the edge of his finger as he sat, fists clenched.

Islington was right, the food was ideal for a country walk, along with a pint for each of us. Well, two for Pierce. This proved tonic for his unspoken tension, and when we spilled out of the public house and onto the road, I was no longer worried.

"To the woods?" Islington then said.

Pierce's shoulders released a burden.

Then.

"Niall?"

Pierce stiffened.

"Niall, is it— Is it you?"

We all turned to see a woman. Older than me, yet still young. Caged, somehow, in the sense of a smallness she could do nothing for. Her dress was clean but faded. Her hair a mouse brown pulled back in a simple bun. Whatever beauty she owned had been worn into the work of her life. But her eyes. They were hungry with hope. And what's more, they were startling silver. Puddled, fresh rain. Pierce's hand began to lift at his side when he saw her.

"Nance," he said, then swallowed.

The worry that threaded her face broke. She took a step, then another, until she was almost at a run, throwing her arms around Pierce's neck, clutching him like she couldn't believe he wasn't a ghost.

Pierce swallowed her into his embrace.

I could see Islington and Hawkes exchanging a glance, and we three took a step back to give them privacy. But I was riveted on the scene before me. When the young woman pulled away, Pierce moved his thumbs beneath her tear-filled eyes.

She said something—half laugh, half cry—gripping his shoulders with her chore-worn hands. He said something in reply and she, nodding, letting her forehead fall so she might lean her head against his shoulder, her own shoulders shaking. He kissed the top of her head. "Nance."

"Look at you," she said, and then what sounded like, "I thought you were long dead."

She buried her face against Pierce's chest, his hands hovering above her frame a moment before he rested them on her arms, waiting until she again pulled herself away. "But you're with friends," she said, forcing her emotion behind whatever propriety she could manage, wiping her own tears now with the edge of her finger.

Pierce stepped back as she did—his left hand still gripping her arm—and turned, opening the private reunion to include us three. "Nance, I'd like to introduce you to my friends. The Duke of Islington, Mr. Nigel Hawkes, and Miss Emma Lion."

We, each of us, nodded in turn. Nance's eyes had grown wide when being introduced to Islington and remained so throughout.

"This," Pierce continued, "is Nancy Pierce, my sister."

It was him speaking the words that nailed everything into place.

Islington: "A pleasure."

Hawkes: A silent, reassuring expression.

Emma: "Very nice to meet you."

"Likewise," Nance replied, not wholly comfortable. But when she looked back to Pierce, she smiled. "Look at you, Niall! A grown man, if there ever was one. You look like…" Then her eyes lit up. "Of course you'll come, you must, Niall. She's home. She's in the kitchen. She'll not believe it."

"I don't think—"

"Come to the house, Niall. She's waited—"

"My friends—" Niall ran a nervous hand through his dark hair.

"We've whatever time you need, Pierce," Islington said smoothly. His tone was gracious, creating plenty of space, no sense of hurry. "Whatever you decide."

Pierce was pressing his lips together.

Then Islington, easy as water in a stream, turned to Hawkes and asked him a question, drawing the two of them out of the conversation between Pierce and his sister.

I couldn't quite do the same.

"It's just down the lane here, surely you remember," Nance said, turning a deeper sentiment into a laugh to assuage the moment.

"Is *he* still there?" Pierce asked, looking past her as he spoke.

Nance's face stilled, old hurts and fresh difficulty evident in her silver eyes. "Niall…"

"Is he still there?" Pierce repeated, now looking directly at Nance's face.

"Yes, of course. But he's ill, a…an injury of the brain. He's bedbound, you see."

An angry, sharp word escaped Pierce's lips.

Nance raised a hand to Pierce's forearm, tight with unspoken strain. "Please come and see Mam. It would break her heart if you didn't."

"You heading there now?"

"Yes. I was just only to pop into the Thistle and Flag to borrow Mrs. Pruitt's red thread, but that can wait."

"Go get your thread," Pierce said. "I'll be here when you come out."

Light flashing in Nance's silver eyes. "I'll be only a minute. Only wait, Niall. Wait for me."

"I'll wait, Nance." He then grinned in a most unexpected, boyish manner. "Get on with ya."

She smiled in equal measure and stretched so she could kiss Pierce on the cheek, then slipped into the Thistle and Flag.

Pierce watched her go. His smile failed. He swallowed. An expression of guilt, of wariness, of affection.

I reached my own hand to his forearm, only a moment's reminder is all. It seemingly triggered a deep breath, and he let it out with caution, turning to face we three. Islington and Hawkes had paused their conversation, waiting. And it was Hawkes who spoke. "Do you need us to wait here, do you need us to head for Stonecrop, or do you need us to come with you?"

Pierce started to shake his head, more to himself than anything. He placed his hands in the pockets of his trousers. "I don't want to inconvenience—"

"What do you need from your friends, Pierce?" Hawkes said. "To wait, to go, or to come?"

Pierce looked down at his boots and let out another breath, lifting a hand to the back of his neck. "Come with, if you like." Then Pierce looked over at me, his mouth turned down in a complicated line. "It looks like I'll be introducing you to my mother, Emma. If you've no objections."

~~"Certainly not!" I said, somewhat astonished for the turn of events~~.

"Certainly not," was what I wished to say aloud but didn't. What actually came out of my mouth was, "Introducing your— Fine as anything— That is…"

Usually, a lapse of communicatory skills would be met with Pierce's mature, somewhat dark amusement. But this afternoon, he kept watching my face, as if it were only he and I, alone in his studio, and he had asked me as honest a question as he could. His focus brought about my own.

"I'd be pleased to meet her, Pierce," I said quietly. "How many years has it been?"

"More than twenty. I've never been back."

"And you truly wish us to come with you?"

Pierce looked over my shoulder to Islington and Hawkes, both still managing to reduce any odd angles as if it were a perfectly normal thing to have one's life's secrets unfolded in a dusty lane outside the Thistle and Flag. "I'm nervous as hell, Emma. I'd like to have you at my back. All of you. I can't—"

He lifted his hand again to brush his hair away. His hand was shaking.

"Niall!" Nance was out into the street, a small basket in her hand.

She looked anxious and disbelieving and joyful mixed together. I tried to see more of Pierce in her but could only see the resemblance in her eyes. "I was worried you would—"

"I'll carry that for you, Nance," he said, taking the basket from her hand, and then offering his free arm for her to link hers through. "Shall we?" He looked over his shoulder.

"Lead on," Islington said.

And so Pierce did.

Trying not to release too loud a breath, I looked at Hawkes. He gave me a small nod, quick and sharp. A carry-on-soldier affair. I returned my attention to Pierce and Nance. They had started talking about old, well-worn things. She couldn't stop looking at his face, wondering. Stepping closer to Pierce only a moment, I slipped the basket from his hand then fell back in step with Islington. We slowed until we were nine or ten paces behind.

"Did you know Pierce was from Derbyshire?" I whispered. I didn't mean for it to sound like an accusation, but whispering does odd things to one's words when sharpened by uncertainty.

"No," Islington replied, the word quiet but prolonged. "Although, on occasion, when he's had a number of drinks, his accent has slid towards Derbyshire, and I've wondered. I certainly never believed him to have grown up so close to where I did. Unlikely our paths crossed, this village having no ties to Stonecrop."

From me, a frown and nod.

Hawkes, trailing thoughtfully behind.

Not long, then, until we'd walked down one lane and then another, approaching what—surprisingly—appeared to be the parsonage. Pierce's shoulders tightened and pulled forward with every step. I hated what I could feel rolling off him.

Nance was doing her best to make us feel welcome. "No trouble at all," she said, when Islington enquired if our visit would be a burden on her mother. "She'll never believe it."

It was a deceptively sunny day.

Incongruous with the weather of a man returning to the home he had fled as a boy.

"Is Pierce's father in the church?" Islington asked me in a murmur.

"I've always been under the impression his father was dead," I whispered in return.

I wonder now, how had I known? What had given me that impression? Was there a moment or a conversation?

I can't recall.

Nance had run ahead into the front garden. I won't forget the scene. A woman now grown, releasing her brother's arm and running ahead, calling for her mam. She was through the door, her voice echoing. Pierce had slowed his step. His eyes travelled the vine-covered parsonage with all the complications of layered dislike. There was anger, too.

In all that sunshine, Pierce was waiting like a destroying angel warring against his past.

A shout from inside the house, and a woman who looked like an older, more sorrowful version of Nance came flying out of the blackness of the doorway.

She did not seem to see Niall.

She was running to her boy, gone at ten or eleven and never heard of since.

Niall's entire body went taut with old pain.

"Mam," he choked as she cried out, her arms around his chest as he wrapped his own arms around her entire person. "Don't cry, Mam."

But there was nothing for it.

The woman was clinging to Pierce, her veined hands trying to find purchase on Pierce's back as if she had to make certain he was standing before her. She muttered and cried into his chest. Nance was also crying openly now, and I couldn't help but look away.

Derbyshire. They had been here in Derbyshire.

And I wondered why Pierce had not…?"

But I stopped myself. It wasn't fair to Pierce. I knew none of the particulars.

Now that I do, I can't fully blame him.

It took a moment for Pierce's mother to compose herself, Pierce blinking away his own emotion. But when she placed both hands on Pierce's face, looking up with disbelief, she said, "I swore it was your father standing in the garden. You look just… My son. You're the age he…"

"I've some friends with me, Mam. Can I introduce you?"

His mother came to herself; she blinked and looked about. There we three stood. "Oh."

"Mam," Pierce put his arm over her shoulder. "The Duke of Islington, Mr. Nigel Hawkes—a vicar, as it happens—and Miss Emma Lion. Islington, Hawkes, Emma, I'd like to introduce my mam, Ann Thomas."

There were pleasant exchanges all around. I thought nothing of the mismatched surname. A few polite questions from Pierce's mother, responses in kind from Islington. But their words dropped away. All sound did. With sunshine, and birdcall, and June all about, green and fresh like a painting, I heard nothing. Sound was lost the moment I watched Pierce, his arm around this woman, this stranger, looking like he utterly belonged to her, and yet seemingly prepared to defend himself against any number of ghosts.

"Miss Lion?"

Someone was saying my name.

"Miss Lion?"

It was Nance. "Would you care to join in for tea?"

"Join us for tea," Pierce's mam echoed.

"Most certainly," I managed, swallowing.

She turned expectantly towards Islington and Hawkes.

"If you'll excuse us, Ma'am," Islington said, "Hawkes and I have a pressing concern to see to in the village. We will be gone half an hour, I should think," a glance at Pierce, who answered with a sharp nod. And with that, the lift of his hat, Hawkes doing his own version of a polite parting, they were out of the gate and onto the lane.

"Let's go inside, then," Pierce's mother said, wrapping her arm around Pierce. "It isn't real until I see you sitting in my kitchen, Niall. Not until…"

Nance, eyes luminous, linked her arm through mine and reclaimed the basket. "A day for some refreshment, Miss Lion," she said.

The kitchen was carefully kept but tired. There were large flat stones, smoothed by centuries of footsteps, old beams ladened with herbs. But it was bright through the windows, for all that, and Pierce and I were urged to sit at the table, to make ourselves comfortable.

Pierce's mother stealing glances at his face, over and over, to ascertain he was real.

"Nance," she said, eyes casting about, "would you fetch some fresh flowers from the garden. This table should be set properly."

"No need to fuss, Mam."

But Pierce's words were ignored as his mother and sister left the kitchen on their own tasks. Pierce stared at the doorway through which they'd gone, focusing rather on some unseeable thing. Before I could ask anything, *say* anything, he reached over and found my hand beneath the table, grabbing hold.

I placed my free hand over his, uncertain.

The sound of footsteps and then his mother entering with a tablecloth of exceptionally beautiful lace. It was clear to see she had again been crying. "I thought this would be nice," she said, spreading it on the table before us, her thin, veined hands smoothing the lace with care.

"It's lovely, Mrs. Thomas," I said. "Truly."

"A gift," she answered, her eyes moving between Pierce and myself. "I had thought to make it part of Nance's hope chest, but it doesn't look— Well, perhaps there will be another occasion."

Pierce released my hand.

And then Nance entered, a wild June bouquet of campion, vetch, and peonies.

"Ragtag, but the garden is flush with 'em," she said.

It wasn't long before a tea had been laid.

"Cake. Poppyseed, actually," Pierce's mother was saying. "I can scarcely believe, as it always was your favourite."

All this while Pierce was nodding along, watching his mother, but his early show of affection had been cooled by an internal caution.

It was Nance who first began asking questions. Nothing too pointed. Careful, perimeter queries.

Was ours a friendship of long standing?

"We've known one another for over a year now," Pierce answered.

How had we met?

"In London, through a mutual acquaintance." Again, a bare description with little detail.

"Are you," Nance hesitated while Pierce's mam stared into her tea, "still living in London?"

"For now," Pierce answered. I did not understand any of their history, none of the many layered reasons he'd not ever once written, but in that moment, I wished to kick Pierce under the table. They were trying tremendously to not pry into the history of this prodigal son, and he was doing his best to tell them naught.

"I thought I saw your name in the paper, a few years ago. With a photograph of soldiers?" Nance said. Then she waited.

Pierce took a sip of his tea. His hand was shaking. (Had I been able, I would have produced a flask and added several swallows of whisky.) "Yes, I work as a photographer. The London papers have printed my work from time to time."

Here Pierce's mother, Ann, looked up. "Is it good work, then?"

Pierce nodded and allowed his gaze to flick to his mother's face. "It is, Mam. Very good work."

"He's tremendously popular," I added, my fork pinning my piece of poppyseed cake in place. "He's taking more society portraits now that he's not following the wars."

Pierce shifted.

I bit my tongue.

Only, his poor mother.

All said and done, I've had many a more comfortable tea.

"Have you always been in London?" his mother finally asked.

"No," Pierce responded. "I've been in America, then doing some far work in places like Africa, Morocco, Afghanistan. Most of my time has been in New York. It's… It's been a profitable place to be." It sounded like he felt he must defend his distance, and that he resented that fact.

Nance looked wonderstruck. "Have you really been all those places?" And her enthusiasm couldn't help but thaw something in the room. "New York! Is it true what they say?" And off she went, drawing up visions of a life distant and different from this small, forgotten village.

Finally, Pierce began to sound like himself, giving her anecdotes and curious details, a smile behind his eyes as he watched his sister's enjoyment. "I think you might even enjoy California more than New York, Nance." A relief, when Pierce's smile stopped hiding, unhindered.

Nance laughed aloud. "California? All the way on the other side of America? I can't imagine."

We all sat thinking something or other. But the silence was given too much space. No one knew what to say next. Until Pierce suddenly said, "Is he here?"

Ann looked up sharply. Nance looked down.

But Pierce was determined. "Nance said he was sick?"

"It was an apoplexy," his mother said, shifting in her chair. "He's bedridden now and cannot speak in any meaningful way."

"How long has it been?" Pierce asked.

Nance shook her head. "Three months."

His mother said nothing, her mouth a thin, worn line.

Then Pierce gave a strangled, bitter laugh. "Almost convinces a man to believe in a God."

"Niall," his mother said, but it was with her shoulders pulled together. She was a woman who was acquainted with fear.

"What?" Pierce challenged his mother evenly. "Are you going to defend him?"

"He's ill, Niall."

"What of all the years before? You always explained away his temper with every reason you could think. He was strained by the work of the parish, you would say. A man of God who, too, deserved grace for his sins. The drinking was never as bad as I made it out to be."

"Niall…" Ann attempted.

Pierce's eyes narrowed. In detachment. In wonder. "You still defend him."

"We must… We must forgive all—"

The sound of wood scraping against stone. Pierce stood, sending his chair clattering to the floor.

"Niall," Nance tried.

"Where is he?" Pierce asked. "I'd like to see him."

"He's an old man, Niall," his mother whispered.

"I have a right to look him in the face. You know I do. Where is he, Mam?"

"He's in the parlour. He requires too much care to be moved upstairs. Only, please—"

Then, three things. Pierce made a move to leave the kitchen. I stood. Ann grasped Pierce's arm. "He's an old man, Niall. If you could see what has happened to his health. His dignity—"

"Why are you defending him!" Pierce cried out, shaking his mother's hand away, his voice sounding so very young. "After all these years. Why can't you say he was a terrible man who was cruel to you, cruel to your daughter, and living hell for your son?"

"Niall—"

"Why is it so hard for you to say the man who stood at the pulpit on Sunday was a brute! Was a liar!"

"If you could but see how he…"

"Oh, I'd like to see him, Mam."

Nance was frozen in her chair, but I followed Pierce.

I couldn't not have.

I would not leave him alone.

Pierce pushed open the door across the hall, and I followed.

It was dim, the curtains mostly pulled although the windows were open. There was a bed, and a man lying within, propped up against some pillows. The left side of his face drooped in exaggerated fashion. He seemed aware, but unable to communicate. And so his eyes, the right one widening more than the left, followed as Pierce came to stand at the foot of the bed, looking down at the pathetic figure before him.

The old man blinked his eyes to focus on the face of the man who stood above him. A look of confusion and then realisation. And then terror.

Pierce, when he saw it, laughed.

I was shocked.

Unbalanced.

I felt cold and heavy as Pierce went quiet. An anger so deep that I took a step closer, lifting my hand as though I might need to somehow prevent a torrent.

It was as if Pierce did not see me, lifting his chin even while his gaze nailed the man to his bed. Pierce stood at his full height, shoulders pulled back. He made a dismissive sound. And then did something I was not expecting.

He quoted the Bible.

"*Is this the man that made the earth to tremble…?*"

The man in the bed flinched.

"Apoplexy," Pierce said evenly. "Many call it a stroke, for they believe the sufferer was struck down by the hand of God."

The man in bed was fidgeting with his right hand. He opened his mouth, and nothing more than a sound came out.

Pierce's eyes narrowed. They pronounced sharp judgement. "I came into this house a boy of seven years old. Old enough to remember the man who held place before you, a man who was more than you ever could be. I'm ashamed to say it now, but I was eager at the prospect. My mother safe. A larger home than our dank cottage. A man to replace the father lost. I regret how quickly I gave you my trust." Pierce's voice was like a frozen sheet of ice. "And you beat me, old man. You beat the hell out of me. For any little thing. For nothing at all. And then you would stand in that church and preach the gospel of Good News. You bastard."

"Niall," his mother said from the doorway, worrying her hands, eyes round with sorrow and fear. "Please, son."

But Pierce's eyes were drilled on the helpless man in the bed before him. "You hit me, at times you kicked me like a diseased mutt and called me such. Do you remember?" Pierce's voice was rising—it rang through the room. "You should have remembered my father. You knew him. Knew his stature. His strength. You should have known that one day you would be helpless before my fists, and I would come raging back into your life and take my due."

"Pierce," I said, my voice barely audible.

"Niall, please don't. He's injured."

Until this point, it seemed there had been a chain keeping Pierce at bay, but his mother's defence snapped it loose. Pierce's gaze whipped up, locking on her face. "He's injured? *He's* injured? You always did this! You stood by. You excused. You wept in your pathetic corner! Too frightened to take your children and leave!" Pierce was yelling now.

His mother fell into herself; there is no other description. Her face twisting in pain as her shoulders slumped, her chest gone concave as if she had been trying desperately to protect herself for too many hollow years. But the fear had never left; it remained, eating away at her chest. Nance stood paralyzed behind her mother, but she was beginning to shake. "Niall," she tried, voice shaking, "we've left it—"

Pierce cut her off. "It wasn't that he was kinder to you, Nance. It was that he always made you guess. At times he'd give you sweets, at times he'd deliver the switch. Your hands. Your poor hands, blistered, bleeding, for your not having the strength of a child twice your age." His attention was shot like an arrow back at his mother. "I've seen more than either of you know. I have seen mothers in war, in famine, in prostitution. And I *cannot* understand why you didn't take us away from this place. Why you felt it your Christian duty to uphold his position despite the cruelty."

"It isn't such a simple thing," his mother cried like a wounded animal. "I had no family—"

"There were people here, in this village, who would have helped—!"

"Niall. Son."

"Had you been more of a mother you would have the right to call me son."

It was Nance who made the sound, a snarl rather than a whimper. She caught her mother, holding her up. "Niall, it isn't Mam's fault!"

Pierce watching the scene from twenty years of distance.

"Niall," I began, but it was the same moment Pierce looked back at the man in the bed.

"You know the Bible well enough. We both do. You hung your own millstone, and when I hear you have died, I will rejoice."

An intake of breath.

I realised it was my own.

Pierce stepped closer to the bed, vengeful prey approaching a caged predator. "You *beat* me. You *hit* me. You belittled and shamed and did whatever else you could to tear me down. But that was nothing compared to your holding me in the river. You held me under the water until I couldn't breathe. Over and over. The terror," Pierce's voice broke, "of your *fist* on my shirt collar. Do you know what that's like, old man?" Pierce moved quickly, grabbing the man's shirtfront. "Holding me under until I gulped for air and only found water! Dark, helpless terror. And you would laugh and say, '*That'll teach you my boy.*'" Pierce was shaking the man, gripping his shirtfront and shaking him hard, voice twisting so tight it was difficult to hear the words. "Even after that, Mam didn't take me away. I tried to tell her. But she wouldn't believe me or wouldn't listen. She did nothing. Later, I would hear her crying in the pantry."

"Niall," I said. It sounded like an order.

Pierce opened his fists, letting go of the shirtfront. The old man fell against the cushions. But Pierce was overwrought, and nothing would stem the tide. "Did you tell them why I left? Did you *ever* tell them why I ran as fast as I could? Why I swore I would never return? You tried to kill me! Bloody bastard. You tried to drown me! You held me under until I passed out. And then you left me for dead in the river. I woke in the dark, washed against the bank, bruised and freezing, barely able to swallow. Damn lucky chance of it I survived!"

The sound of Pierce's mother sobbing, of Nance nervously speaking a comfort she didn't feel.

"You tried to kill me!" Pierce yelled again, and he lunged forward grabbing the man's shoulders. "You tried to *kill* me!"

I was between them before I realised how. Facing Pierce, my hands on his arms. I'd broken the grip of his right hand, though he was still holding on with his left. "Let go, Niall," I shouted. "Let him go!" I looked at Pierce's face, I caught his gaze with mine and held it fast, then threw my arms around him with such force, he could do nothing but stumble backwards. Unbalanced for a moment and then his arms came around me, pulling me against his chest and anchoring himself. Out of breath, half out of his mind.

The press of his cheek against mine made me realise I'd been crying.

"Pierce," I whispered, deliberately choosing his father's surname. "Pierce. It's time. It's time to go. It's time to leave."

His entire body tightened; a storm so strong it felt like holding on to a gale-force wind. He was fighting, fighting. He could not let go.

"Niall."

A rip of a breath in response, his frame quaking with anger, and Pierce let his head drop down against my shoulder.

"It's time to leave this room, to go outside," I whispered. "There is space, there are long roads, your life is elsewhere. It's time to go."

I don't understand why I said what I did, but it was as if he were trapped in a corner not of his own making, yet only he could find a way out.

He held me tightly, and I could feel his nod against my shoulder. He kissed my cheek, eyes red with tears. "Long roads," he repeated. "You're right. We should go."

He released me. And without a glance to his mother or sister, or the man in the bed, Pierce took my hand and led me from the room.

His step did not slow.

Limping, he guided us out of the room, out of the hall, and out into the sunshine.

It was one of the most surreal moments of my life.

Islington and Hawkes were waiting in the shade of the tree across the lane. And I had little doubt but that they had heard it all, the window being open. Pierce walked past them, not seeing anything, his hand holding mine so tightly I had to half run to keep up. Islington and Hawkes fell into quiet step behind us—the sort of solidarity where nothing is asked but everything is given.

Pierce did not lead us back down the lane, towards the Thistle and Flag. Instead, he cut across to a well-worn path crossing a small field towards the woods. Once we'd dropped down into a hollow, and enough trees flanked our way, once we were out of sight of anyone on the lane or at the parsonage, I pulled back on Pierce's hand.

"Pierce," I said.

He kept walking.

"Niall!" Three quick steps and I pulled myself equal to, then ahead of Pierce, turning and forcing him to stop.

He let go of my hand.

The deep well of his mind released him.

He found himself.

He saw me.

"Are you all right?" he asked, half panicked. His hands came up to the sides of my face. "Are you all right!"

"Yes. Niall, yes! I'm fine. Breathe. You're not…breathing. Islington is here. And Hawkes. We're all well. I am well."

Pierce truly saw my face. His hands dropped away, silver eyes ascertaining if I was telling the truth—that I was uninjured, unharmed. His chest rose and fell. He took a step back. He looked about, the surrounds terribly familiar, the river we stood alongside likely where he had almost been killed. How familiar, how unsettling. The anger I hoped was dissipating had not. It had been hidden by bewilderment but was now rising. Like the sour smell of smoke burning something that ought not have touched a flame.

But he was with friends. Friends who claimed no touch on his previous life. And so Pierce took a breath, then another. He took a step back. "My apologies," he said, holding up his hand, so taut the veins crossing over the bones on the back were like ropes. The muscles in his neck tightened. His chest rose and fell. "My apologies, truly."

And he began to walk in the direction of too-distant Stonecrop.

We three stood rooted, watching, weighing.

"What does he need, Hawkes?" I said, grasping at any thought beyond my own.

Watching Pierce, Hawkes looked like he knew, and he was sorry for it. "Before resolution comes the lance, Emma."

And it was Hawkes who followed Pierce across the field.

By instinct or hesitation, I reached my hand out to Islington's arm—asking him to wait, to not follow, just as he was doing the same. "Let Hawkes," I said.

"Yes," he answered. "Let Hawkes."

Islington, still watching the two figures growing in their distance, lifted his hand to cover mine—the same hand Pierce had held so tightly my fingers were pressed red. "Are you all right, Emma?" he asked, still not looking at me.

"I assume you heard the whole?"

"The window was open. Pierce's voice carried."

"I'm fine, Islington. I'm— We are all somewhat rattled."

"Yes," Islington said as Pierce, then Hawkes, disappeared from view. He swallowed and pursed his lips, eyebrows drawn in concentration. Finally, he looked at me. "There is a path running along the river here. If we match our pace with theirs, we will come out a quarter of an hour ahead."

We said nothing more, each of us in our own thoughts the length of the journey.

Two hours across country without speaking. The mystery of Islington's past faded. For a different tragedy, a different broken past had come roaring into the present, consuming everything.

Islington, Hawkes, and I had a single task ahead, that of holding Pierce up.

Other mysteries were to be held at bay.

Other sorrows were to wait.

As we were nearing Stonecrop, we could hear an argument in the woods not far from where we walked. Pierce's voice loud and justified, Hawkes's return cadence one of dancing away from the blows only to deliver his own. As if Hawkes were picking a fight with Pierce's anger, trying to wear it out.

Islington and I looked at one another as we wordlessly walked out of the trees below the lake, crossed the lawn, and were up the stairs to the south portico.

We sat.

It was not the relief it should have been after such a journey.

Hawkes and Pierce broke from the treeline not long after, walking along the edge of the lake.

"Is Hawkes trying to tire Pierce out?" I asked.

Islington said nothing.

We kept our gazes on the two of them, the intensity of their conversation conveyed by the way they paced, the way Pierce lifted his hands in frustration. At a certain point Hawkes broke away, coming towards the house, but not to where Islington and I sat. He walked around the corner, past the front entrance, and disappeared.

Pierce waited by the lake, arms crossed, staring down whatever demons he could not put to rest.

I watched only Pierce for the duration of Hawkes's absence.

Then, "*Ah.*"

Hawkes was returning to where Pierce stood beside the water. He was carrying two sets of boxing gloves. With him was one of the older stable boys.

"*Ah,*" I repeated. Then, "Oh dear."

Islington's expression was even when he said, "Hawkes is going to rip Pierce's anger out at the roots."

That was when a rather refreshed voice startled us both, "I see you're back! Lovely bit of shade, Henry. I'll ask Sarah to bring tea. What sounds tempting, Miss Lion?" Mariana, having spent the day in bed, looked content with her lot in the world. She was smiling as she looked at us, then surveyed the scene before the lake. "Hawkes and Mr. Pierce would like to join, I assume. What is it they're doing?" Pierce was removing his coat and waistcoat. "How strange. Henry?" Then she saw Hawkes, coat and waistcoat also removed, rolling up the sleeves of his white shirt before picking up a pair of boxing gloves. "Goodness gracious, they aren't going to box!"

We neither of us had a response.

"A grotesque sport," Mariana murmured.

Again, we gave no answer.

She then left to see about tea.

In the meantime, with the help of the stable boy, Pierce and Hawkes had both secured their gloves. A few moments of talk, Hawkes raising his glove to Pierce's chest as if in accusation. It looked like Pierce smiled, the first one we'd seen since Nettle, and said something to Hawkes.

It was direct, how Hawkes answered, and must have been a brazen response, for Pierce cocked his head to the side, frowned, and clocked Hawkes in the face with a right hook.

Islington guffawed.

I am fairly certain I cried out as if in pain.

Hawkes, dancing a few steps back, lifted his forearm to the side of his mouth, wiping the blood away, and grinned.

He ran at Pierce.

I closed my eyes at the inevitable, only opening them after the first blows had landed.

Pierce was good, but he was no Hawkes. Strong through the shoulders, but with limited ease of mobility due to his injured leg. Whereas Hawkes was lightning. Pierce had to wait for Hawkes to come to him.

It soon became clear this was not a fight to win.

It was turning into a spar.

A joint practice.

The brutality of the May Day fight with the strongman was a thousand miles away from this exercise. It was Hawkes giving Pierce a way to release fury, bone deep.

Mariana returned, two maids in her wake, and sat beside Islington with a *tsk* that could have come from her brother on nearly any other occasion. As it was, Islington was fully enjoying the spar. "Look at that there," he said. "Pierce was a fighter before his injury. Longer reach than Hawkes. But due to his injured leg, Hawkes can catch him two to one."

Mariana looked first at her brother, then at me. I recognised the well-worn look of Devereux long-suffering. "I am certain Miss Lion's aunt would *not* approve, Henry," she said—to the two of us, clearly.

"There are facts to which you are not privy, Mariana," Islington replied.

She smoothed her skirts and looked straight ahead in response.

I blinked. And did my best *not* to look at Islington in complete astonishment.

Are Devereuxs always so unconventional when presented with a firmer, more starched reaction from one of their own tribe?

Pierce landed a blow, reclaiming my attention. Then Hawkes answered. One. Two. And another as Pierce tried to feint, turned on his injured leg, and stumbled back a few paces with a pained laugh.

I had not realised the grip of fear that had taken hold of my heart until—with the sound of Pierce's laugh—I felt it loosen.

~~I said in relief~~ I said without thinking, "There is far less blood than the last time Hawkes fought. It's more of an exercise, really."

"Exactly," Islington echoed.

Mariana, hands placed protectively over her unborn child, watched a few more moments, then, "I think I'll put my feet up in the library."

Flushed faces, shirts plastered with sweat, the fighting turned towards Hawkes and Pierce discussing techniques, running through repeated motions, punching one another's gloves rather than their persons. They fought until all the energy in their bodies had dripped down to the grass, the long shadows of late afternoon tied to their feet.

Finally, they relinquished, sitting down, facing the lake. Pierce fell onto his back. Grabbing the laces between his teeth and pulling, Pierce loosened the gloves and tossed them to the side, before placing a bare hand on his chest.

I watched as it rose and fell.

I watched for any sign of anger left unspent.

That was when Islington said, "Lion?"

"Yes?"

"Exactly how long have you and Pierce held an understanding with one another?"

Well.

I have had moments of dreaded advent in my life. But none that prepared me for the arrival of Islington's question. We both kept our gazes on Pierce and Hawkes.

"A few months now, since we acknowledged, uh, our feelings," I answered at length, stepping around the words like they were shattered glass.

Islington sat unmoving.

I waited.

Eyes narrowing the slightest degree, as if his interest in the view was increased, Islington still said nothing.

My tiredness rose in a wave. I wanted rest, respite. To escape the complications of the day. "It isn't— We are…"

"You owe me no explanation, Lion." The way he shifted in his seat did not overly convince me he meant the words.

Several minutes passed.

"Why do I have the sense," I ventured, "that you have opinions on the subject which you're choosing not to share?"

"Because you're perceptive," Islington answered immediately. Then, "*Ah.*"

Hawkes had stood, holding out a hand to Pierce and pulling him to his feet. Pierce's limp was more pronounced. Hawkes said something and Pierce laughed it away.

Hawkes had lanced the pain as far as he was able.

Heaven help the rest.

My eyes were feeling heavy, like rain. "I think—" I sat forward.

"Go and rest, Lion," Islington said.

"I'll be down for dinner."

I don't think he believed me. But I believed myself. Thirty minutes of sleep and…

But after I made my way to the tower, removed my dust-covered boots, and washed my face, I allowed myself to fall onto the bed. My mind to fall deeper. I did not wake for hours.

I've now written the night through.

The birds have begun to call.

June 19th

We are all worn through.

I fell back asleep after writing out, wringing out rather, the whole of yesterday, letting it drip onto the page. I did not wake until after luncheon. Rising, washing, dressing, remembering how all my dreams had been drenched in rain, I soon found myself wandering Stonecrop.

Mariana was nowhere.

There was hardly a servant to be seen, and when they did cross my path, I gave a solicitous smile and continued on my way.

I finally found Islington in the library, sitting at his desk and staring at his steward's ledgers as if he were thinking of anything but.

Rapping the back of my hand against the door, I said, "Might I enter?"

Startled, Islington looked up, both relief and worry shifting his shoulders. "You've slept a great deal. Are you feeling yourself?"

I entered, sitting down in one of the leather chairs near the hearth, the one where I could easily converse with Islington while he sat at his desk. "I've been sleeping through all the wrong hours, but I am not ill. Where are the others?"

"Mariana is visiting a friend in the neighbourhood." Islington paused, knowing she was not the one after whom I was enquiring. "Hawkes and Pierce have gone to the river bend."

"They've gone swimming?"

Islington nodded.

It struck me as odd. "Pierce went swimming, you say?"

Islington said nothing.

I waited. And then, "Are you going to make me ask for details of last evening?"

A sigh from Islington. He tossed the pen in his hand onto the ledger. "It was a difficult evening for Pierce. We went to a pub in Lockwell."

A pub.

"And how," I asked, "are all feeling this afternoon?"

"Hawkes and myself are both fit as a fiddle," Islington said.

"There were three of you, if I recall."

"Yes. Pierce needed to be, *ah*, wrung out."

"Meaning he drank himself into oblivion."

"Not quite oblivion," Islington said diplomatically.

I looked out of the window. A bright day, two in a row like lucky coins.

Not so lucky, perhaps.

"Did he speak of what happened?" I asked.

"Very little."

I closed my eyes, scenes from yesterday circling my mind like a bird of prey.

"Might I ask you a question, Lion?"

"I could answer more easily if I knew what the question was." Opening my eyes I looked to where he sat. Islington leaned back in his chair, watching me as if we were playing a game of chess.

"Has Pierce ever been that angry before, in your presence?"

"Certainly not!" The answer rushed out before the question had any chance to settle. "As you should know."

Islington placed his left elbow on the desk before him, resting his chin on his thumb while his finger rested against his lips. "I've known Pierce to maintain admirable stoicism when it comes to temper." A hesitation. "How much does he drink when he is with you at Lapis Lazuli?"

"Are you angry with him?"

"I am worried."

"Worried for Pierce?"

Islington picked up the pen on his desk with his right hand, tapping it absently. "Pierce,"—tap, tap, tap—"for one." When he looked back at me, I understood it was I who remained the unspoken second.

I could not…

Did not want, rather…

Well.

Grasping for some light thing, I said, "You have likely seen Pierce drink more than I, at The Cleopatra."

A nod, but one that connotes internal distraction rather than corroboration.

I had envisioned Islington's high disapproval, upon his discovering how things stand between Pierce and myself. Only, I had *not* envisioned the disclosure happening in such dramatic fashion. In a situation where the instinct of all of us was to steady the ship, keep every man on board. I wondered if Pierce was now regretting asking us all to stay. Or if it is a relief that people who care for him know.

As if Islington could hear my thoughts, he frowned to himself. "I would not have wanted my past to be thrown at me in such a way. Nor do I know how I would behave towards a man who had abused me so, who had tried to kill me. You don't—" Something in my expression must have stopped him, rerouting his thoughts. "Lion, Hawkes and I held him up as best we could."

"What? Oh, yes. Only I—"

What was I to say?

I'm still not certain.

There may be several reasons why I stood, declaring that it was stuffy indoors. Didn't Islington think? A turn in the garden would remedy, to be sure. A single clap with my hands, like a disillusioned naturalist, I said, "Sunshine and birdcall, Islington. Nature's medicine. Are you interested in joining? No? Well."

And I excused myself.

Hawkes found me two hours later, where I sat reading in the shade of the ruins.

Sunburnt and muscle tired, wearing faded blue trousers, a shirt, and braces—Hawkes had the attitude of a sixteen-year-old boy in high summer. His hair was mostly dry.

"Hello, Hawkes," I said as he sat on a bit of stone wall that still caught the sun.

"Hello, Emma."

"This is the third time this year your face has been bruised by fighting. Eccentric, for my poetry-reading vicar. Absolutely appropriate from the leader of The Reprobates Ten. Are you going to make a habit of pummelling and being pummelled?"

Hawkes, sitting just so, fussing with his fingers as he was bent forward, gave his head a single shake. "I've little intention of that," he replied quietly, tilting his head to the side and looking at me.

"More importantly, what are you reading?"

I held up the book he had given me: Wordsworth.

Hawkes closed his eyes, stilling his hands.

Ye slight no life—to God and Nature true;
But death, becoming death, is dearer far,
When duty bids you bleed in open war:

Having no understanding of the context, I simply said, "Amen, Vicar."

"Hmm," he replied, sounding suspect of my agreeance.

"Have you any other Wordsworth on the edge of your brain?"

And Hawkes, shifting, began to speak.

Wisdom and Spirit of the universe!
Thou Soul, that art the Eternity of thought!
And giv'st to forms and images a breath
And everlasting motion, not in vain,
By day or star-light, thus from my first dawn
Of childhood didst thou intertwine for me
The passions that build up our human soul;
Not with the mean and vulgar works of Man;
But with high objects, with enduring things,
With life and nature; purifying thus
The elements of feeling and of thought,
And sanctifying, by such discipline
Both pain and fear,—until we recognize
A grandeur in the beatings of the heart.

He finished, and I was still caught by the concept of "*high objects, the enduring things.*"

After a few moments, I said, "Thank you, Hawkes."

He ducked his head, a pained smile. "I've promised myself I would stop reciting poetry."

"I can't think of a sadder thing."

A shrug of disagreement.

We sat in our contemplations until I braved, "You were with

Pierce? Swimming at the bend?"

Hawkes shifted on the stone. "He came back an hour ago. He was wanting to find you, first thing, but I told him to sleep a while."

I leaned my head against the stone at my back. "*Sleep. Perchance to dream.*"

"*Aye,*" a sigh from Hawkes that was rounded in some sense of human discontent, "*there's the rub.*"

"Did you know, Hawkes? Did you know any of it?"

He looked off towards the woods to the north. "Intimations, shadows. Some I understood. Some I did not." Hawkes reached down and picked one of the small flowers growing over the ruins on which he sat, twisting it between his fingers. "You and Pierce…" He broke his thought off. Something I have no remembrance of Hawkes ever before doing. He stood, a moment of staring north in some indecipherable distance, and then he wordlessly turned, and I watched him pick himself over the ruins to a hidden path on the east side, which would deliver him to his medieval tower.

I tried to open my Wordsworth.

The book remained closed.

Later

I saw Islington and Hawkes having a discussion in the apostle garden. I was too far away to have heard a word said, but the actions were not simple, their shared thoughts were not light. Islington's movements were tight, as he took a few steps to the right, then circled around, not pacing but moving. He was speaking *at* Hawkes, hands lifted as he made his point.

Hawkes was standing with his arms folded, looking down with all the seriousness of a philosopher.

Islington seemed to ask him a question.

Hawkes had no immediate reply.

Islington asked again, waiting.

Hawkes looked up and gave answer.

It caught Islington, stilled him. He stared Hawkes down a moment then threw up a hand.

Be it in frustration or concession or commiseration, I could not say.

Leaving the north walk from where I had witnessed it all, I went to hide myself away on the south portico. That is where Pierce found me, watching a summer wind tossing the boughs of the trees beyond the lake. He eased himself down into the chair at my side. I looked over at him. He avoided returning the favour, but in his right hand, between two fingers, waited a folded note.

His jaw was bruised beneath the shadow of his stubble.

"I was just coming to slide this beneath the door of your room." Now a glance as he stretched out his hand and waited for me to take the missive.

Pyramus and Thisbe.

I took the note, the slight sandpaper sound of sliding it from between his two fingers.

In his ever-familiar hand, it read,

SORRY TO HAVE MISSED YOU, BUT IT'S AN EARLY TRAIN.

I looked at the words, bending the paper absently back and forth. Then, "Are you much recovered?" I asked. He did not blink or look away from me. The same pools of silver as Nance.

"Do you refer to Nettle or boxing with Hawkes?"

I'm not certain I wasn't referring to the pub in Lockwell.

"You—"

"If I—"

We both broke off. Beneath the weight of our mutual consideration, we waited. I waited.

And it was not rue that I read in his expression, but some bitter herb all the same. "I don't know how to apologise to you, Emma. What penance do I pay for catching you in my storm?"

I wasn't prepared for such a question. I opened my mouth, closed it again, trying to discern the root of a growing frustration. Pierce took my pause to mean the penance was more than he could pay.

"I'd understand," he said, carefully, "if it is too much for you. If you wish to end—"

"Niall Pierce," I said, "you are so ready for others to throw you away." I'd meant to be gentle but could not find a way.

I was not waving a flag of truce.

I was drawing a weapon.

But it was *for* Pierce, not against him.

"Did you think," I asked, "that I was made of such thin metal that I would snap for the past of it all?"

He opened his mouth, but either could not or chose not to say the words. Instead, he looked down and released a breath. He stood, placing his hands in his trouser pockets, looking over the expanse where we four have been ridiculously happy together. It was uncomfortable, my still sitting down, and so I also stood, arms folded, staring over the same southerly view.

Pierce tried again. "I wanted to kill him. I wanted to shake the very life from that broken frame. I have always tried to be a better man than that. I have refused violence, unless set upon. And yet I was so angry." He twisted the words with his voice as if to break them. "And for the first time I held all the power. I hate him." It rushed out—a curse, an oath, a relief. Pierce looked over at me. "I *hate* that man. I always swore I would do better. That if I had…family, I would never— But I've had many years of not trusting myself."

It was a sharp soliloquy, a dagger embedded and twisted.

A heavy, difficult cut.

"This is why you said you don't want children." Unexpected relief—to ask a question I hadn't recognised had been waiting in the wings so near the stage.

"One reason I don't care for the idea," he replied. "There are others."

Was it incongruent to the moment, for me to notice the birdcall in the garden? But I did. And it loosened that which had turned our words too tightly. I sighed. "You might have told me. That he had tried to kill you. That you'd run for your life."

When I looked at Pierce his expression was sharp with a habituated distrust, a caution that carried a knife. He swallowed and looked away from me. A laugh then, a tired sound. "Damn it all to hell, Emma."

"If I had known this was home—"

"This isn't home." Pierce cut his words through mine. He lifted a hand to the back of his neck. "Stonecrop is a world away from my upbringing. I enjoy being here. All the best of Derbyshire with no connection to my old life." A pause. "I won't be returning to Nettle any time soon." A second pause. Longer. The sort of deliberate absence that tells one there is more to be said. "I'm going back to London for a few days."

In the rush of worry, I began to think illogical, sideways thoughts. He was retreating to London. He would not return. He would drink himself into oblivion and then disappear. And none of this warranted any of that, did it? So we knew of his childhood. We were bound to, at some point. But that was not his life today. Pierce had distanced himself. He had become a much better man than the one who had beaten him. There was no reason for him to disappear. There was no cause. "But Pierce, Islington's sister is coming. You can't simply… disappear! People shouldn't disappear!"

"I'm coming back, Emma." He was watching me as if he'd understood some new fact. "A few days, is all. Some space on the train, time to think, tasks that need doing. Then I'm coming back."

"Only, I didn't know—"

"I'm coming back."

"Yes, good!" I rushed. "So you've said."

"So I've said," he repeated.

"When is your train?"

"I leave now. Islington is going to drive me to the Lockwell station."

"So you've spoken with Islington."

"I've spoken with Islington."

"Good."

Somehow, in the intervening space between our words and Pierce's leave-taking, we both managed to loosen our shoulders, managed to slow our hearts. When he moved, I thought it was to step past me, but it was to come closer. Pierce lifted his hand, placing it on my neck as if to draw me to him. He did not. But there was joint and bone in the action. Something secured in place. I lifted my hand to the back of his, gripped it one long moment, and we both let go.

June 20th

Every minute of this day has crawled uphill. Bloody knees and scraped palms. Metaphorical but as painful as any physical injury. I keep seeing myself in the kitchen with Pierce's mother, his sister. Their alarm and resilience. The pain of the son who left.

I've no right to say Pierce shouldn't have been as angry as he was.

This sort of human tragedy—violence, cruelty—feels different from the grief of loss. Grief, as tangled as it is, can be more straightforward. You loved them, and they died. No, that isn't quite the truth. Loss is never direct; it never finds a worn path. No matter how, or why. It throws one into the wilds with no path at all. Only… How to write this out? There are some abuses that feel tangled, sticky, every dim feeling invading the peace of one's heart. Cruelty played out over years, and a feeling of desolation and ash in its wake. Human brutality carries its own sting.

Later

It was nearly time for supper when Islington turned the kitchens upside down by ordering that the old dining room—the banqueting hall still intact on the first floor of Old Stonecrop near the tower—was to host our meal.

"Henry, the entire dining room is set," Mariana had countered.

"It can be reset."

"Which will put supper behind. It is ready now. The food will be cold, and Mrs. Knowlls will be upset."

"Then," Islington said in a matter-of-fact manner that reminded me of his London self, "I shall descend into the fiery bowels of the kitchen and face Mrs. Knowlls myself. Lion? If you would be so good as to venture to the tower and warn Hawkes?"

Entering Old Stonecrop by way of the Glass Walk, I found my way to the stairwell of Hawkes's tower. Going up and up and up, then knocking on what I presumed to be his door, I received no answer. Below, the servants were already bustling about, trying to make the banqueting hall presentable in only slivers of time. But where was Hawkes?

If I were Hawkes I would…

My assertion proved correct. I climbed the worn, narrow staircase all the way to the top of the tower. A far more medieval affair than my own—I liked to think of Hawkes in residence here. (One should have a friend who is able to lend a personal tower when visiting.) And when I came out onto the top, there he sat against a battlement, dressed for supper—in a manner of speaking—and reading a book.

After informing him of the change in plans, I spent a few moments surveying the expanse in all directions. My tower did not match the ancient height of the hill, which betrayed a more complicated understanding of the dominion below. Above us snapped the red and green banner, the medieval Devereux crest whipping in the evening wind, two dragons warding any evil away.

Supper in the old room had the unexpected attitude of being festive. The stones worn, the mullioned windows warped by time, the view out over the flowers of the courtyard garden. Enchanting in its own right.

Islington was wearing a green waistcoat with sharp black tails and trousers. He and Mariana batted the history of the place between them. It was the gift of distraction, and we all gained benefit. There was a collection of medieval weaponry on display—

Lion: "Is that dried blood!"
Islington: "It's rust, Lion."
Lion: "Are you certain?"
Islington: "Unless Hawkes has been poaching."
Hawkes: "I rarely poach on Islington's estate."
Islington: "Rarely?"

—among them being two antique foils.

"Those two are not secured in place, if you'd like to spar afterward, Lion."

"Henry," Mariana said, "Miss Lion is wearing a rather nice evening gown."

"I've seen Lion avoiding many a ballroom threat in that very gown. She has enough room to move her feet."

"Feel no pressure, Miss Lion, to be made ridiculous at my brother's request."

"Oh, I would never pass on the chance to run Islington through, no matter how old the foil or how inconvenient the gown."

Mariana, tired I'm sure, said, "I suppose if you phrase it like so."

And so the three of us (Mariana having excused herself to go sit in the courtyard garden) made our way to the roof of the banquet hall—not, in actuality, with the antique foils, but a rather beautifully kept set for which Islington had sent a footman—and Islington taught me the basic lunges and plunges of the sport. I realise those are not the proper phrases, for which I cared not a jot, for it irked Islington.

> Islington: "Your posture is good, Lion, however you need to throw more strength into your forward thrust."
> Lion: "Let's bind you in a corset, shall we, and see how you do with a forward thrust."
> Islington: "More strength in the legs."
> Lion: *Takes an unsportsmanlike swipe.*
> Islington: "What was that for?"
> Lion: "Irritation given."
> Islington: "I think what you meant to say was joy."

Later, as I lay in bed, I thought about the happiness of we four.

How tangibles and intangibles held us together.

How palpable the reality of life that something might crash through and change everything forever.

June 21st

Reading through Hawkes's Coleridge. I've just come across a line that I cannot shake. My eyes keep returning back and back again.

I am too tired to be hunted by a line of poetry.

Later

My heels relentlessly bit by the words, I made my way into the portrait gallery, walking to the far end where *the* portrait hangs. I looked at the three of them and then opened my book to the incriminating page.

> *Fount, tree and shed are gone, I know not whither,*
> *But in one quiet room we three are still together.*

I looked at Islington and his companions—how comfortably linked, how assumptive that they would always exist together—and wished to cry.

"Are you irritated about something," Islington asked later in the afternoon, while he, Hawkes, and I were playing a somewhat silent game of horseshoes.

"No," I huffed, as my first shoe bounced three feet beyond the peg in ~~spectacular~~ grotesque form. "Only life does not play lightly with its human pieces." I threw my second horseshoe and—glory be—it caught hold of the peg and spun around. A ringer.

"Well done!" said Islington.

Hawkes raised his book as if offering a toast—*Meditations*, in Latin, i.e., steal proof from Emma Lion.

But the mortal joys of horseshoes were fleeting.

For I was torn open. All was tenuousness and uncertainty.

"We don't even have a portrait!" I found myself spitting out. As if it made contextual sense. "There is no quiet room in which we will be still together. Don't you see? The four of us? Alchemy ripped asunder with no proof remaining for anyone to know what it was.

Or that it even existed to begin with! Who will know that we— Drat and blast!" I sounded like a lunatic but too much had poured into the verbal river. It was rising over the banks and there was nothing for it. The fields would flood. "Most don't believe in it anyway, the idea that other substances can be transfigured into gold. But we know!" And I swung my gaze like a scythe to where they both stood—somewhat stunned by my ~~outburst~~ painfully delivered exposition.

A moment passed.

Then two.

"He returns on Monday, Lion," Islington said quietly. "Pierce returns Monday. And we four continue."

And I, chest heaving, stood there feeling like all my seams were inside out and frayed. It was difficult to look Islington in the face and take his comfort.

I, who had discovered secrets he'd not shared.

Who had acquired three young ghosts, knowing almost nothing about them.

Who had thrown myself against the torrent of Pierce's wrath and pulled him to shore.

It is not that I am ignorant of the toll of friendship. I am not. Only I wish I knew better how to carry the balance. And then there is Hawkes, whose irksome mystery now feels like a grace, locking me out of a third expenditure I might not have capacity to pay.

All this while I stood there thinking, *Steady on, Emma. Surely you are overreacting?*

"I know I am," I answered aloud to myself. A deep breath. "I understand. Only it isn't…" Wishing I had another scrap of iron to throw, I made an effort to laugh. "Never fear," I proclaimed, dusting my hands. "All is well. I am only trying to distract you from winning the final throw."

Islington tapped his finger on one of the horseshoes in his hand and said, "Little hope of that, Lion."

Needless to say, Islington secured the points he needed to win.

Later

Islington and Mariana have left to sup with family friends of long standing, graciously excusing Hawkes and I from joining.

A quarter of an hour after they left, when I was crossing the hall in process of traversing the house from the library to the south portico, Hawkes said, "Do I need to confiscate Coleridge?"

I stopped and looked up at the grand staircase. Hawkes sat midway up the stair, as if it were a perfectly normal thing. He was looking tired in a way he had not since we arrived.

Some deep internal recess opened to a glimpse behind his eyes, and Hawkes said softly, "*But in one quiet room we three are still together.*"

Dust motes and stillness and late, late afternoon sunshine.

"It's a rather sad line," I replied.

"Yes," Hawkes said. "Breaking and beautiful. Have you spent much time with the portrait?"

Half a mind and half a second, I almost feigned ignorance. But Hawkes was looking like an ancient mystic, serious and dishevelled from a day spent out of doors, and I thought God might frown on my having lied in the face of such honesty. "Their care for one another, so palpable one can hardly bear to look. And yet I keep returning to it, again and again."

"*A friend should bear his friend's infirmities,*" spake the vicar.

How very *Julius Caesar* of him.

"Yes, well," I answered, "in the end Julius was stabbed, wasn't he?"

Hawkes closed the book held loosely in his hand and set it on the stair beside him. "Sometimes we pay high prices."

"How do you bear it, Hawkes?" I asked before I could even understand how much I needed the answer. "How do you serve in the office of vicar and know each painful corner of so many people? Is that why you—" I broke off. There were ten ends to my sentence.

Hawkes simply waited.

I selected the least impertinent way to finish my question, one that walked too closely to the line that Islington had asked me to mind. "Is that why you keep your distance?"

"I keep my distance, not to avoid burden. It is to spare others."

Irritation rose up, a consequence of these knotted days. "Is it only your decision to make?"

He sat looking at me.

I did not withdraw my challenge.

We waited in a stalemate.

Mrs. Harrison and a maid came through. Neither had been warned the hall had become a court where methods of friendship were being tried, but with discreet grace they were gone through to the other side. All the while I stared at Hawkes—a shard of late afternoon sun cutting across his person, his blue eyes lit as if by holy fire.

"It may very well need to be," he finally answered. "But I don't believe my secrets are the ones that have agitated you, Miss Lion." An attempt at a smile. "At least, not at present."

"You think I am angry at Islington—?"

"Not Islington," Hawkes interrupted, his words firm but calm.

"Why would I be angry at Pierce?" I said, as if I wasn't convincing myself. "What is more pitiable, what would draw more compassion, than what I saw?"

"I never said I was speaking about the tragedy of his childhood."

The words cut across my heart just like the light cut across Hawkes.

"I'm not angry at Pierce for— You've no idea what we've… I'm only worried."

"And." Strange, how it wasn't a question.

But there were words behind the door Hawkes opened. "And he needn't tell me everything, but burying it in the manner he does is… difficult."

"And."

"And I wish the two of you hadn't let him drink himself into oblivion in Lockwell."

"And."

"And what if he does not return on Monday because he's not coping in London without us?"

"He has Chambers."

I may have made a sound of disregard. "A small comfort."

"It should be a great comfort," Hawkes replied. "He has saved Pierce before."

It wasn't in censure.

But as it was in truth, I felt a sharp edge. The cut stung.

And I did not know how to ask if Chambers had saved Pierce on the battlefield, from alcohol, or some other way?

"And," Hawkes added, "I sent Chambers a telegram."

Something fell. How else to describe? Something fell from my shoulders and broke against the hard marble of the checkered hall at my feet. Burden, I suppose, would be the name of it. "You did?"

"I did. And I go to St. Crispian's tomorrow morning to give my sermon. Pierce and I will return together."

It was rather dusty in that hall.

The housekeeper should pay more attention.

As I was without any handkerchief to speak of, I blinked it away. No words came to mind and so I followed Hawkes's form. "And."

"I won't leave him behind."

"And."

"We will not be forgotten. The four of us. We are not so easily disbanded."

I blinked again. "And."

"As of this moment, we are friendship-bound. No matter what winds blow, the fact that this has happened is immutable. Everything in the future may change, but our present claims something stronger than change."

"What is that?"

"Truth. We are a truth. You, Pierce, Islington, and myself."

"And?" Now it was a question. Was there more?

"And we followed Pierce to Lockwell so that we could bring him safely home."

A minute, then two.

"Thank you," I managed, in the full vulnerability of honest answers, in the quiet of a great house.

"I don't particularly wish to dress for dinner," came Hawkes's response.

A messy laugh. "Nor do I."

"I'll speak to Mrs. Knowlls to prepare a basket for you, if you'll ask Isla for a pair of trousers."

"Pardon?"

"A golden sun still to set, the smell of moss and mud, crickets, and plenty of pain to wash away. I thought it would be obvious that you would go swimming this evening."

And so that is how I found myself alone at the bend, remembering the feeling of water holding up a body. Green trousers from Isla, a young man's shirt, more movement than I've felt in ages, and the smell of dark, wise water speaking philosophy with the trees.

Later

I was in my nightgown, lying awake, thoughts edging a small, seemingly insignificant place called Nettle, when I heard a knock on the door. Standing, taking three steps to the door, I undid the lock and turned the knob, expecting Isla.

There in the darkness stood Hawkes.

His cheeks were wind-red, eyes bright in the lamplight coming from the writing desk.

He smelled of dusk and woodland and starlight.

"Hawkes, have you been out walking?" I whispered.

"I have," he said, as if he were still out of breath. "I've just returned. Cake?" Then he lifted his right hand, which held a plate of fine bone china with a fat, tired slice of cake lying on its side. Thrusting it towards me, Hawkes waited for me to take it before he said, "Open your window. A scented breeze fit for Oberon's court." Then, "Don't worry, Emma Lion."

June 22nd

I am using a borrowed fountain pen—"Don't fling this one into the shrubbery, Lion"—for as I was writing this afternoon on the colonnade looking over the courtyard garden, I stood without realising my fountain pen from the Jane Eyre Society was half out of my pocket. It fell, landing on the stone with an air of disillusionment and betrayal. But I, stepping forward to pick it up, errantly kicked it with the toe of my boot and sent it flying into a long line of shrubbery between stairs. Just as I was gazing down, determined to fetch my pith hat and enter this Derbyshire jungle, I was called in for luncheon.

Now that I'm sitting down to write, I've remembered my pen abandoned in the shrubbery. Thinking it ~~best~~ ~~wise~~ ~~prudent~~ a lovely evening for a stroll in the verge, I intend to rescue it posthaste.

Later

I had meant to take my lamp, then, discarding it, I took a candle and small vesta instead, descending the staircase. Instead of breaking out on the first floor and walking out onto the colonnade, I continued to the ground floor and quietly escorted myself out of a door that led to the stone walkway below. Doing so, I found myself coming right out to the line of shrubbery where my delusions said I would have no problem locating my pen by candlelight.

Instead, once I'd climbed into the shrubs and forged something of a way through, I found myself eavesdropping on an ~~argument~~ ~~conversation~~ ~~debate~~ discussion between siblings.

"...but Henry, what could you possibly be thinking?"

"Is this about the cricket again? Emma was likely bored stiff from embroidering half the day."

"I'm not speaking of cricket. I perfectly understand women are human beings. It is everything else to which I refer. For example, when Hawkes and Mr. Pierce were fighting—"

"Boxing."

"Whatever you wish to call it."

"This is Stonecrop, Mariana. A gathering of my friends at Stonecrop."

"Yes, and it carries all the leeway Stonecrop affords you. The relaxed expectations, eschewing of certain formal duties, trusted servants, I understand. Only, she isn't your sister. She isn't actually your ward—"

"She is in the eyes of London."

"—and when you promised you would explain the whole debacle, I didn't… I didn't expect—"

A snap from Islington at her hesitation. "Didn't expect what?"

Her words came like a spear thrown of necessity by a regretful soldier, "Which one are you trying to replace, Henry?"

Night silence in the country is louder than one remembers. An owl's call, insects, the sound of leaves rustling. And when one is hiding in shrubbery, one's heart trammels and the air in and out of one's lungs is like the east wind. I was *certain* they both knew I was there but I could not risk the noise of leaving. Nor could I catch a sinking heart at hearing Mariana's question.

Islington's words, when he answered, sounded like the continuation of a sigh. "Neither, Mariana. I'm replacing neither."

"Henry." A pause. "She clearly…"

Mariana broke off her own sentence.

Clearly what?

~~I wished to know.~~

I demanded to know.

"And what if I were to tell you," Islington stated, "that Lion—that *Miss* Lion," he corrected, and it sounded like a response to an expression received. He started again. "If Hannah and Becca were here, she could walk through the door of our friendship and hold down the last corner."

The conversation stilled. Until, "Do you mean that?"

"Utterly and completely."

Utterly.

And completely.

Islington would place me utterly and completely into some corner of his life that I don't understand. His loyalty was a stay as I sat huddled, afraid of the barest movement. Afraid of swallowing too loudly. Afraid that someone was trying to dismantle the four of us, even though Mariana did not sound like she was trying to do anything of the sort. But Mariana was wishing to rein something in that has grown glorious and wild. I could feel the potent freedom of my father against the wise convention of my mother, warring.

Mariana's answering line was severe. "Then you must protect her, Henry. Her reputation. Her standing."

"I will."

"Henry—"

"I won't let her fall!"

I would swear a full minute passed. There was a silence, the meaning of which I was not privy. Then Mariana said, "Oh, dearest."

"I will protect her." It was reactionary, the words loud but sharpened on one side, then as a quieter addendum, "We all will."

"And what of when London discovers you are not, in actuality, her guardian?"

"Mariana," he said her name like it was a complete sentence, in a tone demanding she understand something.

"She isn't Hannah. Nor is she—"

"Please, don't."

"The three of you were young. You were children. You grew up together. There were conventions half ignored because of such things. Henry, look at me. Henry. You are nearly thirty-one years old. You can't pretend…"

"Mariana, this friendship, *these* friendships, the four of us—*this* alchemy—if you could see it—"

"I do see it, Henry. One can't *help* but see it."

An impatient sigh.

"The four of you together create such… What is one to even call it?" Mariana asked. "Just watching you, Hawkes at his ease, Miss Lion fresh and unbroken. She is intelligent." A noise from Mariana that sounded like she was strangling some amusement. "I like her, only she does say the most unexpected things."

A sound of assent.

"As for Mr. Pierce, he is not what I was expecting."

Islington had loosened, they both had, for her comment brought about a laugh. "What were you expecting?"

"We both know that Pierce is the sort of man who wields power simply by existing. Don't look at me so. I *like* the man."

As if their words were stones thrown in a pond, they waited, letting all the ripples settle.

When Islington spoke again, it was confessional. "You know better than anyone, what the last decade cost."

A break. "I do know."

"Then don't, please, don't tell me that there isn't some grace being afforded. I have three friends, these three friends whom I trust with my very life. We've all found something of a respite, something of a—"

"But she is made vulnerable."

Islington answered with frustrated laughter. "I know. I understand, more than you believe I do. There are…dammit, there are complications and plenty of caution to be had, and I am trying to hold my patience in the face of them. But you also have to remember that Miss Lion isn't the daughter of a duke, Mariana. She's not titled. Her aunt may be, but Emma has no interest in this world that you and I are forced to inhabit our entire lives. Emma walks outside so many of these trappings. It's one of the compelling things about her. The circumstances of her life allow this. She is of age. She owns a house. She runs her household—though that might be calling it a bit too rich as it is the maddest, most wonderful place you've ever seen. She works—or attempts to work, when she's not covered in the ashes of some deceased pet. But that's beside the point."

Another space.

Mariana now the first to break silence. "I know her father did a great deal for you, *meant* a great deal. And you wish to recompense—"

"Don't discredit—"

"—him in some way."

"It has nothing to do with Declan! Mariana, I knew. From the first time I saw her last year in that stupid library, attempting—" he took a breath. "She was attempting to explain Pliny in a most erroneous fashion." A laugh then, the sort pulled from depth after depth.

"What did you know?"

"That we share a tangled fate. No, let me finish. Independent of her father, independent of Hannah or Becca or *anything*, she—in and of herself—claims a portion of me. I want her here. I want her welcomed. I want Stonecrop to be for Emma what it is for Hawkes: a sanctuary. I want that for Emma. I want that for Hawkes. I want that for Pierce, of whom you seem to disapprove."

"I *don't* disapprove. I very much like Mr. Pierce and he is welcome here as often as you invite him. He knows a great deal of this world, that much is clear. And so we have you, and Hawkes, and Pierce, and thrown into such a dynamic camaraderie, Miss Lion. One only has to look at her to see how much she believes—"

"What?"

"That every ship can be righted."

The idea shook something loose in me, but I'm not certain what. What did she mean, exactly? That I am naive despite my losses? Or foolhardy? Or blithely optimistic? Or did she mean I'd retained a sense of faith in humankind and…?

Mariana is not unreasonable, and—as acting chaperone—has right to voice opinion. Only her worry kept bringing to mind a future in which I've overcome everything only to sink in the end.

But Islington began to defend, saying, "St. Crispian's is the—"

"St. Crispian's is a wonderful peculiarity which allows you all to think you can write your own rules. Heaven forbid the rest of London ever encroach on the place. But life is not so forgiving. As her friend, Henry—the friend with the most influence and power—you have to protect her better than you are now."

"The entirety of her life is not mine to control."

"You understand what I mean."

Nothing said for a moment, and I, uncomfortable and curious and embarrassed and…astounded, really, let myself sit back on the ground, my tired feet tingling from the relief.

"She has a chaperone," Islington attempted.

A pause with a palpable snap of patience from Mariana. "Who isn't real!"

Islington began to laugh, just then. He laughed harder than I've ever before heard. "You should have seen—" he tried to say but could not finish. It was some moments before the sound diminished and trailed off into the dark.

When Mariana spoke, it was in concession. "As she means so very much to you, the family will act in accordance. We will corroborate your role. I must needs make myself a visible force."

"You don't have—"

"I do."

"You hate London."

"A strong word. I only prefer not to be there. My public approbation of Miss Lion can only help protect her vulnerabilities."

"You don't—"

"I am not saying I plan to turn my own life upside down to do so. I am expecting my sixth child, Henry. Only we both know my calling on her and then inviting her to dine with the right people will smooth a few wrinkles."

Another pause. "As much as I would love, at times, to grant myself the power, I am not here to manage Lion. As Hawkes reminds me."

"Only you are now her guardian, for all intents and purposes. The two of you need to be honest regarding what this will entail. A strategy must be in place. She must understand what is at stake, and I hope you do the same."

"Were you so fastidious with Maggie?" Islington said.

"Maggie has nothing to do with this, Henry. Maggie has always been a relentless fire."

"And every time I wished to rein her in, you would—"

"Maggie was determined to do something brash and foolish. Her eloping with a man of means—a good man, thank God for that—was the best of all pending possibilities. You and Maggie are water and oil."

"We didn't used to be."

"No," Mariana released a breath. "It is regretful. You must remember, dearest, that Maggie was young. She followed Father's lead."

"When it came to her treatment of me. Not in anything else."

"Yes, and as the youngest daughter of this house, Maggie was never going to be left without recourse."

"And neither will Emma."

There was nothing said for a stretch of minutes, feeling so pulled and quiet I almost thought one or both of them had left. Just as I was going to free myself, Mariana began to speak.

"A bespoke set," she said. "I must admit."

"Pardon?" Islington asked.

"The four of you, the friendship. I saw intimations when the three of you first arrived—an envious camaraderie. But Mr. Pierce arrived and a key turned, the four of you locking into place. I can't claim to understand, but I can see what you have, Henry. Unexpected."

"Unexpected," Islington echoed. "And necessary."

"Necessary," I whispered to myself.

We three sat, they unaware of a third party. Once they had retired to bed, I crawled from the shrubbery and—relieved to find the door I had used before still unlocked—returned back to my tower.

Pen from the Janes yet unfound.

June 23rd

A letter for Hawkes has been waiting for his return this morning.

The scent of pear lingering.

Later

Pierce and Hawkes are at Stonecrop.

Islington and I were shooting before they arrived. Bow and arrow, however he tried to convince me to side with shotgun and pigeon. My four pinned butterflies represent all the blood I care to have on my hands at present.

The diversion was a rather silent exercise.

I, spinning through the entire overheard conversation from evening last.

He? I couldn't say. Possibly the same.

(The lot of the eavesdropper is a heavy one. And as much as I think I enjoy knowing secrets, I've decided there is a limit to how much I actually wish to know.)

"Islington," I said, my arrow flying wildly over the straw target.

"That was your poorest shot of the day."

"Oh, I've still plenty of room to disappoint."

He took his shot. Hitting the target but not in any impressive, dead-centre sort of fashion. Out of character, from what I've seen. "You were going to say something, Lion?" Islington shot again. The arrow went wide. "Damn." A frown. "Apologies for my language." He half turned and looked at me. "Why do I recognise that expression? Oh, don't tell me. You wish to confess something. Grant me patience. What is it, Lion?"

I ~~gaped~~ slightly gaped; Islington having rather astutely read my face. "With an invitation like that, one hardly knows where to start."

"Go on."

I could not, I discovered, make myself confess that I had been in the shrubbery. But there were other secrets I did not know how to keep buried. "I've seen the portrait in the gallery, of you and…your sister, and friend." I rushed on so as not to lose courage, "Only, I thought you should know."

Islington nodded, even as his eyes narrowed and he looked towards the lake. Still, he moved his head slightly up and down, as if agreeing with some pronouncement only he could hear. "A fine piece. D'Ouro was the artist, actually. It had been in storage for a number of years before Mariana returned it to the gallery last autumn."

"It's extraordinary."

A caught sound, the single-syllable confirmation that also implied a pain of some sort. "It was, Lion. It was."

We stood there a moment, a breeze promising a clouded afternoon. Whatever else the subtle exorcism had accomplished, there felt to be a measure of relief between us.

"I've been meaning to tell you, I found your pen from the Jane Eyre Society. Yesterday afternoon. It is cleaned and polished, waiting for you in the library."

"Why, thank you!"

"Of course."

"If you would have told me yesterday, I wouldn't have over— I wouldn't have over worried."

And then Pierce and Hawkes arrived.

Hawkes looked tired, but Pierce? Pierce seemed weary to the bone, only just sewn together.

I smiled at them both and tried not to stare.

"Mrs. Knowlls promised something wonderful upon your return," I said.

The last final steps, Islington stepping forward to shake their hands, and I holding myself back when all I wished to do was throw my arms around each of them in turn, and whisper how happy I was to see them both back again.

Later

I lit a candle tonight. I lit more than one, and set them in all the windows, the south tower blazing through the clouds.

June 24th

Maggie and Jonathan Revel have arrived.

And what a blast of gunpowder!

It wasn't anyone's particular intention, but the general hour of their arrival was known, and we had all found ourselves knotted in the hall. So it was only natural we stepped out to greet the Revels upon their arrival.

Jonathan Revel is a lean figure—taut with confidence and natural athleticism refined by tremendous amounts of wealth. Brown hair, blue-grey eyes, immediately likeable presence however sharp his observations, with a sense of unassuming intellect.

He stepped out and offered a hand, which was scarcely used as Maggie propelled herself from the coach. It was not throwing herself from a hot air balloon, but it was with as much command. Maggie looks like a Devereux—same dark hair, positively golden eyes, patrician instinct. But while Islington and Mariana have turned towards elegance, Maggie is all sophistication and untamed amusement.

"Mariana, darling," she greeted first, while Islington and Mr. Revel shook hands.

"Henry," Maggie said, kissing his cheek.

"Maggie," Islington replied.

She smirked at him in a manner that I've decided was, yes, I'm going to write it, decidedly off-putting. Pierce was two steps before Hawkes and I, and he received a king's greeting.

"Pierce, old boy," said Jonathan, and they embraced with a quick slap on each other's back. Maggie had just said something to Islington—I couldn't hear what—and burning with a bright smile, turned to Pierce.

"Pierce! You came just to keep me company, I know it."

And she…

Well.

She grabbed the collar of his coat, lifted herself up on her tiptoes and kissed Pierce in assertive greeting.

It was *not* a kiss on the cheek.

Nary a soul seemed surprised, although Islington rolled his eyes at Mariana, and Pierce held up his hands in self-protection, saying, "I take it you missed me?"

"Jonathan and I are bored out of our minds. Why don't you come for a visit? Why, he'll not even let me shoot a gun if I've had a single drink."

"Oh, she usually manages to find one," said Mr. Revel to an Islington who was using all his self-control to hold his peace.

"Young Hawkes!" Maggie had caught sight of Hawkes standing halfway up the stairs, book pinned beneath his arm, hands in his pockets.

"Maggie," he said with equal affection but less volume, as if he knew she was all antics, and it did not throw his balance.

"Your friendship is one of the few good decisions Henry has made!" she said, blowing him a kiss accompanied with a wink.

It was a rather fetching thing.

At this juncture the grouping had shifted, and Mariana was introducing Mr. Revel.

"A great pleasure, Miss Lion," he said affably.

"I've heard many wonderful things about you, Mr. Revel," I replied.

But when Mariana attempted to make introductions between myself and Maggie, it was as if the youngest Devereux had gone deaf. Selectively.

"Maggie," Islington put his hand on her shoulder and physically turned her around. "This is Miss Lion, a great friend."

"Hmm. Hello." And it was said with less enthusiasm than anything else she'd yet uttered.

"Lion, my youngest sister, Maggie Revel."

"Hello, Mrs. Revel."

Eyes slightly widened. "Oh, let's not do that."

And she turned back around, her arm linked with Mariana's as she walked up the stairs and into the house. The party loosely followed. Pierce, speaking with Mr. Revel as they went. Hawkes, mussing his hair in thought, glancing at Islington and I before he wordlessly followed.

"She," Islington said, "is a treasure."

And we looked at one another, I with some amazement. "Is she always so…?"

"Rude?" Islington assumed. "She's whatever she wishes to be. I'll try to keep her jabs from your direction. I'm usually the one in the party with whom she has her fun. You, however, are not a known quantity, and not primed to find her as enchanting as everyone else. But a little time and you will."

"Will I?"

We began to walk up the stairs and Islington grimaced. "You'll see."

And I did.

Maggie Revel can twist a room around her finger and spin it like a plate. I can only imagine what a regular social gathering is like. She must make everyone eat out of her hands.

But Stonecrop, I suspect, was different.

She was among her own people. They knew her. No one to be dazzled by her charm, beauty, sense of humour, sharpened on both edges. Maggie employed all these, of course, but she was home, entertained to be so. And good to her people.

Except Islington.

We found ourselves in a drawing room, being served coffee and tea, bread and cheese. She, Jonathan, and Pierce clearly have shared a friendship of long-standing. Hawkes, she knows from his visits to Stonecrop. We found ourselves having a lengthier introduction conducted by Mariana and Maggie ~~behaved~~ almost behaved.

"Yes, he's written of you."

I, naturally, was curious *which* he, exactly.

But Pierce had asked her something and her response had made almost everyone laugh.

"Everyone loves Hawkes," was one of the few things said directly to me before supper.

"True," I'd replied.

Maggie actually seemed to respect Mariana.

As for Islington?

"It always feels so lacklustre when I arrive, Henry. The place picks up too much of your personality and we're all left a bit parched."

"Would you like a drink?" he replied, evenly. The looseness I've witnessed in Islington all month carefully locked away.

"Not everything can be solved with the physical. See, that's what I mean, not a metaphysical bone in your body."

Pierce was in conversation with Jonathan Revel, but Hawkes caught the comment, as did I.

That was when Pierce called, "Emma, you should come and hear this."

"You think she would find the stables interesting?" Maggie asked, also coming over and sitting on the arm of the chair where her husband sat.

"Why not?" Pierce asked. He invited me to sit beside him and went about explaining his investments with Mr. Revel, and what they were trying to accomplish with the stables.

Maggie looked annoyed at my interest.

We had a, well, is genial too strong a word? Yes, it is. But it was a conversation nonetheless, about my father, his oeuvre, his ethos. As she was genuinely curious and asked intelligent questions, I did feel interesting for a full twenty minutes.

We changed for supper. Around the table, the Devereux siblings were reminiscing on their childhood. Strange, how they would say "we" quite often, but none of them mentioned Hannah by name.

It was mildly frustrating to find Maggie so amusing. I could see why Jonathan loves her—for he clearly does. Perhaps a portion of their balance comes from his willingness to call out her affrontery with an unserious yet solid retort. Islington mostly takes her humour good-naturedly, although I could see he was thinking beneath thinking beneath thinking. He would take it as jest when she said the like of, "But you've never been one to really lead out with your life, now have you, Henry?"

Twice, perhaps three times, Maggie *did* look at Islington as if she thought him so terribly fine a person, as if her love ran deep as anything else in her blood. But then came dismissal, and a jest filled with disappointment.

And I would try not to watch Islington's expression too long, wondering what he really thought of the scarcely veiled barbs.

She never slighted Mariana.

She never slighted Hawkes.

She never slighted Pierce.

As for me? She seemed to have her occasional fun being mostly splendid and then saying the like of, "They say you are Henry's ward, of which he's never said a jot. But what frilly business. I'm surprised you put up with it all. It takes real spirit, I suppose, not to fall for such limitations."

And I would open my mouth—a time or two with a clever line—that I never managed to say before she'd changed the course of conversation.

There was one moment when Pierce said, "Don't be such a pill, Maggie." No venom, nothing bent out of shape, only someone who wasn't going to put up with her shenanigans.

"You're right," Maggie said, owning herself for a moment. Then, surprisingly, an aside made to me, "There are few people who can catch me up short, Miss Lion. Johnny for one, Pierce a close second. He's never let me get away with anything. There you are, Henry. What have you done with the Rembrandt etching? I was hoping to steal it for my own collection."

After which, she launched into a story of her attempting to acquire a byzantine mural, making herself the fool of the tale, eyes sparkling, brutally honest about every one of her foibles coming to bear in a debacle so entertaining that the entire room was left in near tears. Even Islington lifted a hand to conceal his half smile while declaring her the embarrassment of the family.

The evening finished with Jonathan Revel and I playing a card game he calls Kingdoms, which is all chance and no skill. Back and forth, back and forth, until his luck grew bored and he won the entire thing.

June 25th

The Walk 'Round was planned for today and Hawkes—in an understated yet definitive manner—informed me it was a highlight of a visit to Stonecrop and I'd not want to miss. Pierce had settled himself in the library with a week's worth of newspapers, so I—not wishing the realities of life to crash so headlong into the remnants of my June—decided to join Hawkes.

We followed behind the three Devereux siblings, observing them—as one might a pride of African cats—~~decide~~ ~~debate~~ argue over what improvements and changes, if any, ought to be made during the course of the calendar year.

It was a spectacle of opinion, insult, and crossing enemy lines to side with a former ally.

There were arguments aplenty, and the siblings were not above recalling past slights to bring about their desired result.

Hawkes—who in my mind is never one to be amused by the bickering of others…at least, not too terribly much—seemed to take the entire exercise as a personal entertainment.

"Yes, dear," Mariana was saying, "but you were also the seventeen-year-old young man who believed yellow was your colour."

Islington narrowed his eyes, "Irrelevant."

"Made you look jaundiced," Maggie agreed. "Remember how Walpole wouldn't let you step into the rose garden if you were sporting that daffodil waistcoat?"

"Which calls to mind a certain chartreuse affair," Islington said, a side-glance at Mariana.

"It was for Eliza's wedding and couldn't be helped. Forced couture is a far cry from chosen attitude of style, Henry. Now, the curtains in this room should be cream, with terracotta and olive green stripes around the perimeter."

Islington and Maggie both paused to consider.

Then at the very same time,

> Islington: "Ideal, I should think."
> Maggie: "Ghastly! How staid!"

"Not all of us wish to look like we have joined the bohemian circus, Maggie." This, of course, was Islington.

"No one would credit you with half so much imagination, Henry."

Mariana ignored them both, envisioning her curtains with satisfaction.

"Once I have a wife, neither of you will have the right to utter a single word regarding the decoration of Stonecrop. I should marry just to spite you both."

"Please do!" the sisters said in unison.

"Only, don't make her a terrible bore." This was Maggie. "Marry someone with whom I can have a glorious row."

Islington had moved on. "Next we go to the library. Tread with care. And let me reiterate I've no intention of applying a camel embroidery to *anything*." A pointed look at Maggie.

"If you're looking for something closer to form, Islington, I amend my suggestion to include the jackass."

And with that, she waltzed past Islington while he gave her an expression lined with daggers.

"Do be civil," Mariana chided them both. "I thought we drew the line at animal insults after the baboon debacle five years ago?"

It wasn't long before I abandoned the familial vaudeville and went out to the south portico, finding Jonathan Revel sitting with a paper, a drink, and—of all things—a tray filled with fairy cakes.

"Care to join me, Miss Lion?"

I sat in the chair on the other side of the laden tray. "Fairy cakes, Mr. Revel?"

"Jonathan, please."

"I'll accept your Jonathan in exchange for an Emma, if it suits."

Mr. Revel looked up and smiled. "My youngest sister is named Emma."

"She must be a delight."

"Bit of a prude, really, but your existence balances the weights and measures of this world."

I reviewed my comportment of the last few days and felt he had no grounds to make such a comment. "What have you been told and by whom? I would be willing to sue any number of my friends for libel.

Especially Islington, as he is so comfortably established."

Mr. Revel grinned and took a sip of his whisky. Something about the action caught my attention. And was reinforced this evening once I'd decided to observe. It was this: Jonathan did not seem to need the stuff. A single glass might stretch over several hours. He did not find his way back to it again and again the way that Pierce does...

Bother.

I return to the portico.

"Please," Jonathan said. "Have a fairy cake. The cook makes them especial for my arrival."

"An unusual pairing."

"I like them," Mr. Revel said, his American accent sharpened against the rounder vowels.

I picked up the delicious yellow cake and took a bite. To my surprise, a chocolate toffee pudding waited inside, causing near disaster. But I managed to catch the toffee before it fell onto my dress, turning half away as I handled the unexpected onslaught with sheer perseverance of will, placing the majority of the cake in my mouth as quickly as possible, and using my fingers to wipe the dripping chocolate from my chin.

Most elegant.

Mr. Revel, without looking up, withdrew a clean, pressed handkerchief from his pocket and wordlessly handed it across to me.

"A trifle messy," I said, once I was capable of speech.

Now he looked up. "But ever so good. The cook has promised a tray each time I visit. Have another."

I did. Careful this time to keep the chocolate and toffee pudding from threatening all and sundry. As I ate, I wondered again over the unusual yet...somehow perfect pairing of Jonathan and Maggie.

"You look like you have a question you're not asking. Go on. I don't mind."

"*Ah.*"

Jonathan smiled at me in recognition of the tone. He thought it funny.

"You and Maggie. However did you—? Well, that is, never mind. Even when given permission to ask a question, I don't think it polite to enquire how, er, certain things..."

"How Maggie and I came to be? To put it mildly, she blackmailed me."

I blinked and dropped my fairy cake. It fell, luckily, on the handkerchief spread over my lap. I picked it back up. "Blackmailed?"

"Or would the word be shanghaied?" He said, enjoying my startle. "As much as the Elders of the Devereux family are disinclined to admit, Maggie had decided that a life with me would be a jolly good romp in comparison to anything she could find here in Merry Old England."

"She shanghaied you? But doesn't that imply…kidnapping someone on a ship?"

Here Mr. Revel gazed across the lake and narrowed his eyes in amused remembrance. "It was a rowboat. She had managed to hire two French sailors to, eh, bind my hands and feet and set me down in the waiting boat. Once she had finished her lessons and attended a polite tea with her classmates—under the watchful eye of that dreadful Madame La Coste—she sauntered her way down to the cove and climbed into the boat, laughing that I'd been waiting like a trussed pig for nearly two hours. She then rowed out to sea and proposed. After presenting her blackmail, that is, and all the reasons why she thought we'd get along famously."

I am certain I sat looking like the most disapproving killjoy that ever walked the planet. I couldn't imagine thinking such a thing was acceptable in ~~any~~ most circumstances!

Maggie Devereux, at sixteen years of age, paid two sailors to kidnap, tie up, and place in a rowboat one Mr. Revel, wealthy American businessman ten years her senior!

I. KNOW. NOT. WHAT. TO. SAY.

My entire life of misadventures feels like a pale sham of conglomerate effort.

My dancing on the stage of The Drunken Duck?

Child's play.

"You look shocked," Mr. Revel said, bringing me back to the present. "Perhaps I had misjudged your sense of *joie de vivre*." I daresay he had, to a degree. Emma M. Lion is a great many things, but I have never considered paying sailors to kidnap a grown man and cast off to sea in nothing more than a rowboat. The scenario has never crossed my mind.

Nary a once.

I cannot decide if I am pleased as punch to discover I am a much more conventional specimen than others believe me to be, or if my weak imagination and comfortable courage have let me down.

"Not shocked," I managed to say. (I was shocked.) "Only, how on earth did Islington not perish outright from a fit of disapproval?"

Revel smiled. "Come to think of it, I don't think he's ever been told about the rowboat. He did discover that she had climbed into my hotel room through the outside window—that was small contribution to the blackmail portion of the whole romantic business, but the rowboat..."

I blinked.

I thought of Maggie Devereux climbing into the window of a hotel.

"Miss Lion?"

"Yes," I said, looking at him with untampered honesty. "Such a scheme has never once crossed my mind, and I find myself at the height of disappointment in my own imagination. Troubling, as I've always considered it so very robust."

At this Jonathan Revel laughed.

Before I could further enquire—

What did she say?

What did he think?

—Maggie herself came out onto the portico. "There you are, Johnny. Oh, don't tell me she's baked you fairy cakes. Really. Sometimes I think I married a child. Hello, Miss Lion. You look like a sick trout. Any particular reason?"

"I..."

!

"I've just told Miss Lion how you kidnapped me in a rowboat."

"Impressive," I managed, finding my speech. "An escapade that creates more questions than it gives answers."

Maggie narrowed her eyes at me. "Well played," she said, then her gaze flicked to Jonathan, for whom the two words were intended. "What do you want, Miss Lion?" Maggie continued. "Money? Introductions? Jewellery?"

Before I could say, "Pardon?" I realised the root of the entire game. Mr. Revel had given me something with which to keep Maggie at bay.

Blackmail, if one must use the apt term.

It gave me courage. "I take it Mariana and Islington don't know the whole?"

Maggie narrowed her eyes at me. "Jonathan wants me to play nice with you, Miss Lion. Then nice it will be. What is your price? Since Jonathan here was the one who let the cat out of the bag, I can only assume he's willing to pay from his own purse. You look like the sort of young woman who could use a great deal more money than you have."

She eyed my ensemble—as if I were a dead rat—and looked back up at my face.

I did not mean to say it out loud. It was a thought for my head only. But so potent was the personality of this Maggie Devereux Revel that the thought came with enough strength to be articulated.

"You are odious and fascinating, by turns. I don't know which carries more weight."

The half second and I'd imagined several fates, not excluding a fairy cake smashed against my face. Instead, Maggie tilted her lovely head, her eyes flashing a moment before saying, "There is hope for you yet, I see."

I did not know if this were compliment or insult.

I still don't.

But being willing to brazen it out, I replied, "I like to think of myself as someone who knows how to honour a confidence. I will, however, keep newly acquired knowledge close at hand, should the need arise."

Maggie, eyeing me in that indecipherable manner, leaned over Jonathan in a rather provocative way, picked up his whisky, swallowed the whole without so much as blinking an eye, and dropped the glass. As if from habit, Jonathan caught it smoothly and, without making comment, set the glass back on the table.

Maggie disappeared into the house.

"Pity," Jonathan said after a moment, "about the whisky."

He then reopened his newspaper and continued reading.

The mystery of becoming someone's accidental wife has paled in comparison to having kidnapped one's future spouse and rowed them out to sea. Jonathan and Maggie Revel must have the most amusing, spectacular, and, well, *tiresome* marriage in all the world.

Later

I said something this evening to Mariana and Maggie about the view from the south tower. Maggie interrupted.

"Not the South Tower?"

"Yes, that's where my room is."

Maggie had looked directly at Islington. "The South Tower, Islington? I can't see why that was necessary."

"I thought Miss Lion would like the view," Islington had replied. "You yourself insist on keeping your room in the north for that very reason." And he turned back to Jonathan, with whom he was speaking. But Maggie was put out. "You never do seem to manage, do you Henry?"

And it was one of those misshapen moments where everyone has stopped talking and the words stood on their own for far too long. And as much as I wished Islington to say the likes of, "I seem to be managing you, don't I?" he looked at her levelly and said, "I'm certain I don't do as well a job as you would, but I thank you for your patience."

Mariana, who loves her sister and had had enough, waited until the conversation of the room had returned before discreetly taking her sister by the arm and removing her from company.

I have just heard that—oh so regrettably—Jonathan and Maggie are to make an early start. They'll be off first thing.

Pity.

June 26th

Last night I was awakened by a hand being placed across my mouth. It was terrible, the blink of realisation and then a thrash, where I threw myself out the opposite side of the bed. I found myself staring at Maggie Revel, a single candle in her hand.

"Jonathan and I leave in the morning," she said.

"And you're determined to strangle me before you go, I see," I replied in my fluster.

"I don't like a good many things about you." It was said in independent declaration.

I have been disliked before.

Only Maggie's dislike was like a battering ram splintering every defensible door.

"You do have certain qualities I can appreciate," she added. Also an independent declaration.

I wasn't certain which statement I should distrust more. And just as I was about to say so, she said, "Get dressed now. There is something I've been wanting to do a good many years now and you're going to help me see it done."

And Maggie walked over to the desk, sat down in the chair, and waited.

I had two choices before me. One might define them as Self-Respect and Curiosity.

Having respected myself a great deal over the years, I chose the latter.

And thus it came to be that Maggie Devereux Revel and Emma M. Lion, fitted with all tools necessary, switched the signs on the Stonecrop mazes, renaming the petite, frothy maze as The Gentlemen's Maze, and the challenging, sprawling, sporting specimen as The Ladies' Maze.

Job done, Maggie led us through the Gentlemen's Maze with expert direction, where we climbed the tower in the middle, and spent a few hours glimpsing stars between a fickle covering of clouds. Not much of anything was said between us, Maggie smoking a cigarette with shocking ease all the while.

"I despise this place," she said.

"Why?" I said, my coat wrapped snugly about my person.

She did not answer. Which was expected. She seemed to be the sort of person who liked the attention of a shocking statement without the responsibility of giving it any foundation.

But surprise me she did.

"It's the only place I miss when I'm away. That is why I hate it. Everywhere else, I can take or leave. Most people, too. But Stonecrop?" She smashed her cigarette against the stone she leaned against, the red heat of burning tobacco disappearing into midnight smoke. "It can never be let alone."

I gave her answer no response, but a good deal of internal thought.

And then, "So was it your house? Where he stayed when he was ill?"

A second surprise. "Yes," I said.

"And is he recovered, do you think?"

"I believe he has."

She nodded. Then, "Good."

When I woke, it was in the stiff, invigorating cold of pre-dawn. A silver sky. Birdcall. The surrounding green sleepy and wise. My neck was aching and I was alone on the tower, left to find my way out of the maze.

It took me over an hour.

I am—if Absolute Honesty were required—glad they've gone. It was an amusing splash about, unexpected, painful to observe, and vastly entertaining. I adored Mr. Revel and liked certain aspects of Maggie well enough.

I will, however, allow myself one note. There was a sense that the freedom of all was impacted by Maggie Revel. As if Maggie took the whole of delight on offer to everyone and used it all for her own gain. No room for the enjoyments of others.

Her freedom would always come at the cost of someone else's liberty.

Another way to say it: Fire steals away oxygen, and Maggie Devereux Revel is an unapologetic torch.

Later

I came across Isla walking The Calendar burning sage.

"Oh, hello," I said, brushing the smell of the smoke from before my face. "What, pray, are you doing?"

Isla found it perfectly acceptable to say, "We always burn sage, Miss Lion, all through the house, after Lady Maggie has been for a visit."

Feeling like all of Stonecrop had taken a deep breath and begun anew, I continued on my way.

June 27th

I went down to breakfast just now, admittedly the last to arrive. I had slept deeply for my night in the maze, and it was a task of monumental effort to argue myself away from the comforts of the south tower.

Isla's sage must have done its work, for things felt back to their sprawling field, vine-climbing, elegant state.

Mariana and Islington were discussing cottage repairs.

"Good morning, Emma," said Mariana.

"Hello, Lion. Did you sleep well?"

Light replies and the hasty assorting of my breakfast plate, and I joined them at the table.

"The month gone," I said. "I cannot believe it is our final day at Stonecrop. How shall we while these dwindling hours?"

"Hawkes insists we spend the afternoon playing badminton."

"Ah. What shall be the teams?"

"Yet to be decided," said Islington.

"Speaking of Hawkes," I replied, "Where is he?"

Which was how I was notified that Hawkes had taken the train up the line to a village called Tipsy.

"Tipsy? What does he do there?"

"I cannot speak of it," answered Islington. "For when Hawkes goes to Tipsy, he only invites one person to accompany. And if you speak of it, you are never invited again—which is why Maggie has never been invited. He has a way of knowing." Now Islington stopped. "He had a ticket for you, as it happens, but as you were not awake when he left, he gave it to Pierce."

"Hawkes was going to take me to Tipsy and I missed it!"

"I've only been invited once," said Mariana. "The most peaceful morning of my life."

"And you won't tell me what occurs?"

Mariana smiled warmly and shook her head.

"Well! I'm happy for Pierce. And that means my morning is free to—"

"Finally go riding with me," Islington pronounced. "Unless horses frighten you," he looked at me with something of a challenge.

"Not frighten," I said carefully, "only I've learned through experience—illegal experience, mind you—that fate will sort horse thieves out one way or another."

Islington looked both amused and nonplussed together. "A gentleman's horse is not a joke," he said.

"Alas, sometimes a farmer's is. Now, I will accept your invitation, if you'll make nary a comment regarding wardrobe as I've nothing suitable for riding."

"There are barbarians among us," Islington said to Mariana.

Who, ignoring Islington, said, "You can borrow my habit, Emma."

Later

The excursion on horseback was much more agreeable than I thought it would be, and much slower than Islington had anticipated.

"I don't understand the sedate pace," Islington commented, sitting easily in his saddle, left hand loosely holding the reins. "I've always pictured you riding breakneck across the fields."

"Yes, well, that is an Emma I would very much like to be. Thrill. Chase. The entire persona. However, my parents never owned a horse, and I was banned from my Aunt Eugenia's stables after the incident with the manure. My only truly consistent shows of horsemanship were when Maxwell would take me riding. He would pull me up behind him, and I would throw my arms around his waist, and we would fly." I squinted at the horizon line. For there stood understanding, waiting for me to see. Perhaps the reason I've not cared for the idea isn't Mary and I having flung ourselves off Farmer Strawhun's horse?

Islington, lifting the reins as his horse navigated a tricky bit of field, said, "Was Maxwell your soldier?"

I blinked and glanced at Islington in surprise. "You know something of him?"

Islington shook his head. "Very little. Only that he existed."

A query: Is what I felt in that moment what Islington had felt when I'd spoken of the portrait?

A relief that filled old, complicated corners.

An unobtrusive confirmation of the significance of an old connection valued by a new?

"He was no soldier, despite having become one. But he was a horseman. Maxwell would tear through fields at such a pace, I was certain we were crossing the boundaries of world after world. That the very nature of time could not account for the recklessness."

I was pleased to find it was sweetness, not sting, when I spoke of him.

"But you would never race so when left to your own devices?"

"I rarely rode my own horse."

"I'm not requesting the bending of time out of shape," Islington smiled, "but I do think we might go a little faster than we are at present."

Later

We did play badminton, the four of us. Hawkes and I in fierce battle with Islington and Pierce. I am not a model example of the sport, but Mary and I had won the tournament at Fortitude and were on track to clinch a second trophy when we were discovered by Mrs. Wade. The rackets were confiscated, each birdie systematically plucked before the entire school. There was not a girl left unaffected by the brutal dismemberment.

I digress.

Hawkes and I held our own, although Islington and Pierce did plot and plan their way to eventual victory—five matches to four—despite Pierce's limp.

Preparations are being made for a final bonfire up on the hill. I'm to go down to the kitchens in quarter of an hour. In the meantime, I have been sitting atop my tower attempting to distill my many days in this place down to its essence. And am I changed because of it?

There is a freedom in my body.

It is so very familiar, yet long abandoned for the mandates of adulthood—womanhood, I should say. While I am under no illusions (nor is anyone else of my acquaintance) that I am the ideal execution of what a woman ought to be, I still feel like I've tucked my wings against myself too often. Curtailed? Perhaps trimmed?

My mother had once said something or other about the necessity of this.

But sitting in this high tower, the breeze cooling the sweat on my skin, I have two questions.

When is it necessary?

When is it not?

These long days out of doors feel like coming home to a place to which I've always held the key, but was told it should be put away. But, oh! There has been sovereignty of self in this place—of body, of spirit, of the intangible magic which sews the two together. To shout and run. To lie in tall grasses and watch the wind play the sunlight both true and false. To feel the building threat of rain and watch it crash to earth from the tenuous safety beneath a tree rather than from behind a window.

I am, I suppose, satiating a long drought.

My childhood soul has been left too long abandoned.

How do I best find it in London?

At times I feel my body has betrayed the girl I was, growing past the lithe limbs hewn in independence. We are to be fit for the purposes of adulthood, I know this. Childhood anticipations are traded with the shouldering of heavier things. But these days, these stones-tossed-in-tall-grass days, have stretched my muscles, recalled past forms, and I am remembering how it is to feel, to follow the instincts of something young yet ancient. To step outside the province of maturity and marvel.

Later

As for our final evening on the hill,

> *I count myself in nothing else so happy, as in a soul remembering my good friends.*

And perhaps,

> *Fount, tree and shed are gone, I know not whither,*
> ~~*But in one quiet room we three are still together.*~~
> *But on one quiet hill we four are still together.*

June 28th

The Return to Lapis Lazuli House…

…was lovely.

The four of us sat in Islington's carriage in the same configuration as we had the train, Pierce to my left, Islington directly across from me, Hawkes beside him and at my diagonal. There had been steady conversation all the way home. Nothing too impassioned, neither boring, only summer-mellowed enjoyment. Even Hawkes did not remove his book from his satchel, instead he listened, arms folded, expression sleepy, saying the occasional this or that.

But to turn onto Whereabouts Lane from King Henry's. There, the Reed and Rite. There, the Morrows. There, Mr. Johnson's. And just before the crook in the street, tall and singular, grey limestone with a blue door, was Lapis Lazuli.

My own home.

"Here we are," I said, not waiting for anyone. And I was out on the pavement as Parian opened the front door.

"Parian," Pierce said as he disembarked, "could you give us a hand here?"

Islington was helping with our things. Hawkes having followed, intercepting Cousin Archibald, who was shouting something. Agnes—fresh home from Scotland a week ago—carrying my satchel and pith helmet inside.

The comfortable familiarity in the hall; a hello to Fitz who is still alive; Parian taking my trunk upstairs without a word of complaint; Pierce disappearing into his studio, then reappearing once Agnes had insisted that everyone take tea before disbanding. Cousin Archibald and I managed to remain in the same room, mostly because Hawkes sat beside him the entirety of our tea and listened to every absurd complaint. Islington was listening to Pierce explain another commission he's taken with the British Museum. And I sat in my chair, my own pink chair, and saw that it was good.

The four of us.

We had all been given secrets to keep and we were keeping them.

After, when I went upstairs to wash and change and brace myself for the evening's long obligations, I entered the garret. Tidied and recently cleaned, it smelled of lemons. The bedclothes were crisp. The mirror cleaned. My desk was empty save an inkwell, pen, and a few of the missives Pierce and I had sent through the wall. My green bookshelf—lovely bookshelf—waited with my small but important library. And on the wall, Pierce's photograph of Afghanistan and Saff's sketch of Hawkes. My crown and sceptre had been dusted, and the chair near the window seat waited for me with cushions fluffed. The carpet, as well, looked like it had been taken up and beaten clean.

One should go away long enough to know the cotton-soft contentment of coming home.

The Return to Aunt Eugenia's Ball…

…was a brutal jolt.

If returning to Lapis Lazuli House was a dream, Aunt Eugenia's ball was a night of forced insomnia. Waiting on the sideboard had been an order from said aunt:

Emma,

I send my carriage at five o'clock. I've had Madame Tasset prepare a gown for the occasion. We will sort you into acceptable state here at Spencer House. Be agreeable.

Your Aunt

Thankfully, upon my arrival, Spencer House was in uproar. Decorations, last-minute changes, deliveries and noise. As Aunt Eugenia was nowhere to be found, I was able to make my way straight to Arabella's rooms. I never forget the golden draw of my cousin's beauty, but after a month apart I was reminded why she garners the attention she does.

"You sent me nary a letter, Arabella," I said from the doorway. "Not one."

She, robed and reclining on her chaise longue while a maid set her hair, granted a benevolent smile. "You forget I've heard nothing from you either, my dear Irishman's daughter."

I almost asked if she'd steered quite clear of Lord Croixton, but as Arabella said nothing of the man, I did not wish to tempt fate.

Tea was sent up from the kitchens, and we ate while two maids saw to our toilettes. As for our gowns, Arabella was in sky blue and gold, while my gown was red.

Shockingly vibrant red.

"I will attract every bull in attendance," I muttered as the maid pinned the gown at the waist.

"Did you not eat at Stonecrop?" Arabella asked.

"A great deal. Only, most of the days were spent walking and, well, running about with rackets and nets and books."

"Hmm," Arabella answered in smug yet adoring assessment. "You do look *quite* sporting. Mother will throw a fit."

And a fit she did throw.

We were in the First drawing room, Roland having just arrived. "Greetings and felicitations, chum!" A kiss on both cheeks.

"You smell nice, Roland."

"Something I picked up at that Hound place. The proprietor has the most interesting—"

Aunt Eugenia came bustling in, fan drawn like a Corsican dagger.

"Arabella, Roland." She frowned. "Emma, you've bothered to return, I see. Now— Good heavens! Look how very in the sun you have been. Why, you look positively Iberian!"

"Thank you!"

Aunt Eugenia, working her mouth and pulling her jaw back, steeled herself. It was admirable, really, how she refused to be thwarted. "The violent red was to cast a sickly pallor about your person, but now I find you the picture of health! I implore, nay, I demand you pull every drop of English blood to the surface. The Countess of Ellam is going to be in attendance, you see. As well as her fortunate daughter; fortunate in the basest sense of the word—she's rich. Let us not glorify hermits." With a pause, and a second survey of my person, she managed to convey the entirety of her disapproval. "What was that duke thinking, letting you traipse about—"

"Aunt Eugenia."

"Traipse, Emma! Traipse. I know a Traipsing Woman when I see one, and you fit the very bill. Why, I never saw a woman so Countrified as you this very moment."

"Ma'am," I stated firmly, readying myself to proclaim a Righteous Position I did not hold, "I thought long and hard about how to best aid Arabella in this hour of need, and I've decided to sacrifice myself, allowing a general countrification to occur. My rough-hewn nature will contrast the glorious beauty of my cousin. Isn't that right, Roland?"

Roland, who at this point was gazing with distraction at nothing, was firmly elbowed. "Ouch! Ah, Emma. Yes, whatever you just told Aunt Eugenia."

"That I am a barbarian in contrast to Arabella."

"We all know that," he replied, sliding a golden smile onto his face.

Aunt Eugenia was suspect.

"You mentioned Lady Eloise Silver?" I redirected.

This restored focus. "Yes, yes. *You*, Emma, are to discover what you can about her."

"Really, Aunt."

"Is Eloise Silver going to be in attendance?" Roland chimed in. "I'm certainly glad I came!"

"You," Aunt Eugenia whipped around, pointing the tip of her gathered fan into his chest, "will be glad no way, no how. You are not to look at the girl. Arabella is to be the sole beneficiary of your attentions."

"You do realise I am not the one to which you are trying to marry off Arabella," Roland ~~grinned~~ brazened.

"You do realise that I could scupper any alliance you wish to make in the future?" countered a cross Aunt Eugenia. And before I could recover from her having used the word *scupper* she said, "It appears the first guests have arrived. How irksome. The first guests are never those one actually wishes to see."

And so the ball began.

Roland and I did dance, early in the evening while he was waiting to do his duty to Our Fair Cousin.

"I've missed you, Sport."

"Roland, you goat. That appellation doesn't suit."

"I can hardly call you what I did when we were children."

"The Grand Banshee?"

"The Grand Banshee," Roland repeated with affection. "Did you have a jolly time of it while you were away?"

June and all that came with it.

"Yes," I answered honestly. "Beautiful, unexpected, not simple, yet glorious."

"I can see Islington's as countrified as you."

"He's here!" I glanced around Roland and there stood Islington. Standing amidst the crowd along the floor, wearing his finest evening kit, Islington was speaking with Lord Stringham—adjusting his cuff while he said something, his gaze canvassing the floor. He saw me, the subtlest of nods in my direction. Elegant manners. Chin slightly higher. Islington of London had reincarnated in his full glory.

After the waltz he greeted us both. "Good evening, Lion. Sutherland, a pleasure as always."

"You never said you were attending," I said.

"I never intended to, only your aunt sent me a lengthy chastisement including eight reasons why I had little choice in the matter."

Roland looked disappointed at his hero's capitulation.

But I knew better and was not surprised when Islington finished with, "It was the note sent from Miss Arabella Spencer who clearly—and rightly, I must add—stated that as your guardian, it would be considered gauche for me not to show my face. Shall we dance, Lion? Or would you rather join the men in the library for gambling."

"Need you ask? Gambling!"

Upon which I discovered he hadn't been serious.

We joined the other couples on the floor. Pity.

"I've heard your name linked to mine a dozen times since my arrival," Islington said. "The interest is not worn off as much as I'd have liked."

"Aunt Eugenia likely told some indiscreet person where I spent the whole of June."

And at the mention of Stonecrop, Islington and I began speaking of the place as if we'd not seen it for a year. Joint anecdotes freshly formed. Amusing snippets, such as,

"I don't spoil the hounds."

"You do! To the extreme. Mariana would corroborate."

It persisted most of the waltz and then we fell silent.

Until Islington said, "You're dissecting me, Lion."

And I realised that yes, I had been. "I was wondering if you play your cello here in London."

"No."

"Intriguing. I'm trying to reconcile Islington of London and Islington of Stonecrop."

Eyes pulling slightly at the edges, he said, "I see." And then something I did not expect. "You might be surprised to know there is a difference between Lion of London and Lion of Stonecrop, as well."

"Is there? I should think I'm very much the same everywhere. Now, Lion of London has a lesser knowledge of ferns, but now that I've two volumes on the subject, I expect to become an expert."

"Two?"

But the waltz had come to an end, and we found ourselves with the choice of Aunt Eugenia and her court, Arabella and her attending suitors, or the refreshments.

"A drink before I escape to the club?" Islington offered.

So standing, each with a champagne punch in hand, Islington and I watched the spectacle.

"There are worse things," Islington levelled philosophically.

"Yes," I allowed. "But there are also better."

And at that Islington tipped his glass to mine, the silver sound, and we drank to our private toast.

After Islington's departure, I spent half an hour doing my aunt's bidding—speaking to Lord Brexton, then dancing with Lord Brexton, followed by Lord Abernathy, who kept his gaze on Arabella as best he could, and then I was ordered to accompany Lady Sheridan in asking Lady Cray how her recently married daughter fared. "Felicity and bliss, Lady Sheridan," came the response, as Lady Cray inspected me with a twitching eye. Very reminiscent of my aunt. Speaking of my aunt, she soon ordered me to notify her *the instant* the Countess of Ellam arrived.

"It's vulgar, to have accepted an invitation and arrive so late. Now, Emma, stand by that palm tree over there so you might see the entrance. Do Not accept a dance. Do Not leave for a reason of any kind. Emma, pay attention. Do Not wave at the Clifford girl. Now, as you are wearing red, Do Not smile overly much. It makes one look like a dance-hall girl."

I coughed. "Yes, Aunt."

And so I stood by the palm tree and waited and watched. I knew most guests from sight, if not by name. There was Annalise Clifford, and Miss Hunt with her brother, and Lady Harlow. Viviana West was near at hand, but Lord West was not in attendance. Lord and Lady Brookstone, their sons not having yet arrived. (They never did.) Friends of Aunt Eugenia's, enemies of Aunt Eugenia's—which in London society often makes part of the same list.

Roland decided to keep me company for quarter of an hour while I waited for the Countess of Ellam to arrive. Congenial, amusing discussion, until I said, "I was awfully worried Lord Croixton had wormed his way into an introduction. But he is nowhere to be seen."

"As for that, Emma—"

"Can you imagine a more ridiculous thing?"

"I heard a rumour last week."

"A good one?"

"That Lord Croixton had attended a dinner at which Aunt Eugenia and Arabella were also present."

I guffawed. "Do be serious, Roland. Of course that didn't happen. Why, their social circles are not even the same shape. Aunt Eugenia would *never*."

I brushed the speculation away.

I didn't believe it.

I still don't.

Worry, conjecture. Gossip.

"I'm only saying what I overheard."

"Where?"

But in that instant came the long-anticipated moment. The Countess of Ellam and her entire entourage had arrived in the hall and would soon be coming up the stairs. Leaving Roland, I made my way through the teeming ballroom to find Aunt Eugenia. She listened to the news of their arrival like a battlefield general. Then, taking my wrist, she moved herself to be in prime position for their entrance.

It felt like a shadow of the Montagues and the Capulets, only instead of swords there were smiles.

Which, at times, can be more dangerous.

"Lady Ellam, what a delight. I am happy you were able to join us this evening."

"Lady Spencer," the countess replied, older than Aunt Eugenia, stricter, her chin lifted in a no-nonsense aristocratic manner. "It was kind of you to include us in your occasion."

The introductions began. Beginning with the countess's sister and brother-in-law, their son and his wife. And there, breathtaking and ethereal, standing like a fabled maiden on a solitary beach, was Lady Eloise Silver, glancing about.

She nodded demurely when her mother introduced her to Aunt Eugenia.

"And this," Aunt Eugenia sniffed, "is my niece, Miss Emma Lion. Presently, the Duke of Islington's ward."

At these words, Lady Eloise had looked directly at me. Not at the mention of Islington's name, but rather the mention of my own.

Or so it appeared.

The countess gave an uninterested smile and returned her attention to Aunt Eugenia to finish exchanging a polite phrase or two before they joined the other guests.

I, however, had retained Lady Eloise's scrutiny.

But as the party, having done their duty to the hostess, turned towards the floor, Lady Eloise was already surrounded.

She was asked to dance, with the request of the three dances already following.

Hand tentatively resting on the arm of Lord Stringham, she

glanced about only once, pausing when she found me, still standing beside Aunt Eugenia.

There was a nearly indecipherable resignation in her eyes, the slightest ghost of a doe being hunted.

I wished to rescue her somehow.

I can't say why.

"She's peerless," Roland said from over my shoulder.

"She doesn't wish to be here," I answered.

"If you can distract the old girl, Emma, I aim to ask Lady Silver to dance. I've never seen such a creature."

A sigh.

I could not deny the statement.

"She is the most graceful, otherworldly person I have ever seen," I granted. "I wouldn't mind a chance to speak with her, if only to glimpse behind the placid mirror of her person. Although it appears she'll not have a moment to herself all evening."

I proved prophetic.

And while the evening continued, a success by every measure, the golden sun of Arabella and the poignant, melancholy moon of Lady Eloise, their mamas playing their respective pieces on the board, I felt somewhat sad—watching Lady Eloise glancing over her shoulder, as if she half hoped to find someone she knew she wouldn't.

It was Roland who found me fast asleep in the library at quarter after three in the morning and escorted me home.

June 29th

I slept through the morning, missing the service entirely. The sleep of the dead, as they say. Not even the half waking and turning in a tangle of bedclothes before drifting back to the oblivion of deep sleep. I simply disappeared into miles and miles of dreams, waking with a terribly sore neck from scarcely having moved.

"I hope Hawkes did not read so very much poetry," I yawned as I sat dazed in the breakfast room, Agnes determined to wake me with scones and strong coffee. "I hate to think he's spouting verse without my having heard."

Later

I HAVE SOMETHING FOR YOU, AND I HOPE IT DOES NOT MAKE YOU SAD.

Is it a tragic ballad where the heroine dies leaving the hero a wrecked, discarded man?

NO

Is it a book that was brutally torn from its spine? Or…oh, I know! A badminton birdie which was dismembered, separated from all its feathers! I've seen a good many in my time. I am hardened to the tragedy.

MEET ME BY THE SHARED WINDOW IN THE WEST GARRET.

Later

Pierce. Thank you. You are right to say it is sad.
But not the sort of sadness from which one should run away.
It is a lovely photograph of Tybalt. He looks like a philosopher.

I THOUGHT YOU WOULD RATHER HAVE IT THAN NOT.

Might I ask you something?

YES

Intrusive question, I know. But are you going to write to your mother and Nance?

UNDECIDED

Later

This evening, after Pierce and I had eaten dinner—the entire meal spent discussing our favourite selections from the Stonecrop menu—he excused himself and I sat thinking about what the coming month would bring. And about what Hawkes had counselled, when I'd asked him how to control the reins of my own life.

"Quietly," Hawkes had said.

Quietly.

I shall experiment with this word and see what comes of it.

Later

Agnes informed me, as I was sitting at the kitchen table with a cup of tea, that there was to be a late-night meeting in the drawing room of the S. S. C. S. S. "Only tonight is when the full council can assemble. It being late on a Sunday evening."

"Pardon? The full council?"

"Yes, Miss. If you would give us leave of your drawing room. You'll hardly know we are there."

"When are they to arrive?"

And not half a second later an ordered knock sounded.

"Now, Miss," and Agnes went to answer the door.

I stood and followed Agnes, watching as a parade of solemn butlers, valets, housekeepers, and cooks—all in stiff black—walked into the drawing room with All Due Seriousness. Each greeted Agnes by name, a few asking after her time in Scotland.

Once they'd filled the drawing room, Agnes followed, closing the door behind her.

Leaving me standing alone in the shadow of the hall.

Somewhat amazed.

I sat on the stairs and listened.

Low murmurs. Men's voices. Women's voices. A spirit of solemnity seeping from beneath the door. I sat with my elbow on my knee and my chin in my hand hoping Cousin Archibald would keep to his rooms. Agnes came out and wordlessly rushed to the kitchen, returning with a glass vial. Then a second time, with a tin of powder. The murmurs of discussion, the sound of a man grunting as he stood up. A debate which reached the fever pitch of a man exclaiming, "I say!"

A butler was sent out into the night, returning with a mysterious parcel beneath his arm.

I sat quiet, determined not to embarrass Agnes in front of her compatriots.

Not long after, two housekeepers disappeared, returning less than five minutes later, whispers between them.

And so it continued.

I, at that point, had rested my head against the wall, with images of serious-minded servants in black walking through my sleepy mind.

Agnes, and a small army of fellow cooks, disappeared into the kitchen to prepare tea, returning with four trays of refreshment, and the S. S. C. S. S. persisted.

Finally, just before midnight, the conclave broke.

I was wakened by the sound of applause and general relieved camaraderie. The door to the drawing room opened, and they began to pour out into the hall, handshakes and smiles accompanying the congratulations.

Agnes saw them all to the door.

Hats tipping, one woman pinching Agnes's chin, and they all discreetly slipped out into the dark of night.

"Oh, Miss Lion!" Agnes beamed, dragging me into the drawing room. "We have accomplished the impossible."

She motioned at the floor with exuberance.

The carpet was pristine.

Not a mark of the ink stain remaining, the original colours preserved.

"We would not have done it on the Sabbath, Miss, except Mr. Stanley says removing stains is the work of the Lord."

Well.

It is, I admit, a miracle.

June 30th

I dreamt last night of the tree.

The tree was on the crest of a far hill—strong, wandering branches, and abundant. Then storm and rain, come with lightning. The tree struck, the force splitting it in two. It burned, the bark left charred, marked with lines of spent fire. This was when I became aware of myself being present. In the rain, beside the tree, I lifted my hands to the blackened trunk.

Burned away, no life left.

I knelt. I threw my arms around the trunk and held it, weeping. The night persisted, a cold rain lashing over the hill. Still I clung to the tree. After what seemed like an abyss of hours, the rain abated. The wind also. And I, wet through, pulled myself away. I pressed my hands against the damp, black wood. Tracing every split, every scar.

Hours passed.

I do not know why I stayed.

Then the sky growing lighter. A line of gold on the horizon. And as I continued to press my fingertips to the burned wood, the sound of morning birdcall. From a branch on the left, the smallest bud breaking into leaf, and then a spread of green reaching in the morning. I pulled my hands away—body sore, dress sodden, hands marked in ash—and looked about. On the right, too, an unexpected show of green.

The tree split in two was determined to live.

Dawn illuminated the scene, the morning sun fully breaking, blinding. I blinked my eyes against the molten gold. The blue morning air began to warm.

I awoke.

I have spent an hour sitting, staring at nothing—aware that there is a steadiness beneath my feet. Tangible as the desk on which I've set my hands. I remember the charred wood, the force of the rain, the never-ending night. And then the impossible: hope.

Profound, peaceful hope.

Lifting a finger to the crevice in the wall, I knew.

I knew that I would give the hope to Pierce, if I could.

Every golden coin of it.

I've taken the folded fortune from the back of my desk drawer and find I'm no longer afraid of what it could mean, or what it mightn't. I am neither looking for Pierce inside the words, nor am I afraid of finding him there. As for its meaning? I can't say.

Meaning is the question wise men have asked through all the ages.

Later

Having changed for bed, I snuck down to the kitchen to prepare a contraband cup of tea, and Agnes was sat there at the table, singing as she polished the silverware.

"Hello, Agnes. You must be frightfully tired."

"Almost finished." Agnes looked at me brightly. "I missed you something terrible, Miss Lion. I know I'm not supposed to say. '*A trustworthy personal servant gives no complaint to the absences, however prolonged, of their employer*', but as grand as it was to go home, as happy as I was to be with them all, it was…fitting to return to Lapis Lazuli House."

"I couldn't have said it more aptly, Agnes."

"A cup of tea to take with you to bed, Miss?"

"That is indeed what I came for."

It is the last day of a leafed-out June.

What a tremendous journey.

I can feel the cool of the Derbyshire streams over my feet, the expansive views beyond the edges of my mind, the joyful, heart-rending, complicated weaving of four lives.

If I had to choose the most significant—

Dear me, what is that? I'm sitting in the window seat, my journal on my lap, and I've just seen a shadow approach Lapis Lazuli. Not much else, but there now, a quick rap on the door, and the shadow has fled.

It did not seem to fit any Reprobates I know.

Strange. And unsettling, at this late hour.

However, curiosity.

Later

Complete astonishment!
Utter amazement!
Confusing and terrifying!

I had gone down into the drawing room and pulled back the curtain.

There was nothing, no one in the street. Key in hand, I unlocked the front door as quietly as I was able and inched it open.

Only but moonlight.

Then, as I opened the door further, an envelope fell into the hall, having been propped up against the door's base.

"What, exactly, are you?" I said, picking it up. But when I moved to shut the door, I glanced up and saw a figure watching from across the lane.

~~Not one to be terrified of shadows in the late night…~~

Not foolhardy enough to trust a shadow in the deep recesses of night, I tipped an invisible hat at the shadow—the figure gave a wave—and closed the door, locking it with all haste.

Bringing the envelope up to my garret, I saw that it was bright red.

No more comforting than a ransom note.

However!

I, Emma M. Lion of Lapis Lazuli House, Whereabouts Lane, St. Crispian's, in the Year of Our Lord Eighteen Hundred and Eighty-Four, have been chosen to play a Yet Undisclosed Character in this year's Stirring Rendition of *Julius Caesar*!

I am to arrive tomorrow evening—under the cover of darkness—to a location that will be discreetly delivered. There I will meet the rest of the cast and find out the role I am to play!

But how many women are there in *Julius Caesar*?

Why, Portia and Calpurnia.

It looks as if I will spend the next fortnight as the wife of either a betrayed and murdered Caesar or his traitorous best friend, Brutus.

A strong play for happiness on any account!

Even Later

IT'S PAST THREE IN THE MORNING.

Ah, I see I've been carried away.

DARE I ASK?

Shakespeare. With the intoxicant of intangible happiness incompatible with sleep.

ONE CAN'T ARGUE WITH INTANGIBLE HAPPINESS.

No, indeed.

Pierce?

"Fast asleep? It is no matter;
Enjoy the honey-heavy dew of slumber."

THE PERSONAL LIBRARY *of* EMMA M. LION

As It Currently Stands

The Complete Works of Shakespeare by *William Shakespeare*
Illustrated by Declan Lion

The Holy Bible

Jane Eyre by *Charlotte Brontë*
Gifted by the Jane Eyre Society of Fortitude, A Preparatory School for Girls

Shakespeare's Comedies, In Full
Gifted by Roland Sutherland

Jane Eyre by *Charlotte Brontë*
Gifted by Roland Sutherland

Latin Phrases for the Unrepentant by *Barclay Stafford*
Won at The Dalliance Bookshop

Self-Reliance by *Ralph Waldo Emerson*
Gifted by Niall Pierce

Essays by *Ralph Waldo Emerson*
Gifted by Niall Pierce

Meaning of Flowers
Found in the breakfast room

Vermilion and the Flaming Sword
Purchased without a cover at The Dalliance

Treasure Island by *Robert Louis Stevenson*
Gifted by Young Hawkes

Plutarch's Lives by *Plutarch*
Gifted by Islington

Song of Myself by *Walt Whitman*
Gifted by Niall Pierce

Ireland: Myth, Legend, and History
by *Alistair T. Moddle* and *Jonathan L. Kirk*
(Rapscallion Commentary by Declan Lion)
Gifted by Young Hawkes

Dictionary of the English Language A – J by *Dr. Samuel Johnson*
Purchased from and bound by The Hound
(The entire K section is missing.)

Mixing in Society by *The Right Hon. Countess of ********
Foisted by Aunt Eugenia

Dictionary of the English Language L – Z by *Dr. Samuel Johnson*
Miraculously Gifted by Ben Chambers

The Ferns of Great Britain, and Their Allies
The Club-Mosses, Pepperworts, and Horsetails.
by *Anne Pratt*
Gifted by Roland Sutherland

British Ferns and Their Allies:
An Abridgment of The "Popular History of British Ferns,"
and Comprising the Ferns, Club-Mosses, Pepperworts, & Horsetails.
by *Thomas Moore*
Gifted by Islington

The Poetry of William Wordsworth
Gifted by Young Hawkes

Dear Reader,

As incredible as it seems, here we are in 1884. It's been an eventful journey, to say the least, and life in St. Crispian's shows no sign of slowing down.

Beth would like to thank you, The Reader, for wandering into the neighbourhood and deciding to stay. It is a particular life we live here, good if not ridiculous. And there is much ahead.

Thank you to Beth's family—Kip, parents, siblings, nieces & nephews—who reside in the very centre of her heart. She loves them deeply and is forever thankful for how they cheer her on.

Thank you, Spy Cat Grey. You deserve all the treats.

Friendship is a gift Beth has received in abundance. Thank you, all. You know who you are.

Thank you to the early readers for this volume, Beth's mother, Beth's father, Alena, Natalie, Caitlin, Carlee, Rose, Lori, and an on time yet belated Rob.

Thank you, Tyson Cantrell, for allowing your beautiful design to grace the covers.

Thank you, Ashley Lloyd, for appearing out of thin air to become Beth's trustworthy assistant. You are gold.

Thank you, Ben Unguren, ever the magician, who creates time when he has none.

Thank you, Angie Thompson, for the beautiful copy edits, while still wielding a sword and holding up a light.

Thank you, Allysha Unguren, substantive editor, board member, and fellow in near-hysterical laughter. You have sacrificed so much for all of Beth's books, and it is recorded in her heart.

Thank you, Kip. The one who is the only.

And an especial thank you to Beth's Heavenly Father, who has given her insight, light, and courage every step of the way.

A note concerning the presumptuous Beth Brower, who thought it a good idea to put my journals into the world. She lives with the aforementioned Kip, her chemist husband, and their cat, Spy Cat Grey.

Beth enjoys citrus scents, books, handwoven rugs, and walking in any weather. She listens to songs on repeat. She feels rather fiercely about the ones she loves and needs windows for light and walls for art.

Beth Brower has written the following books:

The Queen's Gambit
The Ruby Prince
The Wanderer's Mark

The Q

The Beast of Ten

The Unselected Journals of Emma M. Lion

You can find more information on her website and Instagram.

www.bethbrower.com
@bethbrower

You can also subscribe to Beth's newsletter and find short fiction about the characters of St. Crispian's on Substack.

Beth Brower Scribbles Away
bethbrower.substack.com

Sincerely,
Emma

www.ingramcontent.com/pod-product-compliance
Lightning Source LLC
LaVergne TN
LVHW102137170926
848365LV00032B/474
* 9 7 8 1 9 5 7 4 9 2 0 3 2 *